Colony's End

Book Three of the New Europa Trilogy

N Joseph Glass

MONOCLE BOOKS, N. JOSEPH GLASS

Copyright © 2022 by N. Joseph Glass

All rights reserved.

No part of this publication may be reproduced, distributed, or transmitted in any form or by any means, including photocopying, recording, or other electronic or mechanical methods, without the prior written permission of the publisher, except as permitted by U.S. copyright law. For permission requests, contact the author at www.glassauthor.com.

The story, all names, characters, and incidents portrayed in this production are fictitious. No identification with actual persons (living or deceased), places, buildings, and products is intended or should be inferred.

| AIMÉE |

The two women hoisted themselves from the floor of the flyer, bruised but otherwise okay. Charlotte screamed, "He's dead. He's dead." They were who-knew-where in a downed flyer with a dead pilot. Aimée thought he may have been into her—she thought that of most guys. The poor corpse's name wouldn't come to her. After some forceful motivation, the emergency hatch let them out.

"We had gotten close, *right?* Signaled our approach to U.A." Aimée intentionally put hopefulness in her tone, as she could see the trepidation in her camera operator's face as clear as the yellow shirt she wore. Aimée didn't think it suited the woman's complexion.

It grew paler. "*Close...* but which way?"

Pointing in a straight line from the flyer's nose, Aimée said, "That way. Looks like we went straight down on our trajectory." Motioning to the sun she continued, "The sun sets in the West. So if that's West, this is South. The colony is South."

Charlotte accepted Aimée's navigational insights, not knowing what a wild guess she had made. At midday, the sun shone directly overhead. Aimée couldn't begin to guess which way it would drift across the sky.

"They'll come looking for the flyer. Maybe it's better if we wait here?"

Not one to let logic get in the way of spontaneity, Aimée balked at the suggestion. *You never get mad at Gift for it, and she's the most logical person you know*, she thought to calm herself. As it turned out, Aimée didn't need to worry about it.

Two unrecognized uniforms came over a rocky rise. Aimée tossed two ideas through her mind: *Are they navy-blue or royal-blue?* After a pause, she wondered, *And who are they?* A few steps revealed the red planet insignia with three letters stitched into the fabric patch: U.R.M.

"Fancy meeting you guys here." Aimée spoke as if she'd passed a friend in the corridor. Charlotte looked like someone had pressed pause. "You just popped over from Mars to say hi?"

The bits after that got fuzzy, as if she'd been with her Russian friends, and partook too liberally of their liquid generosity. *One of them raised his hand with... a taser?*

That's why her memory gaped to this room of a metallic finish of functionality without aesthetics. An unfamiliar and continuous hum pressed on her eardrums. Charlotte moaned, just coming to consciousness. A bunk, Aimée figured, or a holding cell. She couldn't be sure if they were guests or prisoners, but having been tasered and brought there without consent, she assumed the latter.

Aimée slowly rose on unsteady feet. "You okay?"

"Lightheaded. What happened? Where are we?"

"No idea. I think the U.R.M. has us."

"U.R.M.? Here?"

The door slid open on cue. "Yes, we are here." Male, not abrasive or harsh, just stating the fact.

"And where, *exactly*, is here?"

"Words won't do, Miss Toussaint. Please, both of you, come with me?"

He knows me? Interesting. He had come alone in a royal- or navy-blue uniform. The stitching on the silver patch above his left breast pocket read, "CDR. Ryan."

"Come where, Commander Ryan?"

"To answer your question. Don't worry, you are our guests. This way, please."

They followed him through a short corridor of the same unfinished metal—not silver, not gray, but somewhere in between. Aimée felt light-headed too. Or did something else transmogrify her steps? When the door opened, she gasped, and staggered back to feel the safety and solidity of the wall against her back. Commander Ryan steadied her. Charlotte covered her eyes with both hands and stood like a statue.

"How? I mean... where? You... *How?*"

"Easy. It's okay. We are aboard the U.R.M. Santa Maria."

"This is *real*? That... that's... *Earth*?"

"Yes. We are about to enter low orbit."

"Charlotte, you gotta see this."

Aimée stepped cautiously toward an oval window as tall as her, hoping the glass was thick and sturdy. The vision took her breath away and blew her mind beyond her wildest imagination. With everything her eyes beheld since the airlock opened—the sky, the lake, mountains, and waterfalls—nothing came close to this. This had an otherworldly sensation, high above a blue-green marble with swirls of white paint strokes. A single tear made its way down her cheek.

"How... I mean, *gravity?* How are we...?"

"We're under thrust. When the engines stop, we'll be weightless. That will take some adjustment, and I'm to prepare you for that."

When it happened, the closest comparison Aimée could make was being in the lake—the sensation of nothing below her, while the liquid kept her suspended over it. Charlotte had been afraid of the water and couldn't relate. Someone came with a vacuum hose to remove the putrid globs from the surrounding air and take the green-faced woman to what they called sickbay.

***

Commander Ryan presented an abridged history to get Aimée caught up as they hovered over stools. They and the desk were bolted to the floor in a small office.

"We've grown too large, our supplies stretched. The terraforming project is progressing too slowly. Our greatest success is a functioning bio-dome. It's on natural soil but not exposed to the atmosphere. Then we received radio signals from Earth."

Aimée was mesmerized by how her bangs floated over her brow.

"We learned you were able to go outside and had started trading with the Russians. We immediately prepared a mission to send a scout vessel here to examine current environmental conditions and evaluate our return to Earth. After a six-month journey, we're here."

"And you shot down our transport and kidnapped us for...?"

"When we arrived, we found the collaboration between the colonies, and needed to make sure we would have no resistance to our... *reunification*."

"Reunification? You mean you plan to take over the colonies? The entire planet?"

"It is the only way forward." Ryan said it as a given, an indisputable fact she would have no choice but to accept. She didn't.

"And why are *we* here?"

"You are here, Miss Toussaint, because we want you to address the colonies when we're ready. Your colleague is here to provide... motivation."

"Motivation?"

***

The answer came in time, to Aimée's dismay. She had seen Charlotte three times in the days they'd been there, on a spaceship, looking worse each day from space sickness, weightlessness, and vomiting up what food she'd gotten down. Aimée, on the other hand, was treated well, fed twice daily as the crew. They even gave her showers and clean clothes. Showering in zero G meant being zipped into a bag with a breathing tube, the soap and water rolling over her body from top to bottom and vacuumed out. Strapped into a bed sack, she had full sleep cycles.

Flying over the Aurora Borealis presented such a spectacular sight, not having seen it from Earth. Looking down at it left her at a loss for words beyond one. *Magical.*

As the days passed, Aimée got the hang of the exercise equipment, keeping her muscles from atrophying. Her education expounded on their grand vision of the reunification of Earth, presenting the U.R.M. as the saviors of humankind, the only hope for real peace. Aimée exercised caution with her questions. She learned all she could, hopeful something would be useful later when the colonies would surely resist an occupation forced upon them in the guise of peace.

At first, she dismissed the reports of unrest between the colonies as propaganda. Aimée recognized the obvious indoctrination techniques—feigned friendship, the *"we're on the same side"* rhetoric—for what they were. When she heard audio recordings of intercepted radio signals and watched the messages between the N.R.C. and U.A., she saw some truth in what they spewed. What they showed her next unsettled her bones.

Aimée watched in horror as her childhood best friend—looking worn, defeated, and clearly under duress—recited someone else's words. Of course, she caught the *Oh Dio's* and knew Gift had warned them. *Well done, Love.* Seeing the back-and-forth between Raffa and someone called General Xiang of the N.R.C. tightened Aimée stomach—a most unusual sensation in zero gravity. She had to do something.

Charlotte expired.

As Aimée prepared to record her message, she thought about starting and ending with the *Oh Dio* sandwich code. The directive left no room for misinterpretation. "Exactly as we have written it. Not one word added, not one word omitted." Hope in her friends assured her they'd know.

Practicing her lines, Aimée started to see their point. Humans had reverted to being humans. They started fights, created conflicts over misunderstandings, and there had been killings. Besides, as far as Aimée knew, neither New Europa nor the Russian Federation had the means to take a stand against the U.R.M. Attempting it with projectile stunners and sonic incapacitation devices would get them all killed.

Aimée recorded the message.

1

Gift's mind wasn't a reliable source of information, and she doubted her own lucidity. One year of her twenty-seven brought drastic changes, culminating in new oversight in the form of a peaceful global takeover. No, lack of killing wasn't the same as peace. Yet through all these turbulent changes, perhaps things basically stayed the same. At least Gift could easily track her days this time.

Seeing her first airplane wasn't the trip through history Gift hoped it would be. The reality of it was closer to the toy Kofi and Paulina's children made, an outline of a craft incapable of flight. The carcass had once been a flying machine. The large empty tube's height lent enough room for her to stand with little to spare. The length spanned three of her Boxes, but circular. To Gift, it felt like being in a long drainpipe, ready to be carried away like dirty shower water. How she longed for a shower. Outlines of windows lined the floor, and ovals of glass made skylights in the ceiling. Hunger pinched in her belly as Gift counted empty bags of water and food rations in this new cell.

Gift had stowed herself in the gutted, rusty fuselage of an old aircraft repurposed as an ironic taunting of freedom. To have such "freedom" meant trusting in one person, the one person who knew she was alive, where she was, and why she needed to stay hidden. General Xiang.

The "closed" end of the tube had empty spaces by broken windows, where it looked like controls and navigation systems would have been. Gift imagined the one-time flying machine had been ripped in two, leaving its other side open. Nights were cold before the General's first visit on the third day. Using a thirty-centimeter length of thin twisted metal with sharp edges, Gift created a *troglodyte calendar*. Three lines had etched the wall when Xiang appeared. She came on the fourth day. Water and rations for two weeks fell from the general's bags, with blankets and a tablet.

"It's offline," the less-intimidating Xiang had said. No longer her captor, she became Gift's... *savior?* Too grandiose, it supported Gift's disdain for labels. The woman said comms channels were compromised, so on her next visit she'd exchange the device for one with updated vids of Aimée speaking on behalf of the U.R.M. They called themselves the United Republic of Earth.

When Xiang had run her out of the Ops center ahead of the U.R.M. delegation, Gift questioned the change of heart. Ironically, the answer mirrored the reason she and Chan had captured her, interrogated her, and tortured her friends. Those *mal'd* missiles. "It is our only defense, and I must trust your people will use them to free us of these conquerors. You must protect their location," the General had said.

Gift had been honest. She couldn't tell Chan, Xiang, or anyone, how to locate that complex. When she claimed she could find it in a flyer, she had stretched a vague truth. If U.R.M. troops found her, they might think she had value, and not kill her on the spot. That was oddly comforting, and Gift pondered how no matter how awful things got or what deplorable condition people faced, they clung to life. Even in a cell, under the thumb of a madman, humiliated, with her friends being tortured. Humans chose to live. Unbreakable human spirit or blind, stubborn stupidity? Perhaps the truth lay in a blending of the two. Her tummy rumbled again.

Gift's heart leapt inside her chest when she saw Mike walking beside the General. She slapped herself on the cheek to check she wasn't dreaming. Though she couldn't be sure such a gesture proved she hadn't hallucinated. The totes fell from Mike's hands as Gift collided and wrapped him in as tight a hug as her weary muscles could manage. Sacks of supplies delighted and horrified Gift, as she pondered how long she may be in her tube, in isolation. Tear-soaked eyes took a minute to notice his new attire, no longer in the putrid green shorts and tank top still covering her—what she dubbed their prison clothes.

"*Gift.* Oh, thank goodness. Until this morning... I had no idea what happened to you. I figured the U.R.M. had you. Never expected... *this.*"

"I've been here this whole time. How are you? Tina and Matteo?"

"I'm fine. Haven't seen Tina or Matteo, but Xiang here says she'll find them. She found me."

"Found you? Where were you? And what the heck are you wearing?" Gift studied the unfamiliar blue uniform.

"They've been recruiting people to join them."

After a hard slap to the face, Gift hissed, "*What?* How, how could you. You *joined* them?"

"Of course not." Mike grimaced. His cheek was bright red. "Lots of Chinese have, but me and a few of Xiang's people have infiltrated them, *pretending* we buy into the propaganda about this U.R.E. crap. Recruitment training started yesterday."

Gift dropped her head. "I'm sorry... for the slap. And... for doubting you. I'm just not in my right mind."

"I know. No worries. I'd have slapped me too." Mike's smile settled Gift more than she imagined it could.

"Are people buying into... this?"

Xiang said, "On the surface, it is a peaceful transition. Hostilities between your people and mine have ended. There is a plan for unified trade between colonies under their New World Order. For many of my people, they see it as an improvement to their lives from what they were under the N.R.C."

"Is it?"

"In some ways... it is." The formidable woman breathed out a long sigh before continuing in a softened tone. "I was sincere when I said Chan operated outside his mandate. But his actions were not condemned by my government. Aside from the nuances of his insanity—we would never condone sexual assault—our military mistreating people is common. Our people lived under totalitarian military governance. Many welcome this change."

"What now? I mean, if your people like this New World Order, then I just stay here... *alone?*" The single tear snaking down her cheek testified to the weakness in her voice not being physical.

The General said, "We are playing along. Whatever we were, we wish to control what we will become. I will rally my people, and I will find Tina and Matteo. When the time is right, we will overthrow the invaders."

"Talk about irony. That was *us* in U.A. when *you* were the invaders only weeks ago. Wait—" Gift expected more to come to mind, it just needed a moment to get there. "I think... if you take back this colony, what about the rest? What's to stop them dropping bombs or whatever, like when they arrived, and leveling this place?" Gift pointed to her airplane but meant the N.R.C.

"We must act before more of my people accept their occupation and join their forces. That would increase the difficulty of our success."

"Can we work with other colonies? Can we contact them, coordinate our efforts?"

"I don't see how we—"

Impatience brought the general's words over Mike's. "We have no communication besides what we receive from your Aimée person. A traitor to us all. She spews this propaganda, convincing people to join the other side."

"*No.* She'd never. They're making her do this, *obviously*. But I know her... she'll find a way to—" Gift froze as if her brain needed a breath.

"To... what? You just stopped talking. Are you okay?"

"I really don't know, Mike... But for sure she isn't working for them. She'll find a way to help us. Where even is she? Her face looks weird, puffy."

Mike pointed to the cloudless sky. "Up there. She's actually up there, in one of their spaceships."

"For real?" After a contemplative pause full of wonder, Gift said, "Okay, but she *will*... she'll find a way. I need to keep getting her vids. She'll send me a message. Maybe... if you snuck me in, I could see them as they come."

"We cannot risk you being found. We must safeguard the location of our only defense. If they find you, I will shoot you myself to protect that secret."

"Gee, thanks."

"No, Gift, she's right. I mean... not about the shooting you part. I'm working on a back-channel comms link, and may get your tablet online in real-time. There's a broadcast every few days, and you're right. I decoded a message from Aimée about them recruiting guards. That's why I joined up."

Gift's mind jumped. "Good. Told you. Any word from Raff? What about Oksana? She's alone at U.A. Poor thing, she's all alone."

Mike shook his head. "Full comms blackout. Nothing in but Aimée's broadcasts. And Oksana's a strong girl, she reminds me so much of you. She has good people with her at U.A. They'll look after her."

"I hope you're right. General, ma'am, if you can't get me online you gotta bring me these vids more often. When Aimée sends us a message, I need to see it."

"We risk your secrecy and our lives by coming here, and cannot expose your location, or that you are alive. Keeping you hidden and reclaiming my colony are my priorities. They have executed our president, making me the leader of the N.R.C. I must focus on our freedom."

"Mike, I need those vids. Even if you've gotta send a drone or something, I need those vids."

"I'll do my best."

"Do nothing to risk discovery, *nothing*." General Xian's imposing tone returned. "They are scouring the colony for you, and may begin searching surrounding areas. I assume they know nothing about your resilience to the ecosphere, or they would be searching here. But I never plan based on assumption, so we maintain caution."

During a long goodbye embrace, Mike whispered into Gift's ear, "It'll be okay. I love you. We've been through a lot, and we'll get through this. Jailed, caged, interrogated, deprived of food and… and basic amenities."

"Yeah." Gift sniffled.

"But in all of that, Gift… I don't think you've *ever* stunk worse than you do right now. And your breath is atrocious. Really, I may puke."

"Shut up, you dumb jerk." She gave him a smack on the chest and a chuckle. He was right.

2

Patience may not have been her strongest trait, but Gift didn't think herself an impatient person. What resilience remained in her patience after weeks alone?

Mike was wrong, Gift didn't stink. Her body's reeking surpassed disgusting, bringing pre-vomit cramps. Her last shower in U.A. was over two weeks ago. The metal tube that became her temporary habitat—she tried not to think of it as a jail cell—warmed up substantially in the day's heat. She couldn't tell if solar rays absorbing into her skin was better or worse. A pleasant moment in the afternoon shade cast by an outcropping didn't violate the theoretical border fence Xiang erected around her. Hours of *nothing* were the building blocks of insanity. Gift tried every trick she could think of to keep her mind on this side of lunacy, removing talking to herself from the list of its symptoms as she always had the habit of vocalizing thoughts.

"'Only leave the airplane for necessary bodily functions,' she said." The *she* being Gift in a paraphrase of Xiang's unambiguous directive not to go outside except to urinate and defecate. "Bathing is a necessary bodily function."

Gift sauntered in a direction away from the colony, into the wilderness of China. With scatterings of bushes and small trees, it resembled the sandy desert she flew over in Africa more than the lush forests outside New

Europa. Without reason, Gift *knew* a waterfall must have been nearby,. She could use it as a shower. Perhaps a small lake or pond, a stream, a body of water that would remove the sweat and grime and refresh her spirits.

Having left the tablet, her only indication of time was the moving sun—which she hadn't learned to read—her own fatigue, and a best guess. After four hours, maybe five, she had a hike to get back *home.* She figured it best to do that before darkness hid the landmarks. When she had walked back about the same hours, the piece of airplane she inhabited had vanished. Nothing looked familiar.

"Crap," she yelled with all the power she could pile into her lungs. With fists raised, she cried, "Crap. Crap. Crap."

More than ocular input, the chill creeping over her flesh told her the evening had arrived. The twilight spent searching, hoping to find what was the dreaded place of her most recent captivity. Now, she wanted to be there more than anything. The small bag of water she carried had passed half-empty, no matter how she looked at it. Gift searched for another hour under the moonlight, and tried to convince herself optimism drove her, not stubbornness. Her shoulder shrug signaled the end of the effort. She gave the next several minutes to trying to identify the best spot to cuttle up for the night. With no blankets or shelter, she needed protection from what the darkness would bring.

"I need a fire," Gift said to the surrounding night as she piled up dried bushes—remembering they should be dry—and twigs found below the small trees. She had no way to ignite them. Frantically, she checked her pockets for something. The little shorts had no pockets. The waistband held one item, a protein rations bar. Most would be dinner, saving some for breakfast. Her optimism held onto the hope of finding a waterfall, pond, or even a puddle, on the way to her airplane in the morning.

Isolation, desolation. Let it go...

Nestled into a narrow gully, Gift had chosen her bed for the night. The slight wall of dirt shielded her from the near constant breeze that carried the brisk night air over her skin in a soft, frigid caress. "Where was that this afternoon when I was out there dying to death under the sun?" Gift asked the Earth.

...fade away-ay-ay-ay...

"Still need a fire." With her bare hands, Gift dug a basin a half-meter from her bed. Close enough for warmth but not so close she'd burn herself tossing in her sleep. Matteo appeared on her mental display, on his belly digging a hole on the exterior farm. Higher than Aimée was right then and out of his mind. "Those *mal'd* drops." The back of a hand took the onset of tears from under her eyes. Pieces of dry bushes, withered leaves, and small twigs filled the hole, larger branches beside it—everything ready for the fire except the fire.

Her arms ached, and fingers lost their grip on the two hard stones she'd clanked against each other with no sparks resulting. "*Idiot.*" She forcefully dropped the stones. Another search found more appropriate ones for her second attempt. One Gift called flint could have been quartz, the second was a softer stone. Deep in a memory, perhaps from Tom on their journey to meet the Pioneers, a voice said this would work where the two hard stones had failed. Spent forearm muscles, aching biceps, and a bleeding fingertip resulted in a dry leaf catching a spark. Like hope from despair, it smoldered. Gift's sinister laugh was steeped in madness, like a villain in a spy thriller who captured the hero.

Curled up and tucked away in the gully beside the fire, Gift began her slide into slumber. A most unsettling noise revealed she wasn't alone. Had the U.R.M. found her, or was it a wild, ravenous animal on the hunt? Which would be worse? The rustling muted to squeals that morphed into soft, tremulous twittering. Gift mustered the courage to crane her neck and hoist her eyes just above the dirt ledge she lay beside. It was massive at first, but only at first. Its little head was one of the cutest things Gift had ever seen.

Fluffy white ears stood up from its head, a brown close to a soft orange. A white snout held a black button nose, and the moonlight exposed a deep red coat over its body. How it held a thin green branch while nibbling its leaves made an adorable sight. "Ciao," Gift instinctively whispered. Its eyes caught hers and its twittering became hooting, almost a screech, hostile on the ears as it nodded its head slowly. Gift became frightened and ducked into her cubby as the hooting intensified, then ceased.

Not sure what triggered the realization, the sounds of trickling, the pungent odor, or the warm drops splattering her legs, Gift knew it urinated on her. Not only had Gift not found water to bathe, sweat more profusely on her trek, had to spend the night outdoors, now her body carried the scent of some creature's pee on top of its own stench. *That's just great.* After piling larger branches on her fire—still proud of herself for starting a fire—the drift into sleep came.

The sight of Mike and Tina greeting her between slowly separating eyelids was an unimaginable delight. The scene failed the slap test and Gift sat in the N.R.C. with General Xiang, Raff, Nadezhda Anoykina, and Bright. A freakishly tall man from the U.R.M. stood and Gift could see only his chin and curled nose hairs when she folded her neck to look up at him. "The launch codes," he demanded.

"What? No... I don't have those. You're supposed to ask me where the missiles are, and I tell you I don't know."

Raff shocked her by saying, "Tell him Gift."

"Tell him," Xiang, Raff, Nadezhda and Bright chanted.

Gift shouted, "Alright," and entered the codes.

Xiang declared, "Direct hit. New Europa is finally gone."

"*What?* No!"

Crackling sounds ended the nightmare, and dawn's light greeted the landscape ahead of the star that brought it. *You're not gonna pee on me again, buddy.* Gift figured aggression from her superior size would ward off the little fox this time. Or was it a cat, with ears like that? Before leaping into a frantic scream, a little peek over the ledge...

Fear pushed her head down and pressed her back into the security of the dirt wall. Something much larger, two meters long, crawled on all-fours—fierce and intimidating in stature. In a second glimpse, she noticed the ears. Round puffs of fur looked almost comical, cute. Then it stood on its hind legs. Massively tall, shiny black hair like Sakura's, if hers covered her entire body. A bright white patch stretched a 'V' pattern across its chest. It reminded Gift of the type of dress a young girl may wear, except young girls in dresses didn't seem likely to kill you or eat your face. This did.

Tucked back down, eyes pinched shut, as if not seeing it made it not see her, Gift held her breath. Grunts increased in volume, the beast coming closer. *Make a run for it.* No, she'd not outrun the thing at her best, and she was far from that. Her mind called up a memory of not being able to keep up with Tom, and this thing appeared a bit more powerful than him. She missed Tom, and wondered how he was doing through the occupation at N.E.

The loudest snort yet jarred her and dropped specks of dirt onto her arm, face, and leg. Gift felt the next snort as a puff of warm air on her ear. *It's gonna eat my face.* She crushed her eyelids tighter. In time, she courageously peeked to see the giant's bum swaying side to side in the distance... growing smaller.

Roughly a thirty-minute walk. She had been a half-hour from the safety and warmth of *home*. Defeated, she found no water to clean her body—now worsened by dirt, grime, and animal urine—she needed to do something. It came to cutting her drinking rations. With no way to wash her clothes, and a trickle of water over her skin, it didn't come close to clean. Sprawled over a blanket under the setting sun to dry herself, much of the stink lingered, but her nose appreciated what little relief her efforts brought.

Startled by the "Hey, Gift," she jolted to her feet. "Sorry," she said once her dreary eyes found Tina, and reality passed the slap test. The update was brief, more water and food delivered, and the tablet exchanged for the newest broadcasts. Gift's desperate hope to find the hidden messages struggled to assure her Aimée could find a way to sneak more in.

"You see Mikey in the goofy uniform? Such a dork."

"You know he's spying, right? He hasn't joined them."

"I'm not the hermit hold up out here on my own."

"Yeah."

"Hang in there. We're working to get local comms so we can coordinate, keep you in the loop too. Then we'll try to reach Raff, whoever we can."

"I hope so. Tina, I'm... losing it out here alone. I replay Aimée's broadcasts, over and over, all day. It's not even just being alone, you know? It's... it's that I can't do anything to, to help. This... *hiding*, like this? I hate it."

"I know. Most of my day is placating these turds from U.R.M. and doing maintenance. I'm assisting with repairs on the air transports, the Chinese ones they shot down."

"Now that's interesting. I mean, these people came here all the way from Mars—*actual Mars*. They have weapons that could level a colony, spaceships. You know Aimée's up there in one of them?" Tina nodded, and Gift's brain caught up. "I mean, why do they care about *our* stuff? The Chinese stuff, not ours."

"Good point."

"Tina?" Gift said from a soft voice drowning in sadness. "You brought me more stuff. Mike gave me a bunch... You think, I mean, you think I'm gonna be stuck out here a while, don't you?"

"Looks that way. But we'll try to come see you."

"And Matteo?"

"I'll check, try to send him for the next visit."

"That would be great."

3

Alone again, Gift sorted through the bags to find water, ration bars, and a fresh blanket. *Enough stuff to last me weeks. Wonderful.* Her mental voice was better at sarcasm than her larynx. The second bag's contents earned a smile—too long since her lips did that. Apples, mandarins, and strawberries. She had never tasted *baby oranges* before, so started with those. As the juice ran over her chin, she exclaimed with a mouth full of the delicious pulp, "Amazing. Almost as good as honey."

Dropping her hand, Gift Two stiffened. "Nothing's as good as honey. It's the best thing ever."

"I said *almost*. Settle down," Gift One replied.

The joyous occupation of devouring the fruit ended, and she resumed her investigation of the totes. "Irony, you are cold." After having used her precious drinking water to barely bathe, Gift pulled a package of body wipes and tooth sticks from the bag. She laughed heartily for two minutes until tears filled her eyes. They had no joy, nor had they sprung from sorrow. A novel sensation, she couldn't categorize it. "Still can't find me any clo—" The same hideous green shorts-tank top combo bunched up against her nostrils brought an almost forgotten sensation. Clean.

Why am I hiding, again? Right. I have something they want. Gift tried to recall, but her brain had been taking long rest periods of late. It wasn't always there when she requested something.

"Not something I *have*. Something I *know*. They don't know it ... and, and they know that I know what they want to know but don't know. *Yes*. That's it, has to be. Clever, they're real clever, aren't they? But I'm even cleverer and will never tell." Gift spoke to the blanket tossed over a long stick posted in the ground just outside her airplane. A close enough semblance to a human form, she could talk to it and not consider it losing her mind. So far, it hadn't answered her.

In a frantic dash back into her airplane, Gift banged her left shoulder on the side of the door. She ignored the discomfort that may have been pain. The smaller of the holes in the fuselage served as an entrance and exit, but calling it a door lessened the strangeness of living inside the carcass of a metal beast dead for over two centuries. Unsure why she needed to know at that exact moment, Gift got on her knees to check her calendar.

"Five, ten, fifteen, sixt—*arr*. Where are you going? Not sixteen, you stupid idiot. Where was I?" Gift looked up at the skylight and screamed noises without sensible words. "Five, ten, fifteen, twenty. No, no, no. *Idiot*." Following the fifth set of four lines, each of those with a slash through it indicating sets of five, she had forgotten the slashes and the lines kept going. "Twenty-six, twenty-seven, twenty-eight, twenty-nine, thir—"

Two fists pounded her thighs on every "No" Gift yelled, and she yelled several. Her brain had been off doing its own thing. Had she forgotten about the slash trick and just kept etching lines for each day? Or had she forgotten to make the slash but counted the next line as the *sixth* day, making each set of four equal five days? Chan's *Or* came to her mind, and she thought of her thoughts back then, of how a bullet may have been preferable. *Of all the things for my stupid brain to call back now.*

"From twenty-five. One, two, three—" She counted the individual lines to see how many days she gashed without indicating sets of five. "—seventeen." But had she been in her airplane forty-two or forty-six days? No conclusions about why it mattered came to mind, but it must have been something hugely important. Of course, her tablet could have told her the date, but that wasn't the point. *What was the point?*

Rewatching Aimée's vids settled Gift, the lucidity trickling into her. Spotting the clues, codewords, and hidden messages Aimée sprinkled into her words was thrilling. Gift loved spy talk when she and Raff first tried it in a previous life. Once again *Gift* became a secret spy name, even if it was still her real name. Bittersweet sensations filled her when her tablet came online, reducing the urgency for in-person visits. Gift had seen no one in far too long. Comms on the tablet had been limited to only the downloads of Aimée's broadcasts, nothing more. Sitting under the stars, Gift held the tablet so her friend could see. To have someone to tell her if she was right about the secret message or was projecting made her feel less alone. The blanket over a stick still hadn't replied, but watching together, Gift had company. Emily, she called her.

True to Gift's assurance to General Xiang, her friend in orbit had begun slipping more messages into her vids. Gift found them in the combination of seemingly disconnected words. Entire phrases were pieced into multiple sentences and flagged by hand gestures. Sometimes Aimée moved about the ship to show the amiable crew or views of Earth. Those blew Gift's mind, and she could hardly believe Aimée was up there. Gift found no clues in the next two broadcasts. As usual, Emily agreed.

Watching the next episode of *Your Forced Occupation with Aimée Toussaint*—as Gift called it—the head smack came. Aimée held up her tablet while giving clues about sunlight and phosphorescent plants, lacing those throughout her talking points as fitting analogies of the *enlightened* ways of the New World Order. "Like a precious gift, its light will reveal humanity's hidden beauty." To find what Aimée wanted her to see, Gift tried watching in full sunlight. Nothing was there. Or Gift's brain just didn't perform well enough to catch it.

Taps on the tablet, or her knee—Aimée managed to sit cross-legged even in zero gravity and looked lovely—were clues that the word or phrase spoken was part of a secret message. The first full decipher Gift made was in an older vid. By stringing the bits together and trimming what didn't fit, she learned about the secret recruitment of local colonists into the U.R.M. guard. U.R.M. numbers were much lower than presented. Assurance she got it right came not from Emily, helpful as she'd been, but a memory of Mike in that uniform. He'd already found the clue about recruitment, but did Mike know of the U.R.M.'s low numbers?

One decoded thought played the heartstrings of Gift's chest like a symphony of requited love. Aimée hinted about an escape pod and a way to get back to Earth, to come home. It didn't matter in the moment that Gift had no idea how to get herself home, and that Aimée returning from space seemed exponentially more doable than her ever leaving her *mal'd* airplane.

"Gift... Hidden beauty... glowing plants." What was Aimée trying to tell her? On a desperate hunch, Gift searched the exterior of the fuselage for something from a memory. An airplane used by the China of old, it had a thermographic camera which would have an infrared lens. Not there, she had seen it on her failed hunt for bathing water in a scattering of pieces of her airplane.

Being an engineer again thrilled Gift by waking her mind, and it became a delightful preoccupation, a welcome deviation from the maddening nothingness her life had become. The cockpit door became the work surface for Bench-Gift, working her tasks. Tools fashioned from metal shards and strips of wire were rudimentary but functional. The dissected camera supplied the needed parts to create a solution to the problem at hand.

A sound roiled in, *massively* loud, as Aimée would say. Then another, and another. Drops of water pounded the ground with such force it had the clatter of the colossal waterfall Gift had visited with Oksana and Aimée. Her airplane home's metal exacerbated the tumultuous commotion, as the amplified sound reverberated around her like the bullets hitting the Zil in a distant memory. Quickly, Gift gathered her contraption, her tablet, blankets, spare set of clothes, and rations, and huddled everything into the small space of the fuselage not being overrun by leaks. An idea came in the green shorts and shirt in her hand, and she dropped them in the puddling liquid beside a pile of potable water bags.

With the result of hours of work laid over the tablet's display, she would test a theory. Had she correctly interpreted Aimée's code? Would her *Frankenstein* device see it? Playback paused when Aimée deliberately held her tablet vertical with the full back of the device visible. "Let's see if I'm right, and if you'll work, you beautiful, stupid contraption."

> Hi Love. Knew you'd find me.

"Holy crap. It works. It actually works. Emily, it works. *Emily*?" Torrential rains beating down on her, Emily had been left out in the storm, left all alone. At once, Gift set the tablet and her infrared looking-device down, and stepped toward the hole she called a door in the side of her airplane home. "*Emily*." Stepping out too quickly onto the slick mud, Gift's foot slid away from her, rapidly slamming her to the wet dirt. The back of her head took a jolt when it met the ground. The pounding of falling liquid on her skin took her back to Chan's shower.

When her eyes opened, a massive drop brought pain to her sclera and pulled the lids shut. Squinting through her eyelashes, Gift saw dense black and silver above a barrage of droplets pelting her soaked flesh. Rising slowly to her feet and stepping gingerly, she embraced Emily and said, "I'm sorry. I didn't mean to leave you out here all alone. I'm so sorry." Tears joined the rain pouring over her face.

Twisting and pulling, twisting and pulling. The mud refused to let go of the pole's base. Fighting the bullets that were stinging drops of rain, and with all the energy her muscles could muster, she lifted Emily from the wet dirt and carried her inside. Both overlaid in mud and dripping wet, Gift leaned her against the wall where she could see the tablet screen, and sat beside her. "This is the first time I've had you over. Welcome to my home."

> I'm fine. They r few. Fear missiles? More tmrw.

"Emily, she did it. Actual communication, hidden text on the back of her tablet. Good question. Her last keywords: *Ink* and *Kiosks*. I coupled them to *glowing plants* and remembered those stupid 'All Lies' messages in that bio-florescent ink. With no kiosk night mode, I improvised."

Although Emily said nothing, Gift felt her excitement.

"We need to rewatch them all. My sweet Aimée's okay, and she's talking to me... Oh, sweetheart, don't worry. We're still friends, you and me. Come on, let's watch the rest together."

Before playing the next vid, Gift's brain returned to tell her she was still drenched and shivering cold, then kindly reminded her she had a second set of clothes. "No." Those clothes were in a puddle of water from Gift's now less-than-brilliant idea to clean them. Filling that puddle, a gaping hole in the ceiling cascaded rainwater into her home. Stepping under it, she instantly stiffened from the icy-cold bite on her skin. Her resolve to shed the mud from her clothes and flesh kept her there, quivering. When the top and shorts were as clean as they were going to get, she removed them and grabbed a body cleaning pad, giving her a shower with soap and water, and getting her as close to clean as she had been in weeks.

Shaking uncontrollably, she wrapped a dry blanket over the goose-bumps. After changing Emily's soaked covering, Gift continued through the vids and promised to clean the mud from the wall and floor later. She sat opposite the mess to continue her search for clues. The next two vids contained similar messages on the back of Aimée's tablet, telling of her plan to steal an escape pod at a later point. She was staying up there to gather more intel.

Emily was good company, though she said little.

4 | WEEK NINE

Thinking in terms of weeks made it less than months. It nearly destroyed her when Gift considered she had surpassed the two-month mark in her airplane. Weeks were small grouping of days, so Gift thought, *I've been alone for nine weeks.* Staring at her prehistoric calendar, Gift pondered, *When was my last visit? Mike came first, I'm not counting General Meanie. Then Tina.* A mental block kept the next visit hidden behind a wall she couldn't surmount. "Who came? When?"

Suspicions said Emily knew—she had such a good memory—but didn't tell. *It's jealousy.* Emily acted strange since regular contact with Aimée began, paying less attention to help spot the clues. Despite frequent reassurances, Gift could tell a rift had formed and feared it to be unfixable.

There had been one more rain since the downpour that gave her a shower. "*Dai*, it's two weeks ago." Only her second shower in eleven weeks, and she still had no way to properly wash her clothes. That second rain fell lightly, making her indoor shower not much more than a trickle over her skin. Just as bone-chillingly cold, but not very effective for cleaning her body. When Gift first realized her provisions would long outlast her personal hygiene items, she rationed body wipe use to every three days and one tooth stick every other day. Emily didn't mind Gift's stench. Besides, *she* never showered.

"Hey, sweet girl," Gift said when Aimée cleverly disguised her personal greeting as a general one to all watching.

"*Hi, Love.*" Deep in the recesses of her mind, on the days when it functioned, Gift knew Aimée's voice rang only in her head. It was still lovely to hear it. The days with no hidden message tormented Gift, as she couldn't know if she had missed something important. She smiled wider than her lips had in weeks when Aimée cleverly assumed her friend's preoccupation and brought her mind down. On any day without a secret code, the back of Aimée's tablet had a simple message.

> None today. Love you.

"When did Aimée start doing that? Em, do you remember…? Yes, you're right, just before my second shower two weeks ago. Thanks." Gift hoped using the nickname might soften Emily and strengthen their friendship. Not to offend, she waited until Em went outside to check the calendar for the day of the shower.

Gift Two said, "You know you have a tablet, right? It has the date and time on it."

"Yeah." Gift One cared little for Gift Two's negativity.

"Stop with the caveman calendar. It's pointless."

"No. It's very important. It has to be accurate."

Gift Two stood, and put her hands on her hips. "Okay, I'll play along. Why's it so important?"

"When I leave, this thing goes with me." Gift One shook the tablet in her hand. "This calendar on the wall will be the only way for anyone to know."

"You think you're getting out of here? They'll find your withered corpse in here with that stupid tablet clenched in the bones that used to be your fingers."

"No," Gift One shouted.

The uncomfortably warm fuselage became more so listening to Gift Two. Running at all her physical condition could muster for full speed—and no idea how long she ran or in which direction—Gift abruptly halted. "*Yang*. Or was it Wang?" *It's one of those for sure*, she concluded as her mind decided to respond to the earlier inquiry Gift had already forgotten making. *Not Tina, Mike, or Matteo. Not General Stern-Face.* Some guy name Wang or Yang brought her resupply and a fresh tablet. Laying on the dirt when her strength lost its interest in standing, Gift tried to recall the visit.

A warmth filled her cheeks beyond what the sun gave them. When Yang or Wang visited on her second shower day Gift had wrapped herself in a blanket with both sets of her malodorous clothes drip-drying from their not-quite-a-wash in the puddle. The blanket covered more than the shorts and top, yet the embarrassment of not being dressed stung, in the memory as much as the moment. Hopes to at least get some conversation out of the guy, much-needed human contact, disintegrated when it became evident *Hi* was the only English word he knew. Poor guy, it didn't stop Gift rambling on for over an hour.

Wide, wild eyes saw a million stars speckled across a vast infinity. Not since her three-days-outside-the-colony test had she lay flat on her back in the wee hours and gazed upon the magnificence of a middle-of-the-night sky full of stars. "It's gigantic. Like its closer than normal." The night hung a silver ball above her, floating close enough to touch. Silver moonlight gave her incredible vision across the open plain where her eyes spotted the adorable creature that relieved itself on her weeks ago. It headed away from her, and wisely she decided not to say *Ciao*, as the return greeting it offered last time was warm urine. Hopefully there wouldn't be a repeat sighting of Mister V, the enormous black thing that had to be a bear and would eat her face.

Where even am I? She had no idea, and had less than fifty percent certainty which way she had come. "Oh mamma. I'm lost." Rising to her feet, Gift looked in every direction, it all looked the same. She spun around in a frantic search for a landmark, some sign of the way back home. The lightheadedness nearly stumbled her to the ground. Fingers interlocked, Gift rested her hands on top of her head and squinted to see a hint of diffused light several hundred meters in the distance. *No way I could see my airplane from here. Nothing else is out here, nothing anywhere near me besides...* "The *mal'd* N.R.C." Gift had wandered well outside Xiang's theoretical fence and on the wrong side of her outcropping. *How'd I get here? Run back.*

The darkness slowly lifted from the horizon. Not daylight, nothing so grandiose, but the start of morning, the time Gift would catch the first glimpse of sunlight dancing over Colony Lake. It had been so long since Gift swam. Having skipped dinner and being way too many hours since she had a sip of water, her body gave out to the lack of energy. Burning pain covered her knee from the fall but she held the tears in a blink. They weren't for the scraped skin, and she wasn't about to let herself cry for being stupid enough to get herself lost.

Isolation, desolation. Let it go...

Under the intense midday sun, it became impossible to go on, not without water. Small trees with scanty foliage offered little shade. Taking what she could get, Gift leaned against a narrow trunk to sit with shoulders slouched and head down, chin to the breastbone.

"I'll just die right here. *Ha.* Take that. You said I would die in my airplane. Who's the stupid idiot now?" Gift One said in a triumphant inflection.

Gift Two replied, "So you're happy to die as long as it's not in the airplane? That's somehow a victory for you?"

"No—*what?*—hey. Shut up. I mean, *you* were wrong."

"And you are pathetic."

"Why are you so mean?" Gift One asked. "Remember, someone who is pathetic needs sympathy."

"There, there." Gift Two's words dripped sarcasm. It never fit right on Gift One, but Gift Two wore it well.

"Just... shut up."

Gift sat with Oksana in her family home after Nadezhda Anoykina called her back and forbade her to ever return to New Europa. The girl's sobbing infuriated Gift.

"You got her captured and almost killed in Africa. So irresponsible you were with my Oksana. I trusted you."

"No," Gift shouted. "She got captured and almost killed *here*, too. And your creep son... in your own house. You're a terrible mother. She's coming back with me."

Eyes popped open when Gift's slumbering head slipped. The figure they found in the distance looked small and cloudy. Real, dream, or hallucination?

5 | Week Ten

Lucidity came in intervals. At times, increasing in frequency, her brain left Gift in mental obscurity. While she understood Emily to be a coping mechanism, her hope to ground herself this side of sanity permitted the figment of imagined friendship.

To be or not to be. Gift reconsidered those famous words. More than life or death, they spoke of sanity, ramblings from someone on the verge of crossing over. She felt herself teetering on the precipice. Or could she have already lost it? Would she know if she had?

"Real, dream, or hallucination?"

Hunched over beside the tiny tree—barely more than a glorified twig—her arm lacked the strength for a proper slap test. *If it's not hard enough, is it valid?* The figure persisted, small but steadily growing. If not a dream, that left at least two possibilities—not counting insanity. Could her eyes, tired and delirious, have played tricks? The figure didn't appear solid—Gift knew humans were always solid. This *whatever-it-was* approaching appeared part human, part... steam. A darkness like her Box at night returned and everything vanished.

From a distant memory she heard an echo of her name—a question rather than a statement. *Maybe this is what insanity feels like. Was this the kind of scrambled mess going on in Chan's brain?* Alone in the darkness of her eyes and the recesses of her mind, Gift accepted it—she had crossed the threshold. "I've lost my mind."

"No, Gift. Please, you need to drink. Take a sip, please."

An unfamiliar feeling touched her lips and clung to her chin. Moisture. Water. How much she longed for water. Just a sip would do. Her mouth felt weird.

"That's it, swallow. Drink the water."

Was it Gift Two? No, she's always mean, only comes to argue. Emily? Something else, a voice, familiar. Gift fought a battle between the side of her mind leaning into crazy and the one desperately clinging to sanity. *It's not Emily. She's not real.* Gift swallowed and her mouth filled again, cool and wet. Another swallow.

"That's it. Good."

"*Matteo?*"

"Yes, Gift. It's me. You're alright, I found you."

In panic Gift said, "I can't see you. I can't see."

Jarring, the cold sudden splash separated Gift's eyelids to show her Matteo, leaned over her holding the open end of a water bag. A few more sips restored the lucidity that had slipped away.

"When you weren't at the plane, I searched. Walked for hours 'til I saw you. I was so scared something happened."

"Something did. Happen, I mean."

"What? Are you okay?"

"I... What is... *Matteo*, is that you?"

Nothingness enveloped her once again.

The skylight showed its nighttime view, distant stars as specks of light through an oval of glass. At once Gift knew she was "home." *I was in the wilderness, dying. How'd I get here? Must be a dream if I didn't travel. Is this my departure?* The clatter jolted her. Mister V had found her, hungry for her face.

"Oh good, you're finally awake."

"*Little Matteo?*"

"Hey Gift."

"What are... *How*...? When did you...?"

"Found you in the wilderness, remember?"

"*Huh?* Yeah, I think... I saw you. But you were weird, like you were made of steam."

"Okay, sure. And you were a little—"

"Out-of-my-mind nuts?"

"Pretty much, yeah. How're you feeling?"

"I... don't know. How long?"

"If your etched calendar there is correct, three days."

"I was out there three days?"

"Two, and a day here. I brought you back yesterday."

When Gift tried to sit up, Matteo slowly gave her water, which she readily gulped down. Never a fast eater, Gift chomped the rations bar down so quickly the words "inhaled it" would have been a fitting description. A warm smile and a firm embrace reunited brother and sister.

"Nice place. Real... homey."

"Brat." Gift slapped his chest. "Can't believe it's been my *home*—" she outlined the word in air quotes—"for ten weeks already. I'm going a little crazy."

"A little? I saw your *friend*. You called her Em?"

"What, how did—"

"You called to her in your sleep."

"Emily. Thought it might help keep me sane." An apologetic tone came from a scrunched face.

"Yeah, not so sure that worked." Another slap to the chest came with a smile.

"I'm so glad to see you. Tell me everything. Oh, and whatcha got for me?"

Gift crunched on a fresh carrot while Matteo gave her an update on the colony. On the surface, it appeared to be the peaceful transition the U.R. M. promised. Matteo received an assignment in cleaning and had a measure of freedom. "That's the only visible issue for many. The only obvious one anyway," he explained. "We're under curfew, much more restrictive than the N.E. Lights-Out policy."

Outside of work assignments, people were permitted in very few places, and most required authorization. No entertainment vids, vidChat disabled. *Your Forced Occupation with Aimée Toussaint*—they called it *Welcome to the United Republic of Earth*—was the only thing to watch. All colonists attended *Unification Education* each evening, which mixed propaganda with history lessons and what they called the founding tenets of the New World Order.

It delighted Gift to find a new box of body wipes and tooth sticks. She would still have to ration to make them last, as Matteo offered no hope of her getting out of there any time soon. No new clothes or blankets. But the new tablet came with a pleasant surprise.

"Mike told me they can send you brief messages."

"Really? Oh, oh, that's... *amazing*."

"But very limited. Mike told me to emphasize that. Only when *absolutely* necessary. They won't be online all the time, have to be careful not to get caught."

"How do I do it? I just call up vidChat?"

"No, only text chat."

"Like back in my N.E. insurrection-fighting days."

"Mike did it with a Chinese data operator. Remember, if you send a message, brief and only *absolutely* necessary. Don't expect an immediate reply."

"Got it. Oh... *Idiot*. Not you, me. Have you guys been getting Aimée's intel? Finding the hidden messages?"

"Mike's been decoding some."

"Has he found the invisible text ones?"

"Haven't heard about that, so maybe not."

"Necessary? I'll tell him how to see them." A chunk of apple pushed her cheek out as she chewed it into a mush. "Oh. Three days. You said it's been three days? I need to watch her broadcast, look for the messages."

"Mike saw none. Maybe you've got a better eye for it."

"Wait, you found me *yesterday*? Won't anyone miss you, look for you?"

"Got people covering at work, but I'm not sure about missing Unification Education. They don't roll-call, and it's a huge group, so hopefully no one noticed."

"And now? You gotta leave me again?" She pouted and tried the sad soulful eyes on him. "Can't you stay? *Please*."

"Yes."

"*Why not?* I hate it here alone, can't—Wait. Did you... did you say *yes*?"

"I did."

Gift threw herself into Matteo and squeezed as tight as she could with muscles not yet renewed. Welcome tears flowed. The pop put a puzzled look on Matteo's face and a red handprint on Gift's cheek.

"What'd you do that for?"

"Had to make sure I'm not dreaming. Can't... I just..."

"Looks like it hurt."

"Worth it. This is real. You're *really* here... and staying with me. For how long?"

"I had advanced treatments. Not sure how many days I can last, but for now, I'm staying."

After another prolonged hug, they watched the last of Aimée's updates for more clues. Proudly, Gift showed off her invisible text reader. The first vid's tablet raise was the *nothing today, love you* note. The next had more details about their scant numbers and how the U.R.M. were shifting personnel between colonies in the pretense of having larger troops.

***

Days with Matteo passed with no maddening silence, no conversations with herself or Emily—she felt guilty for that. As Gift described her adventures, her first night lost and sleeping outdoors, she learned the *fox* that peed on her was a red panda. Matteo described it as a bear that sort of looked like a fox. He found it odd that it marked *her* in its territory and disgusting that it peed on her to do it.

Matteo had brought cards, so they played Whist and assorted games. He readily joined her in rewatching vids in search of clues she already searched for dozens of times. When it rained one morning, she woke him, made him turn his back and swear to keep his eyes closed, and tossed a blanket over his head so she could shower. He went next with less rigid rules, trusting her back. She used the blanket, taking his shame upon herself.

Using the chat sparingly, Gift learned besides Mike, Xiang had seventeen implants in the guard. Word came of Matteo's absence being noticed, so it wouldn't be safe for him to return—news Gift didn't mind receiving. When the infrared decoder lifted a clue from the back of Aimée's tablet, Gift had to make sure Mike, Tina, and the General knew about it via another *necessary* chat message. No one was online, so Gift typed her message and engaged her patience to wait for their reply.

"Aimee said check their weapons. Something off. If right we can win this."

6

Siblings were not *uncommon* in New Europa, they were nonexistent. In the Pioneers and Ubuntu people, Gift learned she was not alone in having the ability to produce a healthy child the natural way. Those survivors had been doing so for generations. Though high fetal mortality rates kept their numbers low, humans had siblings. Gift wasn't one of them. Yet in every aspect she considered truly mattering, Gift had a brother and a sister. The love they shared resulted not from blood relations, but from real connections.

Her kid sister was fine, she had to believe it. Mike said Oksana was with good people who were looking after her. No reason came to Gift's now well-functioning mind why the girl would be mistreated for being the daughter of the President of the R.F. Even Chan treated her well, and he was far more out of his mind than Gift had gotten, even at her worst. Oksana was fine.

With her little brother there, Gift was no longer alone with only the madness of isolation. Matteo's treatments had limited effect. After a few days his appetite waned, he slept longer, and needed midday naps. *The earth sickness is overtaking him*, Gift feared. Days now included walkabouts with Matteo, exploring the countryside. Gift's disused muscles needed exercise. Plus, not sitting around benefited Matteo. The logical part of her brain said walking in the environment might help his body not get sick from it—theoretically.

"If we could find any remains of those weapons they used against us, find what Aimée hinted us to find."

"Gift, we're like an hour's walk farther from the colony than the airplane is. Unless they were trying to hunt bears, we're not fining any Martian weapons out here."

"My brain's working again." The back of her hand slapped Matteo's chest when he smirked. "*Brat.* You know what I mean. It's... *better.* And I'm not losing my grip on reality or talking to Em. I hope she's okay though, 'cause I know how lonely it gets... What was... Oh, I mean I'm thinking more clearly now."

"I'd say that jumble your words just made argue against that. And is that thought train of yours—or *train wreck*—going somewhere?"

With another playful slap, Gift said, "I just mean you don't have to constantly correct me and worry that I'm out of my mind. I was... you saw that. But now I am. Thinking clearly, I mean. I am. It was more... hopping out loud. Hoping. *Hoping* out loud. It would be great if we could find something. And you don't know, Mister Sane-Brain, if weapons they used could have exploded, broken into a bazillion bits that flung all over."

Matteo chuckled. "Mister Sane-Brain—good one. I'm gonna use that. I see your slightly less-than-crazy point but still don't agree. We're too far and there weren't even any bits around the colony. I wonder if they removed them, like if there *is* something they don't want us to find."

"*Right?*"

"You think other colonies may have decoded Aimée's messages? Maybe found some weapons bits. What if any of them resisted... or got free?"

"Raff's face when they came. New Europa surrendered, like they had no choice. Even after everything, I've never seen her so frightened."

"You think it's over? That we're under this United Republic of Earth, nothing we can do about it?"

"I..." Gift let out an emphatic sigh. "I don't know. *Ma*... I don't... I mean, there is never *nothing* we can do. Beyond our messed-up history, revolutions and wars and all, look at the last year. Our own insurrection, conflicts with the Pioneers, then Ubuntu, governments of U.A. flipping."

"I know, you may—"

"*Yes*. If anyone can get free, overtake these Martians, it's U.A., *right?* I mean, look what they did when the N.R.C. army came. I mean *went*, there, to U.A." Matteo seemed to follow without the *thought train* having to stop to change tracks. "Bright will do it, I'm sure."

"Hundred percent. Okay, it looks like that brain of yours is back. Good, too, we'll need it to get out of this."

"Aimée's note about them being fewer than we think, moving people about to fake their numbers. They're recruiting colony residents, I guess everywhere. Oh, Mike's stupid uniform. Is it the same? Like so no one can tell the difference, who's Martian or... Earthian?"

"*'Earthian'* gives me some doubt about your brain being back." He got another light slap for that. "But you're right. They never remove their helmets, and they do the recruiting in secret, so everyone looks like their soldiers. We implanted some, maybe the other colonies did too."

"Yes, yes. I think so, hope so. Look. We know Sergey fought the Pioneers, back when they were Philistines... to them, I mean. Bright fought the Chinese and won. And at New Europa, Tom beat them too."

"Tom? Was he leading the guards and our defenses?"

"Shut up. You know what I mean. He's there now, and Sara, all the guards. So, if we organize the Chinese, I think, we can get all the colonies back. We can do this. And with them not having an armada up there..." Gift pointed up and pumped her arm. "Limited weapons. We need to find them, learn what Aimée wants us to see."

"Honestly, I didn't believe we stood a chance, thought we'd be under their control, their New World Order, forever." Gift pouted. "No, what I'm saying is that *now?* for the first time, I *do* think we have a chance to send these overbearing overlords back to Mars. And... it's because of you."

Matteo wrapped his arms around Gift and squeezed, infusing her with confidence and gratitude. When its intensity lessened, Gift assumed the moment of sibling affection ended and they'd get back to their walk.

Matteo collapsed; Gift barely able to ease his fall.

"Matteo."

Nothing roused him—not shouts of his name, slaps to the face, not even water splashed in it. He said they had walked an hour from her airplane to wherever they were. An hour of walking under their own power. With no way to physically lift his bulk, Gift pushed her hands under his arms and locked them over his chest. Hunched over and pulling backwards, she dragged him a few centimeters. Another tug. A few more centimeters. The third tug moved him even less, and Gift fell onto her backside. Hopelessness washed over her, and it grew late.

With no way to carry on, Gift looked for a suitable place to stay the night. Fire-making skills again came in handy as the nights saw inconceivable plummets in temperature. All attempts to wake Matteo failed. But he had a pulse, so Gift had hope. Eleven years passed since they cuddled to sleep in a fetal position. This night demanded it, to keep him warm, to keep him safe. More so Gift could feel his back inflating against her chest with each breath.

Darkness ensued, dense at first, until a full moon shone over the field empowering Gift's eyes to see well enough to travel. A ping-pong volley pitted two sides of her now fully functional mind in ruthless battle over rational reasons for her options. In the end, she could make only one decision, so one *had* to be right. *This is the right thing to do,* played on a loop in her mind as Gift walked with soft moonlight glistening on her moist skin. The night's chill shivered bones no longer heated by the exertion of hauling Matteo. Tears scolded her for leaving him unconscious under a large bush between two small trees.

Finding her airplane didn't bring the greatest success. That would come in finding her way back to Matteo.

7

M atteo had insisted on taking water bags, rations bars, and matches, which proved much better at starting a fire than the stones, and didn't damage any fingers. The first marker to confirm her directions, Matteo's left shoe placed in sight of its companion, should have been visible. It wasn't. Memories of getting lost twice in the same wilderness flooded into her like panic—a thought charged with such power it dropped Gift to her knees.

Tears clouded her vision as worry clouded her mind. "Stop it Gift. Get up. Find Matteo." Bolstered by her pep talk, Gift spotted the shoe where it shouldn't have been—she must have walked *straight* back to Matteo in a not-so-straight line. Once passed the matchbox, the next markers would be much harder to spot, so she had laid the matches at shorter intervals. On the distant crest of a small dirt hill, she saw the last water bag. *Doing well, going the right way. Brava, Gift.* The next sight her hopeful eyes captured almost sent Matteo's name slicing through the quiet of the night.

He was up and moving about. He was going to be fine. *Why's he crawling? Must have little strength. Why's he so fat? Mister V Chest!* Gift sank belly-down, grateful she hadn't shouted to the bear, still sure it would eat her face and now overwhelmed with fear it might have eaten Matteo's. Mister V tried to figure out the rations bar, playing with the unusual thing more than eating it. The wrapper must have thrown the creature's simple mind into a state of confusion, unlike anything nature ever put in its mouth.

Not convinced this mountain of a wild, hungry beast wouldn't revisit, Gift prepared for it. In addition to her largest blanket, she had grabbed a bag of nuts and fruit and made the ultimate sacrifice of adding the last of her honey to increase the lure of its attraction. Matteo had shared information about the Asian black bear, and she remembered it ate nuts and fruit and loved honey almost as much as she did. The trail of markers gave Gift an idea. As quietly as she could, crawling low to the ground toward the bear's ample backside, she got within ten meters.

Her first toss of the gooey mixture landed a couple of meters closer to the gigantic face eater. Another managed a bit more distance. One small pile at her location and a toss that hit five meters from Mister V's bottom. Another toss made it closer to three meters, still a decent distance from the nostrils that needed to catch the scent. Thoughts gathered and nerves stiffened, Gift crawled to a tree between her and the massive creature. A pile of treats sat less than a meter from her and one final toss toward the bear puffed up a dust cloud a half meter to its back. Wrapped like a human burrito in her blanket, Gift waited with nothing to do but hope a breeze would carry the fragrance.

She waited.

It ate the last ration bar, the one closest to Matteo, still a safe distance from having his face eaten. Safe if the hungry bear didn't notice him. Gift could faintly see the moonlit blue-gray lump that was her little brother tucked half under a bush, half out. Would unbathed human body odor attract or repulse the beast? Putting her nose to an underarm, Gift considered that if human B.O. would attract Mister V, she was as likely a target.

She waited.

Something caught the attention of the beast that greedily stole her rations bars. In a single blink, its backside became its face and Gift could have sworn it made eye contact with her. Mostly behind a small tree, she allowed her eyes to peer through a narrow sliver in the blanket. After thoroughly enjoying the snack, it followed its nose to the next lump of tasty goodness. Closer to her. The next sweet treat brought the hulk of an animal just on the other side of the thin, bare tree beside her, the only thing separating Gift from the face-eating monster.

Skeptically, its black snout flinched to examine the small mound of food. Scary close, its ears looked so cute, like they belonged on a much less intimidating mammal, something she could cuttle. Mister V merited no such affection. Gift felt sure it would kill for no reason beyond its sheer size. Finished with the treat beside her tree, it lumbered to the next, clearing the way to Matteo.

Commander Tucker's 'hold' order popped onto her mental display. *Don't risk ruining your masterful plan by moving too soon. He'll hear you. He'll eat your face.* Gift accepted her logical caution and watched Mister V make his way through the remaining bait trail. Perhaps puzzled when it found no more treats, it paused, then continued scurrying in the direction her trail suggested.

Repeated tries to wake Matteo failed. Unblanketed shoulders wiggled, and Gift's body protested by riddling her skin with thousands of tiny bumps. Grunts and moans accompanied her efforts to roll Matteo's bulk onto the blanket. Taking some free material to tie around her waist, Gift thought this would be easier than pulling by hand. *The first step must be the hardest*, she thought... until the second. By the fourth, fifth, it became manageable, making her ninety-nine percent sure she could do it. The pull on her abdomen ached, so she grabbed the cloth at her hips and let her arm muscles take some of the pain.

"*Little* Matteo. Guess I'll stop calling you that, *right?*"

While he didn't reply, talking to an unconscious person was saner than talking to Gift Two or Em, so it was fine. She was fine. He'd be fine.

The first signs of dawn restored the color the night had stolen from the metal carcass. Her airplane, safety for her and Matteo. "Just a bit further... I can do it," she said, panting and grunting. "Or is it farther? Never get those right." In what felt like at least three hours, she had gotten her big-and-heavy little brother *home*. "Now what?" To drag him in the opening of the torn fuselage sapped the last of her strength and the distance to the pile of blankets she called her bed could have been kilometers away.

"Matteo, please sweetie, wake up. *Matteo*."

He resembled a pale gray corpse, and Gift immediately fought the image and implications of that word. With no idea how she hoped to do it, she would make him better. Propped up slightly, he seemed to be swallowing some of the water Gift poured in his mouth.

"Good. Water is good." The irony of the role-reversal hit her like a smack in the face.

The one time he came close to waking up, he puked on her shirt. Nothing but thick putrid bile came from his gut. When was the last time he ate? It had been some time for her, but Gift couldn't eat with him like that. She started humming a Nigerian nursery melody she had forgotten until then. Pleasant drifting into the memory put her back in Nonna's arms and freed her mind of Matteo's potential outcomes, which all ended with him dying in her embrace. On her mental display, Gift listed the options, expecting a long list and another ping-pong debate between the two sides of her brain.

There was but one item on the display.

"Well, Matteo... Am I the only one who calls you that? Seems everyone else calls you *Matt*. What does Marie call you? You know, I actually can't remember. But if everyone calls you Matt, that makes it special that I call you Matteo, doesn't it? Not even your mom ever called you her little Matteo, that's just me for sure."

After a minute to recall what she had resolved to do, Gift changed the shirt Matteo puked on, and reached for the same large blanket. With him placed on it and centered, the ends tied about her waist and hands holding onto the loose material, she dragged him out of the airplane. A few steps into her journey Gift paused, turned her head, and glanced longingly over her shoulder.

"Addio," she said to her airplane home, knowing she would never see it again.

8 | WEEK ELEVEN

General Xiang. Cold as stone, fierce, like the face-eating black bear but without the unusual white V on her chest. An image of the general covered in fur twinged the corner of Gift's mouth almost into a smile. Fading as quickly, the mind flipped the scene into Xiang lunging open-mouthed with long sharp teeth about to bite Gift's face off. Oddly, it brought an open chuckle, stopping her feet. Or it could have been the aching in her muscles, overshadowed only by the exhaustion in her bones.

"Water break." With his head propped on the thighs of her folded legs, Gift drizzled a bit of water between Matteo's lips, allowing muscle memory to pull it into a swallow. "That's it. Need to stay hydrated."

Her bronzed skin absorbed the rays of the late morning sun like a dry sponge and became dryer by the saturation. Gift imagined how even the slightest touch of sunlight on the flesh of the last generation before the colonies burned as retribution from the universe itself. The fireball that gave life had cast a deadly judgmental glow over the humans infesting the planet they so carelessly ruined. Just over two centuries later, Gift had spent days outdoors basking in the glory of that forgiving little star, soothed by the comforting warmth it once again shared. *Perspective and circumstance,* she thought.

A familiar feeling welled up, aching for a friend's departed company when left alone, abandoned. Gift reminded herself Emily had been a coping mechanism, but that didn't lessen the impact of the relationship; the way Em had been there when Gift needed her. *Isn't that one of the definitions of a friend?*

"Come on, Matteo. Almost there."

The massive N.R.C. colony came into sight, the tops of the larger domes cresting over the last hill. Dragging her not-so-little *little Matteo* over the incline nearly drained her, yet she moved forward. Her first view of the exterior showed her a colony easily twice the size of New Europa, maybe more. A bit larger than the Russian Federation, which held roughly thirty thousand more residents than N.E.'s fifty.

"We're close now… just hold on… a little longer. Like you're doing… any of the work… anyway… Typical, leave the… real work to me… while you just relax."

The plan was elegantly simplistic. Drag Matteo to the colony then find the secret entrance her friends used to sneak out to meet her, sneak in, and find Xiang or Tina. It was a good plan. Gift may have called it great—until she saw the flaw in it.

"Matteo, where's the secret entrance? How do I sneak you in?"

Gift's mind flashed to a memory, a lesson from Mike using her own words as precedence against her current ideas. That frustrated her to no end. '*There has to be a way in,*' Mike had said in a memory. Matteo played a guard escorting his prisoners. When they reached the entrance to the N.R.C. Ops building, Mike assumed they'd find a way in because they needed to find it. In his absence, Gift brought her own words back on herself. '*Why Mike? Because we need one, there has to be one?*' It was smart when she said it, logical.

Now, less than a hundred meters from the perimeter of the huge colony, Gift would find the secret entrance because she needed to. Her words echoed in her brain, ringing like a klaxon until her head hurt. It had no wall, just an impressively tall fence of linked stiff wire topped with a spiral of metal that looked like it could slice through flesh and bone. Even if not dragging a limp body, she couldn't imagine scaling that. In the next memory, the general caught them outside of Ops. This time Gift wished more than anything for that former enemy, her onetime captor, to be the one to find her. The voice breaking the memory didn't sound familiar.

"Freeze. Hands on your head."

After ten grueling weeks of hiding, torturous isolation to guard her precious secret, the U.R.M. had her. *All that for nothing.*

"I said, hands on your head."

"You also said freeze. So, which is it?" Gift's surprise came not in her wit—though she did impress herself with it—but her uncharacteristic gumption. *Where'd that come from?*

"Hands on head. Now."

Gift unfastened the knot at her navel to gently lower the end of the blanket that kept Matteo's head elevated and protected. As her knees straightened, something hard and small pressed between her shoulder blades. Slowly her hands ascended, fingers interlocked, palms rested on her head, bringing the pain clamoring inside it to bear.

Forcefully she said, "He needs medical attention."

The unseen soldier said nothing. Hands grabbed her wrists and pulled them behind her back. Gift gave a half-second to ponder the irony of being told to place her hands there just to have them removed. The familiar rapid-clicks of zip-tie teeth reached her ears as its pinch tightened on her wrists. One soldier in the same uniform Mike had donned hid under a helmet's dark face cover. N.R.C. or U.R.M.? The English sounded too good to be a second language. No one came to tend to Matteo.

"Come."

"He needs help. We need to get him inside."

"If you wish him to live, come with me."

"If you wished that to sound ominous, it did." So snarky and argumentative, it could have been Gift Two talking. Gift One gladly let her take the lead.

Escorted to who-knew-where, she left Matteo on the blanket under the blistering sun, alone. The power of that mental occupation removed all concern for herself. The locked gate with two soldiers meant Gift wouldn't have found her way in, and she wondered how her allies had snuck out. Less than twenty meters from the gate, they entered an airlock, into a part of the colony Gift didn't recognize. She hadn't seen much of it before her exile.

"Is someone gonna help my friend? You can't leave him out there. He needs medical attention."

"You should be concerned for yourself."

"You said you came in peace… Didn't want anyone to be harmed, or to cause any damage. Prove it."

"Move." He pushed harder, walking her until she came to the center of the small auxiliary dome. The nudges led her to an archway into what looked like a smaller dome twenty meters in diameter. Inside it Gift found a rectangular table with the dull finish of a workbench and a chair on each side. They pushed her into the seat with her back to the entrance of the otherwise empty room.

The door's slam and the clunk of a lock mechanism stiffened her spine. As the minutes ticked, Gift recognized the familiar tactic. The silence and isolation, the suspense meant to heighten her fear. Only it didn't. Had she gotten so used to this, her inner stature didn't summon trepidation? No dread surfaced. "Here we go again," she said to the dimly lit space with green walls. More minutes went by, and Gift worried about Matteo. Were these polite conquerors showing themselves not the monsters they could be by helping him?

A thud brought a flood of brightness to fill the odd little dome within a dome, closing Gift's eyes. Footsteps crept up behind her. Not the heavy boots of a soldier nor the heels of an elegant lady, though Gift had no reason to expect heels or elegance. When her eyes opened slowly for the intensity of light, they saw no one. An empty chair faced her from across the dull metal table, now doing its best to bounce the surrounding illumination at her.

Something pulled her chin up in a swift motion, folding her neck. Rather than the ceiling, she saw a new face, male, but not dramatically masculine, with feminine cheekbones and thin lips. Gift thought the heavy stubble that wasn't a beard rather suited him. When her eyes focused on his nostrils, she saw nothing but hairs in a crisscross pattern. They seemed long for nose hairs, but at least there was no mucus clung to them. Gift remembered Mike once called it *booger*, and she thought it a funny word.

"We know who you are."

"Good." Unable to open her mouth, Gift slurred her words. "That shaves ush like shirty shecons."

"Gift Ojo of New Europa."

"No, shash my nane. You are?"

"Miss Ojo, you don't seem to be taking this seriously. You should be, I assure you," the not-so-intimidating man said. Releasing Gift's face eased the pinch in her neck. "We've been looking for you for many weeks and had expanded our search to include a wide radius outside the colony."

Gift spoke to the empty chair. "I'd say you're not very good at searching. You only found me when I came walking up to the gate."

"Indeed." He walked around the table to sit facing her. "That leads me to why. Why did you come here?"

"Wait. You didn't get Matteo? You can't leave him out there. I told your goon. You need to get him."

"Calm yourself, Miss Ojo. We *have* brought him inside. We mean no one any harm."

"Yet I'm a prisoner."

"Not at all. We are simply having a... conversation."

"Then tell me your name."

"James Morris, U.R.M. I'm sure you guessed that part."

"And *Commander?* Morris, James, why exactly are we having this... *conversation?*"

"Straight to the point, I like that. We knew you were here, monitored the communications between this colony and New Europa. You have some information we require."

"*Look.* As I told the Chinese, one bag of nuts and one scary General, I really don't know much about anything. I mean, I'm an engineer and I know about that kinda stuff. But if you think I know anything you need, anything of... I mean, any valuable information? You, like everyone, are mistaken." A puff of breath punctuated her point.

With a single finger raised, he replied, "If that were the case, we would have had this conversation some weeks ago. The fact that you were hiding all this time tells me we are correct, you do indeed know the bunker's location. Our finding it is imperative to establishing the peace and unity we offer. I assure you... we *will* learn the location."

Gift folded her arms and leaned against the back of the chair, hard against her spine. She stiffened at again being a prisoner, interrogated and threatened over those same *mal'd* missiles. Wishing they had never found them, Gift also considered them the only defense against their Martian conquerors. Silently, Gift stared into the gray eyes of James Morris, letting no words escape her lips.

"Then there is the matter of how you hid from us all this time. We have only begun searching outside. Why now, do you think? You seem like a bright person, I'm sure you deduced the same. We only recently learned of your unique tolerance. This has us most curious... most curious indeed. Of course, we know of the ones you call Pioneers and Ubuntu, their high tolerance for exposure. But they are a unique case altogether, aren't they. Still, *you* surpass even them, by a large margin."

A dry gulp betrayed Gift's uneasiness.

"You're quite special in this regard, aren't you? The key to medical studies to extend everyone's tolerance. You see, we are the same. On Mars, as on Earth, all of us carry the damage of the last decades under the sun's radiation. Generations spent in microenvironments; lives sustained on chemicals after inheriting sterility from before we entered the colonies. But you will help us all reclaim our planet, *our* home. This may be more important to our future than those missiles."

"I see."

"I'll give you time to think about what is best for all, for our future. I'm sure you'll come to see it the same way and do what's for the good of humanity."

9

Under the dim glow of a single illumination panel in the ceiling, Gift sat on a bunk in the same cell she shared with Mike, Tina, and Matteo, now shared with no one. In a mental exercise born of boredom, fright, or both, Gift sought a connection to bridge the prisons of her last few months. Chan's metal hole in U.A. to the shared cell in the N.R.C. Then her airplane, that *mal'd* home which nearly claimed her mind, sending her to the brim of sanity and tottering over its edge. Now alone again, one thing became clear: her endurance had all but waned.

"Isolation for endless days, interrogation, or torture?" Gift asked the cell when she woke. "Isolation seems the play here." Only after her eyes shed the last of the sleep clinging onto them did she notice the coverall folded neatly on the bunk. It creeped her a little knowing someone had opened the cell and placed it there while she slept. *At least I get out of these hideous green shorts and tank top.* "Ooh, undergarments." Experience kept her from voicing her wish for a shower.

On the less-than-comfortable bunk, sitting in silence, Gift waited. Someone must be coming—no other reason to have her dress. Or a mental tactic, dress her in the garb of the New Republic of Earth. Compliance by wardrobe seemed a stretch, yet it made perfect sense as a first step toward indoctrination, to get her on their side, to willingly cooperate, take them to the missiles and help them live in Earth's biosphere. As those contemplations danced in her brain, the friend she missed in her new loneliness was Em.

"Stop it, Gift," she scolded herself. "Not going to lose it again." Time didn't allow the madness of loneliness to overtake her once more. When the squeaking door opened, James Morris hadn't come for her. No single malevolent contact this time. No crazed lunatic keeping her as his plaything.

"Please follow me." The soft voice came from a woman likely older than Gift, possibly in her fifties, with the thin line of an upper lip barely visible over the bottom. Gift had never seen such a pronounced philtrum, made longer by the absence of a top lip. Matching blue and gray coveralls sent Gift's mind racing through ways she could use that to her advantage, blend in and sneak away. Memories of her escapes with Marco flashed—the disguises and crazy hair. What did her hair look like now?

"May I know your name?"

"Corinthia."

"I'm Gift. Where are we going?" Out of the jail space and through the same dome she snuck through weeks before, she wasn't with Matteo—*not* pulling off his soldier impersonation.

"We all work for our future. I'm to escort you to your work assignment."

"So, is this glorious New World Order of yours based on communism?"

"Only in the idea coming from the word community. In your former colony, they had the tenet, 'for the good of the colony.' Ours is, 'for the good of humanity.'"

My former colony? Those words echoed in Gift's mind, slamming into the soft tissue, and short-circuiting synaptic processes to blur most of the walk. She had no idea where they were when they stopped.

"They assigned you to common area cleaning duty. I'm your supervisor. We are part of a team of four and spend our days cleaning toilets and floors."

"For the glory of the empire." Sarcasm came easier than before. "You people know I'm an engineer, right? I mean, maybe I can be more useful—"

"We know who you are, Gift. We have our job, and it's an important one. For now, you clean where the engineers crap. That's as close as you get to the engineering team."

"I see."

The morning passed slowly, cleaning toilet after toilet with Corinthia's watchful eye never leaving her. The other team members, Liu Qing and Zhang Chen, seemed immune to Gift's efforts at small talk. Perhaps they didn't speak English. Corinthia limited her words as if they came at a cost. They took lunch in a small cleaning *office,* not called a closet because it contained a desk surrounded by supplies. Bland rice with limp vegetables and dry tofu became tolerable when Corinthia shared the hot sauce from her pocket. Gift tried to exploit the neighborly kindness.

"So, you're a Martian? I mean, you don't look Chinese."

"*Martian?* We don't call ourselves that. I *was* born on Mars. But that's just it, Gift. We are Martians, and you are what, an Earther? More than that, you are European, and then there are Russians, Africans, Chinese. This is what we need to stop—we're going to stop. We are all *humans*, nothing more, nothing divisive."

"But culture? I mean... we can celebrate that. Diversity doesn't have to be divisive. We've had peaceful relations with the R.F. and U.A."

"And you were practically at war with the N.R.C. Don't kid yourself, you were a long way off from your ideals of peace. We bring that, under one world government."

"Forced on us. I heard someone say how shortsighted that is. You must know... What did you call us, *Earthers?* You must know they'll never accept it. Forced occupation, submission by conquest? It'll spark revolution, rebellion. Haven't you ever seen *Star Wars?*"

"We're no evil galactic empire. We're the republic the rebels wanted to create. Only skipping the oppression, fighting, death, and destruction, to fast-forward to the good part. And it's already done. We've done it, Gift. Most of this colony welcomes us as a massive improvement over how the Chinese ran things."

"And as quick as they were to join you, they'll stand against you when the next thing comes. Or as soon as they don't like something, they'll remember they're unwillingly subjugated and revolt."

Corinthia stiffened her back and sipped water. "There are very few holdouts like you. You'll see, we're already in the New World Order, under the United Republic of Earth. And when the rest of the Mars colonists arrive, we'll all welcome them with open arms."

"And what of those who don't want to come? I mean, it's their home, their lives up on Mars, right? Will they even be given a choice?"

"Finish your rice. We need to get back to work."

The near-silent afternoon shift ended sooner than Gift expected. A few hours, at most, and they escorted her back to the cleaning closet they dared to call an office. Through a door she previously imagined led to a rear storeroom, she entered a tiled space with three shower stalls. Not proper booths with frosted glass walls and door panels, just the back wall divided in three by two thin glass panels offering no modesty. When Gift stepped uncomfortably into one beside Corinthia, she found an unrecognizable cream-colored bar on a tiny shelf under what she assumed was a water delivery system. A circle with a dozen holes attached to a pipe protruding from the wall flashed Gift's mind to Chan's hose nozzle and she trembled.

More than slightly embarrassed, Gift asked Corinthia how to activate the shower and what the odd bar on the tiny shelf was. No splash of warm foam, no blasts of hot water from all sides. When Gift turned the knob on the wall, the jolt of icy water stiffened her, raising her to her tiptoes. Assured it would warm up, Gift stepped to the corner, shivering. When the skin-feel advanced from icy-cold to lukewarm, she finished her shower and used a towel to dry.

No one seemed to end the day as early as her. Desperate eyes searched for Matteo, Mike, or Tina on her way to her hole. Even seeing General Xiang would have been a relief, but no familiar faces found hers. No dinner appeared on the shelf on the door where she and her friends had been fed, and Gift's stomach complained.

Scenes came, vivid and quickly, as soon as her eyes closed. In the exercise room on the U.R.M. Santa Maria, Gift sat next to Aimée, both strapped into a tension post, pulling with their arms to prevent atrophy. They were underwater but able to talk clearly.

"I thought you were dead."

"Nope. Can't get rid of me that easily, Love."

"Your messages. Haven't seen one in days."

"You need to stop this. Tell them how to find the missiles and give them your medical records. Let them dissect you to figure out how we can live outside. It's for the good of humanity."

The door opened and Gift jerked herself in a full-body twitch on the bunk. The cell flooded with light, closing her eyes as quickly as the disturbance had opened them. Slowly, the lids pulled apart to reveal a visitor, James Morris. A wave of indecency swept through her. When he said, "Come," she followed—barefoot and in her bed shirt—through the dome, back to the small dome-like room of their first encounter.

Seated across from him, she could cut the thickened silence between them like dense fog. "James, why am I here? What time even is it?"

"Just past O-three hundred. I have some questions."

"I see."

"We have Sakura Tanaka and her medical records. A file called EXP One forty-two is locked. We require access."

"I don't know what you're talking about."

"Come now, Gift. We know this is about how you came to have your special condition, your childbearing ability, and what allows you to live outside. We know you wish others to have the same, records show your cooperation to that end. That's all we're asking now."

"I think you have me confused with the earth-dwellers we found. *They* have babies without in vitro and have higher tolerance for outside than people of the colonies."

James Morris rubbed the stubble on his air-filled cheeks. The scratch of the stiff hairs on the dry skin of his fingers were like nails on a chalkboard. A long-exhaled sigh flattened his cheeks.

"We know you lived outside since we arrived. Nearly eleven weeks outdoors, and not a trace of illness. You're perfectly healthy. Your friend, on your latest treatment, lasted a few days and nearly died—would have, had you not brought him here when you did."

"He's okay... Matteo? Is he okay?"

"Yes. He's recovering in sickbay. Sorry, in the medical building here. We keep telling you we want the same thing. There's no need to resist us, we're not enemies. Gift, we wish only to work together for the common good."

"*Really?*" The word slipped through an open yawn. "We're having this conversation because I'm your prisoner. You took me from my bed in the middle of the night, marched me here in my underwear and nightshirt. I... I don't see us being on the same side."

"We're back to two points with you. You must see how each of them hurts us all or helps us all. We can only ensure *lasting* peace if we control the missiles. If anyone of N.E. or Russia tried to use them, that's bad for everyone—needless bloodshed and destruction. No one wants that. I know you don't. We can prevent that."

"Ruling by fear. *Your* peace, or else."

"Peace by removing any chance for violence. As people continue to benefit from the peace we bring, they'll be content. Nobody will resist... or want to revolt."

"That's just another way to say the same thing."

"Then what about your medical condition? How does your resistance help anyone? How does it help humanity? There are three hundred thousand humans on Earth, likely many more. And more than one hundred fifty thousand souls are preparing to return home from Mars. Can't you see the good you could do? You help us, everybody wins."

Gift sat silently, arms crossed, wishing to believe the motives of the U.R.M. She couldn't chance trusting them. Aimée's messages intimated a life on Mars more difficult than projected. They came in force to take over, to again be the infectious disease humanity had been, corrupting the healing Earth, overrunning the existing colonies, and hoarding resources. Gift's ancestors on her Nigerian side experienced it in the world *before*. Now they, the colonies of Earth, were the African nations, and the U.R.M. were the European colonizers. No, Gift wouldn't contribute to history repeating this way.

10

Duplicitousness applying to Gift's character—she couldn't imagine it. To make a conscious choice to become perfidious felt wrong, like swimming in Colony Lake for the first time in shorts and a T-shirt—only this time her own skin fit wrongly over her flesh. Gift had seen it in Claudia, Chan, and Xiang. Feigned friendship and *we're on the same side* rhetoric. Now on a first-name basis with James Morris spewing the same nonsense under the guise of a common aim: *for the good of humanity.*

Gift selected the target for her *wolf in sheep's clothing* act. An expression she got, though the visual disgusted her and brought a tinge of sorrow for the poor skinned sheep. It became clear her workmate-guard was a true believer. Her new Martian friend's consistent lecturing spoke of intent to convince her to accept the invasion—conquest of Earth by force—as a good thing.

Not all at once. Let her 'slowly win me over.' By day three, she made progress with Corinthia. With due caution, Gift used the lunch break to question the New World Order, sheepishly challenging its tenets, listening attentively as Corinthia spoke with loyalist fervor.

"So," Gift said after swallowing a mouthful of bread. "You're saying when the U.R.—*E.* has control of the only weapons on Earth, it will somehow ensure peace?"

Corinthia smiled widely, her eyes shining under the soft lighting doing its best to cast a dismal glow in the room. "Yes. Exactly. You're seeing it now, aren't you? To have weapons like that unaccounted for will foster rebellion and desperate and foolish hopes to find and use them against us—*us*, who brought peace back to Earth."

"Back to Earth? I mean, Corinthia... I love saying your name. It's so beautiful."

"Thanks. Lots of people don't say it right or make fun of it."

"You know Aimée, from the update vids? She's my best friend, and people often destroy her name too."

"No way. You know Aimée? She's one of our heroes, bridging the gap, helping people see the big picture and accept our presence here."

If only you knew what she's really doing? Using all her self-control, Gift ensured that didn't escape her lips.

"Anyway, what was I saying...? Oh. What I mean is, well... before you left and we went into the colonies, I guess we finally made peace. I mean, at least stopped hating and fighting enough for the colonies project, *right?* But we were a mess before that, with so many wars, so much fighting and death. And the powerful, the ones in control... they had control of the weapons, much more powerful than the few missiles we know of. Having those weapons didn't bring peace. Working a common goal for our survival did."

"And that's exactly what the United Republic of Earth is doing. Before we arrived, you were on the brink of war. Whether to be fought with sticks and stones or missiles... And *we stopped it.*"

"Well... true." Gift thought that sounded swayed-*ish*.

"I'm glad you're becoming more open-minded. I know you're not convinced, view us as invaders, as conquering overlords, or something... I want to show you something. I think you'll see what we're really doing here."

Corinthia led Gift, fully donned in her sheep's covering, to a large open workspace, and asked Gift to take it all in. Carefully sorting the words on her mental display, Gift sought the best way to give in slightly while not unmasking her true musings. Thoughts of deception and dishonesty dirtied her mind. She became what she had so vigorously defended against when accused by her own people of sabotage. *No. This is justified*, she tried to convince herself.

"Tell me what you see."

"Well... *Allora*... I see people working on air transports, repairing the flyers *your people* shot down."

"Okay, sure. You're right, we did... we shot them down. I guess that's obvious now. And now we're repairing the last of them. We fixed the heavies first so trade could start right away. These are the Chinese light flyers, to serve as transports between colonies."

"And you're fixing them *because*...?"

"We are one. Part of a single human community. It's being good neighbors, fixing the Chinese transports the same as we repaired the Russian ones. We've even given one to N.E. and one to U.A. for trade. Each of the colonies will also have one of these light transports to help unite them further. There's no *us* and *them*, *our* colony or *their* colony. And who do you see working?"

"I see *Tin*—teams. I see teams." Gift hid her giddiness.

"Look more closely. Those are our people working with the Chinese, someone from U.A. All working together on the common goal. This is a small sample, and it's working."

Someone from U.A. she said? That's Tina, dark skinned but from N.E. They don't know who she is. That's good. She had no idea why or how that was good, but she was sure it was.

"And all the colonies... they're all working like this? No one's fighting you, resisting the occupation?"

"Let's say… we have the situation under control."

"I see."

"There's no need to resist this. It's, it's beautiful. Once we have those missiles off the table and you help us make lives outside the colonies, able to support your people and the masses returning from Mars, we move to this glorious future. This is a new age of humanity for everyone."

Gift didn't call Corinthia on how her words separated the colonies of Earth from her and her Martians. Division was there, obscured by the glasses of idealism and blinded by patriotism, but there.

She saw me. Gift delayed long enough for Tina to finally notice her, playing it as cool as Gift hoped she did, not giving away their connection.

"We need to clean the toilets here, or I can't justify bringing you."

The muscles in Gift's neck fought to turn her head. Gift flipped her mind to whether Matteo had recovered as claimed. Eyes scouring the corridors and domes checked every blue-gray uniform and failed to find Mike. *Stupid helmets.* Aimée's note called itself up from memory. They were hiding their meager numbers. No one could discern who were or weren't Martians. Her mind trick worked; she resisted turning to see Tina. Toilets got scrubbed by muscle memory.

"This toilet box is closed for cleaning. You'll have to find another." Corinthia's voice. People often had to pee or do their business right when they were trying to clean the toilets.

"I really gotta go. Not gonna make it to the next box, it's crazy far." *Tina?*

"You have to wait or go to the next box."

Tina pushed her bulk through the Martian as petite as Aimée. "Can't wait. Unless you want to clean the floor and my coverall, it's best if I pee in a toilet."

Too afraid to make eye contact, Gift stood a statue in the corner. Tina did indeed urinate, loudly, making her insistence on getting to the toilet credible. A glance, short and quick, Tina's brown eyes led Gift's to the toilet booth which now needed to be cleaned again. Message received; Gift needed to be the one to clean it. Without asking, she entered the booth. "I'll touch it up, so it's back to pristine before we go."

"Some people have to have their way. Africans. What can you do?" Gift found the comment offensive, being half African herself. It spoke against the *unification and equality for all* rhetoric the woman had spewed for days. Such hypocrisy fortified Gift's resolve that U.R.M. occupation would not bring the glorious New World Order it promised—at least not for everyone equally.

Hurried out of her coverall, Gift got into the shower stall with a head start on Corinthia. Rushing the soap—still amused by how the strange bar lathered on her skin—she finished and hastily dried herself with a towel before pulling the cloth swatch from her pocket. The scribbled message simply said, 'Tmrw. Same time, same toilet.' The wide smile came from giddy optimism tingling the almost imperceptible hairs over her flesh. That may have been the chill of being naked and not fully dry. How would she get to that same toilet box tomorrow?

11

Had it all been for nothing? Gift played along, tough as steel with James Morris, soft and pliable to work her way into Corinthia's good graces, lulling the woman into a sense of complacent victory over her psyche. All the while hoping to find a way to reunite with her friends, as stuck in the New Republic of China as her.

Puff Adder. The name buried itself in an archive file in Gift's memory, stored with other useless facts. The last nature vid she saw with Oksana in her flat. Gift wondered why they allocated the young woman a flat. The Puff Adder hid, blended in, and waited. Unobserved by its predators, it patiently lay in wait for its prey. Eventually, it struck. Deadly.

Getting to the toilet box turned out to be much easier than Gift imagined. Corinthia bought the excuse that Gift left her toilet cleaner, forgotten in the commotion of the rude woman who pushed her way in. Worry beaded sweat over Gift's brow. She hoped the bottle she was to go back to get stayed hidden in the wash bin under the rags. *How will Tina strike?* Gift wondered.

Making herself so obvious Gift's *leash* and work partner had to suspect something, Tina approached. Unsure what to do, Gift continued to the toilets as if she hadn't noticed her burly friend. From in the toilet room, she heard Tina say, "Miss, may I speak to you for just a moment?"

Corinthia's distraction left Gift alone.

"Psst." It came from an air vent halfway up the rear wall. When the metal slated square frame swung open on its hinge, the face behind it shocked Gift.

"*Xiang?*"

"Hurry. Come up," General Xiang said in her *giving orders* voice. It had been weeks since Gift heard it. The last voices Xiang's larynx made at the airplane were soft, strangely friendly. With her head peeping out of the duct and her arms extended down, the general looked like a strange bodiless puppet. Gift grabbed onto the lowered hands and did her best to push herself up the wall. Thinner than Gift thought, Xiang's rail body pressed against the side while she pulled Gift beside her into the metal duct. A metallic rattle slammed from behind.

"Keep going, move."

"Where?"

"One way to go. Stop at the junction."

When Gift stopped, feet came past her face, then legs, a torso, and Xiang's face directly before her own.

"Follow me." The General turned around. They crawled for several meters, turned, and crawled several meters more. The feet ahead stopped. "You hear that?"

"Yeah." The whirls and swoops were familiar vibrations, like the fans on air handler eleven, her first live repair job. It was a lifetime ago, but the failure felt like yesterday.

"We need to pass that fan."

Lifting her head over the General's buttocks to see, Gift considered the spinning of the large fan blades, ready to slice her flesh. The duct expanded to nearly twice its width and height around the fan. Images from action thrillers of an impeccably timed jaunt past such a gauntlet crowded her mind. How they narrowly missed the razor-thin edge of the blade's twirling, millimeters meaning life or death, thrilling the viewer. Gift crawled onward with far less dramatic excitement.

A colossal bang halted the blades. The resourceful General had a metal rod. As Gift shimmied by the vane, she gingerly touched her finger to its edge. Dull, scarcely able to cut the air. In retrospect, it was sensible. Unless a super spy crawling the ductwork of the N.R.C. had been a perceived threat, they had no need for flesh-slicing killer fan blades. On the General's order, Gift removed the rod and welcomed the generous breeze. Beyond the next vent cover, they spilled onto the floor of a dark, cramped room.

"We need to get to my hidden office."

"Hidden office?" Gift felt lost, but not alone.

"A small room, off colony plans and maps. You will be safe there."

"Matteo. We need to get Matteo."

"We get you to safety, then get Matteo. We need everyone we can on our side before we strike."

"*Strike?* We have a plan?" Gift's mood elevated by the prospect of liberating Earth. At least taking a stand against the New World Order—a more realistic goal.

"We are working on one, gathering our numbers." Enemy turned savior, turned friend, turned liberator, opened the door to the corridor. "This area is sparsely occupied. Few people pass here, and most are loyal to me." Creeping along the narrow, dimly lit corridor, Gift's mind began racing as it often did.

"Wait. They'll expect me to go for Matteo," Gift said.

"Yes. I would watch him, use him as bait for you."

"Right, but I've only just escaped. I mean, I guess they know. I don't think Tina distracted Corinthia this long."

"Knowing Tina, I suspect your guard is taking a very long nap, so no one has learned of your disappearance."

"You don't mean... Tina wouldn't."

"I meant *a nap*. I made sure Tina knew how to put her to sleep."

"Then let's get Matteo now. They won't expect it. Once they find out... they, they will."

"You have a point. We have surprise on our side."

"Then let's go." Gift tried on a *giving orders* voice that didn't suit her. "What are we waiting for? Which way?"

"Mike has access to Medical and would have freed Matteo soon. Tina seeing you completely changed that."

"Okay, okay..." Gift's pacing wore a circle into the floor. "Isn't there some vent that goes to him?"

"They are small. We were extremely lucky Tina saw you where she did. Come, it is not safe to stay here."

Gift stopped to face the General. "But you belong here. And no one really knows me. Except the Commander and Corinthia. What if, if we just walk over to Medical? We find Matteo and sneak him out?"

Xiang grabbed Gift by the arm to stop her as she turned to walk, not knowing where to go. "I agree, we have the best chance to get him if we go now. We cannot just walk into Medical, but I have an idea."

Gift followed her former persecutor through corridor after corridor in a series of turns Gift found quite unusual. In three other colonies Gift never saw such a labyrinth of passageways. The narrowness of the dim corridor unsettled her.

"Where are we?"

"Secondary access tunnels on a sublevel."

"I thought it felt like we went down for a while in the ducts. We don't have anything like this in N.E."

"It was unknown for a few weeks before one of ours in that traitorous uniform divulged it. It will be the firing squad for him if I ever find him."

"Firing squad?" Gift asked, puzzled.

"I imagine you do have them in New Europa. We have not done it ourselves for generations, but it is our way."

"I mean, what is it?"

"You are naïve. No, innocent. Yes, and we are robbing you of that. I am sorry for this, truly. When a vile criminal, like a traitor, is found guilty, a line of soldiers shoots him dead. It is justice."

"It's *horrible*."

"Is it any different from you killing Commander Chan? Some people deserve to die. This is simple justice."

"No. It's not the same at all. I didn't even mean to shoot him. I still have nightmares about it."

The stern woman withheld her steps to show a softer face than Gift thought her capable. "It is a pity you have knowledge of those missiles. And your unique physiology. It would have been much easier for you if you were an ordinary young woman. You are extraordinary, and for it you suffer. I deeply regret what you endured under Chan... and what we did to you and your friends. Now this."

Words of gratitude were there, but Gift couldn't bring herself to say thank you to the woman who had been a monster—less of one than Chan, but a monster still. Even after she rushed her from the colony to safety, brought her provisions, sent Tina and Matteo, and now freed her from the Martians, Gift had an inescapable notion Xiang was an enemy. That they shared another enemy wasn't enough to change that, not yet. Keeping Gift safe meant not letting a greater enemy get powerful weapons. Or Xiang could have hoped to get the missiles herself. It may have been an exception to the rule *actions speak louder than words*, because in Gift's mind, the words proved more impactful.

They gave several minutes to the silent walk until the General said they were under Medical. Gift saw no door or hatch into the sub level of the building. Pointing to three large pipes running along the wall and disappearing into the foundation of the Medical building, Xiang said, "One is a false pipe." She rotated a large section in the middle horizontal pipe to reveal an access hole.

Gift shook her head. "This place is *so not* New Europa."

"We prepared for every foreseeable outcome."

"Being invaded by Martians?"

"Unforeseeable."

Crawling through the pipe deposited them in a storage room of dusty shelves full of dustier boxes. The General entered the second aisle of shelving and pulled a box to the floor, flipping its lid onto the concrete and kicking up a small mote cloud. White scrubs filled the box. The two removed their Martian blue and gray coveralls to costume themselves as medics. On autopilot, Gift's mind went to her last attempt to impersonate a nurse in the R.F. and how quickly she'd failed the charade.

"Say nothing," Xiang commanded as they climbed the stairs to the ground level, then two more flights. "He is on this floor." No one waited in the waiting area.

"How do we get him out?" Gift's impatience bled.

"Not we. You wait here, I will get him."

She vanished into the hallway. Before Gift's brain played all plausible scenarios of what Xiang might do, the door opened. She had Matteo. The ensuing hug, intense and tight, burst with emotion. Gift and her little Matteo followed the General down, through the fake pipe, and along the sublevel corridor to her secret office. *Or was it ancillary?*

"Please, may I have the handheld? I know I've missed some of Aimée's messages. I gotta see if there's more."

Sitting beside Matteo, each sipping piping hot green tea, they watched the vids, looking for clues. They hoped to find a way to win. Images flooded Gift's mind of yet more fighting. For liberation, sure, but still fighting. *When will it end? When will humanity ever learn?*

There were no answers, only unrelenting hope.

12

"*L*a speranza è l'ultima a morire." *Hope is the last thing lost. Or is it the last to die?* Something dead is lost, so Gift considered it a decent translation. She had heard it both ways, but *death* had a permanence that *lost* lacked—lost can be found where dead was dead. When hope died, what else was there?

"What was that?" Matteo asked.

"*Huh?*"

"You said something… In Italian, I guess."

"I did? Oh, I guess I did. Yeah, hope… an Italian proverb about hope being the last to die popped into my brain, you know?" Gift looked more confused than him.

Matteo grabbed her hand and cast a gentle glance into her eyes. "We can't think like that, can't lose hope. We've got a decent shot at this. With intel from Aimée, a good chance at overrunning these Martians for good."

Gift's exhalation rolled into a long sigh. "No, it's, it's not that. You know me, always the optimist, *right?* Sometimes even too much. You know, I recently decided that giving things a hundred percent wasn't realistic, so I lowered it… I mean, in my mind, for things working out."

"Let me guess… ninety-nine," he said with a chuckle.

The slap to his chest was playful and light. "Yep. So, I'm not losing that, not totally. *Ciao.* What I mean is, more… It's us. Not *you and me* us, I mean humans us, all of us. It's almost like all we've done since we stepped outside is fight each other. *Ma*, really… the sad thing is it started before I opened that airlock, you know? We did it ourselves, in our own colony. All the fighting. People dying."

"Do you suppose this New World Order may be the way to stop it? I mean, these folks promise peace among all peoples. And… I guess it *is* working… on the surface."

"You're almost as optimistic as me. It's cute. I love you. But no, you're wrong, sweetie. Cute, but wrong. Except that bit you said about 'on the surface.' I believe they're desperately trying to make it look like it's working. Trade, fixing transports, giving a flyer to U.A. I *think?* I think it's all a show. And from what Aimée's been telling us, they're barely holding it together, trying to last long enough to have the numbers when the rest get here from Mars."

"You are exactly correct." The voice reminded Gift of the General's existence. She had been sitting in the room, busily doing something on a tablet. "You are smart, and I see you have not lost hope. Perhaps you are learning to balance optimism and realism. This is good. This balance will serve you well and make you a valuable member of my team."

"*Your* team?" Gift caught her accusatory tone. "I mean, do you have enough people who've not fallen for the New World nonsense?"

Rising to her feet, Xiang replied, "At least twenty of my people are U.R.M. guards. Another forty playing along and waiting for my orders. And we have us."

"*Us?*" Matteo waved a hand over himself and Gift. "You shouldn't put too much faith in us. I mean, look at us. Since they came, we've been pretty good at hiding, and then we got caught."

"You are half right, and missing the bigger part of the picture, as you say. Gift was very good at hiding, but they did not catch you. Gift dragged you here and gave herself up to get you needed medical attention."

"Really?" Gift nodded sheepishly, a reply that brought Matteo in for a tight embrace. When he pulled away, his eyes had moistened. Hers had too.

With bone-dry eyes, Xiang continued, "And you missed an important point that makes you the most valuable part of the operation to free my colony. Not only do you all share the same ideals and optimism, but you are also a cohesive unit, working together, supporting each other in ways I could have only wished for in my people. Your strength is your unity, your combined resolve, I dare say, your friendship. Together, you are strong. I would take you four over a dozen of my soldiers."

"Wow," was all Gift could collect into a reply.

"She's right. Gift, you're the core, the glue. We rallied around you, for you, even when... *she* tortured us."

From behind raised hands Xiang said, "That was regrettable. I, I went too far, justified myself by not being as evil as Chan, that I only did what needed to be done to save my people. It was wrong."

"Incredible," Gift said. "Even when you helped hide me, and brought me stuff... I thought you were acting for your own good, still wanted me for the missiles. I mean, to get them for yourself. When you pulled me out of the toilets, I saw selfish ambition, an act of desperation, not of an ally. So now, now you're saying you finally get that we didn't attack you?"

"Of course," the General said matter-of-factly. "It is clear we were all attacked by the United Republic of Mars. They took out our transports to gain the strategic advantage, keep us from fleeing, unifying, or resisting."

Wheels turned, Gift's mental display connected dots of previous events and anomalies. "And our communications glitches, those scans of our systems, rollers plunging into the ocean, well... an ocean, or a channel they called it, and a lake. By now one's swimming in the Mediterranean too. Sorry. The way Sojourner went dark, those two minutes and thirty-eight seconds. It was *all them*, the U.R.M."

"Here as well. We had these... what did you call them?"

"Glitches."

"They were here as well."

"Let me guess." Matteo postured himself. "You blamed that on us?"

"We could not have anticipated this."

"Okay, okay." Gift patted the air. "We're friends now, good. Well, at least we agree on who the enemy is—and it's not each other. So... *progress*, I guess. Now we need Tina and Mike. Like you said, stronger together."

"Your strength is more than you four. It is your colony and how you united the others. We need to reach N.E."

"The chat," Gift shouted with more excitement than her vocal cords had thrown in ages.

"This connected us to you at the airplane. How does this help us?"

"It can reach New Europa. Raff, she knows how to use it. She knows I'm here. She must be trying to reach us."

Pensive and grimacing, Xiang replied, "We have had it online for weeks and no messages came other than yours. How can we make this work?"

"I can do it. I mean, I imagine so. But I need Mike. He's the one that set it up on your device, right? And your data operator. I can do it, but I need them here."

"Then, Miss Gift, we shall get—"

The door to their secret lair swung open with the force of an invasion. Out of breath, Tina huffed to refill her lungs. Gift grabbed her for a hug. The breathless woman related how, after slumbering Corinthia, she knew she'd have limited time before they came after her, so she made a run for it during a work break. She checked the hidden office, scoured the sublevel for them, and doubled-back to check the admin building in case they had been caught.

"...then I came back here. Didn't know what else to do. And here you are. And you got Matt, nice."

"And Mike? We need him here, and his coder, the one that did the chat. I think, I mean, I can get through to N.E. with their help."

Tina's exhale blended into a long grunt. "Okay. Let me get some water, then I'll go leave Mikey a message. We have a way to sneak little notes to each other."

"We need him and the coder to come here right away."

Tina gulped down a cup of water and took off. A plan formed. If Gift could get N.E. on chat—not anywhere near as sure as she let on—she'd be chatting soon with Raff and New Europa.

"There it is," Matteo said over a wide smile.

"There what is?"

"Your optimism. Hope... *You*."

"You know that Italian proverb comes from Latin. So much comes from Latin. It goes back to an even older Greek myth about this Pandora. Cool name, like Corinthia—maybe she's Greek. Anyway, she had this box—Pandora, not Corinthia—and when it opened, all kinds of evil came. Kinda like when I open that airlock. I mean, good things came, lots of 'em. But lots of bad stuff too. But hope? It was the last thing in the box, *the last to die*. Come to think of it, it was also said that the box was full of blessings, and opening it lost them all. Not sure which fits us best, they kinda both do, I guess. But me? I'm going to hold on to hope. I figure, maybe... maybe we even get those blessings."

"There's the big sister I'm so proud of."

All ate the rice and tofu one of Xiang's people brought them, and waited for Tina, Mike, and the data operator. Gift longed for a dash of hot sauce. Tina arrived first. Message planted, nothing to do but wait. Gift tinkered with the chat code though her understanding of its programing language was worse than her Italian.

The creaking of the door hinge woke her from a nap she hadn't remembered taking and Mike stood over her. They spared minutes for the much needed and extra-tight hug. The uniform was just as dorky as she remembered, and he looked out of place in it. "You smell a lot better than last time I saw you," he said in a playful, teasing tone. It got him a light punch on the arm and a broad smile.

"They let me shower after work. There's this white-*ish* bar thing, solid but a little soft, especially when it's wet. And slippery, I dropped it so many times. They had no suds spray, you had to rub this bar on your skin."

"It is called soap," the General explained. "Only service area showers have it. We have the same shower here, and this will be our home for now."

"Cozy," Tina said sarcastically.

A petite Chinese man stood in the small room waiting patiently. Tufts of puffy white hair reached outward from the rim of the dappled skin atop his bare scalp. His eyes opened less than anyone's Gift had seen, and he had a cuteness to his face and crinkled brow, a grandfatherly quality.

"Hello. Mister Han my name."

"Pleasure, sir. I am Gift. You're the data operator who coded the chat app?" His puzzled appearance spoke to his limited English. "Did you, write, chat program?" Gift gesticulated her words as much as spoke them.

"Yes. Now we fix?"

"Yeah. Well, no, it's not broken. We need to expand it and search for open broadcasts. Come, sit."

Gift, Mike, and Mister Han worked into the night to recode the chat program and upgrade the hardware in the device. Their hope would be tested when Gift turned it on in open broadcast mode.

• ne: Hello?

13

One word swelled their little resistance group into something with the power to act, perhaps even succeed. The raw intensity of that first text unfolded a world of possibilities. It was Red, not called Melody in chat, not when they were again in covert communication. She was Red once again.

- ne: Raff is headed toward the bunker.

- nc: What will she do? Who's with her?

- ne: Boss and Hans. Figure out how to use them.

- nc: Wish there was another way.

- ne: Like Boss said, this is war.

- nc: Yeah. Seems its who we are. Sad.

- ne: Far as we know URM not know location.

- nc: Yeah. Why I hid alone for weeks.

- ne: Good. Well done. Our only advantage.

> - nc: We are planning to take back NRC.
>
> - ne: Here too. And UA and RF.
>
> - nc: Oksana? She Ok?
>
> - ne: Yes. Chatted her at UA and Nailya at RF.

With communication and coordination connecting the four colonies, Gift shared all her revelations from Aimée's secret coded messages. Some Red knew, others they had missed. Only Gift deduced the invisible ink messages and how to read them. Now everyone would have the vital information that U.R.M. forces were more meager than presented and they may not have a fully armed armada in orbit ready to obliterate any uncooperative colony. If it was to be a war, at least it looked to be a winnable one.

> - ne: Coordinating the revolts. All go on same day.
>
> - nc: Smart. When?
>
> - ne: In two days. UA plans to go at dawn.
>
> - nc: UA dawn about same as yours. No idea for us.
>
> - ne: Let me check...
>
> - nc: We are in the future, like RF. They are 6 hrs.
>
> - ne: Right. What time there now?
>
> - nc: 01:48

* ne: You are 7 hrs ahead of us.

* nc: So your dawn will be like 13:00 for us?

* ne: Something like, yes. Can you move then?

* nc: Hang on...

Gift conferred with the General before answering. While they wouldn't have the advantage of attacking at first light, it didn't deter General Xiang. She agreed but had a question.

"Mike, what about the guards?"

"Wait. He's here with us. You said with me and Matteo gone, and Tina taking out Corinthia, you said they'd suspect him. He can't just go back out there."

"Miss Gift, you should let people finish their thoughts. Mike, we had thirty-two guards. Is that still the case?"

"I think they've swayed some. Maybe we don't tell'em all the plan."

Undaunted, Xiang continued, "As expected. There are dozens of guards freely working with the U.R.M. who, I am sure, will fight on their side. I will contact my key men and inform them."

"What do I do?"

"Stay here for now. They put helmets on you to hide your identity. We will use that to our advantage. When we need to move, you will escort us as our guard."

"I'm stuck here too, and Matt," Tina said.

The General turned to her. "As I said, we will all remain here to plan the strike. I learned of your success taking back U.A. from Chan's men. Tina, you are my second and will do most of the coordination. Mike has learned much about the colony layout, so he will assist you. I will be in and out, coordinating with my people. We have one day to plan, and I always plan to win. I am counting on you."

"Roger," Tina replied.

While Gift loved codewords and spy talk, she hated the goofy words in military comms. To her, *Copy* was such a stupid way to say 'Okay.' Now her mind had to devote valuable resources to wondering who *that* Roger was and what he did to make his name synonymous with 'Understood' or 'Will do.' He must have had a reputation for following orders. *What's wrong with saying the actual words?* Memories came of Oksana thinking someone had physically beaten her when Gift used the colloquial, 'I'm beat.'

Gift remembered the open chat. "Do I tell Red yes? We'll be ready to move the day after tomorrow at thirteen hundred?"

"Yes. Tell your Red person we will move at the same moment. All four colonies will be free."

"Got it. I mean, Roger. Whoever that was."

- nc: Okay, we're good.

- ne: Thought I lost you. 13:00 day after tomorrow?

- nc: Already in tomorrow here, so next day.

- ne: Right :)

- nc: Cute. When will Raff have control?

- ne: Hopefully by time we move or soon after.

- nc: Just worried they can still do something.

- ne: Weapons?

- nc: Aimee said limited, but we need to know.

- ne: Oksana can check them. Should know soon.

- nc: Check them? How? Where?

- ne: Bright found large pieces will bring to her.

- nc: Great. Need to know what Aimee hinting at.

- ne: Can she do it? Just a girl, not experienced.

- nc: She can, Im sure. Shes brilliant.

"Can we keep the app open? In case anyone tries to reach us. I mean, is it safe?" Gift addressed the room but looked at Mister Han, who showed her a blank face. "General, little help?"

She asked Han then said, "He says yes. In listen mode, it is passive and unlikely to be noticed. Only when in chat or establishing new connections is it discoverable."

"Good. No one touches it. Leave it on just as it is." As she was about to set it on the desk, Gift noticed it was in silent mode. She quickly set it to audio alert for connection requests and new messages. "Okay, *now* leave it just as it is."

Sleeping everyone in the small office space would be less than comfortable, but Gift welcomed it. So many days and nights in isolation. Now she shared sleeping quarters with Mike, Tina, Matteo and the still intimidating General. Han was not under suspicion, so he snuck off back to his bunk.

Everyone took a shower before bed not to sleep in an atmosphere saturated with a cocktail of body odors. The little shower seemed an afterthought with an opening in the wall Gift wished had a door in place of the synthetic cloth hanging from a pole. Xiang called it a curtain.

To shower, Gift stood directly behind that and felt like she was still in the room with everyone, like the rainwater shower in her airplane with no one covered in a blanket. If not careful, her elbow could have pushed the cloth, exposing her to the room. Muffles of conversation amplified the feeling of showering in the middle of an open space. A brief soaping and rinse under lukewarm water, done. When she stepped out wrapped in the towel, she saw a problem.

"Um, where do I... get dressed?"

"Come Gift, we are all adults here."

"All due respect, General, I can't."

"We'll all close our eyes," Matteo said.

"Like that first time, pretending to be asleep?"

"No one here is twelve."

"And *I'm not* changing out here."

Seeing no other option, Gift gathered her clothes and stepped back into the damp shower stall, stopping Tina from entering for her turn. Changed and with wet spots in a few places on her coverall, she allowed Tina her shower. Then Mike, Matteo, and General Xiang—who stripped in front of everyone and entered and exited the booth fully naked. Her excellent physical condition impressed Gift, tone and fit. Sleep was sound, snoring noises and all.

When the fit General's assistant carried in a tray of green tea and break-fast biscuits, Gift longed for coffee—it had been so long since she sipped her beloved espresso, her last being a less than great cup that morning in United Africa. At least the tea had caffeine. The General reviewed the day's itiner-ary departed to contact her key people. If the military leader had everything planned to the letter, what would everyone do in the comms-dark office all day?

"Tina," Gift said. "Xiang said you're her second and—"

"Yeah, sorry. It's just that she knew about me helping the U.A. with Bright. It wasn't personal."

"No, sweetie, that's not it. That I'm *not* leading this is not a problem, believe me. What I mean is... she seems to have the plan for the colony. So, what exactly are *we* planning here?"

"Our mission is getting Xiang to Ops. Then we'll be in position to gain control of the colony."

"*Mission?* Interesting word for fighting and killing each other. Why don't we just call things what they really are?" Gift wondered if Mission was a military word like Copy or Roger and if those masked some horrible reality no one wanted to face yet everyone rushed headlong into doing. Or was it just a better-sounding word for war?

"We had few casualties in U.A. and no loss of life, on either side. That's the same play here."

"Yeah, not sure Xiang sees it that way."

14

Time could stretch a day forever or pass it by in a blink. Some moments froze and time ceased to exist. Those minutes from 23:45 to midnight that day in the U.A. Ops center wouldn't pass, no matter how hard Gift wished them away. Seconds on the clock hung in suspended animation, taunting her, flooding her entire body with anxious anticipation. But it was fifteen minutes, regardless of the sensation of time's lengthy passage. In this moment at the N.R.C. she had the entirety of a day, and it was somehow worse.

Tina and Mike had the situation in hand, and Gift stayed out of the way, having zero knowledge of the colony—unless anyone needed a toilet cleaned. She wondered if Corinthia had gotten in trouble for letting her escape. She hoped not. Matteo wasn't much use to them either, so he kept Gift company throughout the arduously long day while she replayed Aimée's vids yet again for any missed clues and messages. It gave her something to do. Thoughtlessly, she laid her head on Matteo's shoulder and his arm found its way around her while Aimée talked about improved trade between colonies with some flyers having been repaired by joint teams of engineers from the U.R.M. and people of the colonies. Their New World Order in action.

The joy of seeing her best friend's face and hearing her bubbly voice ached in Gift's heart—she hadn't seen her in so long. The warmth of

Matteo's brotherly embrace felt like a salve on that wound. A spicy lunch gave Gift greater satisfaction than her meals of recent weeks. The crunchy nuts mixed in the protein and veggies added an unexpected and interesting layer to the mouthfeel. While collecting bowls and utensils from everyone, Gift heard it. The chirp of the audio alert on the chat app.

- r: Gift?

- nc: Red, what's wrong?

- r: It's Raff.

- nc: Raff! Grazie a Dio. How are you?

- r: Fine. What about you? Been weeks.

- nc: 3 months!! Fine. Now.

- r: Red told me you were free. Brava.

- nc: Yeah. Almost lost my mind, but ok now.

- r: Cosa?

- nc: Long story. Hid alone. Went a little nuts.

- r: Poverina. You with the team now?

- nc: Yeah. Plus one intense Chinese General.

- r: Xiang? Working with you?

- nc: We have the same enemy... At bunker?

- r: Almost there with Hans and Boss.

- nc: How online?

- r: Just got in range of comms. Transport so slow.

- nc: It's no Zil. Think you'll get in system?

- r: Certo. Ma, will take time. Sergey will help.

- nc: He knows data systems?

- r: He reads Russian.

- nc: Right. Will we have those things when we move?

- r: Not sure how soon. Many firewalls and failsafes.

- nc: Aimée indicated maybe fewer weapons.

- r: Infatti. Nice to know if they can take us all out.

Again, Gift pondered the word replacement, 'take us all out.' Like a lovely evening taking friends for tacos. How Gift missed the group's Friday taco nights. *Focus Gift.*

- nc: You mean if they can kill us all.

- r: Be good to know.

- nc: Oksana on that.

- r: And we need what I'm getting.

- nc: And right back to fighting, war.

- r: We don't have a choice.

- nc: Seems to happen a lot. What if we did?

- r: Have a choice? Don't see any. What you thinking?

- nc: Don't know yet.

- r: Gift, promise me you will keep out of fighting.

- nc: Every time I try I end up in it anyway. Lucky me.

Raff didn't have to say it, but of course she did. As much as Gift wished no one to go to war, *she* wanted no part in the fight. Yet, she often ended up in the middle of conflict and had even killed a man. *It was self-defense, and he was a raging lunatic, a monster,* Gift told herself. It didn't stop the nightmares. Gift took solace in that Oksana didn't have to live with that horror.

- r: Red said they found your medical records.

- nc: Want me more for that now. Pioneers and Ubuntu can stay long. Not only me.

- r: They were not in colonies, not on chemicals. Can't help us, only you.

- nc: They want those... where youre going. Asked me for location. Desperate to find it.

- r: Another reason for Sergey and his men.

- nc: You think theyll come for you?

- r: Have to assume. This is crucial.

- nc: Be careful.

- r: You have someone in data systems there?

- nc: Yes. Xiang has a guy, data operator.

- r: Good. Bright and Nailya too. Need control of systems asap. Only way to win and keep the colonies.

- nc: What about NE? Can Red handle it?

- r: Claudia helping her.

- nc: What!!

- r: I know. But helpful. She found their snooping into the medical records. She'll be able to take back our systems and lock URM out. Red is good, ma Claudia is better.

- nc: Don't trust her.

- r: She wants same as us now.

- nc: Like Xiang. Enemy of my enemy.

- r: Infatti.

- nc: When talk again?

> - r: Red said all online tomorrow after, to update.
>
> - nc: Right. Didn't expect any chat today.
>
> - r: When she told me about you, I had to.
>
> - nc: So glad you did. Grazie mille.
>
> - r: Love you Cara. Be careful.
>
> - nc: Always. Love you too.

***

"Sorry, Mike. I gotta pee again."

"Really? You have the smallest bladder ever."

"She can make it there and back. There's never anyone in the corridors anyway." Tina was right, but they had orders.

"Xiang said not to go alone," Gift replied.

"Mikey, give Matt your uniform. We're on a roll, almost at the Ops center bit and this is the critical part."

Matteo objected. "*Seriously?* I won't fit in his uniform."

"He doesn't know the code words." Mike reached for his helmet. "I'll go. I can pee as well. All that green tea."

"*Right?*" Gift agreed.

The walk to the toilet booth proved Tina's assumption correct. On the sublevel, passersby didn't often pass.

"Glad you had to pee too. I think Tina would've had me wet the floor before she let you take me."

"She's in the zone. But I don't need to go. I just said that to get her off your back."

"That's so sweet." Gift patted his arm in gratitude.

Mike used the toilet, saying he may as well 'squeeze a little out.' Gift giggled at his word choice. It happened. A guard in the narrow corridor.

Mike whispered, "Head down, hide your face."

"Purposeful walking." Gift's sweat glands expelled her anxiety.

Holding her breath and ducking her head behind Mike's shoulder, Gift avoided eye contact—or eye to faceplate contact—as they crossed paths. A masculine voice uttered something indistinguishable. Mike replied with gibberish and paused his step. The passing guard didn't pass.

"This is my patrol," he barked. "Why are you here?"

"Escort for critical maintenance personnel. No one's allowed on the sublevel unescorted," Mike replied.

"Indeed. *Perge*," the guard said.

"*Nam bonum omnium*," Mike said as the two resumed their steps. The guard carried on his way, parroting Mike's last words as he continued down the corridor.

"So, you speak another language now?"

"Just some phrases. Why Matt would've been caught."

"What is it? Is it just a made-up code thing?"

"No, it's Latin."

"No way."

"We don't *speak* it, just some phrases used at the right time and in the right way. If I gave him the wrong reply, he'd have shot me."

"Oh mamma. They shoot each other?"

"This New World Order of peace? It's built on violence with loyalty based on intimidation and fear. There's a ton of dirty crap under the shiny surface they show everyone."

"I knew it. Also too, I don't think you need to specify that crap is dirty," she said in a whimsical tone.

"*So* funny. Now what was that about *purposeful walking?*"

"Something I came up with sneaking through the R.F. when the Pioneers took it. Funny how often I get in the middle of colony take-overs... Anyway, I figure if I look confident and walk like I belong, like I know where I am and where I'm going, people will ignore me. You know, *purposeful* walking." Her smile radiated such warmth.

"Isolation and all aside, you're a real bag of nuts, you know that?"

"And nonsense," she said with a joyous snort. "And you love that about me."

15 | WEEK TWELVE

"Those who deny freedom to others deserve it not for themselves." As Gift recalled, one of the presidents of the United States—remembered mostly for good things—said that. A tall fellow in a silly hat with an impressive beard. Seems if any colony's history tutors taught that, the United Republic of Mars would, having come mostly from the former United States with support of the United Kingdom—ironically once a part of the European Union. Such alliances had fragility and often failed to be united. Chan's words haunted Gift.

He was nuts. But even a nut can be right.

Peeling layers like an onion, Gift saw the foundations of the proposed United Republic of Earth. *They'd shoot their own guards for not knowing the correct Latin codeword in the corridor.* A clarity came to mind. The United Republic of Mars began its occupation with hostility and aggression greater than Chan's polite conquest of United Africa. No, this New World Order of theirs wasn't a path to freedom and peace. It denied such not only to the conquered but also to their own. If the man they called *Honest Abe* was right, these Martians didn't deserve freedom. But did that justify the action about to be taken against them?

No choice but to fight.

Miss Heller's words came back to Gift from a memory well-suited to present circumstance. That made memories valuable, bringing lessons to bear on new challenges and helping clear the debris from current choices. *Was there a choice?* To Xiang, Tina, everyone, they had no alternative but to fight once again. The enemy changed in form and name so many times, but the uprising to war, to violence, was familiar. That dreaded hour fast approached. As the sunlight welcomed a new day to New Europa and United Africa, in the future, Gift had been awake for way too many hours fretting the moment when the clocks would show 13:00 in the New Republic of China.

"Head of the snake?" Gift asked the room.

"*What?*" Xiang barked.

"Chan. He was the head of the snake when we took back U.A. from him. To have him meant the victory would last. The snake died when we cut off its head."

"Interesting analogy," the General said.

"Yeah, but who's the head now?"

Tina's eyes opened from a nap. "You mean if we stop the foot soldiers, the U.R.M. is still there, can undo what we accomplish?"

"Something like, yeah. I mean, even Chan, he wasn't the *actual head*, was he? I mean we got him, and U.A. was free. But then," pointing a thumb to Xiang, Gift continued, "*she* got us. The *real* head, I guess."

"Are you sure, Miss Gift, you have no military training? Your concern is well-founded. I have considered this, but we also have no choice. We must assume the head of the snake, as you call it, is up there, safely in a ship in orbit, just as I was here when Chan took Africa."

Tina added, "The General's right. And we can't get up there. Unless Aimée's gonna go all warrior goddess on 'em up there, all we can do is hit 'em here. So, we will."

A chuckle brought Gift puzzled looks. "Picturing Aimée as a warrior goddess. I think she'd like the image."

"As long as she gets to show her legs," Mike added with a hearty chortle.

"Gift," Matteo said. "We've watched her vids dozens of times. Aimée said more than once they have few up there with her. And she hinted at something being off with their weapons. Like, maybe they're not as strong as they make themselves appear. I think even if we don't get the head, a snake head with no body isn't much of a threat."

"True. And no matter." Xiang stood. "We are about to go. We go at exactly thirteen O-five after my people make the first move. We must be ready. We have one chance to succeed. Does everyone know their role?"

Nods all around and a hearty 'Yes, ma'am' from Tina signaled it would soon happen. Gift had a simple job. She and Matteo would be the distraction, rising to the ground level and dangling Gift as bait. The visual disturbed her more than the mental image of headless snakes. Mike would escort Xiang and Tina to Ops, assuming Han's ability to bypass U.R.M. security codes. Gift's mind wrestled over the General's overbearing positivity being genuine or a tactic. The woman's icy disposition and steel face were impossible to read.

Tina grabbed Gift's arm firmly. "We got this. Mister Han is already in the system, making sure to get us into the building. We just gotta get by the guards. Mike's Latin skills should get us past a few, and we can handle the rest. The fools work as singles, not even paired off. Plus, they'll be coming for *you*, won't they?" She smiled unnervingly.

Gift dry swallowed. "Yeah. Not thrilled to be the bait. Maybe I should've been in the planning chats yesterday."

"It's a good plan, Gift." Matteo's voice had an assuring cadence, but Gift wasn't at all reassured by it.

She turned to Mike. "You're sure the guards will come for me? I mean *all* of them? To clear your path to Ops?"

"We've all been told finding you is our highest priority. Believe me, every guard wants to be the one that brings you in. You'll have so many men chasing you, Tom would be jealous." His playful laugh irritated Gift tremendously until she gave in and joined Mike in it. He had a point. Now she missed Tom even more. They had gotten so close before her last assignment to U.A. Worry for him in N.E. overtook the inner sadness and dominated her.

"Thirteen O-three. We go in two," Xiang said.

Once again, Gift saw the stone hardness in the General, unfazed by the call to action and showing no signs of fear. They were back in Ops, drowned in a fog of red light, with Gift in panicked trepidation and Xiang at her default calm and cool. Now Gift worried for Oksana and couldn't trace the path her crazy brain took to bring her there. She needed to focus, be ready to pop out at the right time to coordinate the others getting to Ops. Instead, she thought of Marco saying they were going to 'pop out' of the maintenance tube into the passageway. Gift clearly had no control of her mind's wanderings and needed to rein it in. They had only a minute before they needed to go, or so she thought.

"*Now*. Move now," The General shouted.

Mike led, with Xiang next and Tina guarding the rear. Along with Matteo, Gift was the last to leave, counting to twenty as instructed before embarking on her part of the mission. Matteo muttered the memorized directions in an undertone as he took the lead in navigating. Gift felt it best as her own sense of direction had often disappointed her. As they slinked down the corridor, the clatter of the uprising's commotion avoided their ears.

"Been like, five minutes since it started. I don't hear anything. Strange. Is that strange? I mean, shouldn't we hear guns and fighting and stuff?"

Matteo kept his eyes forward. "There's a crazy-thick layer of cement between us and the main floor. I doubt we'd hear a bomb go off from down here."

"I guess. Hey, what if we pass a guard?"

"I've got a taser and a pistol."

Gift stopped. "A *pistol?* What the heck? Why do you have that? You can't shoot anyone."

"But *they* don't know that."

"Oh... *Oh*, I guess not. Promise you won't use it."

"Of course not. I don't think it even has bullets. Xiang hogged them all for hers. Besides, the Chinese all know you as the one that shot the highly decorated Commander Chan. They'd think twice before messing with ya."

"Just move."

Gift's nightmare came true, a guard approached. Too early to be discovered, it needed to be upstairs. They didn't know her face, but she was in China and not Chinese, so any guard would be sure to stop her, assuming her to be their prize. Hiding behind Matteo's shoulder shielded her face, but he didn't wear a guard uniform. When the hand-raise of the guard stopped them, her body tucked itself behind Matteo's.

"Where are you going?" A loud female voice barked out the words as a demand. "And who's that with you?"

"I'm Matt and this is Gift, the one you're looking for."

Gift gasped at the foolish bravado. *What the heck's he doing? We may as well have gone to the detention block, been a lot easier.* Before she could gather her thoughts to understand what happened, she saw the poor woman's shoulders shaking wildly, her whole body vibrating. Two uncoiled wires on her chest made their way from Matteo's taser and the nameless woman fell to the ground.

Once he retracted the electrodes, Matteo said, "Come on. That set us back. Need to move more quickly."

Yet again, Gift ran into danger when the mind and body agreed they should run away from it. Miss Heller's *no choice* declaration played on loop, occupying her mental cognition, leaving little resources for what she must do next. She rushed headlong to be a distraction—a worm on a hook like the one Tom showed her when he tried and failed to catch a fish in Colony

Lake. Not only because there were no fish in that water. Gift also forbade him to use such trickery to kill innocent creatures. As she was about to place herself on that hook, she wondered who had it worse, the fish or the worm.

The worm, of course. I'm *the worm.*

Matteo found the passage to the stairs to sneak into the education center two buildings down from the Admin building that held the Ops center. The perfect place to dangle the bait and coax the fish away from Xiang's target. Just then, the image of Xiang being the big fish in the pond with popping eyes and puckering fish lips lifted the corner of Gift's lips. They climbed the stairs to find the ruckus Gift's ears had missed below.

To recognize the sounds of bullets leaving barrels and piercing the air disturbed her. It should have been unknown. A more worrisome idea came in being the destination of those bullets, so Gift ducked even though safely behind the solid concrete wall of the building. She found it curiously silly how her hands instinctively cupped her head as if they would stop a bullet from meeting her brainpan. Now she had to show herself, the last thing her logical brain and melting nerves wished to do.

"Okay, this is it." Matteo's confidence remained. "What we're here for. We need to go out there, but not make it look like we're trying to be seen."

"Oh mamma. How, how do we do that?"

"Act like we're trying to sneak by, don't want to get caught."

"Not hard to fake that. I don't wanna get caught."

"Me neither. But our friends need us, or *they* get caught and the whole thing fails."

Bent at the waist and keeping their heads low, Matteo pulled Gift by the arm to the door, ready to go into the openness of the dome, the war zone. Gift pulled back on Matteo's hands, his grasp painfully tight.

"I don't know about this."

Ignoring her hesitance, he pulled her into the open. Sounds of gunfire saturated the surrounding air and her headache pounded relentlessly. As

Matteo led her along a path toward the opposite building, Gift's frightened eyes couldn't look for soldiers, not ready to see the danger everywhere around her. If she didn't see it, was it real?

"You there. *Halt*."

16

If a fish took the bait, the fisherman had one fish. This is where the analogy ran aground in Gift's mind. The mission failed if they caught one fish. They needed the pursuit to draw all the fish in the pond to the same lure, playing on the selfish desire of each guard to be the one to get it. Mike said they'd *all* come for her. But if the first fish swallowed the bait, the others would scatter to find another meal.

"Run," Matteo shouted, then pulled.

To run away made sense in the mind and the emotional pulp her nerves had become. They needed to be smart, something the flight mode of fight-or-flight didn't consider when panic and fear made decisions. Matteo led the way—his head a bit cooler. They passed another guard, sure to show Gift's face as they did, and kept running.

"Come on Gift." Matteo yelled her name for all to hear, alerting them the catch of the day entered shallow water. And the fish came. A glance over her shoulder let her eyes find a gaggle of guards in pursuit. Ahead of them a dozen, several meters and closing. Matteo ducked into a narrow alley between two buildings and Gift hadn't a clue where they were. The shots fired avoided their direction, Xiang's people and the guards targeting each other. Again, Gift felt the unfairness of genetics as Matteo outpaced her, nowhere near as winded.

"This... better... work. Hope... Xiang... got in." Gift's lungs sneaked the words between gasps for air.

"If Han did his job. Ours is working, lots of guards on us."

"Speaking of... *run*." Gift saw guards enter the alley just twenty meters from them.

Matteo took a hard left onto a wider avenue. While the narrow alley made Gift feel trapped, these open surroundings left her exposed and vulnerable. Stomping feet from behind vibrated as waves dotting Gift's flesh and raising the hairs on the back of her neck. They entered a building. It looked familiar. As they hastened deeper into the structure, Gift asked where they were.

"Same education building we came from."

"Trapped?"

"No, we'll lead them down. We got many following but if we go down to the sublevel, they'll call for more. Give Xiang the time she needs."

Racing down the stairs, pops winced Gift's shoulders as glittering motes fell like mist. Each pop darkened their steps more, extending the chase a few precious seconds.

"Came in handy after all." Matteo waved the gun, holding the barrel.

"Which way?"

"We should split up, divide them."

"No... They don't want *you*."

"Sure they do. Just want you more. Besides, they won't know which one they're following."

Tears drowned Gift's eyes. "No! *Please*, we need to stay together." The begging tone was justified as the thought of being left alone terrified her.

"Okay, I hear them. They figured out where we went. Come on." Clasping her hand, Matteo dragged Gift down the corridor, broke a light, then stopped. He spun around and pulled her past the stairs and into another corridor.

"Good thinking," she said, proud of him.

It was unmistakable, the sound of bodies rolling over each other down the stairs. The image of guards falling like dominos played in Gift's mind. The first part of Matteo's ploy worked. Now if they'll follow the broken lights. Behind another door, Matteo found the set of stairs he sought, having recited the directions as they walked. A Plan B of sorts. They surfaced in a small workshop full of shoes in various states of disrepair. An obnoxious blending of foot odor and adhesive resin offended their nostrils. With great care, Matteo peeked over the counter of the front room to check the coast was clear. Gift followed as they stepped onto the avenue, once again in the open. The rumbling of guards in the shoe shop hurried the two along.

"Here." Matteo pulled toward a small dome-shaped building, Gift's every muscle resisting, yanking him back. "What is it?"

"There's no way out. It's an interrogation room."

"They'd never suspect us going in there."

"No. We'll be trapped. This way."

Gift led with no idea where to go. In seconds, guards spotted them, the first pack gaining on their rear. In full sprint they emerged in a wide-open space the Chinese didn't call a piazza but was as large as Marienplatz in New Europa's Citadome One. Matteo took over navigation and tugged her in the only direction not presenting an oncoming wave of blue and silver uniforms. It wasn't the same narrow alley but felt as cramped and hemmed in as they ran through it. By now, every guard in the complex must have been giving chase with nowhere left to hide. Gift questioned her judgment about the small dome. Too late to second guess.

She didn't notice entering the building. When Matteo tried to call the lift, they immediately realized biometrics were needed. If it was the same as their colony, Gift may have had a way up. Slowly, she swept her hand in circles over the wall beside the shiny metal doors of the inaccessible elevator.

"There has to be a trigger, a switch or something."

"What the heck are you doing?" Matteo whispered.

"If I'm right…" The click came and the wall broke the seam beside the lift frame and released outward. Gift pulled it open to uncover a narrow stairwell. "…a way up."

"Whoa. How'd you know about that?"

"Same as N.E. Doesn't even look like a door. Hopefully the guards won't know about the stairs."

After closing the wall-door behind them, they climbed. When Gift pushed the door, they spilled onto the rooftop terrace—bare where the ones in New Europa had plants and comfy seats.

"Bet you didn't know this was here either."

"Never even been in a housing building."

"*Really?* You gotta come over to Oksana's then."

They sat on the floor, a welcome break after so much running. Sounds lifted from the ground; stomping boots mixed with guesses stated with authority as to where their prey had gone. No one mentioned their building. If they checked it, they likely ruled it out for the biometric lock on the lift.

"We can't stay here too long, need to keep the chase going. Maximum five minutes." Matteo was sensible, a trait Gift only found appealing when it didn't mean risking her life.

"Why? They must be in the Admin building by now. If not, they've been caught, right? So many guards chasing us, why aren't they fighting? Where are Xiang's people?"

"No idea. But we knew the Martians outnumbered us. And with you on the loose as bait, maybe they have half their guards fighting, half chasing you."

"You don't think the fighting stopped because we won?" Gift reached for optimism, but it buckled under the stress.

"Let's just worry about this legion of soldiers on our tails." A snort-laugh escaped as Gift found the image of her and Matteo having animal tails hilarious. "I think we need to get them on the chase again."

"But they know I'm here... Hopefully not *right here*. I mean on the loose. Maybe hiding here while they search is better. They'll get every available guard to join."

"Maybe."

"I worry for the other colonies. They had no me, I mean no distraction. I hope Tom's okay. He must be in the middle of it. And Sara. I'd like to hope Oksana stayed out of it at U.A. but knowing her..."

"What about Raff? You think she's in the missile control systems yet?"

"She's the best. If anyone can, it's her. If she's even there, I mean. Our pitiful ground transport is *mal'd* slow. Also too, she said it'd take time once she got there."

"You're right, she'll get into it. Then we can show these U.R.M. folks who's in charge."

"I just don't know," Gift said and melted emotionally.

"Know what? Getting these colonies free only works, long term, if we control those missiles and tell those *mal'd* Martians what to go do with themselves."

"*Matteo.*"

"Am I wrong, Gift? Am I?"

"Well. It's just... Look at our past... from *before*. Having such weapons never brought peace."

"Yeah, because everyone had'em. But now we'll be the only ones. Right now, they have the upper hand, literally, in orbit. We don't know what they've got or are capable of. Aimée gave us hints but doesn't really know, needs us to check. Raff getting control of those missiles turns the table, stacking the deck in our favor. Whatever they have or don't have, *they* know it too. Why in the middle of an uprising they're hunting you. They don't get those missiles before we get control, it's over for them."

"I hate it. I hate all of it."

"We'd better get back down, ready to run." Matteo stood and held a hand to pull Gift up to her feet—aching feet tired of running.

But it wasn't that, not the tired muscles and sore arches that withheld her agreement. A quietness crept in to replace the thunderous roars of clambering boots. No shouts of *She's in there,* or *This way* floated up to the rooftop. Gift crawled to the edge to peek over the parapet wall. The empty piazza, or whatever the Chinese called it, seemed to be waiting for something. The eerie silence beckoned something dreadful.

17

The trickery in fishing bothered Gift. It was lying to the fish. This school of fish, U.R.M. guards, thus far hadn't gotten their free meal and now seemed to have lost their appetite for the bait, for her. Calling a group of fish 'a school' sounded wrong as Gift had learned in times when many children needed to be educated—most didn't have private tutors—they went to a place called *school*. She could never connect the word for an education center to a bunch of fish.

"What do you suppose they're doing? It doesn't seem like they're still looking for me."

"Can't imagine they just gave up on you. What do you think happened to Xiang's people?"

"*Boh*," she replied with a deliberate shoulder shrug. "I mean, if we were successful, these guys would be caught, surrendered or something. And... if they were still fighting..."

"This doesn't look good," Matteo said in dread.

"I haven't heard a gunshot in a while. No commotion. I hope Mike and Tina are okay. You think they're okay?"

"No way to know." He immediately course corrected. "I... I'm sure they are. Probably hiding somewhere safe, like us." The words brought Gift no reassurance.

A parade of footfalls resumed five stories below. Gift peeked to see a procession of blue and gray-clad soldiers marching toward the center of the square, pushing along about three dozen prisoners of war, all with their helmets removed, all Chinese.

"What's happening?" Confidence vanished from Matteo's voice.

"Looks like the general's freedom fighters, I guess they are, right? It's better than calling them rebels."

"Gift," Matteo said impatiently. "What's going on?"

"Right. Looks like we lost. About three dozen of Xiang's people are in the piazza, square, whatever they call it."

"Oh no…"

"What?" A new trepidation sat her back down. "What's 'oh no'?"

Matteo placed his hands on Gift's shoulders, his face full of melancholy. "They're either going to shoot them all or use them as bait to lure you out."

"*What?*" Her volume scared them both, but however ground-level voices lifted to be clearly heard on the roof didn't work the same way going down. Matteo's quick check confirmed no one heard them.

"They are, they're gonna shoot those people. Moved them to the side, along a wall. The U.R.M. soldiers lined up facing them. It's a firing squad."

Before Gift could think how to prevent this execution, an amplified voice filled the dome. "Gift Ojo. I know you can hear me." Female voice, not Chinese. The accent was British, like when Charlie used to put it on. "As we have said from the start, we wish this to be a peaceful coexistence. No one need be hurt on either side. I offer you my word, Miss Ojo. No one will be hurt if you show yourself. You have two minutes."

Matteo grabbed Gift's arm to forcibly restrain her from standing. "No Gift. One of two things is going to happen now. One: they shoot those people down there, and we stay hidden. Two: we give ourselves up, they get you, and they shoot those people anyway."

"We don't know that. We don't know the U.R.M. And so far, they *have* been mostly peaceful."

"Right, like shooting their own guards for not knowing a codeword. *That* kinda peaceful? Gift, all you've done for eleven weeks, it's for nothing if they get you."

"But... all those people." She dragged the words into a plea for a way to save them, even at the cost of herself.

"They're dead either way. You can't save them."

Sad as it was, he was correct. She had to accept it. They couldn't trust the sort of fishermen who'd drop explosives in the water, killing hundreds of creatures, to get the one they wanted. *The nameless British woman of the U.R.M. said I had her word?* Gift saw no value in the word of a stranger, a stranger who'd come in conquest. They'd stop at nothing to get her, and all she had endured, the isolation and near madness, would be for naught.

"Miss Ojo. This is your final chance to surrender."

Pressed thigh to thigh, Matteo turned and grabbed Gift in a tight squeeze bracing for what was coming. For as long as she lived, Gift would never be able to unhear the rampage that assaulted her eardrums in that horrific moment. The pathways etched in her brain tissue were unable to be removed or archived, part of her now.

Could I have saved them?

"Gift, we had no choice." Matteo offered consolation. How could it be enough? Still suffering the nightmares from taking the life of a raging lunatic, teeth latched onto her arm and desperate to kill her, what layer of guilt might this day pile on? How could she ever be the same? Matteo held on tight with arms of a strong, warm comfort that kept Gift this side of rational to the situation's helplessness.

As much as her logical mind accepted she had made the right decision, raw emotion took full possession of her faculties and commanded brain and body as if someone else were steering a transport. She had no control.

There was no way to know how many minutes passed or if those minutes had collected into hours. Lesser sounds of movement scaled the building to spill over the terrace wall. New feet walking, but few. Sweat glands kicked into overdrive as Gift contemplated what could possibly come next, too afraid to look.

"Miss Ojo. We have captured two of General Xiang's command team, and... they are *not* Chinese. Do you find this interesting, Miss Ojo? I thought you would. One is an infiltrator in our guard, the other a female African warrior. If those helpless people you did nothing to save were not enough, can you live with the guilt of two of your close friends being executed because *you* wished to save yourself from being taken alive, *just to talk?*"

"No, Gift."

"I have to. Let me go. I'll scream."

"This is the same. Nothing you do is gonna change what they'll do to Mike and Tina."

"I have to try."

"No. We can't give in to them. They *will* break you, Gift. Everybody breaks. You'll lead them to the missile complex. Then they'll experiment on you until they find out how to live outside. They get everything and we lose. And they kill you like a lab rat in the process."

"Fine! Better me than Mike and Tina."

"No, Gift. It will be you, Mike, *and* Tina. Me too, for sure. They'll kill us all once they don't need us. You know it. Look what they just did to Xiang's people. And the U.R.M. gets control of the missiles. You can't let that happen."

"Just... shut up."

"Listen, they know your friends are the only leverage they've got. If they killed them, they have nothing. Did you notice she didn't give you a time limit, like the others?"

"Yeah. No two minutes," Gift said through sniffles.

"Right. So, they threaten to kill them until they get you and keep them *alive* long enough for that to happen."

"You sure? I can't let them die."

"I... I'm only saying... what makes sense."

"So, we don't know for sure. And if they don't shoot them, they'll torture them to get me. They—"

The amplified female British voice interrupted. "Miss Ojo, come to the Admin building within the hour for an exchange. You for your friends."

Matteo dared a peek to see the lead woman walk off with guards prodding Mike and Tina to follow along at gunpoint. The relief that overshadowed Gift was potent but fleeting. Her friends hadn't been shot dead yet, but the U.R.M. had them. All that happened was a stay of execution, nothing more. They desperately needed a plan to save them. *Where was that mal'd General Xiang?* A handful of soldiers mingled in the open area and in the surrounding pathways and alleys. Matteo thought aloud, trying to plan a route to one of the access points to the sublevel. He knew of only two and soldiers stood in their way.

Faint at first, it suddenly surrounded them, vibrations filling the air of the dome. A familiar buzzing hum intensified. They came as a swarm, a dark cloud into the center of the dome at high elevation. Dozens of drones, the familiar mechanical whir of electric motors rapidly spinning tiny turbines, cutting and pushing the air, exacerbated by their number. *Could it be called a school of drones?* Within seconds, before the two could retreat to the stairwell to find cover, one of those flying cameras fixed on them. Gift's first thought wasn't of getting caught. The emotion that riled up over her wasn't fear. *Why didn't they do this* before *killing all those people?* Matteo was correct, they were dead no matter what Gift or anyone else did.

To signal her surrender, Gift raised both hands and Matteo followed her lead. An idea so raw, so instinctive flooded her mental display screen. Might Gift have found a choice in this choiceless situation? She hated those one-choice scenarios because having only one choice meant having none. She stepped to the edge of the terrace and climbed onto the parapet wall.

"Gift. What... *Gift*, get down," Matteo shouted.

"You said it, and you were right. If they get me now... all we did, all I did for three months, was for nothing. They get me, they get everything. They win."

"No Gift. Not like this," he frantically pleaded.

"It's okay... my sweet little Matteo. I love you."

Gift felt a wave of calming peace as her eyes shut out the light. She leaned forward to let her body's weight pull her over the edge.

18

Never had Gift's resolve been tested to its limit, never reached the tipping point. Until now. In this moment of clarity, the choice she discovered filled her every fiber with conviction. This was the right move, the one in her power to enact. A small sacrifice, her life for the greater good. *For the good of the colony* expanded into something grander. An ultimate step taken in full satisfaction she'd done her part, given her all. Full of gratitude for her life and the wonderful people in it, Gift leaned forward.

The ground below drew closer.

Time stopped to mourn.

The sensation of touch threw her brain into a state of confusion. Before she understood it, the yank flipped the dome. Her contemplation of departure paused gravity's pull just enough for the spry young man to launch himself up and grab her. On the rooftop, she laid on Matteo, his arms squeezing her so tight she ached.

"You were gonna do it," he said in shock. "You... were really gonna jump."

"And end this. It was the only way. Now I have—"

"No," he said with ear-piercing volume. "We'll find another way. We will. We're better in this with you than without."

"Now they get what they want. What if they get those missiles? Then we've got nothing. And we'll become their stupid United Republic of Earth."

"Who cares. I'd rather have that *with* you than freedom *without* you."

"Did you ask, like, I don't know, about two hundred fifty thousand people if they'd say the same?"

"Promise you won't try that again." He held her tight.

"Well... now I, I can't. Thinking about that ledge makes me feel like I'm gonna pee myself. I *was* ready... I made peace with it. You took my one chance from me."

"Promise me you won't do anything that stupid again."

"It's me. I'll do lots of stupid things."

Their shared chuckle expelled more tension than joy as a desperately needed release.

***

The voice that taunted Gift's surrender before snuffing the life from nearly three dozen human souls came from a British female. She had a face, perfectly symmetrical with sky-blue eyes and the fare skin of healthy youth. Her nose was neither too thick nor too long and her lips were full, but not overly so. To Gift, she should have been a broadcaster in a glamorous outfit, out-of-place in a military setting. *How did someone so pretty become a soldier?*

"This would have gone easier if you'd given yourself up. Some... *regrettable* things could have been avoided," she said as an opener. In the large white office behind a desk made of some type of faint brown hardwood, a serious stare captivated Gift. Standing in arm restraints, Gift stared back from across the desk.

"It may make you feel better telling yourself it was my fault *you* slaughtered thirty people. I won't take your guilt, lady. It's yours to own." A silent gaze blanketed the soldier woman. "Where's James?"

"Excuse me?"

"Commander Morris. Did he outlive his usefulness?"

A puzzled look came over the stern, stunning face. "All you need to worry about is how to help your friends by cooperating with us. We can reach an accord and maintain the peaceful transition we began since our return."

"Where are they? Mike and Tina? I'm not telling you anything 'til I see they're okay and have assurances they'll stay that way. And Matteo. Where did you bring him?"

Alone in the oversized office, which Gift assumed had belonged to the former president of the N.R.C., Gift presumed this new woman in charge, James being her underling. Interlocking her fingers and flipping her hands around, she pushed her palms out toward Gift with loud crackling pops. The still-interlocked hands rotated and rested on the desk. "When Mister Morris spoke with you, he asked questions and conscripted you to a work assignment. He was not harsh, did not intimidate you, and never harmed or threatened you. The goal was to show you our way was working. We have united the colonies and work together for the good of all."

"What happened to Corinthia? If you shoot your own guards for forgetting some dumb phrase, what'd she get for letting me escape?"

"You will soon learn *I am not* James Morris, and you will not be treated as well if you don't tell us what we want to know."

"How do I know you'll keep your word and not harm my friends?"

"I have given no word to keep. When I offered those rebels' lives for your surrender, I would have kept my word. I held your friends out like carrots, and you didn't bite." Gift didn't get the carrot reference and tried to fit it into her fishing analogies. The picture of a carrot on a fishhook looked wrong. "You didn't surrender under any terms. We found you. That means that you work with us and... we'll see how best to reward such cooperation."

"I see."

After a lengthy back-and-forth about the location of the missiles, the conversation shifted to Gift having been outside the colony for over ten weeks. Not even the Pioneers or Ubuntu managed that, and the nameless blue-eyed beauty practically drooled over Gift doing so. Lingering silence was Gift's only reply. Threats came against Gift and her friends, bringing an uncomfortable anger at Matteo to her gut. Stopping her self-sacrificing fall led her here, keeping him and Mike and Tina in danger.

The woman stood, tugged her waistcoat, and instructed Gift to remove her shoes. A hum that hinted of a tiny electric motor landed on Gift's ears as the woman moved behind her and cut the tie pinching her wrists. She raised Gift's hand to meet a cold metal clamp that made its way around the wrist. Then the next one. The hum returned, raising her arms until her heals lifted just off the floor, the balls of her feet keeping contact. The taut pull ached Gift's stretched muscles.

Sitting again at her desk, the interrogator continued, "We didn't install those. The Chinese president had them here, liked to keep a prisoner in front of him, often left them there for days. He wouldn't speak to them, simply had them watch him doing his daily work like they weren't even there. Miss Gift, *you do not exist* until you tell me something we wish to know."

After thirty minutes—perhaps an hour—of using a desktop terminal display in stony silence, the woman rose and left Gift in the office.

The room flooded with intense light as bright as the sun at midday when no clouds floated between Earth and sky, and Gift's eyes pinched closed in response to the sudden exposure. She pondered her new predicament, and the fury of emotion that held onto Matteo's selfish act. The hours dragged on as the night left her strung up, saturated in the illumination.

General Xiang led the investigation while they left Gift hanging from afflicted Y-spread arms. A hard smack to the cheek brought added pain as the bony knuckles of Xiang's backhanded slap abused Gift's flesh. Only at that point did Gift realize she'd been stripped naked.

"And how did you stay out so long? Why don't you get earth sickness? How can you make babies when no one else in the colonies can?" For an unknown reason no logic could justify, this embarrassed her more than nudity's shame.

A snort twitched her nose. Scene change. The General came to visit Gift and Emily at the airplane. Em ate all the apples while Gift sucked down the honey. The unlikely friends laughed when Em misused a Chinese colloquialism Gift oddly understood. She had been talking about her post in the ground and described Gift putting her on the pole as fàng gēzi. The usually stern military leader chuckled as she explained to poor innocent Em what it meant to stand someone up.

Awoken by a heaviness in her bladder, Gift hung under the blinding light holding her eyes hostage. Her hands numbed for lack of blood. "*Hello? I need to pee. Hello?*" After a few seconds of no reply, she screamed, "Hello," three more times. Familiar to Gift from experience, the warm sensation affixed her coverall to her thigh. "Figures." When she woke next, the unpleasantness in her nostrils didn't overpower them.

When the leader with the British accent entered and took her seat at the desk, the lights returned to normal.

"I peed myself. Can I get cleaned up?"

The woman didn't reply, look, or break her movements over her desktop display. The squeak of the door opening behind her brought a glint of hope to Gift that they might address her request. They did, but it would have been best to be ignored. Two guards cut the coverall off her with large scissors. The blur of the human figures vanished, leaving Gift still unclean, hanging by throbbing, sore arms in nothing but her undergarments—slightly better than the nakedness she dreamt.

Gift saw the malevolent genius in the silent treatment. It was maddening, frustrating, and made her feel invisible, inconsequential, and valueless. Hang there until she died or gave them what they wanted. Given no food or water, Gift watched the woman sip Earl Grey tea made from actual tea leaves.

A rich gingery fragrance snuck up to tease Gift's nostrils, restoring partial consciousness. Lunchtime. The woman ate at her desk in front of Gift. Suspicion ran high she intentionally amplified the chewing noises. Gift craved the food and her dry mouth lusted over the water, callously gulped between mouthfuls of garlic-ginger tofu and rice. Having drunk nothing in two days, little came when she urinated again, yet its whiff carried greater potency. The hard Martian continued working unfazed, whereas tracing the sensation of a drop snaking down her leg occupied Gift's mind as a respite from the reality engulfing her.

Visitors came and went, all ignoring Gift as a sconce on the wall. More so. A group of three sat behind her. Gift stayed conscious, seeing only the woman at the desk. Of course, nothing confidential dared escape any lips. They acted like she didn't exist but were fully aware of her. Perhaps that was the failure of the pretty lady's plan to make Gift feel nonexistent and inconsequential. She still did.

On a late afternoon vid chat, most definitely staged for Gift's benefit, a male Chinese voice with a poor command of English grammar updated his counterpart on the status of Mike, Tina, and Matteo—in isolation and being deprived of food and water. The woman ordered him to intensify the efforts tomorrow and get results. While an obvious ploy, it worked.

What did Matteo say? Everyone breaks. Gift wondered when that moment would come and, if an inescapable fact, what was the point of holding out any longer?

19

One enemy of Gift's had slid closer to a friend. Sara. Not Guard Sara, Gift never considered her an enemy for doing her job. Shower Group Sara. To say 'friend' may have stretched the term. As amicable acquaintances they chatted in the shower queue, though Gift hadn't been in as many since Oksana got a flat with a private shower. The memory may have lifted the corner of Gifts lip. Would seeing the half-smile cause an increase in the applied duress? It didn't matter. Gift's head hung from a neck too weak to support it, and the tiled floor filled the slits between her eyelids.

A familiar rumble chased the sudden boom. Initial conclusions flattened into wishful thinking. Her friends were captives so the distant noise couldn't be the disturbance of action, a hope for freedom. Gift's irises rolled nearly into her forehead to see her captor's face. Desperately she looked for the twitch in her eye, the British beauty's only tell. Glimpses barely worth the effort made Gift's eye sockets hurt.

When the door creaked from behind, Gift assumed the Martian Lady's torturous lunch delivery. The idea nudged her closer to her breaking point. The promise of a sip of water had the power to advance her beyond it. Her arms reached upward like petrified tree limbs. Numb. Dead. The stumps her legs had become tingled. *Everybody breaks.*

"Good. Secure the room," the tormentor from Mars said to the guards just before she slumped in her chair.

"Gift," someone may have said.

Like lead weights, Gift's arms fell and crashed into her thighs. Strength-less, Gift's legs buckled, and she collapsed but didn't slam onto the floor. Mustering all her might, her finger pulsated as it reached toward the desk. "Wa…" came from her mouth when her mind said *water*.

Relief finally came to her lips in liquid form and filled her mouth. As it poured down her throat, she instantly felt its recuperative power, like life surging back into her. Her muscles politely requested more time. Arms had wrapped around her, supporting her slouch from under her armpits and over her chest. Voices came from every direction, many with the sound of her name. Then sliding. Falling. *I must be dreaming, still hanging in the office, detached from consciousness. The fall will wake me…*

***

In an unfamiliar room, Gift's eyes appreciated the duller lighting on a soft gray ceiling. Under a blanket in a bed, she became uncomfortably warm. The fatigued arm that flipped the cover off pulled it back quickly when she realized no clothes hid her shame. A face appeared beside her as she turned from the ceiling to see Xiang. Gift supposed it was a dream.

"It is okay, Gift. We are back in my secret office."

"How?"

"I caused a diversion, a minor explosion. I used that to free your friends. It was easier to get them first."

"Everyone? Where?"

"They will return soon. I knew the governor would immediately call for security and I intercepted the call. I freed your friends on the floor below you, and we came for you."

"How long?" Gift's thoughts required great effort to push enough air from her feeble lungs to expel words.

"Sixteen hours. We gave you nutritional injections."

"I'm... um, my clothes?"

"You soiled your underwear so I wiped you the best I could."

The fierce general became a soft motherly figure and helped Gift to the shower stall after giving her some much-appreciated water. Mental clarity being elusive, unsure of realities or dreams, no shame visited the awkward scene as Xiang helped her bathe and dress. Body washed, dried, and in a clean coverall, Gift ate a bowl of rice with broccoli and some kind of protein. Three glasses of water later, her thirst finally relented. Strength filled back into her, aiding her back to herself.

"Are they really free? Matteo, Mike, and Tina?"

"Yes Gift, as I told you. Tina carried you here after we disguised ourselves as guards to free you."

"Where are they?"

"Preparing our escape."

"You mean, leave here? To go where?"

"United Africa. The only colony we know is free. They were successful in their revolt where we failed."

"I see. No word on New Europa?"

"No. We will get to U.A. and check on them from there. Your friends are readying a flyer. Tina knew of one close to being finished before she became a fugitive. We will go at dawn."

"What time even is it?"

"O-three nineteen."

The General raised an eyebrow to Gift's spontaneous half-snort chuckle.

"No, it's just funny. As in ironic, I mean. My nose itched like crazy the *whole* time hanging there. Couldn't scratch. Drove me insane. Now... *nothing*. Figures."

Gift saw General Xiang laugh for the first time.

"I admire you." Xiang's words caused thoughts to crash and spin in Gift's head. "You stood up to Chan and to me. Again, I apologize for my role in that. You spent weeks in hiding and you helped with those hidden messages. Now humiliating torture by the U.R.M. Gift, I believe you are the strongest person I have ever met."

"Wow. I mean, *thanks?* But I'm not, really. I've mostly been tossed in cells or hid out alone. Not exactly heroic. It's just... more like getting captured a lot and not dying."

"You have my deepest respect. I am grateful Matteo pulled you from that ledge. You showed true heroism and bravery. I agree with him, we are better in this fight with you than without you."

"He told you?"

"He is very proud of you. We are all proud of you."

Pensive, Gift momentarily considered not saying what came from her mouth next. "Well, I must admit, it's been... *difficult* for me to, for us, to be on the same side. I mean, you helped me escape and hide, and brought me supplies. And now you re-rescued me again from those Martians. Washed me and helped me shower." Gift's face withdrew. "I'm still super weirded-out, not comfortable with stuff like that. But... thank you. Now we're planning our escape together, and in this battle for liberation from the U.R.M. It's just... all so strange."

"Understandable."

"Oh. I... when we, on the way. Did I fall or something? I fall a lot in my dreams, usually wakes me. Sometimes I end up falling in real life too."

"It was more of a slide. I was the only one besides the president aware of an escape hatch in his office with a sloped shaft to this sublevel."

"And the pretty woman, did you call her governor?" A head nod confirmed. "Did you... Is she...?"

"Stunned. But Gift, after what you said, are we okay working together? To follow my plan to flee to Africa?"

"This is where we are now. What we need to be. That's what matters in the end, I guess. And I agree about going to U.A. first, yeah."

Gift woke to familiar and welcome faces. The reunion was short and sweet, with firm hugs for all when her dear friends returned to the secret sublevel office. The light air transport was in working order and prepared for the flight to U.A. First-shift workers would soon crowd the corridors, providing the opportunity to slip through the hustle and bustle without suspicion.

All in U.R.M. guard blue and gray and under face-hiding helmets, they entered the workspace with flyers in various states of disrepair and found crews getting tools ready. Tina took the lead on this phase, pointing everyone's eyes to the flyer they were about to steal.

"Wait." Gift found a flaw in a plan she didn't know. "How's Mike gonna get in? He'll be over by the door."

Tina smiled. "No worries, we won't leave Mikey. Good catch though. Once he opens the hanger hatch, we move. We'll fly with the door open, drop beside Mike, and he jumps in. Nothing to it."

"A lot can go wrong."

"They will not see this coming," Xiang replied. "According to maintenance records, none of these flyers are ready for flight. We fixed it ourselves. We will be gone before they know what happened."

Mike raced off to handle the door, and Tina and Matteo approached the flyer repair team as a distraction. Xiang and Gift strolled through the workshop like they belonged there, straight to the transport with no one paying them any mind. Soon Tina and Matteo climbed in and took their seats, leaving the access port open. The General, the only one who could fly the thing, sat at the pilot's controls and pushed *Start*—a button oddly labeled in English.

Nothing happened.

20

General Xiang's biometrics wouldn't start the flyer. When Xiang asked if Mike successfully bypassed the biometric scanner for the transport's flight controls, Tina confirmed.

"Doesn't seem like he did it right," Matteo said.

Quicker than a blink, Gift dropped to her back at the general's feet, arms extending under the flight control panel. In a muffled voice, she said, "He said he did flight controls. Sometimes you gotta be specific with Mike. *Flight controls* aren't the same as the security to turn the stupid thing on, it's on a completely different system."

Tina asked, "How the heck do you even know that?"

"The R.F. flyers are the same." After a hearty grunt, Gift continued, "Sergey told me they're like that so no one can hijack the thing after it starts or is in flight. Had to ask what hijack meant. Anyone got a screwdriver or something?" Someone's hand gave her the tool, and she fiddled for another minute under the console. "Not sure where the word comes from. Sounds like a greeting to some guy called Jack, but it basically means stealing the thing. Without biometric security clearance, you can't operate it even after it's on."

"Can you fix it?" It sounded like Tina's voice.

"Not broken. I guess... I'm... hijacking it." An "ouch" followed a deeper grunt as Gift continued working. "Almost got it."

"Door's not open yet," Matteo pointed out.

Xiang answered, "He was told to wait until we flash the forward lights to know we were ready. If he opens it too soon, it can be closed by an override. We have one chance at this. The timing must be perfect."

"Gift?"

She grasped the nervousness in Tina's inquiry. "Just a sec."

"Matt, strap in. I'll get Mikey at the hatch." Tina's voice trailed off with her pounding footfalls.

"Try it now."

The low hum of live circuits trickled over Gift's ears and the current flowing through the wires fondled her fingers. System activated, ready for flight control, the flyer lifted. That it wasn't the best timing to scoot out and get up became evident when Gift toppled and slammed into the wall. Low and moving slowly, the transport didn't come to a full stop at the access door. Gift turned to find half of Tina with a firm grip on a handhold above the hatch. In one quick motion she fell back, pulled Mike in, and yelled, "Go. Go."

Metallic pops ricocheted off the rear, chasing them away from the colony. They were gone, airborne and on their way to United Africa. Xiang leveled off, allowing Gift to stammer over to Mike for a hug, mouthing 'thank you' to Tina over his shoulder.

"What took you so long?"

"Just needed to get everyone settled." Gift didn't want Mike to feel bad. The flight controls were working perfectly, as they had asked him to do. *Mike being Mike.*

"Good work, everyone," Xiang said. "Get comfortable. It will be several hours."

Gift peered out a window. "Anyone following us?"

"Nope," Matteo said. "We took the only working flyer."

"Only working one at the N.R.C. They have a few others in service, but we checked." Tina had worked on them all. "There are little ones at all the colonies and two working heavies are both at the R.F. for some reason. We should be clear."

"Also too, I'd guess they may think we're headed for N.E. anyway."

Xiang lifted her eyes off the controls. "I would not make that assumption, and I do not think the governor will either. They likely do not know we are aware of United Africa's liberation, so it is safe to say they would not guess our destination."

"If not N.E. or U.A., where would they think we're going?"

"Gift, what has this entire issue with you been about?"

"The miss—*oh*. They must think we're going straight there. And they don't know where that is to send anyone after us. I know I missed most of the planning for this escape, but... why aren't we going there?"

Piling more seriousness onto her default expression, Xiang said, "So, you *do* know the location?"

"Well... no. Not *exactly*. I told the truth. But I also said I may be able to find it in a flyer. And well... I'm in a flyer."

Mike replied, "Nothing we could do there, anyway. Besides, we don't want to risk anyone following us."

"No flyers," Gift countered. "Matteo said no flyers could be following us."

"I would send small transports from New Europa and the Russian Federation to look for us. We believed from the start the location must be between the two colonies."

Smiling at the general, Tina said, "It helps to have a military mind on our side."

"And when they don't find us? They'll head to U.A. then the Ubuntu village. Process of elimination at that point."

"Matteo's right," agreed Gift.

Tina leaned forward. "It's why we're not staying long at U.A. We get an update on weapons, get Oksana, and get outta there."

"And go where?"

"If N.E. is ready, we help liberate them. If not, we hide out for a while. Too many variables to make a solid plan. Sorry for the chaos, Gift." Tina was thoughtful and correct. Gift needed order and symmetry to quell the dull pain.

Mike added, "Plus, we're going in a straight line, best speed to U.A. We'll fly a wider pattern to N.E., so we won't be spotted if they have flyers looking for us."

After a lunch that called back all those nutrition bars Gift consumed in her wilderness sabbatical, conversation shifted to what Aimée meant them to find out about the weapons. Pure speculation, but Gift's confidence was high the power looming over them, keeping the colonies in total submission, may have been far less threatening than portrayed. Gift allowed optimism to return, having noticed how much of a void its absence left.

"What on Earth is that?" Matteo's words dripped childish wonder.

"How tall you think it is?"

Mike replied to Tina, "Eight hundred meters. That sucker's tall."

To see the mystery object, Gift had to get up and push her face into the window. Not a natural wonder, a marvel of engineering touched the sky. A giant skeleton of a building with a patchwork of glass panels, from broken to gone, speckled over it as rotting skin clinging to metal bone. The impressive tower stretched above them from its base—murky water on one side, sand dunes on the other.

"Dubai. That was the city. And the tower was called the Burg, no, Burj Khalifa. Don't ask me what that means. It was once the tallest building in the world." Mike didn't even need the handheld to tout those facts.

"Pulled that one out of your butt, did ya Mikey?" Tina's interesting expression sent Gift and Matteo into a giggling fit. Mike took no offense and offered no sarcastic comeback, making Gift proud.

"Why'd they make it so tall? Looks like they had plenty of land."

Gift raised an eyebrow at Matteo. "Hubris."

"Plus, cities were all about cramming people into as little space as possible. For some reason, there was this... competition almost, to make the tallest building. Every few years they made a taller one." Mike always lit up when spewing useless history.

"Like us in the colonies," Tina said, chuckling. "Living on top of each other, I mean. And now that we have the entire outside, no one wants to be overcrowded. I can't imagine people choosing that."

"It was a very different world. Let's hope that's one old way we don't revert to."

All agreed with Mike as Gift distributed the next round of rations. In a memory, Gift heard Sergey's words, 'they give no joy.' Matteo inquired of the source of her chortle, and she related the story, minus the part about where Sergey found the frog and what else his eyes found at the little lake. Gift had gotten to the point of being able to enjoy parts of the memory without other details souring it—proud of herself for it.

They lurched forward.

It felt like hitting a massive bump in the Zil when racing to save Miss Heller's life. *What could we run over in the air?* Gift wondered in the split-second it took her to realize the ground's rapid approach. The face she found on General Xiang increased Gift's fright. Never had the woman shown fear or anything less than calm confidence, not even in the shaking office when falling bombs were about to end her existence.

"Strap in," someone yelled.

21

S low time had been a perception, an unusual phenomenon Gift compared to walking through water. Normal muscle contractions moving body parts with greater effort and less result. In each *slow-time* experience, visuals of people moving at half speed enclosed her in a foggy mess saturating her sense of reality.

It surrounded her now.

The descent took mere seconds from the clock, yet eternity passed over them. Slowly, Gift watched her hand reach up to pull the fastener of the safety strap. As the smooth metal buckle latched into the clasp at her hip, the click sharpened the reality—they were crashing. A hunk of metal and polymers plummeted toward the ever-approaching ground, the solid surface waiting to consume it, grind it into a masticated mess, and vomit it out over the arid land.

Words melded into diluted and warped background noise, becoming sounds of fear with no further meaning. None needed. All onboard shared the same dread, the same helplessness. All except the pilot, drenched in her own sweat as Gift had never seen emanating from a human brow. Her always straight, horizontal bangs melted into black spaghetti strands sweat-glued to her forehead. Intense focus from her midnight-black pupils could have shot lasers. The woman's thin, toned arms shook fiercely as they gave every bit of their energy and strength to controlling the manual yoke.

The light brown that filled the forward windscreen teased hope as hints of green drew a thin line across the top of the glass panel. A hint of light blue descended like a camera slowly panning upward. Xiang gave her all to leveling the craft, pushing glimmers of promise into her passengers like a drug, but not strong enough to quell the panicked fright stiffening every one of Gift's muscles.

The fall jolted them violently, like a nightmare throwing Gift off the sofa onto the floor intensified by an order of magnitude. Movements were brief and unsubtle as Gift's head jerked forward and slammed back into the headrest. A rushed glance found everyone locked in the same position, pressed into their seats like corpses propped up on display—a mental visual Gift found most peculiar, never having seen or conceived of such a posturing for dead bodies. Perhaps the lifelessness of their blank stares summoned the image.

"Everyone alive? Everyone okay?" Gift shouted.

One by one all confirmed the crash hadn't taken their lives. Matteo said his head pounded, and all confirmed the same hammering in their skulls. The powerful General moaned. Hurriedly, Gift unstrapped. "General, are you okay? Are you hurt?"

From a face scrunched into itself, she replied, "Fine." When Xiang reached to undo her strap, her deep inhale sounded wet. "I may have broken a rib or two."

Gift climbed behind her to free her safety harness and heard the clicks of clasps releasing her friends. Those straps saved their lives, Gift was sure of it, thankful to the engineers who'd been thoughtful enough to install them. Overflowing gratitude came for Xiang's piloting abilities as she turned a sure nose-first deadly impact into a survivable crash-landing. Thoughts shifted momentarily to that Russian pilot who likely did the same to save Aimée at the loss of his own life, and Gift failed again to remember that poor hero's name.

Mike tried to slide open the emergency hatch Tina had pulled him through on their escape several hours prior. "Any clue where we are? How close to U.A. we got?"

"We were not far, an hour out, maybe less." General Xiang pointed forward. "The green ahead is a good sign. We crossed the desert, which is good for us going on foot."

"*Almost* crossed. I mean, I see green, but it's a good bit ahead of us." Gift hated to be the pessimist of the group, but they needed a dose of reality to figure out what to do next.

Tina packed supplies into backpacks, getting ready for the trek. "If we were an hour out—hopefully we weren't more—how long on foot, do we think?"

"Got it," Mike exclaimed. The clank of the rear hatch's locking mechanism echoed in the enclosed space.

"Maybe a day, no more." The impressive General held her midriff with one hand, pulling a tablet from the flight control console with the other.

As they made their way out of the flyer's rear hatch, Gift asked again if anyone had pain or was hurt beyond their initial assessments. It seemed, thanks to Xiang's skillful fortitude, all were relatively unscathed—amazing considering the mutilated mess the flyer had become. It had gotten late. The sun had recently set but hadn't finished lifting the last of its illumination from the landscape.

"Where we shot down?" Tina lent no fear to her words.

Mike looked around the landscape, then asked Xiang, "And will they come to finish the job?"

"No other transports were anywhere in the area. And I do not think the U.R.M. shot at us from an orbital vessel."

"What, then?" Matteo asked.

"Most likely a malfunction." Xiang turned to face Mike and Tina. "You did excellent work on short notice, getting the transport repaired and fly-able. We could not know which of its systems were damaged or how badly."

"So, you're saying we missed something?"

"No, Miss Tina. The flyer had many problems, and we could not have known them all. Now I suggest we move out for United Africa."

Gift readied herself for the trek. "Which way?"

Pointing toward the distant green assumed to be the desert's end, Matteo hoisted a bag. "That way. Sun went down there, so that's West. We go West toward U.A."

With loaded backpacks slung over their shoulders, the group of escapees-become-crash-survivors headed West, with the General leading the way. Carrying herself as if in perfect health, she made Gift forget her multiple broken ribs. The first hour added weight to the pack pulling Gift's shoulders, and she found gratitude for the walk beginning after the sun departed, carrying away the day's heat.

The distant delineation of the desert became dissolved shapes of bushes and trees just beginning to take form like a Monet landscape. Unlike the impressionist's paintings, the weary travelers' hopes were for greater clarity to come into crisp detail when they got up close. Once the patchy up-shoots of grass and weeds thickened into a carpet over the land beneath their feet, Gift requested a needed pause. Grains of sand had hitched a ride in her shoes and reached various other places she didn't care to mention. Carrying on, the moonlit trek pushed them well beyond physical exhaustion, but Gift didn't want to be the one to ask the robotic Xiang to stop again.

"Guys, I'm dead. Can't we stop? *Please.*"

"*Yes,*" Mike enthusiastically agreed with Matteo's motion. Tina added her support. The incredibly fit General—who Gift thought could go for days, not hours—conceded to the repeated mumblings of complaint. Tina,

Mike, and Matteo gathered sticks and twigs for a fire, and Gift seized the opportunity to check on her former captor.

"How are you, really?"

"As I told you, I am fine."

"I see you holding your side and how your face cringes every now and then. Now, I mean, walking all this way, with broken ribs?"

"I appreciate your concern, Miss Gift. My injuries are not severe, and people can walk quite well with broken ribs. You do not need to worry."

"Just Gift, please. What can we do? I mean, to help with the pain?"

Unzipping her coverall and freeing her arms of it, Xiang said, "Help me wrap myself." She withdrew a long strand of blue cloth from her pack and handed it to Gift.

As Gift wrapped the general's torso, she asked, "Where'd you get this?"

"There was an extra coverall in the gear pack on the flyer. I cut this from the lower hem to the collar to make a compression bandage."

"When?"

"When we were loading the backpacks, before we left the transport."

With a firm yank, Gift said, "Is that good? Too tight?"

Xiang grunted, "Perfect," and tucked the end into the taut fabric. "Thank you."

"Welcome. You really think we can find the colony? And in a day?"

"One day was a best guess. And we are heading West, which is good, but I am not sure we are at the correct latitude. I assume we must veer slightly Southward."

"What do you keep looking at on your tablet? Will it help us find the colony?"

"Perhaps. It is a topographical map of the area around the colony, but it is difficult to determine our relative position this far out."

"I see."

"Gift,"—she didn't say Miss— "one of us must remain awake, on guard."

"Why? We're sorta in the middle of nowhere."

"I saw something before the flyer crashed, but I do not wish to alarm everyone. It was a flash of light... from the ground."

"Wait. What are you saying? Someone shot us down... from *the ground?*"

"I believe so."

"What... I mean, who? No one knew we were coming."

"True. I am afraid we do not have the answer yet, so we must be cautious. You are the one who slept last night. I ask you to take the first three hours on watch and I will take three and let you sleep."

"Okay. And what if I see or hear something?"

"Wake us."

The wood gatherers returned and made quick work of starting a fire. It wasn't wintery cold by any means, but the night teased the chill it would lay upon them as they slept. A circle of human bodies formed around the warmth that would help fend off the brisk nip creeping in the darkness. The one on the watch would feed the fire as it consumed the wood giving it life. Gift hoped humans wouldn't repeat past sins by again consuming the planet giving them life.

22 | WEEK THIRTEEN

Wondrous sights and adventures expanded with the new world Gift and her friends discovered stepping out of that airlock a year prior. From her beloved Colony Lake to the splendid mountains of what was North-Central Europe to the unimaginable thrill of being in an unending ocean. While Gift would readily say she loved her life in the New Europa colony of before, this new life offered by the Earth on which she lived and explored, soared kilometers above any dream—and she had some wildly vivid dreams.

Every good has its bad.

Where did that notion come from so suddenly? It must have been connected to her favorite band preserved from before, one of many things that made her music so much better than Mike's. The singer's melodic voice conveyed such raw emotion—pain and passion with equal depth. She would listen to Bono singing U2 songs for hours. Her favorite was called *Bad*. It played in her mind on loops when she was alone in her airplane all those weeks, and may have helped her hold on to sanity in those moments when she didn't let go. *Let it go... Not fade away.* Those lyrics certainly fit the situation and soothed her out of and back into lucidity on several occasions.

Isolation, desolation. Let it go...

This experience felt different. Their new world—which Gift called an 'undiscovered country'—once again heaped misery and unwelcome situations upon them. But this time she'd not endure it alone. She had her friends with her, some of them at least, and the stern Chinese general. They had survived an air transport crash Xiang thought may have been an attack from the ground. What might that mean?

"Gift." Tina said her name as a statement.

"Yeah."

"I asked you if you were ready. We finished our pitiful breakfast, took care of necessary business, and you're just sitting there. There, but somewhere else. You alright?"

"Lost myself in a song inside my mind is all. I'm ready."

Predawn light guided the trekkers, and Xiang pushed on with greater strength and stamina than anyone with a fully intact ribcage could. Gift had to admire her for that. No longer the evil monster dominating her, interrogating her, or torturing her friends, the general herself became a friend. No, that wasn't the right word. Colleague, team member, ally? Better words, if not a perfect fit. The postulation of how much more difficult accepting Xiang must be for her friends raced in to fondle dormant synapses and fire them up into thoughts. If Gift had been struggling to let go of resentment when she had only been questioned by the woman, how must her friends have felt? A space on the brain cleared to ponder their remarkable fortitude and her heart swelled with pride and gratitude for her dear friends rising above petty resentment—or not so petty after being brutally abused—to willingly follow that menacing soldier now leading them.

"Breathtaking."

"Amazing."

"Absolutely gorgeous."

Words lacked the intensity to describe a glorious vista they gazed upon as the morning sun began its ascent. The canvas of a master artist stretched from the horizon and filled them with awe and humility. At least that's how Gift imagined everyone feeling while struggling to define the sensations surging within herself. Whatever their circumstance, whatever the challenge, whoever may have shot them down, all disappeared to give this moment the glory and honor it deserved.

The purple haze had been wiped away to overlay the canvas in a burnt orange that slowly morphed itself into the intensities of the red spectrum, turning into brilliant lavender as it stretched above them. The distant fireball appeared massive as it crested the horizon, igniting the few puffs of clouds that dared inhabit its sky. Colors of light silhouetted the trees as black limbs stretch skyward, greedily soaking in the warmth and energy the sun freely shared. The yellow of the Earth's favorite star blended into oranges and reds and turned the sky reaching out in all directions the most magnificent blue Gift had ever seen. A single tear gently crawled down her cheek to pay homage to the scene only nature could present.

As they carried on toward United Africa, Gift struggled to keep her optimism, setting it at her new default ninety-nine percent. A dose of realism hit like a palm-smack to the forehead, telling her she hadn't had many things reach that in recent weeks. Instant melancholy overwhelmed her, sweeping through her flesh and weakening her bones. In truth, her confidence didn't come near ninety-nine, though she tried to present that to her friends. Her reality whirled in dread she was unable to dismiss over who shot them down, why, and where they were now.

Uncomfortable wouldn't be a strong enough word to describe the effect on Gift to have Xiang squatting right beside her when they stopped for a much-needed break. The unnaturalness of this new positioning next to her, when both needed a little extra time as well, was too much.

"I do not want to startle anyone, but—"

"You startled *me*. Can't I get a little privacy?"

"I thought we were above this. I am sure we are being followed."

"*What?*"

"Shh. Let us not have everyone panic."

"But who? How?"

"Whoever shot us down."

"U.R.M., you think?"

"No. Whoever they are, they were in the wilderness. Not likely they knew we were coming or who we were. I hoped they only wanted the flyer and would leave us to ourselves. But I do not plan based on hope and luck. I have been watching, turning our course in ways they would take for us being unsure of our navigation. I believe they are at least five, perhaps more."

"Oh mamma. Now what?"

"Our best option is to take them by surprise before they can ambush us. If I were them, I would make my move in the rocky terrain ahead. Plenty of places for them to hide. We will surely end up in a place where they will box us in and take us easily."

"I don't know. I mean, I don't even see or hear anyone."

"I have an idea."

"I'm sorry, I can't do this. Would you give me a little space to finish up here?"

Reluctantly, the general finished her business and left Gift to do the same, able to do so now with some restored dignity. Cleaned and decent, she readied herself to continue the conversation, as much as she feared the topic. Xiang lifted the secrecy as everyone needed to know this plan of hers. Soon all understood the situation and who took charge of it.

"But we've got no weapons." Tina's objection was sound. How would they mount an offensive against an unknown and unseen enemy that had the means to shoot down an air transport? What else did they have?

"Surprise." As the only soldier in the group expounded on her plan, it became clear as day why she was a military commander. Her mind displayed an ability to strategize and coordinate like no one Gift had known, likely more than even Sergey. In the end, the plan was simple, and she was correct. Their greatest weapon, their only weapon, was the element of surprise. They had to hope, no, Xiang would not use that word, *expect* their enemy would not see it coming.

Act natural. At their action point, as Xiang called it, the rising walls and tables of dirt and rock folded shadows like a curtain. Acting natural was as unnatural as Gift's first attempt at swimming. Trepidation crept over her flesh. Lined in a single file, they looked to the general for the signal. Each step took minutes while they raced toward the next battle in haste. *The inevitable fight, the destiny of human creatures*, Gift lamented.

When the military commander placed her tablet in the side slot of her backpack and pulled the zipper up, they leapt into action. Xiang ran directly along their path, into the center of the oncoming storm where their unseen foes no doubt planned to ambush them. Gift and Mike flanked the left while Tina and Matteo took the right, hoping each pair would come up behind their would-be attackers. Just as the general foresaw, they caught the band entirely unawares and got the jump on them, as Mike put it.

In slow-time, Gift watched Mike's movements along with her own. He hung on a thick man's back with his arms wrapped around his neck while the man twisted, attempting to shake him off. Gift pulled off the *two knees* trick her mind had only envisioned working on Chan, this time succeeding in the reality. When the thinner of the men turned to face her, her left knee crushed his testicles, bringing his head down just as Tom said it would. Her right knee then cracked his nose, falling him to the ground.

The slam to her jaw came from the darkness. Gift had seen the woman move out of her periphery and presumed to go for her next. That thought surrendered to the heated excitement of the moment. The closed hand she took to the face reminded Gift of the woman's existence. It surprised Gift how it ached her muscles to swing her fist as hard as she could and miss, the air taking the full force of the blow. The lunge of the nameless woman, a match for Gift's height and build, took them both to the ground in a strange embrace they held as they rolled intertwined down a slight slope, becoming enveloped in a cloud of dust.

A sound that could have only been a bullet piercing the air came from somewhere. A shot in the distance with the fright of it by Gift's side, knowing her team had no guns to shoot. The second rang much closer and Gift's left thigh felt the pressure of being squeezed in a vise and set on fire. The woman underneath her squirmed. Assuming Tina's persona on herself, Gift's elbows raised, and her fists flew into the unknown lady's face. The woman's squirming stopped, but the throbbing agony and fire-hot pain in Gift's leg remained.

Mike's guy lay out cold on the ground, tied up. Mike bound a rope around the one Gift left with the assaulted manhood and broken nose. Gift rolled off the woman who'd shot her and fell onto her backside with her hands on either side of the entry wound as if they could bring some comfort to the unrelenting pain. As Mike came running over to her, she saw the testosterone of frenzied victory fade into dread at seeing her damaged thigh.

"Restrain her first," Gift said.

Another bullet broke the air and rattled Gift's bones, distant again, surely seeking Tina, Matteo, or Xiang. As Mike finished the knot securing the unconscious woman, Gift tried to stand, bellowed a noise of agony, and fell on her bum. Mike reached his hand under her thigh to examine the underside of the torn flesh.

"There's an exit wound, that's good."

"*Good?* That I've got *two* holes in my leg... is *good?*"

"Good there's no bullet stuck in there. Let me help you up."

As they stood, Gift hobbled aimlessly. Irrational thinking moved her toward the ruckus of gunfire, and Mike tried calling her back. As if on cue, someone fired another thunderous shot. Then another.

"No," Gift screamed to the air, the enemy, the world.

"I need to help them. You stay here."

Fuming over Mike's reasonableness and barely able to hobble, she determined to run to her friends' aid. The images racing through her mind were unstoppable. Gift saw her friends being blown away. The brain allocated no space to contemplate fear for how she and Mike were the next bullets' destination until he ran away, headlong into the battle to be killed.

23

Throughout her life, Gift's unrelenting optimism spilled over to those around her—sometimes to the point of annoyance. More recent experiences tried their best to rob her of that, and she had fought pessimism like Captain Arcadia defending the Banzai, losing only one of the one hundred percent she wished everything had. Now that internal battle escalated to war, and Gift knew she was kidding herself—which is to say she wasn't—when she tried to hold to that ninety-nine percent.

After handling the assailants on their side, Gift had no idea what her friends were up against or what General Xiang encountered running the charge straight down the middle of the battlefield. Now alone with one knee to her chest, the thrashed leg out straight, thoughts flashed in her mind, drowning her in chaos and dread. *We lost. Everyone is dead. I'm next.*

New shrieks drowned the last two ear-piercing pops, the snap familiar. Gift was certain she heard it before, knew what made such a *theew*. Projectile stunners. A second attempt to stand failed but Gift's determination swelled. If wrong, at least she wouldn't just lay there waiting to be killed. With all the strength her arms could summon, she propped herself up on one leg then had no idea how to move forward.

"*Gift.*"

Before her eyes found anyone, she knew the voice she had missed hearing for so long it hurt. "*Oksana.*" The young woman rushed herself into Gift's arms, nearly knocking her to the ground. A hug better than a warm blanket on a frosty night, even better than espresso, wrapped her in loving reunion with her kid sister. Was the latest of her battles over? Battles she only now realized were smaller parts of a grander war. "Is it over?"

"We got'em all, yeah." No pride of victory ignited the girl's words, only an unplaced sadness. Perhaps she lost her thirst for violence, only there in the heated moment of rage, pain, and regret, when she almost killed Chan. Oksana said in a disheartened whimper, "Tina."

"Where is she?" Gift asked in fearful impatience. The answer tormented her, a picture she couldn't face, so she hit the off switch on her mental display.

As a statue of a man captured by the sculptor in the moment of pent-up fury before an explosion of rage, Mike stood, bathed in silvery moonlight. Gift could see the hate and thirst for revenge swirling in his eyes, electrifying the squiggled red lines like bolts of lightning in his scleras. Matteo knelt beside her, wearing eyes a vastly different red as Tina lay there. Silent. Still.

Hobbling along with most of her weight on Oksana, Gift made it as far as the large woman's feet and collapsed. On her knees, leaning over her dear friend, she sobbed like that little girl whose crayon Aimée had broken, only this was guttural, not forced, not faked. There were no last words, no goodbyes. The answer to her next question lay in two torn holes in the fabric over Tina's chest. Gift's mind resisted, she needed to ask, to understand what those bullets had done. What they had taken.

Matteo answered, "We almost had'em, Gift. We found two women and three men on our side. And, and… Tina took the first two guys out in seconds. I got the third, and then we went for the women. Tina jumped one, and I pulled the other to the ground. Her knee, it… she slammed it into my groin and, and stopped me cold."

Gift felt her heart beating, the arteries swelling and contracting.

"She ran and pulled a rifle off the ground but didn't aim it at me. First... she, um, she shot the general. Shot again and grunted. I think she missed Mike with that one. Then she saw... she saw you, across the path... Aimed and said, 'Smile, you're dead,' and pulled the trigger."

Gift's trembling hand brushed a strand of hair from Tina's face.

"From nowhere, Tina leapt in front of her. She... she was hit in the chest. Somehow... I, I don't know how... she stayed on her feet, between you and that rifle. Tina stayed up, Gift, like she... just *couldn't* let you die. She had to, had to stay on her feet. Took another one to the chest and still didn't fall. She rushed the woman with the rifle and knocked it out of her hand." Matteo paused for a wet sniffle. "Tina dropped to her knees. That woman reached for the gun. They got her, Bright and Oksana, with a projectile. Took the guys out that were fighting Xiang and Mike, too."

From a face overtaken by tears, Gift asked, "They shot Xiang?"

"*She's* fine." Mike's words frothed with an anger Gift doubted centered solely on the bound woman, the murderer who had killed Tina. "Bullet ran clean through her shoulder."

"Tina," Gift bellowed. Through a fountain of tears and warm mucus, she cried, "I'm so sorry. I'm sorry Tina. I'm so, so sorry." She lay herself over her friend, the gentle giant she had called her, though never to her face or to anyone else. A moan came from somewhere deep within, deeper than her diaphragm, more than guttural. It rose from the marrow in her aching bones, from the essence of her soul. Raw emotion erupted into a stretched sound that never formed a word, didn't need to. It said all that could be said for the loss of an incredible friend and an exceptional woman.

Who took this beautiful life and robbed it of its decades to come? Of love and memories yet to be made. Why?

As Gift learned months ago, days didn't stop to mourn, and this one kept moving on despite Gift's fervent desire to crawl up into a ball and cry beside her lifeless friend for the rest of her days. The hard stance of Mike's pose broke with a twist of his torso, the scurry of his feet, the clenching of his fists. He hadn't turned toward the woman with the rifle, the one who pulled the trigger. He lunged at the general.

Becoming a stature herself, Xiang stood still and took the full force of the blow Mike solidly planted on her cheekbone. In the glow of Bright's torch, she readied herself for another, but not in a brazen or spiteful manner, not taunting Mike or egging him on. Gift saw something else in the woman of stone. She saw regret. A face steeped in sorrow didn't line up with who Gift knew, had assumed, Xiang to be. Bright intercepted Mike's second fist, catching it like a ball in a mitt. Standing between Mike and General Xiang, the mountain of a man said, "That's enough."

"It's because of *you*. She's dead because of you. You and your *stupid* plan." Mike was seething, ballooning his chest as he sucked in gasps of air with drops of spit foaming on his bottom lip. "For all we know, these people meant no harm, maybe wouldn't have attacked, not have killed us. Now she's dead and… it's *your* fault."

Xiang remained silent as if taking the scathing words as deserved punishment. Gift ceased moving her hands over the wounds on Tina's chest, feeling the tattered threads of the cloth around the holes torn by the bullets that took her. Something about that tactile sensation solidified the reality in her mind. The words Gift needed didn't come. It shocked her to find herself searching for words to defend the militant woman who recently had tortured Tina, Mike, and Matteo.

"*No*." Bright's voice was an army. The power it commanded could cripple flyers and melt bullets in the chambers of enemy guns. *If only that were true*. "Xiang made the right call-*Oh*. These people tried to take over after we defeated the U.R.M. Before we could exile them, they stole weapons from us, including the RPG that shot you down. It's better to die in the flyer than let these savages catch you. They would have done terrible things before they killed you all."

Helped to her feet by Oksana, Gift welcomed the young lady's arm wrapping around her waist in a tight squeeze, fastening herself to her big sister's side like she never wanted to let go. As much to support herself as to return the shared connection, Gift laid her arm over the girl's shoulder. Also shared between them was the disaster the emotion had wreaked on their faces, swollen eyes still red and cloudy.

"Bright's right, Mike, everyone," Gift said. "This was our only play... and we all agreed to it. These people tried to kill us when they shot the flyer. Only the general's skills kept us from being crushed to death in a mangled mess of twisted metal and... stuff. And they were *not* following us for nothing. Xiang was a hundred percent right. They were set for an ambush right where she said they would. If we didn't do this, all of us would be lying here dead, not just—" She couldn't say it. "Also too, if she didn't say anything, we'd have walked right into it."

"And what about these... monsters, then? Savages, he called them. We don't just let them go. Tell me we don't let them go."

"No Mike, of course not." Gift spoke so sure of herself but had no clue what to do with them. "What did you say, Bright? They'd do terrible things to us before they killed us. Oh, you mean like..." Fear held back the thought.

"Savages." Mike asserted his condemnation. "They get what they deserve. What goes around comes around. Karma and all that crap."

"That is not the meaning of karma," said the Chinese General. "But I agree. We cannot take them back with us, and their actions are deserving of death."

"Hold on a min—"

Before Gift could get her thoughts out, Matteo woke from his grief coma. "No. We're not that sort of people. I mean, we can't be, right?"

"Wait. How long ago were they banished?" Gift did the calculations in her head, knowing the folks from U.A. had progressed little beyond seven days without intense cases of earth sickness which, if untreated, would eventually prove fatal.

"Four days. They will die out here soon-*Oh*."

"So, we leave them here? You looked at Mike like he was a monster when he suggested we kill them. Now leaving them here to die like that... Who's the monster?"

Gift marveled at how the same words can be used for or against someone with slight changes in circumstance. Matteo's words almost parroted Xiang's when she accused New Europa of using missiles to enforce peace by intimidation.

"Maybe we're all monsters."

"No Gift, we aren't." Matteo sounded adamant, like he couldn't stomach them reverting to animalistic human tendencies they were so proud to have shed.

While Gift was proud of him, she wondered if he had been wrong. Mike wanted blood for blood, and Gift considered you don't get more carnal than that. Oksana had nearly shot that lunatic Chan. Gift herself had just pummeled a woman. Could it have been that only in such extreme situations the animal part of the human creature manifested? *Is it ever justified?*

"They are our prisoners, tried and sentenced by United Africa. We will handle this." Bright commanded the situation with the strength conveyed in his voice. Whatever he meant to do to handle the matter, Gift thought it best to let him do so. He was right, after all, about it being a U.A. problem. True, it brought itself to them and snuffed the life out of her friend, but a U.A. issue, nonetheless. Had they not happened to fly overhead and get shot down, these people would have died in mere days.

That's a pretty feeble justification, Gift. A copout.

Time being of the essence as it tended to be, Gift still insisted on a burial for Tina. No one objected, and all took turns with the one small shovel from the transport, with others lighting the deepening hole with torches. Gift tried to offer some words in eulogy but choked on them. Mike and Matteo expressed their thoughts of friendship and respect. A half smile briefly moved Gift's lips when Mike mentioned how Tina loved his jokes. Her mouth quickly leveled, and Gift managed to push out a few words.

"Goodbye, my dear friend. Your advice was never crap. I love you."

Mike and Matteo joined the embrace between Oksana and Gift, and the four shed more tears before being pulled away. The day continued. The fortress of a man sent them along to U.A. in the ground transport after he wrapped Gift's leg and Xiang's shoulder to stop the blood loss. Bright told them to send the transport back with his lieutenant as soon as they got there. Mike and Tina had done an excellent job with this transport, pulling the weight of five with no sluggishness.

Driving into the vast night without Tina pained Gift with all kinds of wrong. Leaving her behind. Her life had been sacrificed to save Gift's when Gift would have chosen it the other way around every time. The twisted knot relentlessly tightened in her stomach. Mike barely stopped in time on her frantic demand to allow her to vomit over the side of the vehicle without falling out.

24

A shared silence accompanied them as everyone grieved without words. Perhaps no words could be summoned for such an occasion. With no way to articulate the hurt and loss, the anguish of grief too fresh and strange, no one knew what to do with it.

The midafternoon sun warmed the ride, and Gift's anger at the haunting passage of time vented itself as anguish. Losing Charlie taught Gift how grief encompassed a host of powerful emotions beyond sadness. Sometimes dramatic swings in her mood or sharp snaps of her tongue, seemingly coming from nowhere, found their source in the deep loss and drew their strength from it. Would the lessons it took months to learn in mourning Charlie help her in this new transition to life without Tina?

Not likely.

"How'd you find us?" The agonizing silence needed a break, and Gift figured she'd strike the first chord if no one else would.

The puzzled look on Oksana's face lasted through her reply. "I increased the range on the monitor sensors after we kicked those U.R.M. turds' butts." Gift smiled to mask the pain of the callback to Tina's word for Max.

"You did? Brava."

"We expect them to come back, in greater force. Of course, we've got reasons to believe they may not have much greater force. From Aimée, I mean. Plus, I'd think if they did, they'd be back already, right?"

"She is smart like you." The general spoke from the back of her head, not bothering to twist her neck from the seat beside Mike.

Perhaps subconsciously, Gift had sat between Oksana and Matteo, recalling the crush. Of course, the way the girl's earlier hug hung on him like a wet sweater reminded Gift how many times Raff broke up her own embraces with Mike, helping to reinforce the idea and the need.

"Smarter. Way smarter," Gift replied.

"We picked up the flyer just before it went down. If they'd have shot you a few seconds sooner, we probably wouldn't even have seen it."

Matteo asked, "How'd you know it was us?"

"Didn't. We expected to come out to find a bunch of dead Martians in the wreckage. Came to salvage what we could from the transport is all."

When Mike failed to swerve the vehicle around a rock and the transport bounced, Gift's brain pulled a file from its archive. She, Mike, and Tina were speeding along in the Frankenstein monster of a transport they had assembled at N.E. for their trek into the forest to upgrade the remote monitor sensors. If every little thing was going to remind her of Tina, how long would it take for those memories to consent to smiles replacing tears? It took months with Charlie, and this had only been hours. The throbbing in her thigh brought her back to the moment.

"And you stumbled into a firefight, guns-a-blasting and all." Mike's tone lost its hateful bite, his normal voice a welcome replacement. "Good thing you had those stun rifles on you."

"Bright insists we take'em everywhere."

"He's *that* afraid of the Martians returning?"

"Yes, Matt. Plus those criminals. They dropped them far from the colony and away from the Ubuntu village." Gift marveled at the maturity in the young woman. The experiences she'd endured piled on years.

"Oh, I almost forgot..." Gift pulled Oksana into a hug. "You turned seventeen."

"Yeah, like a month ago."

"Sorry. Been a little busy." The two shared a grin, neither ready for a chuckle or anything more than a slender lipped and quickly withdrawn smile.

General Xiang asked, "Do we have functioning comms on this transport?"

Oksana said it didn't, but her handheld did.

"Perhaps you should alert the colony of our updated passenger list. It left with you and Bright and is returning without their commander and they will see Mike and me first. I would like them not to shoot us."

"Good point." The sharp military mind continued to impress Gift.

"Yeah. Also too, they still aren't so keen on the Chinese. Nothing personal." Gift caught how Oksana had picked up her quirky mannerism, saying 'also too' as she did. Having been told many times it was redundant and not proper English, Gift didn't care. It was her way. She could no sooner change that than accept chaos and disorder. Her logical mind wrestled with that paradox for a while. Her last few months were filled with nothing but chaos and disorder.

***

As bitter and disappointing as the U.A. coffee always tasted, Gift delighted in her first sip, taking it before a meal, shower, or anything else. By the time she finished her cup of black liquid delight, Bright's lieutenant—a tall thin fellow called Samuel—took off in the transport. The colony's chief Medic, an older woman with puffy white hair named Helena, tended to the bullet holes in Gift's leg and Xiang's shoulder. The thick white goo filled the holes in the front and rear of her thigh and became extensions of her skin. The numbed muscle mass between took on a constant tingle the medic said would rebuild the tissue. Xiang received the same for her shoulder and proper bandages for her ribs.

Moving among the U.A. residents, the general said little and smiled at everyone. Worn like a mask, it softened Xiang's demeanor—perhaps a restraint not to upset anyone by her presence—a sound precaution with Chan's invasion fresh in everyone's minds. While Oksana expounded the details about their time under the occupation, Xiang's softness firmed up to interrupt the energetic teenager.

"My dear, we must hasten. I agree the U.R.M. will attempt to reclaim this colony. They are also no doubt already on the hunt for us, for Gift especially. Time is a luxury we cannot afford. We must discuss *pertinent* details to our next actions and find a means of travel."

"Oh, travel won't be a problem." When Xiang and Gift showed confusion, the young lady elaborated. "Shouldn't be, anyway. We've got an *almost* working flyer here, the small one from the R.F. That's why we were going to salvage yours. We should be able to get ours going if we can get some parts off it."

"How'd you get a flyer?" Gift asked.

"Fortunately, it was here when we fought those jerks. One of those idiots tried to take off, escape in it. Crashed it before he got two meters off the ground and damaged the stupid thing a good bit. That's what happens when you disable the biometrics and let anyone fly it—or try to. I fixed what I could but hit a snag without the replacement parts."

"Well done, young lady," the general said.

"*Ma*, you came back with us before you got to the flyer. We didn't get any parts."

"Bright knows what we need. I've been teaching him about engineering."

"Brava, Oksana. Really... well done. Let's hope the parts weren't damaged, and are compatible—that one's Chinese, yours is Russian."

"*Ha,*" she heartily replied. "Russian engineering with parts made in China. I'm sure we can make it work."

Standing from her seat at the table, General Xiang apparently had enough of the chitchat. "I understand you were looking into what Aimée told us to check regarding their weapons, the ones dropped when they arrived."

"You mean when they announced their *polite* conquest of Earth," Gift said.

"Right... General, ma'am. This is huge, actually. Aimée was right about something being odd. Bright brought me all kinds of goodies from two of whatever fell just outside the colony. Gift, you gotta see them."

After a hurried dinner, the group moved—Gift limping on a crutch—into the maintenance dome, where several parts and large hunks of something were lined up and orderly. Greatly appreciated by Gift, she loved how she and Oksana had that in common.

"...so those three pieces came from the same one bomb, or whatever. Only it wasn't a bomb. See, I think they could've done some actual damage if they wanted. So that part of the first broadcast was true. Basically. If any of these hit a dome? Pretty bad, lots of destruction. But here's the thing... They wouldn't have exploded, at least not much."

"Wouldn't have exploded *much?*" Gift scrunched her face. "Sounds like we're back to that *less lethal* nonsense. What do you mean?"

"This first one looks like some kinda huge maintenance drone. It has fuel cells that could explode easily enough, but like I said, it wouldn't have been a gigantic explosion. That sucker was heavy though, so when it smashed the ground just outside, the whole place shook like we were being bombed."

"That must be what happened in the New Republic of China. The domes shook, but we sustained no damage."

"Yes ma'am. General, ma'am." Oksana seemed unsure of the woman's role, beyond the obvious intimidation. "This other one, weapon, I guess...

but not really. See, I think it was a terraforming drill. Another enormous boom, shaking the Earth around us. This thing was the size of a heavy flyer, and solid, with a massive drill bit. But I'm pretty sure they didn't mean for it to *drill* into us."

"Okay then, my brilliant young protégé. What's your conclusion? Impress me."

Oksana flashed a wide smile. "They were dropping junk on us to scare us. I mean huge, massively huge hunks of junk. Even so, the Martians just dropped it on us. Or... *near* us, I guess. And the final blow that rattled above the Ops center? I think that was their heavy lander hovering with breaking jets blasting. Not so much a flyer, more like, like, a dropship."

"So, you believe Aimée's rumors mean they're out of weapons?" As much as she trusted the intel, Gift found it hard to believe the U.R.M. came to conquer them with no weapons.

Once again, Xiang applied her military intellect. "Or perhaps they dropped these items, wishing no damage at first, to save their weapons to use against us later."

"Fair point," Gift agreed. "But why didn't they respond yet to the U.A. uprising? I mean, they've been free for a few days, and nothing. If Aimée's right about their limited manpower... barely holding control of the other colonies, they've got no one to send here. Can't spare the soldiers. So, if they had any weapons up there trained on the colonies as they threatened, why leave U.A. free for days? Why not make an example of us... *Them*. U.A.?"

Wearing a smile Gift grew to like on her, Xiang said, "You are smart. I am again very glad Matteo stopped you from jumping off that ledge. We need you."

"Wait. *What*? What ledge? What jumping?"

"Another time, Oksana. So... so much has happened. I promise I'll catch you up when things settle."

"Fine, but I'll hold you to that. Now, I know you'll want to see this last one for sure. But we gotta go outside to see it. It's mostly intact and way too big to haul in here. But it's too dark now that it's, oh my, almost two."

***

After coffee and a meager breakfast, a twenty-minute walk took them to what Oksana so eagerly wanted them to see. Mike joined them after a longer sleep, having gone to bed earlier. Mike always said he could be a professional sleeper. Gift envied that about him. Right away they saw something very different about the fallen object. A large oval, crushed at the bottom with its metal wrinkled and folded, yet its middle and upper parts were almost completely intact.

Mike whistled at it. "It looks almost like they engineered it to do that. I mean to crumple, to keep the rest sound."

Gift took in the sight. "I agree."

"That's exactly what I thought when Bright showed it to me. And I confirmed it when I went inside."

"*Inside?*" Mike and Gift said in unison.

General Xiang stayed eerily quiet, an observer of the goings on, nothing more. Perhaps the military brain didn't consider itself fully compatible with the engineer brain, and they outnumbered her three to one.

"Not a lot of room, so you and Mike climb up in there and have a look? I'll wait with the... um, general." Oksana didn't seem pleased by her own suggestion.

25

"A stonishing." Mike oozed an electric curiosity. Gift looked at a piece that didn't seem to fit, recalling the old expression to her mind of a round peg put into a square hole. *Or was it the other way around?* Seeing this unusual peg, Gift's mind started modifying the shape of the hole. "It's some sort of... ship, I guess. What did Oksana call it, a dropship?" As she studied its modest interior and reflected over the crumpled state of the exterior, Gift reached a different conclusion.

"Escape pod. Look at the limited controls and these two seats. Significant absorption cushioning and super thick padded safety straps. Compartments for provisions and spare oxygen. And how it crashed... but I mean, it sorta crashed... *safely*, right?" Looking around, Gift answered her own question. "Nothing in here was damaged. Well, a bit, actually, but I think it's because it fell harder than designed, like they disabled the breaks or something. *Ma*, it's like the bottom's some kinda crumple zone to keep the passengers safe. Not meant to fly, just land. It's an escape pod."

"Makes sense."

The two faced each other kneeling on the black cushioned seats, which were positioned back-to-back with barely the room for elbows to extend before hitting the sides. Gift's right leg already had the pre-sleeping-limb tingles from sparing her injured leg any of her body's weight. No one was meant to spend much time inside of the thing, just drop, land, and out.

The port hole then entered through—a half-meter square with rounded corners—was just large enough for a body in an environmental suit to exit.

Mike pushed every button he could reach. "It's dead."

Gift readily agreed when pounding fists failed on all controls... but one. A deafening swoosh saturated the cramped space. Neither could fathom a guess what the noise meant or what had made it. The tiny capsule's interior became cast in a yellow tint—an unexpected transition from the soft white light of the morning sun's rays slipping through the hatch. "What the heck just happened?" Confusion overlaid a tinge of anxiety.

"I'd say you triggered the parachute." A curled chin emphasized Mike's point. "If you're right about it being an escape pod, that makes sense. It's the breaks that were disabled."

A muffled, "Gift. Mike," came from outside the shell that contained them.

"We're alright, Oksana," Gift yelled towards the port hole with the cloth draped over it.

"What the heck did you guys do?"

"Mike thinks we opened a parachute. Our best guess is this thing may be an escape pod."

"Yeah, figured that bit out right away when I first saw it. But that, what did you call it? It shot the para up from the top, a fabric like a giant yellow blanket. It shot up about twenty meters with a bunch of thick cords connecting it to the pod then it draped over the thing. Was pretty cool, actually."

Xiang said, "If this is an escape pod, are there any bodies in it?"

"No," Gift shouted out. "It's empty."

"Any sign people were in it and got out?"

Oksana answered, "Don't think so. When we got to it, the hatch was still sealed. I'm pretty sure it came down empty."

Inspection concluded, the two freed themselves of the cramped space. When she set her foot on a hold, Gift's damaged limb crumpled under her and she fell from the hatch, sliding the curvature of the vessel. The swish of her slide under the thick fabric roared over her ears. With what no one would mistake for skill, she rolled onto her knees and up to her feet to reclaim her crutches. Mike came down with more finesse.

"Why would they send an escape pod empty?" Mike asked. "Its whole purpose is for people to escape."

"This is part of what Aimée said... about their weapons, I mean. They... *Ciao*. Let's think about this." Gift put on her thinking face. "The U.R.M. was the only colony built off-world—a couple hundred thousand colonists. All their resources had to go into critical supplies. I mean, what enemies did they expect to find in space or on Mars? Never found any hint of alien life and no one believes in Martians. That stuff's only in bad sci-fi, right? So, they wouldn't... they *don't* have warships. Why would they? Their fleet was all cargo ships and migration vessels."

Oksana said, "They dropped it empty for sure. Used as a weapon, not an escape pod. I agree with Gift. Aimée wanted us to see they have no weapons."

"Unless they built weapons and warships in the last two hundred years."

"Mike," Gift began her retort. "Why would they? Look, I love science fiction as much as anyone, even the bad stuff. On Banzai they found Martians, I mean, not like how we call U.R.M. people Martians, actual aliens. Well, actors in makeup. That's fiction. The U.R.M. had no reason to waste any resources on weapons or warships."

The spindly index finger of the dour general extended toward Gift. "She is correct. I have given this much consideration. Why did the U.R.M. choose to come now, attack now? They must have been monitoring us, learning we had gone outside, and that Earth could support them if they returned. Given the time it had taken their colony ships to travel between

Earth and Mars, it took months for them to arrive here. I would estimate they initiated their preparations to return a short time after your people of New Europa first went out and began open communications with the R.F. They would not have had time to design and build weapons."

"Exactly. Thank you." A smile fought its way through the dread to reach Gifts lips. "They threw what they had on their colony ships at us. Think about it. A huge repair droid, a massive drill, an escape pod. And like a bunch of stupid idiots, we all just assumed they had an armada of warships and could wipe us out if we resisted. It's what they hoped we'd fall for, and we did. That's what Aimée suspected. She was right."

Mike pinched his chin. "Okay, but it *is likely* they have some more junk to drop. Kept some for a just-in-case scenario. Not for nothing, we can't assume they used it all up at once, can we?"

"I need to catch up on Aimée's broadcasts. I'm sure she sent me more clues. She was onto something with the weapons, she may have more intel for us. Oh... *Oh*. She said something about an escape pod she hoped to use. I hope this wasn't it."

"They had several pods on each cargo ship." The history buff in Mike activated. "Seeing what they dropped... That explains why they have limited personnel, not being a transport ship full of passengers, but a cargo ship loaded with all that crap they dropped on us."

"That means we can take back the colonies and not worry about them wiping us out. What are we waiting for?"

Oksana's rush to battle worried Gift. "First, we need confirmation from Aimée. I need to see the update vids."

Walking back to the colony at Gift-on-crutches speed, the conversation continued. Xiang exuded confidence in them having the superior firepower, a cache of tactical missiles opposed to objects dropped from orbit. They could target the U.R.M. ships and end the occupation in one swift, decisive action. It embodied a perfectly rational military strategy from a brilliant soldier's mind.

Gift hated it. She had to believe they could find another way. *Could it be concealed in what the general once called peace by intimidation?* Gift wondered if this situation may perhaps have been a justified cause for that. *What would humanity be afterward?*

"What missiles?" Oksana asked for the third time.

"In that first bunker that your br... Where we found those rogue Russians." *Good save, Gift. No need to mention Yuri and upset the girl.* "It's connected to a missile launch facility. Somehow survived the unified decommissioning of all weapons for the colonization project."

"Yeah, it was Russia, Gift. I'm surprised they only kept one. And you mean to tell me my idiot brother was sitting on a cache of missiles?"

"Missiles have navigation systems that do not require pilots."

"Another of our expressions, General," explained Gift.

"It is imperative we gain control of that facility and target the ships in orbit." Xiang's words left no room for counter argument, presenting only one way forward.

Gift couldn't see the alternatives she desperately wanted to find. "Raff is there. Been there a couple days. If anyone can get into those systems, gain control, it's her." Thoughts of Raff had not visited Gift's mind recently. She missed those thoughts and gladly welcomed them back.

Oksana said, "Yeah, but the last I heard from N.E., they were stumped. And we haven't heard from them since their uprising failed."

"Failed?" Mike questioned.

"Wait, what?" Gift asked over him. "What happened? How's Tom... and everyone?"

26

Sorrow amalgamated with pride in Oksana's words. "It seems only United Africa was able to stand up against these jerks. Far as we know, the R.F. isn't free. But I'm basing that on not being able to reach them. Also too, that Sergey wasn't in it. I think they'd have won if he led them. We heard nothing from Red after N.E.'s revolt failed."

"What happened at N.E.?" A freneticism in Gift's words worried her, but the moment called for it, the answer not coming fast enough.

"We got one message from Red then she was gone. Been trying to reach her again ever since on the chat app. Nothing."

"My *goodness* girl, just tell me what happened. *What was* Red's message?"

Oksana tensed, never having been on the receiving end of this side of Gift's character. It obviously unsettled her. "Um... well..."

Taking the nervous teenaged hands in hers, Gift said, "Sorry. I'm losing it a little here. I need to know what she said. What happened?"

The softer tone calmed the young woman. "Just one message. Red, I think it was her, she just said, 'We failed. Traitors among our guards.' That's it."

"Anything else? Any word on anyone, the status of our guards? Oh mamma. Tom? Sara? Is Red... is she okay?"

"That was the complete message. Nothing since."

"We need to keep trying them. Why aren't you trying?" Gift's voice elevated; her words hurried over themselves. Oksana withdrew once again, hunching her shoulders like she wished to curl herself into a ball and hide.

Mike eyed the body language. "Let's pause and think. Oksana said they've been trying. I'm sure she means that Bright's people in Ops are continuing to try to reach N.E." A nod confirmed and the girl's shoulders shed a degree of tension. "Good. Gift, we'll keep at it and hope to hear from them soon. Where does that leave us? I mean, I'm not sure going *there* is the best idea."

Ending the barrage of frenzied questions, Gift apologized through a whisper as she held Oksana in a tight embrace. Reciprocation soothed her worry, telling Gift the apology had been accepted and the heat of the moment understood. Yet again, Gift marveled at the young lady's maturity, unsure she would have been as quick to put off taking offense.

"This modifies our plan," General Xiang said. "Mike is correct. It is not safe to go to New Europa until we can be certain they are free. Unless..."

"Unless what?" Gift's hard tone returned. Confidence was high that the general would be immune to it.

"Unless we can assist in liberating them."

"Yes. Yes. Brilliant. Let's do that."

"Gift, settle down." She saw Mike was about to be the voice of reason he so often was. Hot-headed in moments dominated by emotion as much as she, he was level-headed and reasonable when he needed to be. Gift didn't want that now. It was a time for action, not reason.

"Don't tell me to settle down. We need—"

"We need to be rational and calm. A wrong move here could end this, end us all. If we rush up to N.E. not knowing the situation there, we'll only fall into their hands or end up dead."

"And the flyer's not fixed yet," Oksana added.

"Everyone, let us sit and discuss this. Of course, Mike is again correct. Gift, I did not mean to suggest we go there without a plan. We must not act in haste. Call everyone together, please."

Even tacking the word please onto the end didn't fool Gift into thinking the general asked. Xiang gave an order, taking charge once again. It seemed clear the trained military mind should head the strategizing and lead any mission to help liberate New Europa. At least, if they wanted it to have any hope for success.

***

In Bright's office—the one that used to be Blessing's, the one where Gift watched helplessly as Chan robbed a brave woman's children of their mother—they gathered. As Bright set the last of the added chairs in the room, Xiang waved off his motion to sit, standing to preside over the group, her little army of ill-equipped and untrained warriors. Except maybe for Bright. Gift figured him an army in a single human form, stronger and fiercer than any Chinese soldier she had met.

Whatever this group could be called, a reconnaissance team, a tactical insurgency, an invading army, or armchair warriors, they were what Xiang had to work with for now. Bright and Gift—both leaders of their respective colonies, envoys at least—with Mike, Matteo, and Oksana. When he declined to invite his lieutenant, Bright explained he needed him to stay to look after the colony while he joined the mission. Bright's eyes could have shot lasers at Oksana, melting her face, when she objected to his joining them.

"The flyer we have," she spoke with full confidence they would get it flying, "holds five. It's a small one."

"Then *you* stay here, little girl."

Before Oksana could erupt in a fury of heated exchange, Xiang replied, "We need everyone in this room on the mission. I am familiar with the Russian flyer; it is the same design as the Chinese ones. We can modify its seating configuration and it has ample power for the weight of six plus whatever weapons and equipment we need."

"How soon can we get going?" Gift's anxious worry hid from no one.

"I share your urgency to get there as soon as possible." The general spoke softly. "Again, this is no time for haste at the expense of caution. The U.R.M. is no doubt on heightened alert after losing this colony and fighting off uprisings at the other three. I would be."

To interject, Mike raised his hand but didn't wait for Xiang's approval. "I'm with Gift, of course. It's our colony, our families, our friends. We want to get there yesterday. But when will we even have the flyer ready?"

"Oksana?" General Xiang's question set all eyes on the junior engineer.

"How close are we, sweetie?" Gift inquired.

Turning to the big guy she responded, "Bright, did you get all three of those parts I asked for from the downed Chinese flyer?"

"We did-*Oh*. And plenty-plenty other parts we took as spares, whatever we could salvage, as you asked." Turning to the group, he added, "She is an excellent engineer. She will get us flying soon."

Gift took that as an apology for how the burly man snapped earlier, though she was aware Oksana didn't slide easily into resentment. She was the sort of person who proved anyone wrong by her actions.

"But... sorry if I got this wrong, General..." For the first time, Matteo joined the conversation as more than an observer. "Even if the flyer were ready to go today, you're saying we can't go until we contact N.E.?"

"That seems the wise course, or we could fly into an ambush. I assume since the U.R.M. have not found her yet, they must be expecting Gift to go to New Europa. If that is the case, then it is likely the most heavily guarded of the remaining colonies under their control. It is what I would do."

"I'm just a farmer, basically, so I don't know. Maybe waiting here isn't the best idea. It's possible the U.R.M. may come back, try to take this colony again. And the longer they don't find Gift heading to any other colonies, the more likely they'd check here. We came here because it's the only free colony. They'll figure that out."

"But they didn't know about our chat, that we knew U.A. was free, or knew anything, really." Gift stood, with renewed strength in her leg to support her if she didn't lean too heavily on it. "I'm not saying we stay here, and if we can't go to N.E. yet, we need to get closer at least. I mean, so we get there quickly when it's time."

"But the chat." Blank faces told Oksana to elaborate. "It won't work on the flyer. It can only contact the colony on open channels. Once we leave here, we won't be able to contact Red or anyone on our side in N.E. until we're practically there and are on their monitors."

"*Crap*. She's right. It needs the repeater network."

Mike's face lit up like the sun. "No. I mean, right, you and Oksana are right, of course. But we *can* use it, tap into the repeater network, I mean."

"The signal is point to point with no way to intercept or hijack it." Gift had done enough work on the relay system to understand that much.

"Right. But I worked on it more than you, and I know how to tap in at any of the signal transfer stations. If we get physical access, I mean. We can get a handheld online and use the chat app."

Unable to restrain herself, Gift hobbled over to Mike and leaned over him from behind. Falling onto him when she asked her leg for strength it couldn't give, she turned her blunder into an embrace. "You're a genius." She turned to the General. "Let's do that. Get as close as we can and make contact."

Xiang panned the room with no expression to hint at her thinking or reaction. The pause was infinite. "Agreed. We take provisions, as we do not know how long it may take to make contact. Where do you suggest we find one of these stations?"

"*Mike?* Which is closest to home?" Hearing the word home escape her own mouth and fondle her ears gave Gift a warmth that felt like pain. Home. How long had it been? How was everyone at home and what would they find when they finally got there? The heaviness the emotion carried sat her back in her seat.

"Paris. It's in what used to be called France."

"Very well," the general said. "We leave as soon as that air transport is ready for flight. We have three engineers and three parts to replace. Get on that now, and when you say everything is ready, give the entire craft another inspection." Obviously, she wasn't familiar enough with Gift to realize how completely unnecessary it was to add that last bit. "Bright and I will remain here to discuss strategies and gather weapons."

The self-professed farmer stood. "What do I do?"

"You gather food and water, a medical travel kit, and whatever else we will need. Be sure it is enough for four or five days. We do not know what to expect or when we might establish contact with New Europa."

27

Working alongside Oksana and Mike felt like coming home. Gift got to be an engineer, laboring beside two beloved bench-mates. Tears visited her eyes a few times while repairing the air transport with thoughts of Tina. While the aching went beyond tolerable—or just this side of it as she carried on with the day—the notion persisted that she would start finding joy in the memories sooner than it took with Charlie. Not for who either of her departed friends were to her, but for how she had grown and learned to balance grief, settling its chaos.

The young apprentice moved with all the proficiency and skill of a master, keeping pace easily with Mike and Gift to get the parts replaced, tuned, and calibrated. Tests confirmed they were functioning properly. Without a pause or a word, she and Gift began giving the entire flyer a once-over, checking every system in exhaustive detail. Both were so wrapped up in it, so focused, they hadn't noticed Mike leave until he returned with food. The sleek black air transport had been connected to the power grid and the dull hum of its recharging cycle became the background music for their meal.

Gift fully swallowed her lump of pounded yam with a finger-pinch of stewed vegetables. "How long to reach Paris, you think?"

"Six hours. I made the trip here from there once, after checking that equipment not long after we installed it. You should have seen Tina climbing that tower."

Glossed-over eyes saw Matteo come with his third load of supplies. Bright followed with a small cache of weapons, including projectile stun rifles and standard guns. Gift's protests over the guns fell on deaf ears. They were ready to go, but they weren't. Missing was the one person who could fly the thing.

"Where's the General?" Gift asked Bright.

"Sleeping. As the only one who can fly the machine, I told her to rest while I load the supplies."

"I can fly it," Oksana said with heightened enthusiasm.

Utterly surprised, Gift asked, "*How?* When did you learn to do that?"

"One of the few real friends I had was a little older than me. He did the training to be a pilot and got time in a simulation, the full setup with virtual reality and everything. He let me do it a few times. It's fun, and not really that hard."

"It's not the same as the real thing." Mike was always good at pointing out the obvious.

"I flew a real one a couple times."

"What? You said your first time in a flyer was when you came with me to New Europa that first time. 'Never been outside the wall of the R.F.,' you said." Gift felt reasonably sure of her memory.

"No, actually... you *assumed* I hadn't been in a flyer. I never said that. And what I said about the wall was true, from a certain point of view. I had *flown over* the wall, but never been on the ground beyond it."

"Well... we'll debate the details of that conversation another time. But good, you can be our second then. For the trip, Xiang is the pilot. She's real good too. We'd have died in a mangled wreck if she hadn't leveled the flyer."

Mike would often be the voice of reason, but Gift didn't appreciate it when that voice conveyed a pessimistic realism. "Haven't we concluded the U.R.M. had been crashing the flyers? The Russian ones and the ones from the N.R.C. both?"

"Yeah," Gift replied.

"I mean, we're getting into this thing and headed toward New Europa. Paris, sure, but in the general direction of N.E. Not for nothing, no one else thinks they'll try to blow us out of the sky?"

"Oh mamma. I hadn't even thought of that."

"I have." General Xiang appeared from behind them. She constantly thought about strategy and military tactics, always a couple steps ahead of everyone else. "We know they want Gift. If they suspected she was on a transport, they would hesitate to shoot it down and risk not taking her alive."

"Also too, don't forget Aimée's message. Not just about the weapons we now know are nothing more than them dropping space junk on us. She said they can't actually shoot down any flyers, don't have weapons to target and fire. They used spies and sabotage. Think about it... We were flown to the N.R.C. and then we flew here. Well, almost here. And nothing. If they could shoot down flyers, they'd have hit us both times. I mean, not the second time... if they had gotten us the first... you know what I mean."

"How'd you confirm that? When?" Matteo showed a puzzled face, knowing they had all barely slept and Gift had been busily inspecting fake weapons and repairing the transport.

"Caught up on Aimée's updates. Rechecked some older ones."

"But, *when?*"

"Please. I hardly slept. *She,*" Oksana jabbed a thumb at Gift, "didn't sleep at all. Our tent glowed all night from her tablet. There were, like, a thousand gross bugs all over it when I unzipped it this morning."

"We will fly throughout most of the night, so everyone must sleep onboard. No tablets." On that final word, or command, from Xiang, they climbed into the hull of metal and polymers and set off once again, defying gravity and fate alike in hopes of liberating a second colony. How they might have hoped to handle the Russian Federation and the New Republic of China were *tomorrow problems*, as Gift called them, not to be occupying today's mind.

***

Dreams were the only wondrous sights this new voyage brought. The dark of night that blanketed the ground and rode the waves of the waters below hid the Earth from view. Sheer exhaustion dominated Gift as she spectated her unconscious mind's visions with scenes changing from joyful memories to impossible scenarios that seemed so grounded and real in the dream state. In bizarre curiosity, Nadezhda Anoykina had been a recurring character in the drama series of recent weeks. Often, she would obliterate Yuri in a puff of purple smoke and vanish herself, either of her accord or at the unpleasant end of Tom's taser coils. If meaning laced itself in dreams as Gift's ancestors believed, she couldn't find it.

"The kid's really flying," Matteo said in an excited tone. Gift's eyelids parted in time to see the frosty glare *the kid* gave Matteo. Being called 'a kid' by the older boy Oksana crushed on must have been a devastating blow of reality, deflating the unattainable fantasy. She immediately returned to the joy of piloting the air transport, no doubt staving off the offense by believing she'd prove her adulthood to him without needing words of refutation.

"Just there. Do you see it?" The hardened, near-robotic army creature who had barely shown signs of being a human had become a gentle mentor figure leaning over Oksana's chair. She very nearly reached nurturing. It could have been Aimée or Gift herself with the young lady. Xiang made a habit of showing Gift sides of herself she had up to then kept carefully guarded and hidden.

"She's landing us?" Mike's voice blended shock with complaint as he shared his morning breath with everyone in the confined space.

They descended with scarcely noticeable sensations of movement. The aircraft touched down gently, as good as any landing Gift had experienced with seasoned pilots. Cheers and congratulations came from all, and Xiang patted the young woman's shoulder and said, "Well done." A genuine and innocent smile drew itself on Oksana's face, and Gift gazed upon her kid sister with such pride and love.

When the flyer's hatch slowly opened, they were in a huge rectangle, a patchwork of weeds and dirt with small mounds scattered about as if a giant had run through it, trying to squeeze a fistful of sand that slipped through his fingers. A sweet fragrance fondled Gift's nostrils and she saw bushes with branches reaching and twisting upward as if trying to escape the ground's hold. It brought Gift no dull pain as she admired the disarrayed beauty of a space nature had rescued from mortality and sculpted into something vastly different from what men long since dead had shaped it to be.

When Gift turned around, an impressively engineered structure greeted her. Like the carcass of the once glorious building they passed fleeing China, except this one didn't hold the same incompleteness. As much a metal skeleton as the other, but not meant to be adorned with glass skin nor to shelter the parasites called humans. Though badly deteriorated by the unkind effects of time, Gift thought it perfect just as it stood. Bubbling with anticipation, they approached lugging bulky backpacks. Impressive to look upon, standing at the base of one iron leg grew the giant as its neck stretched to touch the empty blue sky. The morning's first sunlight caressed its side, giving life to the behemoth that shone like the sun had risen just for it.

"We're not really seeing the iron." Mike entered his full history tutor mode. "They used to have to paint it all the time to keep the metal from corroding, then they invented a new latex resin said to last two centuries."

Matteo whistled as he folded his neck for his eyes to find the top of the thing. "But I *do* see rust and corrosion."

"That's because they added that two-hundred-year coating something like two hundred fifty years ago."

"I see."

"You will," Mike replied. "Wait till we reach the top."

"We have to climb all the way up that?" Gift imagined them scaling the structure like monkeys—proud of herself for remembering the long-tailed animal's name.

"There's stairs inside."

Relieved not to be the only one huffing her breaths, Gift emoted gratitude for the pause when they reached the second platform after close to an hour of relentless stair climbing. Although able to walk unassisted by a crutch, her healing thigh muscle slowed her ascent. Bright stood tall, breathing normally, as if he'd strolled in from the next room. Despite a plugged hole in her shoulder and mending ribs, Xiang appeared the second most fit, with only a slight elongation in her breaths. In a memory, Gift tried to pace Tom and now she missed him even more.

"More steps on this next part," Mike said. Gift hated him at that moment, seeing it as his fault the stairs existed. A flashback of Aimée saddened her. 'People equate the messenger with the message,' she once said. At least she knew Aimée was okay, seemed to be anyway. Yet that knowledge lacked the capacity to take away the pain of being separated for so long.

When they reached what Mike called the observation deck, everyone did what people from *before* used to flock to this spot to do—gawked in wondrous amazement. The flyer looked so tiny, like a toy version of itself in the distance. The portrait of a once bustling metropolis painted a surreal image of a city known as a center of fashion and art. Reduced now to shells of buildings, yet it looked much like the Paris eyes of spectators from before would have beheld. Practically mathematical, the symmetrical layout presented a soothing order reaching an almost exquisite beauty. The city of art and culture, itself a work of art.

Looking from the other side, Gift found more of the same symmetry. Clusters of buildings separated by streets in a giant V shape as if designed to be gawked upon from above long before anyone had conceived of the tower from which to witness its splendor. Plopped in the backdrop from a vastly different time, the skeletal remains of taller buildings in the distance seemed out of place, detracting from the classic style and simplistic elegance of the ancient town. Intriguing to Gift's engineer brain, the ancient structures had fared much better against the ravages of time's passage.

"Careful," came with a yank on her arm. Matteo pulled Gift back from a gaping hole in the floor.

"What the heck? I mean, what stupid idiot put such an enormous hole right here?"

Mike had the answer, of course. "It used to be really thick glass people walked over to see below."

"I'd pee myself standing over that, no matter how thick the glass was."

"Let's get to the transfer station." Mike added, "And everyone be careful."

28

Gift knew so little about the lives of those who populated this city and thousands like it spread across the planet. The ones who squandered the world they were given and ruined their home. Empty, decaying structures lingering through time as proof they once existed, once thrived in a society she couldn't imagine being part of herself. Life was simpler when New Europa was a little enclosed colony, a world of its own, on *Mars*.

With a handheld jacked into the communication array in the signal transfer station, Gift attempted to reach N.E. in the chat app several times, grunting after each no contact notice. The restaurant at the top of the Eiffel Tower would be their home for however long it took to reach Red or anyone at New Europa. Their backpacks overflowed with rations bars, water bags, body pads, and tooth sticks, and each had a sleeping bag. General Xiang commended Matteo for doing well in his packing. He had even thought to bring a few decks of cards.

For the third time in as many hands of Rummy, Gift asked Mike if he had the chat app on the handheld in open mode to receive incoming messages. Each time he had to answer the same question his tone's annoyance increased. Between each round, Gift checked it anyway, and tried to send a message at least twice or three times each time she did. Nothing.

"I have a game that requires skill over luck." General Xiang appeared to have tired of the gameplay of Rummy. "It is called Dou dizhu. It is hard to master, as it requires mathematical and strategic thinking and carefully planned execution. Playing it keeps the mind sharp and will help us be prepared to plan our victory."

Surely, it proved a true test of the general's patience to teach everyone the rules of play. With two decks of cards, they could play the less popular multi-player version. As much as Briscola had been difficult for Gift to learn for the ugly and confusing Italian suits, she found Dou dizhu much harder as the game ignored the card suits completely. It blew her mind when Xiang won with four twos, weak cards in most any other game Gift had ever played.

Oksana pulled her sleeping bag directly alongside Gift's to cuttle-in for the night. The chill didn't have an overly harsh bite in the restaurant they made into their habitat for who-knew-how-long. The sleep sacks were made from the same impressively warm material as the blankets and jackets Sergey shared on that infamous road trip that felt to Gift as a million years ago. One side inflated somewhat to offer a needed cushion against the solid flooring. Body heat had nothing to do with the youngster choosing to sleep almost touching Gift. Gift also wanted her kid sister close to her.

The morning left Gift alone in the company of General Xiang when Bright, Mike, Matteo, and Oksana decided to explore the area, to take in the sights of Paris like tourists from a forgotten era. Despite her best protesting against anyone leaving and a sickeningly mother-like demand for Oksana to stay, they descended the unending stairs. Gift watched them like ants walking away with the pressure in her chest of saying a goodbye that meant she'd never see them again.

"You didn't want to go see the city, or what's left of it? I told you... I'm fine staying by myself, to man the chat app. *Woman* the app? Whatever."

"I did not stay for you, Gift. When we make contact, I must speak to them to coordinate their plans and see how we might assist. It is very important I speak to them."

Checks of the device and repeated unanswered chat attempts occupied the morning and afternoon, while a surprisingly talkative Xiang filled most of the time with anecdotes. Gift chimed in, asked a question here or there, but the general went on and on about her life in the N.R.C. To cap the political talk, she voiced a long list of complaints against its former president. There was no mourning of his death, though she didn't relish assuming his position as leader—little as it meant under U.R.M. occupation. Life in her colony touched nowhere near the joyous and carefree living Gift enjoyed before those conspiracies, secrets, and sabotage turned her colony upside-down. *Those mal'd All Lies messages.*

It shocked Gift to learn Xiang and Chan were once promised in Union, 'engaged' as she put it—a new context of the word for Gift. The president himself had ended it for 'security concerns.' That, and his insistence on proper military behavior, forbidding a high-ranking general to be involved with and to *marry* a subordinate officer. Gift had learned the term from the Ubuntu, and that partners were called husband and wife. The need for the words eluded her, and then she brought her mind back to Xiang's stories while she checked the handheld again.

"While it hurt like no one should have to hurt when it happened, you can see why eventually it ended up being a good thing."

"*Huh?*"

"Dividing me and Chan."

"Oh, right. Him going crazy and all. I guess it spared you a real mess. *Ma*, wait... You knew he was off his rocker before you sent him to U.A. with nine dozen soldiers?"

"I never said I sent him. And I warned the president when I started to see it. I did not imagine it was getting so advanced. And Gift, again, I am very sorry for what he did to you."

"You've said it enough. We don't need to relive that. Besides, like I s—"

Chirp.

On her feet in what passed almost as negative time, rising before the alert from the handheld had beeped, Gift clasped the device.

- ne: Hello?

- ua: Yes. Red?

- ne: Oh thank goodness. Oksana?

- ua: No, Gift.

- ne: No way! You made it to UA?

- ua: Yes. NRC failed. UA free. What at NE?

- ne: Didn't go so well here.

- ua: Tom? Sara? Everyone? How bad?

- ne: Less than terrible, got stopped quick.

- ua: Tom and Sara okay?

- ne: Yes. Some of ours infiltrated URM guard but then turned on us. Tom said they did it in the "best" way. I know. But he meant they leaked the play but not the players. Tom and Sara okay.

- ua: Oh good thanks. Now what?

- ne: Tom is ready to move, but low on manpower.

- ua: We're coming to help.

- ne: Really! When?

- ua: Not in UA ma don't want say where. Close.

- ne: That's amazing.

- ua: We need proper military strategy and coordination. Is this guard with you or able to join the chat?

- ne: Who is this?

- ua: With me, grabbed device. She needs talk to Tom.

- ne: Who?

- ua: General from NRC. Helping us.

- ne: Wow. Okay Gift, if you say so. I'll patch Tom in.

The General had to forcibly extract the device from Gift's hand after allowing a minute or three of back and forth between the two, obviously involved and in the throes of painful separation from each other. While Xiang planned with Tom, Gift read over her shoulder and had a thought. "*Marco.*"

"Who is that, and why did his name have to damage my eardrum?"

"Sorry. He's my friend, nice young guy—"

A stiff hand-raise stopped Gift's words cold. "Relevant to this mission, please. What do we need to tell Tom about this Marco?"

"Right. You're right. Sorry. He's in maintenance and he knows how to sneak around in the shafts and ducts and stuff. He'll give us an incredible advantage. Like how you snuck around at the N.R.C."

"Now that is relevant. I will tell this to Tom. We can use this to plan a much better strategy. Thank you, Gift. Very smart, as I have said."

Minutes passed over the tiny device as Xiang's thumbs hit the keys, her eyes reading Tom's replies. A plan came together, and Gift got excited. For the first time, it looked like they had a chance, especially with Gift's idea of using Marco. The General gave the device back when Tom said Claudia needed Gift. On the first message, she pulled the device from Xiang's view and asked for privacy. The shuffle of feet signaled the return of the explorers, and Gift's mind came down from the worry for her friends. In the app, that once vile woman typed text messages as if none of the sabotage had happened, reducing the insurrection to a footnote in their colony's history, nothing more than an interesting anecdote.

- ne: They know everything about your condition.

- ua: Everything? How?

- ne: I found where they hacked into the medical files after Sakura told them nothing.

- ua: Is she okay?

- ne: Fine. A strong woman. Charlie was a lucky man.

Was a lucky man? Charlie, the guy who's been dead for over a year because of the insurrection and violence you *started. Him? He's a lucky man?* The boiling point reached, Gift's thumbs had so much they wanted to say. Not the time, Claudia was helping now. Once again, Gift had to force herself into the present moment and leave the past ones in the past.

- ua: Yeah.

- ne: I hijacked their comms. They've been after you for the missile facility for a while. Your exile drove them mad. They learned about your immunity to earth sickness and now they found about the getting pregnant thing and they are more desperate to find you.

- ua: For that? Why?

- ne: Found some of their messages. They have not had a childbirth on Mars in 20 years. In vitro stopped working for them. This is more than the missiles, more than earth sickness. They will stop at nothing to get you.

- ua: Why are you telling me this now?

- ne: You said you were coming here. You are in hiding and safe. Stay there. You can't let them get you. If they use you to solve their baby problem, they may just end us all with our own missiles. Start over with them having the whole mal'd planet for themselves.

- ua: I don't know. I need to process.

- ne: Don't come here. If you do, they'll get the missiles and use them against us. Experiment on you to solve their health problem. And then we're only in their way. We'll be done for sure.

- ua: Put Tom on. Private.

After composing herself, determined to go ahead with the mission and ignore Claudia's warning, she wished for nothing more than to chat with Tom all night. Sleep wasn't needed, the world became irrelevant. They spent some minutes blissfully alone in chat. It never got mushy or overly romantic, but their genuine affection expressed itself clearer than ever. As the next words came to her thumbs and conveyed their intentions on the tiny keyboard, she knew in that moment, all doubt removed, if any ever existed.

- ua: I love you.

- ne: Love you too. See you soon.

29 | Week Fourteen

I t had been days and they had not yet cracked it. Raff and Hans were still working at it, according to the last update Red shared. Gift didn't tell Red, Tom, Raff, or anyone else about Tina, not the time for that sort of news yet.

- ua: Yes, I'm fine. Oksana is with me.

- r: Good. Where are you?

- ua: Not far from NE. Ready to help them at dawn.

- r: Careful Gift. I say that to you a lot.

- ua: Right? This is nuts, just crazy.

- r: Ma Claudia is right, you need to stay out of it, stay safe. They want you. If Aimee is right, and you saw what they dropped on us, they want this complex, they can't find it. They lost everyone at NE who knew. We're all here. You are last one.

- ua: I know. They get me they get the missiles. And now this other stuff. Why did it have to be me?

> - r: Mi dispiace. My fault. If I hadn't taken you here, you
>   wouldn't be able to find it. They wouldn't have hunted you
>   for three months.

No, Gift didn't blame Raff. If anything, her curiosity was to blame. Being one of four Board members aware of their existence was bad enough. Worse was being one of three who could find it, and Gift thought she could, even if not certain. It's what helped her hold on to her resolve to tell Chan, Xiang, James, and that gorgeous nameless governor lady she didn't know the location, and that was technically true. But in a flyer, she felt confident she could find it, set to ninety-nine percent.

> - ua: Not just that, they want me for my crazy genes, my con-
>   dition. I don't understand why they're doing this.
>
> - r: Cara, they're desperate. Mars not doing well, not able to
>   have babies, not even in vitro, Claudia learned. They are
>   dying.
>
> - ua: I get that. But if they just asked for our help, we'd have
>   helped them. Why this? Why always this?
>
> - r: Sorry.
>
> - ua: Me too.
>
> - r: They must think you can help save them. I agree what
>   Claudia told you, that is more to them than the missiles.
>
> - ua: Pioneers and Ubuntu can have babies. Without in vitro.

- r: But only you can help us and URM. Those people were not in colonies, not on treatments. And they lose many more than they have. Dozens of miscarriages for each birth. URM very interested in you for how to get back to nature and survive as a species.

- ua: As Martians. We were surviving fine on our own.

- r: It's late. Big day tomorrow. Get some sleep.

- ua: Yeah right!

- r: Please consider sitting this one out.

How Gift would have loved to sit this one out. *No choice but to fight*. Did Miss Heller have any idea how often those words would ring in Gift's ears like an echo in an open cave? She couldn't have, no one could. Once again, Gift found herself in the middle of the issue of those missiles. How to get access, and what to do once they did. *Those mal'd, stupid missiles.*

- ua: Still no access to systems?

- r: Progress. Found targeting and launching control cannot be operated from the bunker. We got through a firewall and into systems that controlled security, found a tunnel to the platform and command center. That's what we need. Working on getting into that for two days now.

- ua: Progress I guess.

- r: Once we have these, we end this.

- ua: Peace by force or threat.

- r: We didn't ask for this. Is what it is.

- ua: I guess. I gotta go Raff.

- r: Love you Cara.

- ua: Love you too. Best to HF, Boss & Sergey.

Sleep wasn't plentiful, coming in short doses between the mental gymnastics that drove Gift crazy. Twice she lifted Oksana's arm off her, and once she'd gotten up to pee. When it was time to pack their things and head down the infinite staircase, the sun had not yet arrived, but sent an advance of illumination as a hint for the night to take its leave. Like an action and adventure vid, Gift watched herself board the flyer. Another person, a character in a story, headed off to war. She was no soldier.

If the timing was correct—and it was crucial they timed it right—Tom would already be mobilized by the time they arrived, and his distraction should allow the transport to land close enough to the colony without being ambushed on deboarding. If the timing was spot on. They were about to find out.

***

The distant sight of home melted Gift's heart in joyous pain. The world had unfolded, and she'd seen more of it than she imagined when the airlock opened, more than she cared to. New Europa was world enough for her, was her world. Her loved ones were there. Tom was there, somewhere in the domes coming into view. Xiang landed by the lake, and when they exited the flyer with backpacks on, they were greeted by Marco and Sara, just as planned. They needed to move, but the reunion demanded hugs before anyone was allowed to go.

Snuck in through the airlock in the back of the secret farm off dome four, they were in New Europa. Gift was finally home. She thought of the Pioneer refugees who had been staying in Charlie's shelter and wondered if they were still there or had been given better accommodation. In Dome Four, outside the rebuilt storage building, they found early morning commotion as passersby passed by quickly, scurrying off like something pulled them all in the same direction. Tom's distraction.

At passageway Six-One, Marco opened a wall that didn't appear to be a door and waved them all through. Bright, Xiang, Oksana, Mike, Matteo, and then Gift, followed by Marco, with Sara taking the rear. Up two flights of stairs, they entered a place familiar to Gift and ducked to waddle through the low shaft to the access ladder and up to the catwalk stupidly devoid of handrails. *Why didn't I install them on one of my committees?*

"Sorry for the lack of handrails, just be careful." Marco showed a posture of control and manliness Gift found assuring. Pointing to Bright and Xiang, he said, "You two follow Sara. She'll take you to meet Tom and help subdue the guards at key positions as planned. The shift change happens in under fifteen, so you need to move."

Sara led them away to do their part of the job. Mike and Matteo knew their role and Mike led the way, having been in this place once before, he had clear in mind where to go to find air handler two. That left Marco with Gift and Oksana. They followed him down from the scary catwalks to descend a different two flights of stairs to ground level.

"From here we take the maintenance tube between the cultivators' habitats and the passageway. We can get to Dome One and then I know a way to get close to the admin building."

"Like old times, except I'm not stupidly wearing a black dress to wander through maintenance shafts."

Marco smirked. "I liked the black dress."

"I bet you did, jerk." She slapped him playfully on the chest and smiled.

"You got the masks?" Oksana asked.

"Yep, just like that general asked."

"Told is more like it. I think Red and Tom could feel the commanding tone when Xiang typed."

"Yeah. So, how'd you end up with a Chinese general, anyway?"

"Long story."

Oksana said, "One of many I'm still waiting to hear."

"Let's focus on now. It's time for action, not stories. We need to time this right, be in position when Mike and Matteo do their thing."

As Gift spoke, Red and Claudia approached in the maintenance tunnel. It thrilled Gift to see Red—Melody, but on a mission, she was Red again—and she got a hug while Claudia got a disdainful look. It was Gift's first time seeing her since she was taken from Raff's bench a lifetime ago. Gift had so much to blame her for, so much hate to pile onto her, the kind that had a place and felt right. But this wasn't the time. In this moment, Gift forced herself to see her only as someone helping them.

They followed Marco to get into position. Without being exposed in Dome One, the one where most of the guards patrolled to protect their governor in the admin building, they could only get to the opposite side of Marienplatz piazza. The only things standing between them and the Ops office were the statue of the founders, a few guards, and biometrics they couldn't open. Nothing to do but wait for the signal.

When the klaxon sounded, they raced out of hiding in the education center, passing the founders with a new contempt for them, the ones who built the colonies had fostered the development of the U.R.M. Guards had dispersed as expected, the mission being expertly planned to the detail by General Xiang. Red and Gift quickly opened the access panel for the biometric systems for the side entrance and had the door open in under two minutes. All according to plan so far.

"Masks," Gift shouted in a whisper.

Marco handed a small clear nose and mouth mask to Red and Claudia, then finally took one for himself. Gift and Oksana didn't need them for this next part. Masks strapped around their heads with mini oxygen cylinders adding pure air to the filter, the three readied themselves to go up one level. The two engineers broke from the group, leaving Claudia and Red to accompany Marco to the Ops Center to reclaim admin access to key computer systems. From Gift's office, she and Oksana could tap into the security system and monitor the most crucial locations and access points.

"Matt did it. Look, he did it." Oksana mentioned only Matt, Matteo, when he and Mike had done it—but mostly Mike—by activating Sakura's knockout gas, as Mike called it. The screens showed the two guards in Ops lying on the floor. Just then, they watched Claudia and Red enter view, stepping over the unconscious Martians and starting their work. Gift frantically switched from camera to camera in a desperate search for Tom... and the others.

"Flashback, right?"

"*Huh?*" It took a second for Gift to get Oksana's point. "Oh, you mean you and me monitoring a battle to take back a colony—*again*. Yeah, *our thing* now, I guess." They found a chuckle in the chaos. "*Ma*, minus a raving Chinese lunatic this time."

"Well, we *do* have that general." Oksana smiled at her own humor and she was beautiful. How Gift longed for this to be over so they could get back to sharing happier moments.

"There," Gift shouted, but not to the teenager beside her. The camera had found Tom with Xiang and Bright, several U.R.M. guards on their knees around them. Perhaps playing that awful Chinese card game had helped them gain the victory.

Darkness fell over her eyes, and the world disappeared.

30

Things are not always what they seem. How many times Gift had said those words to counter jumped conclusions and halt ill-conceived actions. This time, the situation couldn't be anything other than what it seemed. Or so it seemed. When she woke groggily on the gently rocking air transport, her eyes immediately found Oksana slumped over the seat beside her. It took effort to raise her head to check her surroundings. Even before the blue and silver uniforms manifested, Gift understood what had happened.

"Where are you taking us?"

"Be quiet... if you don't want another dose."

"Dose of what? What did you do to us?"

Turning from the seat in front of her, a muffled voice replied through a face shield, "What part of 'be quiet' did you not understand?"

"If my choices are shutting up or nag you with questions... I said, where are you taking us?"

"Russian Federation."

A quickly pulled back smirk hid Gift's satisfaction in how she'd won that little battle of wills. Of course, the guy's Russian accent told her their destination, but she wanted to make them tell her. Pressing her luck, Gift tossed a wild theory at the fool. "So, the R.F. *is* working with the Martians.

Yeah, I assumed as much." She hadn't, having just thought of it—perhaps a premonition from a dream.

The pilot answered in American English, comparable to Mike's enunciation and cadence. And pride. "Been doing so the whole time; before anyone realized we were even here. Now it's too late..."

It started coming together. Yuri's hints of a greater danger weren't about the New Republic of China nor a desperate bluff for his tribunal. *No wonder he looked so smug when sentenced. Jerk.* He knew nothing about the N.R.C. They only reacted to the U.R.M. having taken down their transports. And if the Chinese flyers went down by sabotage and remote signal, as Aimée suggested, then the N.R.C. had spies among them as well—the U.R.M.'s only true weapon. Perhaps worse than a physical arsenal, now they could have been anywhere, anyone, in at least two colonies. *Are there any spies in New Europa?*

"...and your pathetic little uprising will be dealt with soon enough."

The threat Claudia and Raff cautioned her about, the reason to stay out of N.E. and not risk getting caught. They had her now, the high trump card—*or a set of twos in Xiang's stupid game*—with the worst yet to come.

"Well, we'll see about that. You realize you picked a real loser to work with, don't you? Come on, *Yuri?* First, he's a stupid idiot. Second, he cares only for himself and will surely turn on you in a heartbeat."

"Talk all you want lady—it's already over. That child of a grown man is of no importance."

That the harsh comment about Yuri came not from the Martian but from the Russian fascinated Gift. Even *they* knew the man was worthless, only a means to their end. Conceivably, Yuri was the only one who didn't realize it.

"Nadezhda Anoykina?"

A deliberate helmet nod answered Gift's question. The sinister smile beneath the faceplate didn't need to be seen, Gift felt it. Hit over the head by a memory, one word in giant letters filled her mental display, *OR*. Was the Russian President feigning cooperation as Bright and Xiang had done, *or*—Chan's little word again held power over life and death—*or* was she being complicit, siding with the perceived stronger party, taking the safe way out. What gave Gift's newest *Or* such intensity came in the unsettling notion that Nadezhda Anoykina may just have been the sort of person who would save herself and let the world around her burn. That idea rattled her shoulders more than the flyer's rocking.

***

Grumbles from her stomach suggested Gift had been knocked out again for a while, maybe hours. In the admin building, Gift woke exactly where Yuri had been seated when she first met that vile creature and his sister—a girl blasting her brother with more unbridled rage than Gift had ever seen before or since. When Yuri entered the room to complete the role-reversal, Gift found it morbidly comical.

"You see, Yuri said you would visit me. Such a lovely gift for Yuri." His hand cradled her jaw and her eyes rolled away.

"You're still a creep."

"And you stole my missiles."

"*Your* missiles?"

"Is pretty-little head just for looks? I am told you are smart woman. Still, you do not see, do you? No matter, Yuri keeps you for your beauty. You are nothing more. *Nothing*."

"Then what about you? No brains *and* no beauty. You knew nothing about the missiles." The pieces were coming together, just not as quickly as Gift was accustomed to. *Side-effect of the knock-out gas?*

"You disappoint Yuri. My people occupied bunker for attack to your pitiful New Europa. We took their food, weapons, and one of my men found evidence of missile launch facility."

Never good at hiding her feelings—not having a decent poker face, as Mike called it—Gift's confusion was clear as she wore her conclusion over her face like a mask.

"Ah, your brain, it works again. If we found missiles so long ago, why the fuss for to get you helping us find it? Of course, the Chinese had no idea, and torture you, my poor dear. Not to worry, Yuri will not harm you. But you ask why the U.R.M. need this informations from you? Is good question."

"The answer's staring me in the face: you're an idiot. You learned of its existence, but not where it was."

"Soon you learn to be nice to Yuri. We spend much time together. Da, much time. The man who found about it, good friend of Yuri, was killed when Sergey's men attacked. He was pilot. Only one who knew location of bunker."

"You're a real turd, you know that?"

"Ah, Yuri knows this one. Is not nice word coming from such delicious lips." Yuri grabbed Gift's jaw and squeezed it. The pressure on her cheeks puckered her lips and he placed his disgusting mouth against them. It was wet and vile, but with hands tied and strapped into the sofa chair, Gift couldn't pull away.

"Enough," an unfamiliar voice said, strong and manly. A glint of irrational hope extinguished itself as Gift saw it wasn't Bright but a new guy with the same empowered depth in his tone. "Leave us."

As Gift suspected, and the talking Russian guard confirmed, Yuri was a puppet and too stupid to realize it. The commanding voice before her must have emanated from the local governor. What could that have meant for Nadezhda to have someone else in charge? He gave no name or rank, only questions. It started the same as with Chan, Xiang, and James Morris. After going on for a while about the missiles, he shifted to the health matters, which Raff said—Claudia said it first, but Gift still hated her—were of greater concern for the Martians.

Standing two meters tall, and so close to Gift his legs pressed against her knees, the man was a mountain of intimidation. Perhaps Gift's familiarity with such fierce, nameless interrogators had hardened her to their tactics. Channeling her mentor, she stayed as calm and collected as Raff, with no wish to be a turtle. She wished for a box of body wipes, tooth sticks, and a hose, to wash the filth of Yuri from her lips. When instinct pulled her bottom lip between her upper and lower teeth the gag reflex tugged her shoulders forward. Yuri's saliva dripped from her lips, and she'd taken some of the disgusting substance into her mouth.

"Tell us about your condition."

"I'm a bit tired. Been a long day. Also too, I think I'm gonna puke."

"We will not play games here, young lady."

Young lady? A closer look showed an older man's face, worn by years of long-hour days riddled with anxiety. Gift surmised him to be in his fifties but with life showing more years on his leathery skin. His questions continued and increased in specificity, making it clear the terrorist-turned-ally that used to share a bench with Raff was right. The U.R.M. had learned everything about her condition, and despite all Sakura had accomplished, her work hadn't cured either earth sickness or the sterility problem. Not yet.

Progress had been steady; Sakura did an amazing job. In fact, she had gotten many New Europa residents to classifications rated in days rather than hours and had improved the in vitro mortality rate significantly. Now the U.R.M. needed more and Gift truly had nothing more to offer. All they could get from her was her—her genes, her body—and experiment on her until they found something useful, or she was dead. Most likely both.

Focusing on the positives, Gift wasn't hanging by her arms in her underwear and none of her dear friends were being tortured. *This is how it always starts,* she thought. *Nice*-ish, *but only at first, maybe some of the 'we're on the same side, want the same thing' nonsense. Then their peace-loving ways inevitably turn. The mood sours, and the gloves come off as they apply duress to get what they want.*

Gift clung to the truth of not knowing the exact location of the complex and spoke to her unique medical state, simply saying she got nothing of the medical jargon beyond how it affected her. When her lack of useful information became evident, what would follow? Peace by threat, Gift assumed.

"We ordered New Europa and United Africa to stand down and restore our governors."

"And you actually think they're just gonna do that after kicking your butts? For humans, you idiots know very little about human behavior. It seems you've been on Mars so long... you *are* Martians now."

"We think we understand your people well enough. Our message to all colonies showed pictures of you and Roxanna with strong implication that their surrender would be better for both of you."

"Who the heck is *Roxanna*?"

"Whatever the name of Nadezhda's brat daughter is has no importance. That we have her, does."

"Your plan is for colonies of tens of thousands of people to lie down and surrender because you have *two* people? And one is from a colony you already occupy? Delusional much?" Gift learned that 'something much?' line from Mike months ago but hadn't tried it until now. She thought she used it correctly.

"You make a habit of underestimating your value. But we have more cards to play than just you two queens. The message is being broadcasted on a loop to both colonies. Surrender or lose you and the girl is a main part of it. And we are done wasting time. If they don't surrender by noon tomorrow... your beloved New Europa will be a crater, and we just may keep you around long enough to see it."

Keep me around. Not such a clever way to say you'll kill me after you kill everyone else. While the man appeared to speak in earnest—as serious as a faulty inverse reactor in a power cell—he didn't appear to be bluffing. But no matter how good his poker face was, it had to be a bluff. He knew nothing about Aimée's hidden messages, or that Gift knew the Martians didn't have the firepower to carry out such an empty threat. *How much falling space junk would it take to completely level two colonies?*

That they dropped an escape pod suggested they exhausted their supply of large objects. Plus, Aimée didn't think they could do it—that was solid enough for Gift. *This guy must be an incredible card player.* Perhaps the mind shifted into escapism as a defensive measure, or Gift's usual mental ramblings had taken over. There was ample room for that possibility. The figurative smack to the forehead felt like it hurt when Gift realized she had finally been to N.E. and hadn't seen Tom.

Relief came by the exit of the nameless inquisitor, and the peace of the empty room fell upon Gift as a much-needed respite to let her mind come down. When Nadezhda Anoykina entered next, Gift's brain had a new and interesting curiosity to ponder.

31

Yuri Anoykina had a bigger role, grander ambitions, than Gift could have imagined. It came together as she pondered his part in the hostility toward the Pioneers, his tribunal, and his callous attitude that bled like an open wound when they convicted and sentenced him. He had been colluding with the U.R.M. So obvious in retrospect. *He hadn't meant to find the missile complex and didn't know it existed. Just an accident of freakish luck.*

Further clarity came as Gift scrolled her mental display. Yuri's thwarted attack on N.E. was to be the first wave of the U.R.M. action plan, the invaders kept hidden until the right time. Gift was sure of it. His failure moved them to take an unplanned detour. Not having come as a navy with weapons to forcibly take the colonies, they plotted to do it from within. Gift found hope in that they weren't fighting a well-thought-out military strategy.

The United Republic of Mars had turned some in the R.F. and N.R.C. into spies. Did they have people in New Europa on their side? The light of intel shone too dimly to make that call. Agents of the U.R.M. had likely been the ones to sabotage the air transports, remotely triggered from the fleet above, hidden beyond the clouds. *The two minutes, thirty-eight seconds. Yes, the scans of our systems, the way our rollers went screwy, the network flukes.* Gift saw it. It must all have been from those U.R.M. ships trying to assess the colonies, hack their systems.

They hadn't learned the vital information they sought, hadn't been able to overturn the colonies on the ground. As a result, they had spent their supply of *weapons*, which weren't even weapons, on the first facade of an attack to occupy all known societies of Earth. They already played their hand and the charade game they'd been performing now lost its luster, crumbling like a house of cards. Their needs were on the table, and they yearned to satisfy their hunger.

Nadezhda Anoykina stood before Gift in silence while the guard who escorted her in took his leave. Gift's arms passed the initial twinges of fatigue and progressed to aching from being tied behind her, and the tingles of onsetting numbness crept over the skin. Chan's *Or* taunted her as she came to the disturbing realization that—given what she knew of the Russian President—she could have been on either side of it. Raising her head despite the complaints from her neck muscles, Gift met the indifferent eyes of the woman of such daunting intimidation.

"Gift, my dear, am sorry of this."

A memory of something Tom had taught her came to mind. *Let the examiner talk as much as possible.* On the flyer, the poor fool posing as a tuff-guy told Gift much more than she hoped. Maybe Nadezhda would do the same? No, this woman was clearly more intelligent and cautious than that guard had been. The empty stare lasted an eternity.

"Gift, you must cooperate. I am accepted it is over, they won. I was not working with my Yuri. He was acted alone. But I accept U.R.M. occupation, there is nothing we can do. Nothing. They will get what they need. As you say, in the one way or in the other. It is better for you to cooperate."

Holding to her new plan of silence, Gift saw something in Nadezhda's eyes hinting at closed lips being the desired outcome. Curious. The woman's foreboding movement to position herself behind Gift hung in the room like a specter of imminent horror or torturous pain. Silk-thread-thin hairs over Gift's skin stood in fear of the warm breath on her ear.

"We must *not* cooperate," Nadezhda whispered. "Be strong and say nothing."

A ploy to lower her guard or sincerity? Nowhere near ninety-nine percent, Gift couldn't guess which side of the *Or* the president played. Chaos flooded her brain, bringing that dull pain.

With a raised head Miss Anoykina spoke in normal volume. "Da, it is better for you. Tell them how to find complex of missiles. You must be cooperated with them for earth sickness and pregnancy. Is for all of us, helps all. You can see this. I know you can."

Returning her lips to Gift's ear, Nadezhda again spoke softly. "We must assume they are hearing all. I worry for my Oksana. We must get you free. Sergey is not here. No one here knows to find bunker. Only you. I have people, loyal to me, and soon we get help. Tell nothing."

With a not-at-all-faked slap to the cheek, Nadezhda shouted, "You stubborn girl." The woman cranked the volume to a full eleven on Gift's one to ten scale. "You make things hard for yourself. When the Governor comes, tell him what he wishes to know. Tell him!"

Expecting the Governor to enter next, Yuri's entrance brought disappointment on many levels. Not only did he disgust her for his abuse of his sister—a monster she deemed unworthy of mercy—Gift despised him as a loathsome creep, a soulless being. She had thought him useless, proven wrong by his role in preparing a group of chemically enhanced rogue guards to take the bunker, kill innocent Pioneers, and plot to overthrow New Europa. Tossed in a tiny cell and tortured at his mother's order, Gift again considered Yuri inconsequential, to once more be proven wrong.

"Beautiful Gift." He leaned his unhandsome face too close for comfort. Anywhere in the colony would have been too close for her. "You must see you cannot win. It is over. *Over.* The R.F. and China are ours, the two strongest colonies. Very strong. If you think your uprising yesterday makes difference, you are stupid girl. We have ships in space and weapons. You have nothing."

"*We?* You think you're one of them, a Martian? I'm not the stupid one if you think you mean anything to them." To break her rule of silence here felt justified. When his buttons were pushed, Yuri easily lost his grip on self-control. His backhand to her cheek told her she got to him. His mother's hand had reached her face with greater force.

"Foolish girl. Yuri is in charge here. My mother is old, weak, finished. Goes along to save skin, but no... she has no power. No power. No saved skin. And Yuri will be the one to skin her alive. Now we have plan to go to N.E. and end their little rebellion. Combined R.F. and U.R.M. forces. If they resist, all are dead. Your people... Dead!"

Gift didn't have to try hard to get him talking. He revealed information the U.R.M. likely preferred to keep secret. They were gearing up combined forces to leave, creating the opening the Russians loyal to their president could use to make their move. Hopefully the conversation was being monitored and Nadezhda heard that bit. A guard and the tall man coming in hastily addressed Yuri's indiscretion. Seeing he was about to be less than politely excused, Yuri leaned into Gift's ear with his grimy hand on her shoulder. Her flesh crawled but couldn't get away, so it sent shivers of complaint over her skin.

"You know, I am sure, what happens now. Now I have Oksana. Yuri will tell her is because you did not cooperate. You did this to her. Then... Yuri comes for you."

A thick wad of phlegmy spit landed on his eye and ran down his nose. The guards removed the vile thing in human skin from the meeting room and out of Gift's sight before he could retaliate. Heavy lumps of flesh where her arms used to be hung from aching shoulders pulled over the back of her chair. That discomfort sunk kilometers under the one Yuri left Gift in, with anxious dread for Oksana dominating her thoughts. Would he have an opportunity to hurt her again *Or* would Nadezhda be able to stop him this time? The weight of that paltry word was too much to bear. *That mal'd Or.*

"You must see now... resistance is futile." The existence of the tall man died in a distant memory until he spoke. "There is nowhere left to run. We will soon have our lost colonies secured and once again under our control. A new world order is coming. You can take your place there. Help us ensure peace by telling us the location of those missiles and how we gain control of them. Then we can work together to learn how to benefit all humankind by understanding your unique physiology. You can be the key, Gift, to our new human society. Think of it, you will help *everyone*. We will be one unified people under a new flag, the United Republic of Earth."

The time for silence had passed. "United republic? Do you have any idea what that even means? Such hubris... and stupidity. I assume you don't, or you'd have chosen a different name. A republic is run *by the people*. Its strength is in the people choosing their leaders, not having 'em forced upon them. I don't know who's really in charge of you Martians, who you so-called governors report to. But I know this... you are a monarchy or an evil empire or something."

"You are right about one thing: you do not know who is in charge. The U.R.M. adopted the corporate structure same as you, and it worked for a while. In recent decades, with certain *evolving* conditions, more authority naturally shifted to the chairperson of the U.R.M. Board of Directors, and the position was renamed *Chancellor* and granted expanded powers. That created a more efficient government unburdened by bureaucratic red tape. Such a benevolent chancellor working with a cabinet of advisors is how we maintain order, and in that order, peace."

While not being familiar with the red tape reference, Gift got the gist of it. "Yeah, you just described an empire. And, and your peace by order is peace by force. If this new world order of yours was really *for* the people... you would cease this occupation... or, or adjust your approach from the unambiguous message your people are sending. We won't stop revolting against forced rulership. Eventually, it will fail."

"All governments eventually fail. History teaches this. It also teaches us we must make the best of our current situation and establish law and order, or we're nothing more than wild animals... eating, sleeping, breeding, and killing each other. We will finally break that cycle."

"You've gotta have some real nut-job zealots if anyone believes that. And I've met some of 'em." Gift's words came on their own—her mind agreed retrospectively.

"Let's get back to you, Miss Gift. You appreciate, I'm sure, that everyone breaks. It's simply a matter of time. Perhaps you think this axiom doesn't apply to you because you have withstood several intense examinations, even tortures, if you will. And you've bravely resisted in the face of your friends being tortured."

The tall man shrunk down to eye level when he knelt beside her. Wiggle lines on his forehead were stacked one atop the other, rising to connect his furled brow to his bare, sand-colored head. Like a rock in a stream eroded away by rolling currents leaving a glossy surface smoothed by the flowing water, his hairless scalp shone under the overhead light.

"Oh yes, Miss Gift, we know about each of your detentions and interrogations. From your suspicion in your own colony's sabotage to Commander Chan and General Xiang to Commander James Morris and Juliette Foster. And there's another thing you must consider if you think you can endure..."

The man paused to brush a curl from Gift's face and force eye contact.

"In each case, your... *motivational* sessions, were cut short. You are truly alone. No one is coming to save you, I assure you. We will get what we need, it is merely a matter of time. Once you see it that way, the one consideration for you is how difficult you will make it on yourself before your inevitable break."

Any silence didn't emanate from firm resolve, nor from Gift deploying anti-interrogation strategy. Her pensiveness sprang from weighing her options. *He said I'm alone. Is that true? Or is Nadezhda Anoykina trustworthy? That* mal'd *Or again. Are her people ready to move and take advantage of the window about to open, the slip of tongue Yuri generously offered? What about Oksana's fate in Yuri's hands?*

"Put me on a flyer. I can find the missile complex."

32

Everyone breaks, it was an inevitable fact. Resistance only prolonged the unavoidable outcome that would always be reached, making it nothing more than an act of futility. As much as physical strength, emotional fortitude and resilience had their limits, endurance eventually falters. Like a dried leaf that sensed the oncoming of winter, Gift's perseverance would wither. She tried to fight it, to hold on to autumn and stave off the next season's bitter cold. An impossible task?

More than ten weeks she spent in isolation, in hiding, to prevent the enemy from getting what she now willingly handed over. Without a fight, no torture to endure, and no friends threatened. But that wasn't entirely true. *No choice but to fight.* Miss Heller's words again played on a loop, spurring Gift on from one battle to another before she realized she had been reluctantly drawn into a war. *And we're losing.*

Reveling in victories found in tiny skirmishes might have improperly emboldened her and her friends. The allies Gift gained, including General Xiang with her military prowess, restored her *mal'd* optimism. In the best of many worst experiences, Gift's stubbornness had conceded just one percentage point, the ninety-nine clinging to her belief they would win. Streams of data flashed before her as Gift processed the weightiness of her decision. *'Put me on a flyer. I can find the missile complex.' I said that, agreed to take them.*

That beautiful governor of the N.R.C.—Gift heard her name but hadn't the room in her brain for such non-relevant data—came the closest to reaching Gift's breaking point. In fact, she *had* broken her. The decision to give in had been prevented only by a daring rescue by Xiang and her friends. Tina was in the group that saved her. Perhaps that heaviest of weights to carry led Gift to this decision. 'Stay strong,' Tina once told her from a face swollen like a balloon.

Giving in is failing Tina. She fought so bravely to prevent them from getting the missiles, getting me, getting what they needed to conquer us once and for all. And she was killed saving my *life.* Pangs of guilt from her decision to guide the U.R.M. to the facility piled themselves on an already insurmountable blame Gift laid upon herself for Tina sacrificing her life. Had Gift squandered it, relegating it to a wasted gesture? How she wished their roles would have been reversed, to have offered her life for her friend's.

But they have Oksana. To identify the greater threat confounded her, and each option brought Gift a fear so real it rattled her bones. That bald man hinted at something awful for her and Oksana, after getting the girl's name wrong. *He's governor of the R.F. and working with Yuri, thinks he's working with Nadezhda, and he can't even get her daughter's name right? A bunch of stupid idiots, and they hold my life and so many more in their hands. No, the worse threat to Oksana is Yuri.* She could only hope, given the pretense of authority dangled before him, he'd not be able to hurt his sister. Gift needed to rein it in.

It's a simple plan. I can do it.

Matteo had robbed Gift of the choice to use the ultimate power she possessed over the Martians, her only power. Selflessly offering her life would have saved her friends, maybe the known world. Not that she had a hero complex or thought of herself in such grandiose terms. That decision had come to her with such profound clarity it wasn't even a choice. And she had done it, she leaned over the side. And now she knew. *If Nadezhda fails to act, I'll kill myself.*

Thankful for small favors, the mission to fly Gift around to locate the missile complex required a bit of preparation time and daylight. U.R.M. guards talked openly in front of her about their plans, perhaps considering her on their side. Of course, they could have seen her as irrelevant and talked as if she weren't there. Demanded by the brain, Gift gave the seconds to consider which of those were worse. She finally stopped the endless volley of ping-pong balls as the evenly matched players on both sides of her mind could have debated the subject indefinitely.

They think there's nothing I can do, Gift realized. All things being considered, that turned out to be the perfect strategy. *When your enemy thinks you're defeated and out of options, they'll not see it coming.* Their callousness may have given Gift the upper hand. If a force in the R.F. will rise, as their President proclaimed, Gift had until morning when she would board the air transport and Nadezhda would free her before that. If not, she planned to get on the small flyer taking off with a heavy transport packed full of soldiers whose objective differed from hers.

No choice but to fight? Not true. This time the choice she found wasn't in *how* to fight, not exactly. If a fight had to be, it wasn't hers. It would be up to Miss Anoykina to rescue Gift and Oksana. If the fight didn't come, Gift would take herself out of the equation. A careful observer, she had learned just enough from recent experiences on the flyer to crash the small air transport once it cleared the colony. She would finish what Matteo only interrupted. Press Play after he had pressed Pause.

Delight filled Gift when, after an extensive debriefing, they escorted her to the home of Nadezhda Anoykina to spend the night. Oksana was there. When Yuri entered, the delight became the vile clear Russian liquid pouring into Gift, turning her cheeks green and giving her symptoms worse than any earth sickness sufferer. Even if it were merely psychosomatic, the disgust felt all too real.

"What's he doing here?" Gift asked Nadezhda.

"Am sorry dear. Orders by the U.R.M."

Yuri put on a smirk which hung on his face as a sinister sneer. "Is my home too, lovely Gift. You may share Yuri's bedroom. Very comfortable for two. Very comfortable."

"You listen, you slimy little creep. I'm cooperating and here as a guest of the governor. You don't get to talk to me. Or your sister."

"No, my dear. Let Yuri tell you—"

Stopped dead in his tracks by his mother's palm, Yuri's face morphed into a misbehaved four-year-old about to be scolded. The fierce tone of the words needed no translation. With thirty years of hatred and bitter resentment setting his eyes on fire, Yuri complied, to Gift's joyous disbelief. The U.R.M. guard in the dining space with them said nothing, as stone silent as the two guards by the flat's door.

Potatoes and roasted vegetables didn't make for much of a last meal. Unsettling Gift's stomach more than the cabbage, she considered how any action to retake the colony and save her life needed to happen soon, and Nadezhda sat there having dinner. Musing shifted her mind back to the mal'd *Or* as Gift couldn't be sure the woman with lava flowing through her veins just blew smoke or really planned an eruption in the uprising she teased.

"Oh no, we're *not* doing this," Gift protested when the guard entered Oksana's room with her.

"This is my room and we're going to sleep. You need to stay out." Oksana's commanding tone failed.

"I cannot allow that," the female guard replied.

"My Oksana sleeps with me. Gift may have the room."

"I'm sorry, Miss Anoykina. It's a show of good faith to allow your children and Miss Ojo in your home for the night. But no one is permitted to be together unguarded."

"The young ladies may share Yuri's room, and you may join, dear guard." A muffled voice of the vile creature came from behind his bedroom door.

"Shut up, jerk," Gift hissed.

"You will remain in your room alone, Mister Anoykina." The command in the woman's voice neared Nadezhda's authoritative tone.

"I'll take the sofa. It'll be a little less weird than sleeping in a bed with this... *masked person* watching me all night." Looking at the tinted face shield, Gift asked, "By the way, do you have a name?"

"Of course."

"I see. You know, you remind me of another guard I once had. Funny, she was also ordered to come into my home and watch me all evening. Would you believe we're good friends now?"

"Do not expect the same outcome here."

Using Oksana's shower transported Gift to the young woman's N.E. flat—she had been indulging in the full-pressure luxury almost daily. She didn't consider it abusing her role on the Board, just taking up an offer from a friend, so it was fine. Less fine, the guard stood beside the shower booth, which had no frosted glass or modesty panels.

When Gift settled in for the night, she tried to make herself comfortable on the sofa. A task considerably easier than it had been at Oksana's flat that first night she spent in N.E. These sofas were more spacious and pampered Gift in luxurious contentment. It almost made sleeping in her coverall passable. With Yuri in the next room, she'd not wear anything less.

As Gift lay wide awake, booming thuds roused the guards.

33

U.R.M. guards standing sentry at the gate outside the Anoykina home's entrance must have been taken out of play—Gift heard limp bodies smacking the floor. The guard beside her sofa rose to her feet, weapon drawn. The other two on her side of the door took the same posture with the advantage of guns fixed on a funnel point, ready to pick off the rescue forces one-by-one. It lacked the brilliance of a Xiang-planned military action. Fear rode on the thought Sergey wasn't there either and this coup could very well end badly.

"Should we open it?"

"Negative," Gift's personal escort replied. "Call out. I'll try the two-way."

"Miller? Saxon?" The door offered no reply to the shaky voice.

Touching her shoulder, the nameless female guard said, "Miller, Saxon, come in."

Room-filling silence fell over the scene. The smell of fear saturated the air, the guards drowning in it. When the door to Oksana's room opened, a hollow version of the young lady stood a statue of fear shrouded in resurfaced memories. A blade at her throat held her life on its edge. Yuri's tousled hair shielded the eye peering around the young lady's head.

"Tell them we will kill the women," he barked to the guards at the door. One parroted the words at the silent entrance.

"Oksana, sweetie, it'll be okay. I promise." Gift had nothing on which to base the assuring proclamation. Did the girl see the trepidation in Gift's eyes betraying her false certainty?

"If door opens, she dies." Yuri's face held a frenzy that transferred Gift back to that madman Chan. The same hysteria in the eyes, a raging storm that cared not for the damage it would inflict.

"He has a knife to her throat," she yelled at the mute door.

A visceral need pulled Gift's eyes back to the helpless girl, as if to confirm the danger. She knew full-well Yuri was the sort of lowlife scum that would take his sister's life as readily as he had taken her innocence. No tears flooded the young aqua-blue eyes, only the blank, empty stare of a story's ending. The emotional nothingness of surrender shrouding the girl in darkness. If it were made of glass, Gift's heart would have shattered into a million pieces.

Her next two quickly drawn breaths took hours, then Gift addressed the living example of how low humanity could sink. In desperation she cried, "Me for her."

"Nice try, my lovely Gift." Yuri flashed a sinister smirk. "You will have your turn. Do not worry."

A memory on her mental display flashed. Aimée said he wasn't very bright, that was unquestionable. But she also said he was a self-serving weasel interested foremost in his own survival. *Sort options. Select.*

"She's nothing to them. Your mother's people want to free *me*. And the U.R.M. wants *me*. Think about it Yuri, you're smarter than this. *I'm* the more valuable hostage."

Before Yuri could react—his face considering it—the female guard turned her gun from the door and touched the muzzle against Gift's temple. "She is correct. And we have them both."

Well, that backfired pretty huge.

A silver canister about the size of a handheld, if it were cylindrical, rolled by Gift's foot. An intense flash lit the walls on fire, blinding eyes as if lightning had electrified the room. Her ears blared like amplifiers playing the rumbling echo and the room became cramped. Footfalls behind her were the driving beats of neurotic music played as if underwater.

Something crashed violently into the nameless guard beside her, falling her to the floor at hyper speed. The door closed over the brother and sister still locked in the death waltz Yuri choreographed. The mind struggled to process, to understand the flood of impulses from the optic nerves. To Gift, the chaos felt like what pre-colony people had called modern art—it meant something to the ones who made it, but she had no clue what that could be. Yet she stared into it, analyzing the color palette and brush strokes.

Caught in a spiderweb of confusion, Gift had been captured. No, the arms of Nadezhda Anoykina steadied Gift on her feet. Guards loyal to their president had the three U.R.M. goons in the flat bound on the floor. The door opened, revealing the dozen guards who started it all unseen, the horror of noise that created hysteria as the opening sequence of a macabre stage play. It had a second act.

"Oksana," Gift shouted.

When two guards forced her door open, they found an empty bedroom. Unable to accept that as reality, Gift stammered into the ample suite, pulled up the mattress to slide it off the bed frame, then ran into the ensuite bathroom, stepping into the shower to check, though it had clear glass. In a frenzied state of uninhabited delirium, Gift pulled everything from the wardrobe, sure that Yuri had her holed up behind the few clothes that hadn't been taken to Oksana's flat at N.E.

"How? Where is she?"

From an unbelievably calm voice, Nadezhda said, "Gift, she is gone. Each bedroom has emergency escape. Is how my guards entered to take these U.R.M. trash. Yuri has her."

"*No. No.* We have to get her."

"We will. I will not let him hurt my Oksana."

From deep within a box she thought she had locked and tossed in the farthest corner of her mental archive came words summoned by raging fury. "Like you kept him from hurting her before."

"What is this hurting before?"

As little as Oksana had ever broached the subject again after that first night, she had begged Gift to never tell her mother. Now a gaff of an emotional outburst destroyed that trust and could devastate the young woman—if she survived this without a slit in her throat. In a mind clouded by heightened emotion, Gift searched for words to salvage the situation.

"I'm sorry. When the Pioneers held her hostage... that was Yuri's fault. He started that whole thing. I'm sorry, I'm just upset."

"Mm... And we made him pay for this."

"Where would he take her? We need to find her."

"This I wish, of course. I cannot save my daughter until we have colony. Yuri works with U.R.M. I am not knowing his dealings. *First*, we must take colony. *Then* my Oksana."

A deep-voiced guard spoke to Miss Nadezhda in Russian. Gift felt the urgency in words she couldn't understand.

"He told we must move from here. We have safe place. Secret place."

Two guards crawled in first, then Nadezhda, Gift, and two additional guards. The escape hatch behind the bed in the President's suite opened to a low, narrow tunnel that went on forever. Gift's knees ached by the time they emerged in the triangular room that looked nearly as large as the bunker by the missile complex but held a heavily stocked weapons cache. Xiang or Sergey could no doubt successfully win a war from this location and that's exactly what Miss Anoykina planned to do.

When the helmet came off the lead guard, it uncovered a familiar face. "Vitaliy Filatov," Gift excitedly said, then gave the burly bodyguard a hug he didn't expect but readily accepted.

"Hello Gift. Good seeing you. Not in this way, I wish."

With no time for pleasantries, Nadezhda commanded her man's full attention, and they conversed in Russian for a few minutes. The president's head nodded often, but Gift only understood her classic, "Mm." Translating what must have been the highlights for their brevity, Nadezhda said, "We have guards distracted. This is part one. This makes possible entrance of the Phil—*Pioneers*. They will help. To breach wall as first time. My men work with them, take my colony back from Martians."

"Then I'll go and find Oksana. Can Vitaliy come with me?"

"This is not plan. As I told, we take colony first, then get my daughter. We find her easy when fightings are finished. To look now is dangerous. I know my Yuri. Is an idiot, da, and now is desperate. He will kill his sister if cornered like wild animal. I much prefer to get my Oksana back to me alive."

"Okay, of course, yes, we gotta act smart. Save her without risking her life. What can I do?"

Vitaliy replied in English, "When Pioneers attacked us, you remember what guards did?"

"Yeah. You locked down Dome One, stopped'em from getting too far. But it didn't work, not really. I mean, they had hostages. And the U.R.M. have Oksana now."

"But now we wish Pioneers to get far. Are with us this time."

"Oh, we gotta *prevent* anyone sealing Dome One."

34

For the second time, Gift found herself helping the R.F. with an invasion by the Pioneers, this time assisting the incursion's success. As lost as ever, Gift followed the president's personal bodyguard through a maintenance shaft. Sounds of violence waited as the assault held for the Pioneers to breach the perimeter wall, which they were actively doing, so Gift needed to hurry. Once again, she became the object of an extensive search, so Vitaliy avoided open corridors and passageways. They reached a small building in Dome Three labeled Седьмой протокол. Unable to read it or even identify some of the letters, Gift asked for a translation.

"Seventh Protocol."

"I see. So, we skip the first six." Gift smiled at herself, having no idea what seventh protocol meant. "And the controllers for the safety hatches are in here?"

"Da. No problem for you, signs in Russian and English."

"Small favors. I had to work on ours when we had airlock issues and didn't know about the air outside."

The center of the room held a two-meter-high column of dull gray metal in a cylindrical shape with a large access panel. "The master," Gift thought aloud. As students gathered around a tutor for a lecture, individual dome and passageway controller modules—like the ones Claudia had targeted in her vicious endgame—encircled the master, crowding the room. Gift knew the systems well but had thus far only worked to *repair* them. Minutes took their time as she considered breaking them, or at least getting them not to engage when called to do so. Claudia's solution to blow them up was quickly dismissed as an option.

"If they want to lock down Dome One... they'll come in *here*."

"Da. Is why you must be fast."

"How much time?"

"Miss Anoykina is moving our men now. Maybe thirty minutes they are in colony. This is when men come here to seal dome."

"Oh mamma. Less than thirty minutes. Wait, what was the plan if you didn't have me?"

"You were plan. Is why we first freed you."

"I see. Then I'd better get this done. Got any tools?"

He pointed behind her to a large toolkit which she happily rummaged through to find everything she needed. Short of destroying the systems, Gift determined how to disabled them so repair time would exceed the duration of the battle. It had to be enough, so she hoped it would be. Starting with the master controller, Gift opened the panel and pulled the main board forward. The screech of metal scraping over metal stiffened her neck.

Yes, that's it. The crystal co-transaction module.

Modifying the format alignment of the gemstone chips while slipping one crystal into her pocket would make the system appear online but not pass its command signals, making it impotent. "I bet it'll take them a while to figure that one out," she said, with a glint of pride for the clever idea. Anyone who understood the basics of how the system worked would logically move to the individual units to manually key in the commands to seal the hatches in each dome and passageway. "Time for phase two."

One by one, Gift moved through each unit, removing the subroutine coprocessor from the main board and each redundancy. A physical match, she replaced each of them with quantity flow regulators, recreating those now infamous dummy-redundant chips of Mike's discovery. That added a few more minutes to any troubleshooting process, and Gift figured this battle might need those minutes.

"Time?" Gift shouted over her shoulder as she worked on the second to last module.

"About two minutes before Pioneers are known."

"Almost done... Okay, moving to last—"

The bang of the flung-open door cut her words. A blue and silver uniform ran in, stopped face to facemask with Vitaliy, and started shaking uncontrollably until collapsing onto the floor. Not knowing beforehand how quick the massive bodyguard would have been to kill a Martian, Gift became immensely grateful for the use of the taser.

"Thank you for not killing him."

"Some are ours. Traitors, da, but ours. Russian or Martian, they will be captured and tried... when this is possible."

"Let me do this last one."

"No. We leave now. More soldiers will come."

"Can't leave that one. They'll know we were here, they're more likely to find what I did and fix it."

Unable to complete the task, Gift masked her presence on the other units not to give away her sabotage. When she opened the door, the man on lend from Nadezhda Anoykina dragged the Martian or Russian out. As quickly as possible, they slipped into the closest maintenance hatch and out of sight.

"Which is one you did not finish?"

"The last passageway control unit. I think it was for Two-three. Will it be a problem? If they manage to seal the one bulkhead, I mean."

"No. We will plan for this. You have done very well."

"Hope so. Now what about Oksana?"

"You know the orders. We wait."

"Don't you need to go join the fight somewhere? I mean, we're done here, right?"

"Da, this part is done. Miss Anoykina wishes you to be protected. I have order to keep you safe, not let them catch you. I will die before I allow this."

It seemed Gift's fantasy of having her own personal bodyguard wasn't so far-fetched after all. That Nadezhda gave him to her settled that mal'd *Or* once and for all. With two free colonies and the R.F. poised to be next, Gift wondered if they would be victorious or merely prolong the inevitable. Would thirst for freedom plunge humans into endless conflicts, violent uprisings and coups, insurrections, and an eventual civil war? It was becoming imperative to find a better solution. Gift had no clue what that could be.

"So, we just wait here? How long?"

"No, this place is not safe. Too close to Protocol Seven room. If they find sabotage, they will look here. I would do this, and some of them know what I know."

"But they didn't know about the escape tunnels in Miss Nadezhda's home."

"They do not know *all*. But they have Yuri. Is good for us he is not bright boy."

"Or maybe... I think... he's just a selfish jerk. Didn't tell them in case *he* needed to escape."

"Da. This is most likely. He is selfish."

"Where do we go?"

Moving through the narrow maintenance tubes proved a difficult task, especially lugging the unconscious guard that turned out to be a Martian woman. While the rock mass of a bodyguard surely could have tossed her over one shoulder, the tight spaces forbade it. With Gift holding her ankles and Vitaliy taking most of her bodyweight from under the arms, it was exhausting. The wet fabric of the coverall stuck to Gift's back, pulling the skin with each twist of movement. When wakefulness reentered the Martian, a gag came from somewhere and Vitaliy bound her mouth in silence. At least she no longer needed to be carried.

Stealth action reached its end when the maintenance shaft ended over twelve meters from the hatch leading to the secret triangle armory that served as the temporary R.F. command center. The existence of two patrol guards complicated things. They had expected them to respond to the incursion and internal uprising. Gift suspected they had reason to be where they were. Perhaps Yuri knew the general location of the secret hideout.

Taking an elbow to the gut followed by a firm knee-jerk to the groin, a distracted Vitaliy doubled over and turned red in the face. The Martian pushed Gift forward out into the corridor and called her fellow guards to assist. *So much for 'I will die before I allow this,'* Gift thought. Guilt came next for not being worried about the poor guy with the crushed testicles.

In a flash too quick for anyone to understand or react, Vitaliy busted out from the shaft fist first on an extended arm. The first guard went down in a half-second with a broken visor clinging to a cracked helmet. Next, the thick arm of the Russian wrapped around the second guard's throat to put the guy into a deep sleep.

The woman holding Gift's arms from behind seemed to have no clue what to do without a weapon. She blankly watched the other two guards go down until a fist met her face, laying her out on the floor, slipped back into an unconscious state.

"What... How? I thought she took you out of play."

"No. I saw no other way to pass the guards."

"You let her escape and take me?"

"Da. To get all three in one place."

"You were *amazing*. Oh, but she really got you good in there," Gift said, pointing to the maintenance shaft. "How are... I mean, how are... your little soldiers?"

"I have been hit in testicles many times."

"O... *kay*." Not being able to empathize with a man being brutalized in his manly parts, Gift couldn't imagine having it done many times made it any less painful. This was one tough Russian bodyguard. Nadezhda had chosen well.

"We go to Miss Anoykina and see how good was your work."

35

Unable or unwilling to imagine the girl's horror, Gift needed to find Oksana. Forceful words came from fear, anxiety, and desperation. "Why aren't you doing something? We've gotta get her. She can't be with Yuri. You need to let me go save her."

"You do not think I wish this? We must not move until operation is finished. So many places for Yuri to hide, and too many guards making movings."

"Sorry. I know you want to get her too. It's just... how long before we can go look for her? Me and Vitaliy can go find her. You stay and run your war from here."

"Watch with me, dear. Let us to check how is going this war."

Pointing to the two tablets left of her view, Oksana's mother invited Gift to see what she was watching. Eight vid windows on each screen, each flipping through images every few seconds like cards being dealt from a deck. Faces flashed by in yellow or red circles, scrolling Russian text beside them too tiny and changing too fast even if Gift could read the strange alphabet.

"Facial recognition... running simultaneously on sixteen screens?"

"We see sixteen in one time. Many cameras check faces we do not see, searching for Oksana or Yuri. You see, *I am trying* to find my daughter. Is better than running through large colony for needle in stack of hay, as you say."

"Maybe... I shoulda asked. Sorry, I just can't think straight. And the other two?"

"Two what?"

"Your other two tablets. What are they doing?"

"Take your lookings. All domes and passages are open. Your job is well done. Well done. No way for them to seal and stop us attacking."

"I missed one. I think it was Two-three, into Dome Three."

"Nothing. Look to here." Nadezhda pointed to one of the monitors. A bullet-like exit wound had ripped through flesh made of steel. The Zil could have driven through the yawning hole. "Once we know this one is missed, we blow hole. My men advance from Six and Pioneers moving from Dome One. Soon they push U.R.M. forces into corner and we have them."

"Where are *we?* Which passageway?"

"Out from door is passage Five-six."

Desperate to act, Gift had no doubt the theoretical bindings would become physical if she tried to go find Oksana. And from recent experience, she knew not even a solid knee to the nuts was going to get her past Miss Anoykina's stone wall of a bodyguard.

"So, they've passed us. We can go."

"I must command my men from here."

"Vitaliy and I will go. And if you see anything, if your face-scans find her, you can tell us. We have two-ways?"

When the tree-trunk of a man stepped between Gift and the door, she assumed it the physical part of keeping her from running into an abyss of unknown chaos. She had never been so thrilled to be wrong.

The big guy said, "I agree with her. You are safe here, Miss Anoykina. I can take Miss Gift to find your daughter. I fear what Yuri will do when this ends."

"He'll kill her. Or…, or worse." Gift had to tread lightly not to betray Oksana's trust.

"Go. Make my Oksana safe."

The corridor outside the secret or ancillary command center greeted the pair with the eerie calm of a normal day. The only sound came from Gift's stomach. In the chaos, they skipped the morning meal, going from their middle-of-the-night rescue straight into battle. *There must be some famous saying about not going to war on an empty stomach*, Gift had to assume.

"Any idea which way? Places Yuri might hide?"

If Gift found trailing Tom in a flat-out run difficult, with Vitaliy, it was exponentially harder. Strong as the Zil and fast as a flyer, Gift moved like a turtle trying to keep up with him. Those odd creatures were better at hiding their heads than they ever were at running. Anxiety spiked when the near-superhuman Russian disappeared around a corner. They were well behind the advancing troops, but that fact lacked the power to overcome the trepidation of getting shot to death. A tight grasp latching onto her arm startled her.

"This way. Yuri keeps a habitat here."

Vitaliy practically dragged Gift into the housing block and down a corridor. It could have been a habitat block in New Europa, identical down to its beige concrete floor, pale-yellow walls, and endless rows of habitat Boxes. Only the occasional illegible sign showing non-alphabetic letters or symbols or whatever they were gave up the colony they ran through. Yuri's Box was empty and filled with the stench of an exterior cultivator's sweaty body odor at the end of an extensive work shift—an offense her nostrils had often endured with her little Matteo.

"Not here." Vitaliy stated the obvious. Gift understood the need for words to make a situation real.

"Why would he even have a Box? He lives in luxury at his mother's flat. That place is like a palace, with fantastic cooks, house cleaners, showers."

"Best not to ask such things. Let us go."

"I see."

The search guided them through domes Five, Six, and One. A secluded storage building in Dome Five had been a favorite spot of Yuri's. Vitaliy explained how he held secret meetings there when he thought not to hold them at home with his sister listening from the next room. Three more possible hiding locations found nothing, no sign the siblings had been there. A pause for Gift to rest gave the bodyguard a moment to check in with Nadezhda to inquire about the camera monitoring and facial recognition software. Neither it nor the President's eagle-sharp eyes had spotted her.

"*Idiot.*" Vitaliy turned a harsh eye in Gift's direction. "No, I mean me. *I'm* an idiot." The heat was gone, but the man's face said he needed further clarification. "Does Yuri know about your secret tunnels and maintenance shafts? Any way to get around and not be on camera?"

"Of course. He worked with our Rosgvardiya."

"And he knows about the escape routes from their home, of course—used them to take her. *Idiot.*"

"Why this word again?"

"Just takes me too long to figure things out, is all. I'm turned around and lost. Take me to the Anoykina home."

Racing again, this time at Gift's speed as she pleaded with the man-shaped machine to slow down, they arrived at the door. His biometrics opened it, which she thought peculiar. As paranoid and controlling as Nadezhda Anoykina was, Gift wouldn't have expected her to allow anyone access to her home. Or perhaps it was *because* of the paranoia.

Stepping into Yuri's room creeped Gift, but not in the way she expected. Disgust overtook her as if Yuri again slobbered over her mouth. Gift slept on the sofa because there was no guest room. She and Aimée had spent their nights in the Anoykina home in Yuri's bedroom. The shiver that crawled up Gift's flesh and shook her shoulders brought a more intense reaction than anything the ice-water pond under the waterfall had done to her body.

"Miss Gift, why would they be here?"

"Because even he knows no one would search here. I did something similar myself, my first time here, actually."

"They *were* here. Look to the cracked mirror, the tilted picture on wall, the lamp on the floor. There was struggle. No struggle in rescue earlier. Yuri took Oksana from *her* bedroom, not his. Da, they were here, not long from now."

"Oh mamma." Gift imagined the worst possibilities if that walking sack of rubbish took his sister back to this place. "Where's his escape tunnel?"

As they crawled through the dim, cramped ductwork passage, Gift couldn't picture Oksana cooperating. She must have put up a fight with the scrawny inhuman thing keeping her captive every step of the way. Did he hold some power over her, the way Fred's eyes always froze Gift, trapping her under his spell? Not like that, Fred just intimidated her, but she never needed to consider how far his dominance might reach. Moving farther through the darkness, Gift heard sounds, muffled and distant. A thud echoed as when Gift's knee fell too harshly onto the metal floor, only louder.

"Oksana."

The speed of Gift's crawl increased, fueled by hope and desperation. Still muffled, the recognizable mumbling of a gagged mouth tried to call out for help, shattering the darkness. A frenzied hysteria moved Gift's hands and knees with Vitaliy's head pushing her bum to go faster. Relentless hope floated in the air's thickness. They'd save her, capture Yuri, and this would soon be over. The crash of hope taking on weight and hitting the ground came after successive thuds. Louder, closer, but equally muffled and distant.

"*No.*" The Russian behind her explained, "They are in other shaft. Exited through Oksana's room."

"No. No," Gift yelled, banging the side wall's thin metal with her fist until it bruised the lump of flesh under her pinky. "*Idiot.* That's the way he got her out the first time. Where's it go?"

"He will exit in maintenance corridor. We will exit in storage room by main farm."

"Gotta move. Come on." Like some malformed insect, Gift moved gracelessly with limbs pulling and pushing her to the end of the shaft into the storage room. As Vitaliy emerged, she asked in a voice drenched in panic, "Which way?"

Pumped full of adrenaline, Gift ran at what must have been the fastest speed her legs had ever accomplished—she thought she could have outpaced Tom. They entered a maintenance corridor where Yuri and Oksana had to be. They weren't there. Without words, the bodyguard yanked Gift by the arm and pulled her along for several hurried meters. When they stepped out of the narrow, dim passage, they stood in a maintenance bay, its wide door open to the landing pad where they helplessly watched two heavy transports lifting off the ground.

"*No.*"

36

"The Russian soul is a dark place." Russian author Dostoevsky supposedly said that, but Gift never understood it. When her literature tutor, Miss Van Burke, said it in her introduction to Crime and Punishment, perhaps the author's most famous novel, the image of Russian people it presented to young Gift was bleak and unwelcoming. Perhaps this sparked a mental battle she'd fought since meeting the people of the R.F. and working with several of them. Could it be why she had, at times, been so distrusting?

When her Sojourner blipped, she rushed to blame them for spying and sabotage. Questioned them regarding their troubles with the Pioneers, accused them of withholding medical information, and made a rash judgment against them for siding with the U.R.M. in this conflict. Could that man's quote have been so profound, influential enough to stay with her, shaping Gift's thoughts and feelings into something she despised? Was it fuel for bias?

Oksana is Russian. Love for her kid sister, family in the most meaningful sense of the word, spoke strongly in argument against Gift's prejudice and brought her mind down. And she had many friends in the R.F. she trusted implicitly. Friends such as Sergey and Vitaliy, in whose hands she placed her life on several occasions. More than once she stood up for them in defense of accusations from Chan and Xiang.

The rage buildup surging in her veins wasn't biased, not dredged up from a murky sludge of misplaced pride. No negativity brewed within her for the people of the Russian Federation. *It's one man, who inconsequentially happens to be Russian. He's nothing more than vile scum inside the skin of something posing as a human.* To an even greater degree than with Claudia, the anger belonged here.

Oksana has a lovely soul. Bright, gentle, and true. Dostoevsky must have been wrong. Or, conceivably, Gift misunderstood his words. There was ample room for that possibility. The name of the guy from the story must have been somewhere in her archive. Gift could almost see the letters in her mind taunting her, staying just off the mental eye's periphery. He had been a vile criminal, a remorseless murderer without regret. Yet the guilt came, a little late and only after being prodded. Did he repent at the end of the story? 'That's debatable,' Miss Van Burke had said, presenting valid arguments for and against.

If Yuri had a conscience, he buried it much deeper. If it existed, it didn't want to show itself. Or maybe it had died, or never sprouted. His own mother and sister condemned the creep in word and via tribunal. *No, his soul must be a dark place indeed.* And he had Oksana.

"We gotta go after them."

"We cannot. No other transports here."

Heated to the boiling point, Gift's mouth raced ahead of her brain to verbally rip the massive bodyguard in two. Thankfully, it stopped itself to consider his word *'here.'* Cloudy from waking in a post-drugged stupor, Gift knew she arrived in a small flyer. The two that took off were heavies.

"The small flyer, it's here. Where is it?" Desperation dripped from her words and spattered drops of saliva onto the muscular chest at Gift's eye-level. At least she hadn't spat in the guy's face.

"If is still here... behind Dome One."

Caught in a vise grip mid-turn, Gift couldn't move when Vitaliy's hand clamped onto her arm. Her look could have melted his face. "We gotta go. We need to get Oksana."

"Status of colony is unknown. I must contact Miss Anoykina. And, sorry Miss Gift, we do not have way to track transports. We cannot follow."

As much as she resisted, fought, squirmed, and pulled, there was no escaping his grasp. No escape from his logic either, which her brain used in a desperate battle against the more powerful emotional forces running amok. Sand stirred by a wave settled when the water retreated to reclaim its place in the ocean. *Breathe, let this settle.* Emotions calmed, the mind regained control.

Not even a hint of resistance encountered them along the corridor leading to the secret command center and armory. The halls teemed with Russians wearing smiles and hurrying off as if they had something important to do.

"They're rushin'," Gift said with a smile.

"Da. We are all Russian."

"I mean, the Russians are rush-*ing*. You know, rushin'."

While Vitaliy didn't get it, or perhaps didn't appreciate the attempt at humor, it served as a distraction against foreboding dread for Oksana and what Yuri might do to that poor girl. Gift had no spark left in her soul and the defeat of letting him take her, of losing her, became a devastating weight. Now she had to tell Oksana's mother.

When Nadezhda was not in the hidden room, a sense of relief swept over Gift like warm shower foam. It meant victory. Relief, as glorious as it came, got cut short when Gift recalled the U.R.M. still had ships in orbit and she only assumed, by secret messages from her dear friend in outer space, they lacked the manpower and weapons to destroy the colonies. She briefly wondered what odds Mike's stupid gambling app might put on it.

As a queen perched on her throne, Nadezhda Anoykina sat in her office like it was just another day. Hopeful eyes dimmed. Under laser-intense irises and a lowered brow, inflated bags of anxious exhaustion below her eyes distorted the countenance of her entire face. They dared enter her presence without her daughter. Not Gift's mom, all her tutors combined, not even her interrogators—and she had had many—assaulted Gift's ears as this.

But it wasn't the President of The Russian Federation yelling and screaming. It was Oksana's mother. She was only that, at a moment that demanded the role. It didn't break Gift's heart. The flyers lifting off had done that, leaving little left to trample. Nadezhda's pain found what remained and stomped it into a lump of mush. Gift slumped. "It's my fault. By time I figured Yuri's play, it was too late."

Breaking the fiery stare locked onto Gift's eyes, Vitaliy stole Nadezhda's focus. "No. Is no one's fault. Miss Gift searched, ran, fought, and did her best to find your daughter."

Rising to her feet, Miss Anoykina hunched forward, curled her fingers into fists, and rolled them onto her desk to support herself with slightly bent elbows. The primate posture was every bit as full of intimidation as intended. She disgorged her words in Russian, and Gift felt their heat as they passed her and drilled into the bodyguard's soul. No translation needed. She must have beaten him senseless with blame. Gift could see the guilt and shame casting a shadow over his entire being, taking the failure solely upon himself.

Waiting for a break to cut in, Gift took advantage of a lull when the raging woman needed to catch her breath. "Where could they have gone? We've got a flyer; we'll go get her."

"If I had idea, would we be *still talking?*"

The yelled question was clearly rhetorical, but Gift needed words to calm the room and move toward a plan. If any amount of screaming would get Oksana back, Gift would have lost her voice to the effort.

"Let's think it through. You have the same perimeter and airspace monitors we do. If they were active when the heavy transports left, we should at least have a general direction. We can start with that."

A deliberate flicked hand gesturing toward the door came as the only answer the still enraged and red-faced woman would offer. Something about hell's fury and a scorned woman popped onto Gift's mental display. It prompted her to leave the office unscathed—beyond some damage to her eardrums, that is. The hefty bodyguard followed, and Gift wondered how that quote went in Russian.

In the Ops center, Gift and Vitaliy checked the sensor data and pored over the logs. Then he remembered the cameras and replayed video from the landing pad that caught the takeoff of those transports. It confirmed their fear as they watched Oksana being dragged into one with Yuri and many guards. Between Russians on Yuri's side and their U.R.M. associates, they were a small army. Well-armed and in full battle armor, Gift reckoned they stood a good chance of taking a colony. "But which one?"

"Sorry. Which one what?" The Russian giant appeared visibly confused and Gift realized her thought escaped as words, as they often did.

"Which colony do you think they'll try to take back?"

"I do not know this. We assume they still have China. Africa would be easiest, but this is no sense. No advantage. To come back here would be foolish."

"But Yuri's an idiot, so..."

"He is not in charge. I think your colony, if any."

"Oh mamma. Too bad Yuri's not in charge."

"Can N.E. defend against them?"

"Well, we did overthrow them. And we've got pretty decent defenses, kept three heavy flyers full of Chinese soldiers from taking New Europa."

"I heard report of this. Most impressive."

"No. Oh no. Those N.R.C. soldiers that attacked? They had no idea what defenses we had, so we caught them completely by surprise. I gotta think Yuri's guys and the Martians know exactly what we have. Martians occupied us, had control of everything there, for three months."

"Before to speculate, let us see which way did they go."

"*Crap*. Look." Gift pointed to a spot center-right on her display. "East. They turned East as soon as they got in the air. Nothing's that way. Why'd they go East? You think to land and regroup?"

"This is possible, but I do not believe so. Martians are smart. To start in direction of nothing... they could turn to go anywhere."

"Are you saying they went that way to trick the sensors, then turned to go the way they really wanted once out of range?"

"Da. Is excellent strategy."

"So where do *we* go? If you don't think they'll come back here, I mean. I think, do you, I mean... we should go to New Europa then?"

"Agree. I will inform Miss Anoykina."

"Good, we need to move fast. I'll send a warning to N.E. as well, so they can prepare... Oh, wait. Do you... 'cause I can't. Can you pilot the flyer?"

***

The flight from the R.F. to N.E. took longer than any journey ever had in all of history. Gift passed the time looking down for any signs of that *mal'd* bunker. A landmark, anything familiar. Perhaps her optimistic view of her chances of being able to find it in a flyer were slightly over-inflated.

Everything looked the same from above. In this moment, she needed to find Oksana, not the missile complex.

"You wish to learn to fly?"

"*Huh?*"

"Is easy. Come, you take seat and I show you."

Learning to fly, to pilot the air transport, invigorated her. With almost two hours to go when the lesson began, Gift soaked in all Vitaliy taught her, making slight maneuvers and plotting a course in the navigator.

The sweat glands amply responded to the suggestion that Gift land them outside N.E. Flying was one thing, much easier than she imagined. Landing the thing proved something else entirely. While it wasn't the smoothest touchdown in aviation history, Gift had to allow a trace of pride to consider she'd had worse landings with experienced pilots.

Prior to contacting N.E. operations to tell them she was on approach, Gift saw herself running full speed, straight to the Admin building to find Tom. She hadn't even seen him in the brief time she spent there helping to liberate her colony. Three months had passed over the couple with nothing but a single chat app conversation of typed text between them. The one that ended with an exchanged 'I love you.'

Failure never felt so wonderful. Gift happily conceded she'd not execute her plan of racing to meet Tom, falling into his arms to vocalize the words she previously had only typed. Through the lighted crack in the opening hatch, she saw him. His body anxiously swaying side to side, her palms clammy. The eagerness radiating off his face melted her heart and affirmed the meaning in the emotional chaos she'd bounced between the figurative organ and her mind for longer than she had realized.

His firm embrace was the warmest and deepest she had ever experienced. Being in his arms felt like home. It was passion, and it felt right. In unison they said, "I love you."

37 | WEEK FIFTEEN

Endlessness couldn't be considered a measurement of time. For Gift, it came as a sensation when a moment consumed her and stopped the passage of time just for her to stay in it forever. Gazing at the stars on her stolen glimpse of the night sky may have been when she first noticed the phenomenon's glorious existence. Many experiences since had stretched 'endlessness' beyond its infinite border. Wonders of nature gifted her by Mother Earth elevated minutes and hours into something more, something endless.

They squeezed each other tightly, never letting go.

Gift had been in Tom's arms forever as an explosion of romantic heat surrounded them like a third set of massive arms joining the embrace. It was their first genuine hug, yet she had always been there and always would be in his arms. The feeling of endlessness surged through her every fiber, wrapping her in a warmth previously unknown and joyously welcomed. Questions were no longer needed; their answers were clearer than ever. Gift had a deep love for Tom, a bond unlike any she had experienced, and she absorbed his equally fiery passion pushing through his loving arms, infusing her.

In a brief eruption of melancholy, Gift pondered if her mother had ever felt it. She had never talked about the captivation of love or the passion of romance. Gift had always considered herself the center of her mom's life, the source of her joy and the focal recipient of the woman's boundless love. For the first time, she considered herself selfish for it.

Sara found them at the landing pad with the Russian Bodyguard and led the three into the admin building, into Gift and Raff's office. Red sat at Gift's desk, her green eyes aglow with the data stream's reflection like sparkles of starlight. A most unusual blend of sensations filled Gift when her stare met Claudia, pompously seated at Raff's desk. Emotions, thoughts, ideas, and memories, mashed together into a pulpy mush she had no mechanism to understand or control. It brought chaos, that dull pain in the back of her head, overtaking all thought and action. At least, she blamed that for what happened.

Having found herself unexpectedly in an embrace by the saboteur, the terrorist responsible for the insurrection and for Charlie, the body reacted. Gift couldn't recall balling her hand into a fist. Her knuckles hurt and two fingernails broke the skin of the fleshy part of her palm. The pain called a flashback to the wilderness outside U.A. Twice she had punched the face of the wild woman who shot her in the leg. No pop or crack came off Claudia's face. Gift hadn't broken the vile creature's nose. Peering around Tom's head—his instincts stepped him between Gift and the villainous woman—Gift saw Claudia palming her eye and rocking.

"Sorry... I don't... Sorry." She wasn't sorry.

"I get it. It's okay... Well, no... but, I get it."

Red said, "She's helping us now. Been invaluable."

"Melody, why don't you and I give Gift a full status update," Sara suggested to Red. Gift was unsure if she was Melody now that the occupation had ended, or if she was Red because they still had liberation work to do.

New Europa was free. The few U.R.M. guards—actual U.R.M. from Mars—were locked up or had fled on a small air transport. Sara offered a tactical update. The colonists who were conscripted or had enlisted into the service of the Martian guard would stand trial for their actions. They had learned many saw no choice. Two had ratted out their first takeover plan but hadn't given up the players involved. Feeling helpless, they said they struggled to find a balance to appear cooperative while not being traitors. Tribunals would determine their fates.

Given Gift's non-at-all-hidden contempt for Raff's prior bench-mate, Red handled the technical status report. She and Claudia—Red humbly acknowledged she'd not have been able to do it without her—had regained full control of the systems and locked the data stream to external access. They had been able to fully trace all U.R.M. activity on their systems, and verified their heightened interest in Gift's medical records.

Claudia interjected she had confirmed the transfer of Gift's entire medical history and all of Sakura's research to Martian data storage devices. Sara reported that all perimeter defenses were back online and under their control. Because she's Gift, she made Sara go through the three systems one by one, verifying functionality, and had Red access and recheck the controls for each. Tom questioned Gift's cautiousness, wondering if she suspected the U.R.M. to return.

"No idea, but yeah. We gotta be ready. And they know our defenses. The ones that ran away from the R.F. were in two heavy transports full of soldiers. We lost Yuri, and he has Oksana. If they don't come here, Tom, we *gotta* go find her."

"Any idea where?" he asked calmly.

Gift's head dropped. "No... What about the N.R.C? Are they still occupied?"

Red Replied, "Xiang tried to contact her coder. No reply. We must assume they are still under Martian control."

"Crap." All eyes fell on Gift. "I bet Yuri took her there. And the rest of the Martians too. They'll regroup and make a move, and we gotta assume they still haven't found the bunker. That leaves me. *Here.* We startled them, but they'll be back in greater numbers, with all they have."

"We'll be ready for them," Sara confidently declared.

Pointing to the ceiling, Tom asked, "Are we sure they don't have weapons up there? We need to prepare our defense, and that's a game-changer. If we only need to defend on the ground, we can hold them off."

"I need to check Aimée's broadcasts, but I think so. Oksana confirmed they were out of weapons from their first warning attack. They dropped space junk on us, even an escape pod. To me, they threw everything they had. I trust Aimée. They don't have weapons up there."

"We need to be sure. How many ships do they have in orbit? Could be more arrived since first contact." Tom was quite logical in Tom the Guard mode.

"Where's Ticker?"

Puzzled, Tom considered Gift. "Commander *Tucker* needs to be briefed and will lead the defensive planning."

"Good. Then Sara, would you go to him and do that? Tom, I need you—I mean... for the ships and weapons. I need you to review the broadcasts with me. Red, you and her—" she couldn't speak the evil woman's name "—run full diagnostics on all our systems, priority to the defenses. Make sure nothing got missed."

"Miss Gift, what can I do to help?"

Prior to the offer, Vitaliy's existence had been wiped from Gift's mental display. She sent him with Sara to assist Tucker in defensive planning. Given what Gift had seen of him in action, she knew he'd be useful.

After a brief visit to Gift's mom that wasn't very brief, Gift took Tom to the secluded little patch of grass in Dome Three. Her childhood friends' meeting point could always calm her and offered the physical and mental seclusion she desperately needed. With tablet in hand, she sat on the grass beneath that sorry little tree with Tom sitting close, fingers interweaved, joined as one. Tom held the tablet as Gift swiped and controlled it. As much conversation occurred as searching the vids; she had so much to tell him.

Starting with Chan—he had previously only gotten the overall story—Gift summarized each of her captivities, all the interrogations, isolation, and eventual rescue. Fire-red heat burned constant in his brow, being most intensified when Tom learned of Chan's attempted assault. At one point, Gift swore she saw steam rising from his head. Tom's eyes carried a fierce strength enough to have snapped the Chinese Commander's neck with a stare.

The stories continued up to the point of seeing Tom at the flyer. His eyes blinked hard and reopened with a look of amazement for all Gift had endured. A silent hug paid respects to Tina when Gift choked on the story. He offered such compassionate ears, fully involved in active listening and asking discrete questions for clarity but not interrupting her flow. She tried to reciprocate kindly, but Tom had far fewer experiences to share.

"I was worried sick." His soft words came out under glossy eyes. "I never lost faith in you. I just knew you were handling whatever crap they gave you. I know how strong you are... I never doubted that, not for a second."

"That's so sweet," she replied gently. "I was crazy worried for you too. I missed everyone, but... I just couldn't wait to see *you*. Can't believe I came here and didn't even see you."

"I was devastated. Searched the entire colony for you."

"*Really?*"

"Twice."

The tender peck on his cheek overflowed with loving appreciation. The conversation paused from time to time for the couple to watch the broadcasts. Aimée had written a message. Gift raised the tablet running the infrared app of Red's design—called IR Reveal—so Tom could see it.

> Love, only 1 ship here
> No others on way - yet
> No weapons, nothing left to drop

Another message showed on the back of her tablet in a short update vid from three days later.

> 5 people up here
> Few left on ground
> Careful. Love you

Tom relayed the new intel reports to Tucker. He and Gift breathed a little easier, knowing they only had to deal with the remaining forces on the ground. More messages came. Aimée must have curried favor—likely by flirtatious methods—or had been extremely clever in information gathering. She brilliantly used two tablets in one update to relay a longer message.

> URM crashed flyersNE vs NRC their doing
> Sabotage From insideWanted us think URM
> Wanted us fightingis only way 4 peace

The *failed* unity and cooperation of the colonies hadn't failed. The conflict had been manufactured by the United Republic of Mars so they could assert the need for peace and sell the idea they were the only means to obtain it. And some bought into it. There were U.R.M. supporters in each of the colonies, some willing to join forces and actively work against their fellow residents. All for a facade of some New World Order that would be just another dictatorial empire, bringing oppression in the guise of order and demanding subservience for a utopian peace put over the domination like a mask.

38

Hollowed and empty, peace and unity came wrapped in a pretty package of deception. More lies. Only, this would be a world empire built on them. No conspiracy theories would sprout two centuries later to question the foundations of society. Like those four wrought-iron feet standing the Eiffel Tower up to the sky, the footing supporting the promises of the United Republic of Earth was openly exposed. They brought a New World Order of oppression by conquest of—might over right.

Never admitting it openly, Gift had briefly considered going along with it. Deep down, in places of her soul she had believed to be pure, she found a desire for one world government to end the conflicts and stop the fighting. Could rulership by the U.R.M. bring order to the chaos, ending the endless cycle of violence and war? Or were those the musings of a spirit broken by abuse and ready to yield to torment, nothing more than the byproduct of duress?

Staring at the darkness, Gift lay in her bed for the first time in ages. Practically roommates, she had been spending her nights sleeping in Oksana's flat and indulging herself in her shower before they left for U.A. months ago. A remarkable tranquility settled over her on the foam bed cushion of her Box's familiarity. It wouldn't be much sleep—never enough. Her review of Aimée's messages and talking with Tom stretched the evening into what became the wee hours of the early morning. Set to rise at six, this would be little more than a nap.

Every minute awake robbed Gift of needed slumber, but her brain was on fire. General Xiang was correct. Submission by conquest wasn't the same as peace. Even the most benevolent of monarchies and so-called republics couldn't provide that for their people. The U.R.M. was far from benevolent. Their deceit and trickery cost lives, started a major conflict between colonies, led to Chan's occupation, and brought everything Gift had to endure. No, this needed to be resisted.

Gift had fought off the N.R.C. in United Africa and won. Wrestled against the U.R.M. occupation in China and lost. Raced through a frantic mission to save Oksana while the R.F. took back its colony but failed to free the girl. Failure was a dress that didn't fit right. The fabric twisted and pulled and brought an unscratchable itch worse than when her restraints kept her fingernail from her nose in that stunning woman's office.

When sheer exhaustion finally shut off the mind, Gift found herself a bride again, but not in her short paper-thin prison gown. An elegant dress overlain in ivy lace adorned her body. A walking goddess wrapped in silk. Tom waited for her approach in this happy Union ceremony, and the tear streaking her cheek in the dream dripped just as wet when she woke. While not typically believing in messages divined in dreams as her ancestors had, this one had something to say. Any future they would have, anyone would have, could not be under Martian occupation. That of all humans on the planet, Yuri Anoykina—who barely classified as human to Gift—was the one working with the U.R.M. solidified it, if it needed any further solidifying.

***

After Gift and Sara had been stunned twice testing the remote-operated projectile rifles mounted around the colony's perimeter, they assumed their bodies could take a bit more abuse. The impact of the sonic blasts was far more horrific. The near-vomit-inducing dizziness lasted longer, and left Gift's mind swirling in a pool of mud for over twenty minutes. They were ready to defend the colony with weapons functionality confirmed.

Next, a quick check-in with Mike, Karl, and Marco, to see how their project was coming along. They worked on a brilliant plan Mike proposed on the flight from Paris. Back then, Gift fully expected to be the engineer working beside him. Being kidnapped again stifled that idea. Mister Karl graciously followed Mike's lead, lending his expertise and decades of experience to the effort. Red was in and out for coding support. Progress looked good, and Gift called Sara to help them implement it sooner than possible.

More of a delay than losing track of time, Gift's lingering over the bench made her late for her afternoon coffee appointment. Not that she was too busy for the break—and she was—she had zero desire to sit and sip a coffee with *that* woman. Nonetheless, there Gift sat, sipping her fourth espresso of the day with two hands around the tiny cup to keep either from forming itself into a fist.

"Thank you for giving me a few minutes," Claudia said.

"Mm-hm."

"I wanted to say how sorry I am about Charlie. I know what he meant to you. He was such a great guy, eh?"

Not the right opener. Gift mumbled another "Mm-hm" while biting the inside of her cheek to keep her tongue in check, for now.

"Look, I admit I made mistakes. I was... over-zealous, maybe, about getting the truth out there. But I never meant for anyone to get hurt. And I didn't know how some who agreed with me, joined my cause, were going to act. They... *they* escalated it into violence. Sabotage, yes, that was my plan. The first farm fire and airlock were tests. I mean... if you hadn't stopped it... But the ancillary farm was always the plan. That was the airlock I knew I could open to expose the entire colony."

"People got hurt, though, and some died. Charlie di—" Gift gagged on her words. The lump in her throat left no room for them.

"I am *truly* sorry. And... I don't imagine for a second what I am doing now makes up for any of that. How could I ever? I fully expect to return to fulfill my prison sentence after this is over."

"Why are you telling me this?"

"I don't expect or deserve forgiveness, and I'm not asking for that. It's just, I thought, you fought so hard for this colony... and you've lost *so much* that, I don't know, I just needed to tell you... that I'm truly sorry."

"I see."

"Okay... I'll get back to work then, I guess." Claudia's countenance of semi-apologetic became the disappointed confusion of a child expecting a special present that never arrived. Gift had nothing but a blank stare to offer the woman. "Thanks for your time."

"Mm-hm."

Forgiveness was a lot to ask, but Claudia hadn't asked for it. Still, Gift had to think not asking for forgiveness when admitting you were wrong and saying *I'm sorry* was, in all practicality, seeking forgiveness. The unburdening of the conscience of its guilt would yield basically the same result. Gift wasn't ready to offer that, not yet. Though the idea of whether that made her somehow a bad person, or at least a lesser one than she cared to be, would plague her for some time. Alone at the table, Gift took the last of the cooled espresso from her cup as a drop of bitterness on her tongue. She thought it a fitting analogy for the conversation she just had.

What remained of the afternoon was for Tom, although not in the way she desired. She would have wished to extend their previous evening together into a lifetime. If only she could. No, this was work. As a guard, he had been two meters to her back for several days while she worked at her bench. This greatly improved upon that as they would be working together. Among all the chaotic fear and anxiety over the what ifs, there was a comforting niceness in that.

"I gotta admit, this was a great idea," she said in a flattering tone.

"Not even my idea. Just copying."

"True. But copying the R.F. defensive strategy *was* your idea," Gift replied with a wide smile.

"I hope Yuri and his guys don't guess our play. Could ruin the strategy and make this all for nothing."

"Nope," she replied confidently. "First, Yuri's an idiot. I mean, he's got no strategy or brain for this sort of thing. I'm quite sure the Martians will be leading the invasion."

"And second?"

"*Huh?*"

"You said first... so I assume there's a second reason."

Gift smirked. "*Second*, we've improved upon the strategy."

"How so?"

"Watch and learn, my cute man. Watch and learn."

The watching and learning took Tom on a tour around the entire interior of the colony assisting Gift. The hours passed over them as if time knew they were in love and ceased to tick its clock for the enamored couple. Tom turned out to be a decent engineer's assistant, though Gift only needed him to hand her things and carry the toolkit. Still, she smiled at the idea of him being very good at it. Effortlessly, they found a naturalness in how they worked together and conversed the entire time. It dawned on Gift what they shared reached beyond the work to themselves, their souls, their lives. Perhaps that's what made two people one.

It wasn't the complaining of her stomach that told Gift it was well into dinner time. She'd been ignoring that, and Tom never complained or requested a pause. Still working on their project, Gift and Tom observed people going to food stands for dinner or heading home with packages from the little grocers to prepare simple meals. Everything about the scene looked so normal, it disconcerted her and felt oddly comforting at the same time.

Tom eyed the crowd. "How can they just carry on like nothing's happening? Like nothing's *about* to happen?"

"You know, I remember something you said to me. Not said *to me*, but yeah, I guess, it was in a vid message. You said it was cute how I worry."

"It is." His smile stretched lips desperately reaching for his ears. Gift blushed in response.

"But you also said to me—in person, I mean, not over vidChat—that you loved my optimism."

"Really? I mean, I do. Always have. But wow, you've got an amazing memory."

"Yeah. Sometimes it's great. But there's things I wish I could forget, you know?" His somber nod said he did. "But anyway... what I mean is, I think these folks *are* worried. Have to be. Also too, I'm not the only one who prefers to be optimistic. I mean, we all do, to some degree. I suppose they want life to seem normal for now... before it isn't. This way they can hope it will be again."

Tom looked into her eyes with such beaming wonder. "Yeah, you may be right. I think that's what this is, in a way, too." He moved his hand back and forth between them. "Having this, with you... and last night? To talk, really talk, like you and I were the only ones in the world, were the entire universe. I have hope that after this is all over, we'll always have this together."

When she pressed her lips to his, a warmth filled her entire being and melted the anxiety she'd been carrying. She saw it in him too, the softening of his stiffened broad shoulders that came with the pleasant surprise on his lips.

"Let's grab some tacos. I think we're done here."

Halfway through their rushed dinner came the dread they expected but still had hoped not to hear. The klaxon sounding the alert of incoming flyers.

39

As many times as Gift heard similar calls to action and felt their fear overtake her mentally, physically, and emotionally, and as much as she expected it, she wasn't prepared. Not that she hadn't prepared. Since returning from the Russian Federation, Gift devoted every waking moment to that goal. Would it be enough? She had to hope.

Together with Tom, who paced himself with her, Gift ran to the Residential Maintenance building in Dome Two to meet Marco. Red and Claudia were already there in the little makeshift Ops center they had created with Mike in a workshop space Marco cleared for it. Part of their strategic planning, they'd coordinate and run the defensive action from a secured and unknown location. All that awaited the intruders in the Ops Center in the Admin building were carefully laid traps. Gift brimmed with pride at Mike for his brilliant idea.

Anticipation crowded the space that looked huge when they started. Filled with displays and holographic screens, it was a command center above and beyond Nadezhda's secret room. Hers was a glorified observation station in an armory, while what Mike built here was a Strategic Operation Center, which he insisted on calling the SOC. At least, yielding to Gift's protest, he said the letters rather than his original pronunciation of it as a word. Images of feet with only one sock distracted Gift. At once, all display screens came alive with laser diodes pushing light to form images sent from the exterior and interior cameras.

"And the drones?" Gift asked anyone.

Red shoved a tablet at Tom, which he grabbed. His hand starting swiping over it before she let it go. "Got'em. Sending to the holo-screens."

The wall-filling holographic displays became windows to the sky, looking out into the openness between the treetops and the stars. They were dots when Tom spotted them. Gift couldn't make them out from the night's sickeningly dark backdrop.

"Five," he excitedly exclaimed. "All heavies."

"N.R.C. heavies held three dozen in each," Gift offered from a voice drenched in the words' fright.

Mike asked, "Do we think they have that many left?"

"Aimée says no," Gift answered.

General Xiang's abrupt entrance pulled the four walls inward, lessening the freedom of the already crowded space. Gift felt relieved to see her again. While it brought an intriguing oddity to ponder, that consideration wasn't for this moment. Xiang would lead the troops from here with Tucker on the ground, ready for phases two and three. Even she, with all her military training and strategizing experience, had generously shared high praise for what New Europa had done to prepare for this.

As if she'd been there the entire time, General Xiang joined the conversation. "We do not know how many they have from R.F. or N.R.C. Expect them all to be full. Fifteen dozen troops. Get ready for phase one." She appeared, dropped the statement, and gave the order with no greetings. It was go time and Xiang came in already going.

"Ready," both Mike and Gift said in unison.

Unsure she really was, Gift had to play the part. When the pressure mounted, she hoped to be up to it. In her mind, she lay belly on the ground, pointing her stun rifle at purple shadows emerging from the trees. She didn't fire on the approaching Pioneer refugees but thought she could—if they had been the marauders they believed them to be. That same blend of trepidation and confidence were present now as they were then. In both instances, Gift wasn't certain which would dominate. Could she pull the trigger?

But she had taken a life. *Why now? Not now, stupid brain.* She tried to get the image out, focus on her role in phase one and be ready. Chan's round face haunted her like a ghost from a horrible memory. When Gift heard Mike shout her name, she realized he had repeated it.

"Yeah, Mike, I said I'm ready."

"I said two minutes out. Now one-thirty."

The general said, "Tom, stay on them with the drones. You are Mike and Gift's eyes. Mike, Gift, take aim. We will be in range of their sharpshooters before they are within our weapons reach. You must fire as soon as possible."

Sparks of light started popping off the air transports almost on top of them, with muzzle flashes of sharpshooters leaning out of open emergency hatches. Yuri and the U.R.M. knew of the exterior mounted projectile stun rifles, and Xiang had correctly concluded they'd try to take those out from the air. Again, Gift was dazzled by the woman's skill—a skill they desperately needed as much as Gift wished they didn't.

As the five flyers hovered, nearing Domes One through Five, they assaulted the mounted stun rifle defenses. In unison, as a machine-turned gear rotating with precision, tooth by tooth, they shifted toward Domes Three through One. They had the range Xiang said they would, taking out many of the stunners before coming close enough for Gift and Mike's little surprise.

A thunderous roar from air transport turbines pounded the dome with a barrage of forced air like a wave breaking on Gift's chest, stepping her deeper into the oceanic abyss, farther into the unknown. Mike and Gift were ready on their terminals with the commands keyed and fingers hovering over the Return key. On Xiang's order, each pressed down. Watching screens in the remote Ops center Xiang called *N.E. Actual*, the muzzle flashes ceased their relentless blinking, the invaders no longer shooting at them. They saw what they had hoped to see. The air transports wobbled with reduced mobility, one in an uncontrolled spin just meters off the ground.

Skilled pilots managed to land four of them just outside Dome One, with the last spun off course toward Colony Lake. One drone followed it to see it laying on its side with a helpful tree trunk obstructing its rear door and trapping the occupants with the emergency hatch in the dirt below it. That reduced the enemy's theoretical number by three dozen. A stroke of luck brought on by the sonic disruptor array helped to even the odds a bit. The success of phase one rushed into the Ops center with triumphant cheer. But it was far from over.

Claudia and Red—Gift buried the name Melody as this was time for Red to be Red—were frantically banging on their keyboards, preparing for phase two. Gift and Mike busily entered the commands for phase three. Drone vid showed exactly what they expected. All troops marched to infiltrate Dome One and take the Admin building, to claim the seat of power from the colony. Those pawns chasing the queen had no idea they weren't in a chess match but in a game of musical chairs. The seat they eagerly pursued had been removed.

Tom and Marco ran out to take position for what would come next. Tucker had guards on tablets operating the surviving mounted rifles, with only two that could shoot projectiles between Dome One's access point and the landed transports. Expectation of fear was a new terror. Gift watched in silence as soldiers spilled out from the flyers. Hurried calculations—too dark, the camera too far away for a sure count—less than three dozen evacuated each. Good news that barely shook off a drop from the ocean's worth of dread drowning Gift.

The first few ineffective projectile shots failed to stall the soldiers' advance. Their self-contained electro-static modules had insufficient punch for sending their current through what Xiang said must have been rubberized vests. Before she could relay the news to Tucker, they saw one invader drop. Then another fell to the ground spastically. The remote operators must have adapted quickly to target areas not under the thick black skin. The holo-display went dark, then showed a faint-gray message. No Signal.

"Must have shot it down," Mike yelled. "Sending the other, those guys by the lake aren't going anywhere."

General Xiang gave the order, "Phase two, *now*."

Claudia and Red responded with rapid keyboard clicks.

"Anything? Did it work?" Gift demanded.

"We have no eyes," Mike said. "Okay... drone's back."

"You gotta be kidding me," Gift shouted in disbelief.

The second drone's vid found the foot soldiers still on foot, still advancing toward the dome entrance.

"How'd that *not* work?" Mike's frustration saturated the air. Phase two used his original sonic defense that helped stave off Chan's forces a few months back. Its boosted signal had activated, Red confirmed as much. But it had no effect on the Martian troops—with a high probability of Russian and Chinese mixed in with them.

"The Martians knew our defenses. Must have." As Gift had feared. "I don't know... could they have blocked their ears or something?"

"Exactly why we anticipated this, and are not relying on those defenses alone," the general replied. "Stay sharp. Be ready for phase three."

Gift doublechecked her eyes on the live vid feed. "*Wait*. They split up. The larger group is storming Dome One, but look. Two groups took off.

One went right, the other left. They'll enter through other domes. I guess Six and Two."

"Um... guys? We're in Two," Mike pointed out.

Raising both her arms, Xiang made a *calm down* pose. "We planned for this. I would not send my entire battalion through a single bottleneck entry point where they may get picked off. Attacking from three entry points is smart and was expected. It spreads our people thinner and gives them more of an advantage. Gift, Mike, be ready."

"Are they in for a surprise when they breach those hatches." Mike's words exuded prideful confidence.

When they lost the second drone's signal, they were blind. Soldier ants had marched into position and were ready to infest the colony, to attempt to assimilate New Europa into their New World Order. Claudia hurried to do some keyboard magic and threw vid coverage of the three ingress points onto the displays. What happened next would be precursor to phase three, so Mike and Gift stayed at the ready.

As if the colony had sprung three leaks simultaneously, a flood of black uniforms poured into domes One, Two, and Six in unison. Human eyes counted what the camera eyes pushed to them. About two dozen each in Six and Two. The rest poured into Dome One, about four dozen there. The slowing of their rushed advance, which each group did autonomously yet in sync, was undoubtedly brought about by confusion. They met no resistance, no force to hold them back, to defend the colony. *What must they be thinking now?*

A similar thought may have brought a rise to the corner of Xiang's lips. "Timing will be critical on this, so watch them closely."

The order wasn't needed. Mike and Gift gave the displays their undivided attention.

"Mike, you got Dome Six. I'm on Two."

"Copy."

"Are all housing blocks sealed?" Xiang asked.

"Yes, ma'am," Gift replied. "Residents in their Boxes and emergency bulkheads are closed."

All watched in silence as the confused ants in rubber body armor carefully considered their steps. One in each group had a hand to their shoulder and talked into it. As expected, the Dome One battalion marched steadily toward the Admin building. The others made their way towards the passageways that would connect them to Dome One to join their colleagues. Not a soul stirred in any of the domes besides the encroaching enemy forces. Once the groups reached the archway of their respective passageways, they increased their movements to a military jog.

"Ready... Be ready..." Xiang repeated. "Now."

Gift and Mike each took to their keyboards and sent the commands to seal the emergency bulkheads to Domes Six and Two. The soldiers in each spoke stopped to look at a metal wall where they had stepped through an archway a moment prior. They turned with increased speed toward Dome One, as expected, to see the bulkheads in front of them already closing.

One in passageway Six-one tried to make it up the rising wall, only to fall and clutch his knee in a show of intense pain to the camera. All those hours Gift and Tom spent preparing those bulkheads had paid off. Phase Three worked brilliantly. They trapped two groups of soldier ants in the passageways.

The rest was up to the guards. Tom was one of them.

40

Tucker and Xiang had worked out the details of what should happen next. All went according to plan. They had U.R.M. troops trapped in two passageways and N.E. guards were on the move.

"Fish in a barrel." Another of Mike's expressions. Gift suspected he enjoyed having her ask him for clarification, so she did.

"He means we have them trapped. They're caught like fish in a barrel." Red offered translation with authority, but without clarification of its meaning.

"Okay. But you don't catch fish in any barrel. Tom explained it to me once. You use a slimy little worm." Gift's face cringed at the visual. "It goes on the hook *alive*, poor thing. Then you attach the hook with the worm on it to a line and drop it into the water. The unsuspecting fish, victim, comes along for a free meal and—" she slammed her palms together for dramatic emphasis "—it's caught. Worm's dead. Fish is dead... It's just awful. But there's no barrel."

"There was this saying about shooting a bullet into a barrel full of fish," Mike explained. "The bullet will hit at least one. Can't miss."

"Shooting fish with guns. That may be even worse than fishing. Who would do such a thing?"

"It's not that people *did* it. It means when something is easy, it's *like* shooting fish in a barrel. Sure success."

"Why do so many of these dumb old idioms have to injure or kill some poor animal? And I suppose those soldiers are now sitting penguins? We can't forget that they're people. Human people."

After a chuckle he failed to retract, Mike said, "No one's forgetting that. And we're only taking these folks out of play, not killing, or even injuring them. And Gift... it's sitting *ducks*, not penguins."

"Whatever. Can we just see what's happening to those fish, penguins, ducks, whatever they are?"

"On it." When Claudia offered a few swipes across her display and hit her keyboard, the two holo-screens came back to life projecting each of the blocked passageways onto what was a bare wall a second prior. Both groups were huddled around the small hatch in their respective risen bulkheads. Sixty centimeters of solid metal between them and their target dome.

Gift knew those as well, and what it took for her to open one—Mike on one side, she and Tom on the other, and Raff sending code. "These clowns won't get through those hatches and out of those spokes."

A swarm of N.E. guards entered the frame, pressing in on the huddled team in passageway Six-one. With fifty to their rank, they were greater than two and a half times the Martian number. Hands rose over heads and knees took to the floor with no resistance. They made quick use of bounding the infiltrators with zip-ties and a small set of N.E. guards took a post watching over their captives. When Mike spelled the word *pow* letter by letter and made it plural, Gift couldn't guess his purpose beyond an odd way to emphasize the blow they'd dealt the Martians. A real *pow*.

Eyes shifting to view spoke One-two found black ants clustered at their hatch. They had at least managed to get the access panel off and pulled some boards and wires. They didn't stand a chance to open the steel barrier between themselves and their goal in Dome One. Anticipation for the swarm of N.E. uniforms to make quick work of subduing the enemy ended in despondency. Before any other human forms entered view, the soldier ant horde turned in unison and sparked violent bursts of fiery white light. The air in the SOC rattled as it filled with sharp pops, pop after pop after pop.

The bullets' destinations stayed off screen. It had to be the N.E. guards shifted from the other passageway. They arrived in a short time thanks to Marco guiding them through the maintenance tunnels. Tom was there, being shot at. As the relentless popping continued, Gift's ear caught the *theew* whistles ripping the air. The first ant fell. Many more pops and white flashes came, sporadic *theews* between them. Gift had to hope their guards had found cover while the Martians were in the open. Better armed, and shooting to kill, but they had nothing to hide behind, giving New Europa the vantage point. Or so Gift desperately tried to tell herself.

A bloodcurdling scream assaulted their ears. Someone was hit, not by a projectile stunner. Images of Tom's bloodied corpse filled Gift's mind, its eye unable to look away. She lost him already, he was dead. No more to have those moments of normality he said they'd have when this was over. *Theew*. *Theew*. Another Martian fell. Another. More flashes, more deafening pops stopped the *theews*. As if underwater, an amplified whisper of a prolonged and wobbly sound rang in Gift's ear canal. The last soldier ants standing fell with their comrades.

N.E. uniforms swarmed. With zip-ties drawn, they subdued and neutralized the second band of intruders. Eyes desperate to find Tom among the guards struggled to see greater detail than the black uniforms, indistinguishable one from the next. Gift couldn't tell if Tom scurried among them or lay with the fallen, a dead hero in the fight for liberation. There was so little comfort in him being remembered in such a way, it was none at all. Dead was dead. But she didn't know, and it was killing her.

"Can we get contact? *Anyone*." Gift shouted panicked desperation. Her plea was replied to with an *I have no idea* shrug from Red, who instantly started racing her fingers over her keyboard.

"Found a message," Red declared as a victory. "Sending to your display."

> Message from Thomas Mills

"*Play*," Gift shrieked.

"Gift, I'm okay. A few of ours wounded but none killed. We're moving onto the Dome One operation. Love you."

He was okay, for now, but this wasn't over. He was about to go up against a greater number—twice the force that fought back so fiercely they'd injured some, almost killed a few. *He'll be okay. He'll be okay*, Gift repeated on a loop in her mind. She came close to convincing herself of the truth in those words until she acquiesced to the uncertainty. No words had such protective power, such assurance. They were just words.

Dome One had been evacuated. Locked doors on the admin building were the only deterrent to the band of nearly four dozen trying to ingress and take the seat of command. Gift had earlier expressed her concerns that not finding the guards there protecting the building would seem wrong, signaling U.R.M. troops something was amiss. After hearing her out fully, General Xiang had said, 'They will consider we are fighting on three battlegrounds and dispersed. Placing a few guards on that building would be their death sentence, a meaningless sacrifice. The U.R.M. will be preoccupied with guarding against ambush.' She was right, again.

Claudia pushed the admin building's exterior camera feeds to the holo-screens. One view focused on the main entrance and one on the side door to the meeting room with the comfy sofa chairs. At each entry point, one of the ants knelt before the door with their fellow ants blocking a clear view of their actions. Xiang confidently declared they would use explosives to breach the entrance and Mike asked to confirm the building was empty. Gift appreciated the concern.

The plan was a good one. N.E. guards to reached the residential flats across from the Admin building. It had a lovely rooftop terrace. Marco kept them hidden most of the way. With a three-meter gap between the buildings, Gift had the idea to use greenhouse support posts to construct a bridge from the terrace to the admin building. A team had removed a glass panel in the Broadcast suite at the building's rear and stretched out the supports to fashion an overpass from the terrace to the vacant window.

"Can we check the bridge?" Gift asked.

"On it." Claudia tapped and swiped on her screen, and hit her keyboard with a few strokes. One of the smaller displays showed the empty overpass with no one yet on the terrace. More waiting tested everyone's patience. Half the guards were to enter the admin building via a crossing four stories up, the other half through the ground-level doors behind the ants.

Its boom was imagined, not falling on their ears as the cameras supplied views without audio. Too fast to be seen, the aftermath was large puffs of smoke and particles of debris around the entrances. Mike hurried himself out of the SOC to join thirty others as a contingency to surround the building. The U.R.M. uniforms disappeared from the holo-screens as they filed into the two gaping holes where doors used to be only seconds ago.

"There," Gift cried. "They've started across the bridge. What about the others?"

"Team two in position. I see them holding until Team One enters above," Claudia reported.

"I'm going to internal cameras." Red pushed camera images onto the displays.

The ants crawled through the building, searching the ground level, and moving to the next two floors. Tucker's team positioned itself on the level above the dismantled Ops Center. Tom led a team to take positions at each entrance. They'd enter on the signal the ground floor was clear. All expected close combat as the Russians knew the last defense—the knockout gas in the Admin building Ops Center—and wore filtration helmets.

With a handful of guards left on the ground level, and the troops moving toward the stairs to advance to the upper floors, Red sent the call to action to Tucker and Tom on their handheld devices. Tom's team then disappeared into the building. Gift thought she saw Sara in the mix, but it could have been anyone.

Red exclaimed in a deafening high pitch, "Guys... I got something."

41

Never show your cards. Raff had repeated that many times before finally giving up trying to teach Briscola to Gift. While Gift would say she gave up the game for the ugly Italian suits that troubled her card tracking skills, she knew she had tried Raff's patience to the limit. The lesson was sound, in card games and in war—perhaps more so in war. Don't let the enemy know what you have.

Masterful planning by General Xiang employed the same strategy, dividing the defense into three phases and those into stages. More than once she had said, 'They do not see what we have until we use it.' Adding, 'They do not know what we will do until we have done it.' It appeared the U.R.M. had their very own *General Xiang*, though not nearly as clever a *General Xiang* as the real deal. They held some trump cards back to play them at the right moment.

Red exclaimed in a deafening high pitch, "Guys... I got something."

"What? What now?" Gift shouted.

One holo-screen replied by showing five swiftly moving figures under the blanket of night. They came from one of the transports and raced past the Dome One entrance in the direction of Dome Two. Something looked off about their movement, it lacked the near-ant-like precision, the oneness of thought and action thus far seen in the enemy troops. Despite the camera's inability to add clarity to the approaching faces, Gift knew.

"They're only in five. Send some guards to get them. Red, switch the camera." It took time for Gift's mind to come down to a level where her sharp outburst from the moment's heat made her feel bad.

"There, the Dome Two entrance."

"Thanks Red... And, sorry."

"No worries. But guys? Don't forget the little war about to go down in the Admin building. By now they've reached the Ops Center and found it disabled and empty. Our guys are above and below them. A lot more stuff happening there to worry about than the five coming in here."

"Yeah, but we're in here." Claudia outwardly expressed the panicked anxiety everyone experienced within.

Red exclaimed, "There. Look. They're stepping through the entrance to Dome Two. They're here." When Claudia turned to see, Red barked, "Stay on the Admin building. I've got these."

"What do we do? What, *what* do we do? We gotta do something." Gift threw her pleas to the general, who responded with an open palm to Gift's cheek. The pop and sting brought her back to clarity. "Okay. Thanks... *Ouch*, but thanks."

As a reminder to all, Xiang said, "The focus is on the Admin building. Maintain eyes on that. Help where you can. We cannot use the gas as they are obviously wearing protective masks that got them past the entrance. This will be a close-combat engagement."

"Oh mamma. Red, get me a closer look. I'm afraid..." Gift stopped her words, not wanting to vocalize what she both feared and hoped in the same twisted knots in her stomach.

Red zoomed in. "The lead guy's waving a big handheld like—"

"They have us."

"*What?* General, what do you mean?" Claudia's dread fell from the words, crawled across the floor to Gift, and snaked up her legs like panic.

"We have emptied the domes and corridors. They are scanning for heat signatures, bodies. They will find our location shortly, if not already."

Gift said confidently, "We won't let them in here."

"They are here for a hostage exchange." The image on the holo-screen confirmed the general's hypothesis. Yuri lurked behind the three soldiers. One hand clenched Oksana's arm and the other pressed a handgun into her side.

"I have to go." Gift squirmed as Xiang restrained her. "Let me go!"

"They will have you, and Oksana does not go free. Not like this."

"I'll trade myself for her. Let me *go*."

"Listen." General Xiang commanded authority in her voice, transporting Gift back to that interrogation room, immensely intimidated by the woman's presence. "You running into their arms does not free that girl. Me joining you, and you doing exactly as I say does. It is the only way we get her back safely, the only way we keep her alive. Understood?"

"Yeah... So, can we go now?"

In reply came a single, slender raised finger. Addressing Red, Xiang directed, "Keep on them and let me know the moment they appear to have found us, or if they move toward this building." Red nodded and returned to her system. "Claudia, what is the situation in the Admin building?"

Claudia's eyes moved to the smaller displays. "They're in Ops and still wearing their gas masks. They're crazy upset. This one guy shot at the wall for a bit. Seems we really tricked them, eh?"

"And our people?" Xiang demanded.

"Right. Ready to descend on them. And the ones on the ground level have taken out the soldiers there. They're ready to advance upstairs and ambush."

The stoic general went pensive. "By now, they must be expecting this ambush. We let them reach their goal only to find it a dummy, a ploy. I hope your guards are up for this."

The displays darkened, as if the cameras in the Admin building had decided to look away in fear. When Gift inquired, Claudia reminded her she killed the lights as part of the ambush plan. All camera eyes were still open, looking, still sending digital signals being reconstructed as images on the displays. Those images were ghosted in darkness until sparks of violent light intensely burned as flickering stars and extinguished in an instant in the confined space.

"I don't hear anything. What's happening?"

"No mics in there," Claudia replied.

"Can we see? What's happening in there?"

"Gift, we can do nothing more for them. Claudia, watch for a signal from Tucker or Tom for the lights. Get them on *as soon* as they call for them. Red, where are—"

"Found us. I think. Looks like the guards tried to play it cool, faking like they're still scanning. Yuri's looking right at this building."

"He's a stupid idiot," Gift spat.

"So, we're letting them come here?" Claudia's fear had lessened—the concern differed this time, its focus shifted from herself. "If they find us here, take the SOC? They could turn this around. What do we do?"

"That is why Gift and I are leaving. *Now.*" Xiang grabbed Gift's arm and pulled her out of the office and down to the ground level. At the door, she looked Gift in the eye. "We must not let them into this building. And watch your words. We were hiding you in there, that is all." Gift's nod wasn't at all convincing and she felt it herself as clearly as it showed in Xiang's eyes. "You can do this, Gift. I know you can. You are one of the strongest people I have ever met."

After a more reassuring nod Gift only pretended better at offering, she said, "Ready."

"Just as we discussed. Deep breath in... Out... Go."

To push that door open—a hinged double door for the habitat maintenance repair shop—was the hardest thing Gift had to do, but the simplest choice she ever made. She was going to save Oksana from danger, from her hostage takers, from her contemptible brother. Whichever way this would end for Gift didn't matter if Oksana got to safety. Good thing for Gift, her confidence in General Xiang exceeded that in herself as the door swung open, stripping any sense of security from her bones.

Gift stepped out. Hidden behind the building, she needed to step into the open, make herself known. She'd also let Oksana see she came for her, assuring the girl it would be all right. It had to be all right. Deep breath. Her feet needed all the mental pushing her brain could offer. Slowly, full of trepidation, they moved.

The five positioned themselves fifteen meters away from where Gift stepped into their sights. Her stiffness came not from dread or panic, but from Xiang's coaching—which Gift took as orders. Rather than rushing toward her, they stopped their approach as if her appearance had stunned them. Maybe it did. Not having announced their presence or intent, their primary target presented itself. Knowing the U.R.M. wanted her alive, needed her alive, made Gift invincible and unafraid of the bullets in the soldiers' guns. Mostly.

"That's far enough," she shouted over the smooth concrete separating herself from them. They had already stopped moving. "We need to discuss how this hostage exchange is going to work."

Perhaps embolden by the sight of her little unarmed self, Yuri stepped from behind the protective cover of the soldiers. "Hello again, my beautiful Gift. No discussion here. You will come... and I will take you."

"Oksana goes free."

"Of course, my Gift. Once I have you... Yuri has no need for child. On this I give my word."

"Your Word? You've gotta be kidding me." Gift stalled, having been told to extend this part as long as possible before anyone started moving.

"You see these soldiers? U.R.M. Here for trade. Think as you will about Yuri, you know these people are honorable."

"Honorable? You must be drunk. And a stupid idiot. They came by force and conquest... to subjugate us. *Honorable?* They're killing and causing the fighting, all of it. It was them. They crashed all the flyers. Ours, I mean, yours... not *yours*, the ones from the R.F." *Focus, Gift.* "And they shot the ones from the N.R.C. They made us fight each other. Our colonies were at peace before they came. We can get back to that. Yuri, we can settle this... if you let Oksana go. Just let her come to me, and you can go free."

"You say give up, walk away? You say this to Yuri? No, my Gift. Your peace was weak, not to last. Yuri sees this. Is so clear. My mother is blind woman, sees nothing. *Nothing.* When U.R.M. contacted Yuri, I see opportunity for power, for peace. The restoration of Russia. Is good." *That's it, keep talking.* "They wanted for peaceful takeover... was good for everyone. No, Gift, you fool. Is *you*. You and your *precious* little New Europa. You ruin everything with your fighting, resisting. And for what? Soon we take this colony again. Soon Yuri has you."

Emboldened by his own words, Yuri took a half-step.

"Everything done is for nothing. Waste of time. This violence, killings..., is all your fault. Not U.R.M. Not Yuri. *You.* Is you who did this. All you had to do was be cooperating." She got him going as hoped. "To tell where missiles are. Share medical data. Give yourself to help all. This was your role. Was easy. Now, we get what we want the same, maybe you become dissected... *like rat.* Ah, but not before Yuri has his fun with you. You see, outcome is same, but fighting and death is because of you."

If Gift had been right about one thing planning this standoff, it was how easily she'd get Yuri monologuing. The unknown bit was how long the soldiers would allow it, being likely to recognize the stall tactic long before Yuri ever would. That they hadn't intervened told Gift they were Yuri's men, poorly trained Russian guards, not the Martians he claimed. He'd given General Xiang all the time she needed.

"You're not making such a good argument for me to come over there. And thinking of being... *with you?* I'm a bit grossed out now, and may puke."

"You will come to Yuri. Is only way you save brat."

"If these Martians are as honorable as you say, we do this honorably then. I'll surrender myself. I'll come to you. But... you send Oksana at the same time. You'll forgive me if I don't trust you."

"This is acceptable." Yuri pulled on Oksana's arm and pushed hard against her back with the tip of his gun.

She began stepping forward, stepping toward Gift. That she had no tears spoke of her bravery and strength. Perhaps to the inferno of her anger even more so. Gift took her first step, then another. Another. She lingered with hands raised until she was almost beside her friend, her kid sister, one walking from an unimaginable nightmare, the other heading into one.

42

After they conquered the world, Gift would be theirs to poke, prod, stick, and dissect as they pleased in their attempts to counteract the result of centuries of human ambition. They wanted to come home, and she was the biometric key to unlock the door. Fate—not that she believed in it—didn't let her take her life on that flyer. She could save the world and keep breathing.

Dai, save the world? Sanctimonious much, Gift? A sacrifice for one young woman carried no less importance, suffered no loss of grandeur. For the world or for one teenage girl, it was the right thing, a noble and worthy martyrdom. While contemplating giving herself to Yuri, she thought ending her life was a better option. Her eyes stopped the racing of her mind when they met Oksana. One more step and they'd be side-by-side for the first time in forever.

In a swift jerky motion, Gift twisted her torso, shuffled her feet below it, and lunged at Oksana. Tackled to the ground, the young woman fell beneath Gift, the momentum rolling them on the ground behind a fruit and vegetable stand. When the rolling stopped, Oksana lay on top of Gift, and they stared into each other's eyes for an endless moment. When Gift folded her neck to search for Yuri and his soldiers, Oksana followed suit.

Chin to chin, they observed as the guard beside Yuri disappeared in a blurred flash of gray. A surreal scene unfolded upside-down in Gift's sight.

The next one thrust his chest forward and flapped his arms. Gift recognized the bodily vibration of close contact taser shock. The speed and precision of the attack—along with the utter surprise of it—slowed the gun draw of the third of Yuri's thugs. General Xiang's first punch turned his head with such force his entire torso twisted to follow it. In seconds, they were all down.

Yuri stood as a post, as lifeless as Emily. By the time his limited brain functions signaled his hand he had a gun, he didn't. With his own weapon pointed in his face, Yuri's hands went up so fast they could have caused a sonic boom. That powerfully impressive woman neutralized the threat, returning Oksana to the safety of *home*.

On her feet after pressing a bit too firmly into Gift's stomach to raise herself, the liberated youth marched to her brother and sent the echo of her slap reverberating under the dome. That open palm became a fist and broke his nose. Without seeing it, Gift knew the crack's noise. Two arms from behind and pulled the girl from an attack she looked nowhere near ready to end. Gift whispered, "Shh," into her ear, and firmly braced her. In a concession to quit her retaliatory aggression, Oksana spat a full, thick wad of phlegm in Yuri's face.

She turned to the General. "That was... *amazing*."

"Wow. Just... wow." Gift's brain misplaced the rest of her vocabulary.

To Gift's shock, General Xiang pulled Oksana in for a hug. "You are welcome, my dear girl. I am glad you are home and safe."

Gift had to wait her turn but got her kid sister in a long, tight embrace of her own. Gently she tacked on a soft, "I love you, sweetie."

"Thank you both," the girl whimpered until gratitude and relief unleashed the tears her strength and anger had withheld. Looking to Xiang she said again, "Thank you."

Gift asked Oksana, "Are you okay?" Her shy nod said, *I don't know yet.* "We can talk about everything later, okay?" A more deliberate nod stated her agreement.

"Is it over?" she asked Gift or Xiang or both.

"Oh mamma. We don't know. The Admin building."

Gift took off toward the passageway to Dome One despite Xiang's calling her off in a forceful tone. By the time the general and Oksana reached her, Gift had the panel off the small hatch in the risen bulkhead. Xiang rested a hand on Gift's forearm and pushed it down from the control module.

Gift grimaced. "We need to get into this spoke and get to Dome One. We have to help them."

"No."

"Shut up. I'm getting through this."

"And if you do?" Gift's mouth opened for a rebuttal, but Xiang continued, "Then, in much time from now, you find yourself in Dome One in one of three scenarios. One: they are still fighting, and you cannot help them. Two: it is over, and we won without you helping them. Three: it is over, and we lost. You cannot help them, you get caught, and no one cannot help you. You need to think through your actions."

"*I can't.* Do you... I can't think straight." Oksana took Gift's hand and Gift smiled at her. Noticing how quickly the young woman had gained her composure and taken a confident posture amazed Gift. "What do we do?"

"Check the situation from N.E. Actual."

"What about these...? What do we do with our prisoners?"

Xiang withdrew a small silver canister from her military cargo pants full of pockets. "Remain here. Stand clear." With Gift and Oksana watching from a safe distance, she popped a cap off the top of the cylinder and tossed it by the tied guards sitting on the floor with Yuri. In seconds, they lost consciousness.

Margaret Heller sat waiting for them in the makeshift Ops Center Xiang called N.E. Actual. If she had to choose one, Gift preferred Mike's SOC, if he didn't pronounce it as a word. She pulled her mind back to the moment. "Miss Heller?"

"Gift. Oksana, sweetheart, we're so glad you're okay. We were all so worried." An uncharacteristic hug followed.

"Thank you."

"What are you doing here?" Gift asked the Chairperson of the Board of Directors of the colony what she was doing in the defensive command center during an attack. Her mental palm-smack to the forehead was well-deserved.

"Claudia has kept me looped in, sending me vid feeds and updates. When I saw the hostage standoff, I came to assess the situation and see if I could help."

"How did you even get here?" Gift inquired.

"I stayed home, in my flat in Dome Three. There are no sealed bulkheads between me and here."

"Gift? Why did we come back here?"

It took Gift a moment to comprehend the general's question. "Oh. The Admin building. What's the status?"

Claudia answered, "Took a while. With the lights dark, our people had an early advantage, having night vision visors for their initial attack. Used it to take out a good few right away."

"An early advantage? Initial attack? What happened?"

"Martians had night vision too," Red replied.

"Yeah, but we took a bunch of 'em out before they got theirs on. Timed the lights out perfectly for our guards." Claudia's prideful words angered Gift. *She's helping, it's fine.* It wasn't, despite what she told herself.

"Of course, their people have guns, while we've got tasers and projectile stunners." Red gave the update like reading a diagnostic report. The fear departed from her voice, settling Gift's nerves a little. "Still, we took the building. A few tried to escape, but our tertiary forces were there."

Claudia had more patting herself on the back to do. "Right, because we had a perfectly timed lights-*on*, too. At just the right moment, all of ours shifted from night vision to solar shade mode and I hit the lights on at full intensity. Those suckers get mad bright too. That gave our guys the ultimate advantage to take out the rest and get them all rounded up."

"Nice work," came out before Gift could stop it.

"Well done, everyone. And Gift, excellent planning. Very impressive." A complement about strategic planning from Xiang floated Gift higher than all her excellent marks from the tutors ever did.

"Yes," Heller added. "You all did an outstanding job."

"And from what Aimée said, and what we've seen, this should be over, *right?*" Copying Red's voice, Gift's lost its dread. "I mean, it seems like they threw everything they had at us."

"We must not assume anything. We do not know if they have... *thrown everything* at us, as you said. We have only speculation on the weapons with ships in orbit, and no status on the situation in the N.R.C."

Gift said, "Oh, General, I'm sorry. All this focus on *our* colony, and all your amazing help... I forgot how you must feel about your colony, still under their control. But... for those reports, from Aimée, I mean. We can trust her. She said they've got limited manpower and only one ship with no weapons."

"I do not doubt this Aimée person. She has provided excellent and useful intel. However, we must consider she is a guest up there and likely has limited access to their ship and data. They may also have fed her bad intel to leak to us. I do not underestimate these Martians."

Miss Heller had her *no choice but to fight* face on. "Agreed. That's why... it pains me, but we must move on to the next phase. Gift, we need you at the bunker."

"*What?* We can't, can't be considering actually using those missiles. No good's ever come from having them. I… I wish we never found 'em. Also too, we've already won."

Heller replied, "Not really. This was the third assault on us, counting Chan's first attack. Presently, there is no way to tell how many people have sided with the U.R.M. in each colony, perhaps even here, and we have no idea how many in the N.R.C. Their number there may be substantial."

"But I'm not needed at the bunker."

"I highly doubt that. An engineer such as yourself could be useful." Miss Heller paused to gaze into the hazel irises of Gift's piercing eyes, eyes pleading for other options. "Plus, I'm not confident it is safe here for you. Even if it is just to protect the location, to protect you, I want you at the bunker. Then there will be no one here who knows how to find it."

Claudia's face showed genuine surprise. "Wait, so *you* don't even know where it is?"

"No. We immediately decided it would be wise to limit that knowledge. One guard may be able to find his way there, but not likely. And that information is unknown, or they would surely be a U.R.M. target too. Any Russians that know the location are there now as well. So, once Gift is safe, the location is safe."

"Guys," Red shouted.

"Now what?"

"Some guys entered Dome Two but—"

"Oh mamma, not again."

"No, let me finish. They entered, as I said, grabbed Yuri and those guards, and ran back out. They're piling into one of the transports."

"Where'd they come from? More hiding in the flyers?"

"Yeah. Seems they held a few back."

"Can we stop them?" Gift asked.

Red frowned. "No. Already taken off and avoiding our sonic cannons."

"*Crap.* How many?"

"A couple dozen, no more."

"And we've got no idea where they're going?"

"I agree with Miss Heller." Xiang ignored the question. "We should get you to the bunker right away."

"Wait, I don't..., *We?*"

43

Restare: an Italian verb meaning to stay. How much Gift wanted to stay in New Europa, to stay home. The word obviously connected her mind to the English word rest—and where better to rest than at home? It had been so long since Gift rested. She felt beyond exhaustion in every *-lly* word she could think of to describe herself: physically; mentally; emotionally.

Morally?

Back home at last, and now asked once again to leave. To go on the run to protect those *mal'd* missiles Gift came to wish they had never found. Fleeting surges of victory quickly fled her bones when Miss Heller pointed out the logical, if not obvious. They weren't sure of the forces orbiting above, outside their sight and well beyond their scanner range. And the U.R.M. still held the largest and strongest Earth colony, the one with the most powerful army and a fleet of air transports. It was premature to declare victory, to rest.

Might the missiles be the only way we end this?

It annoyed Gift how often Miss Heller's words came back, haunting her head like a ghost in a nightmare and creeping up for a jump-scare at the most inconvenient of moments, pulling her out of her skin each time. 'No choice but to fight.' Gift believed Raff would get control of the launch complex systems and be able to send those missiles wherever they were ordered to go. But would they target the orbiting ship—ships, if Aimée was wrong—and put an end to the threat? Were they even sure it *would* remove the danger? After their arrival and dropping what weren't weapons, the U.R.M. ground forces, not any ships, had been the tangible threat.

New Europa wasn't yet safe. None of the colonies were secure, and no one in them could sleep well at night until the imminence of this forced occupation was completely neutralized. Every fiber of Gift's being screamed '*No*' at the thought of using the missiles in such a way. One word kept bouncing through her brain, *murder*, no matter what anyone called it. Beyond the idea of destroying that ship with Aimée still aboard, more than potentially killing however many others, worse than potentially turning an occupation into a war, it felt utterly wrong.

"It's wrong. It's just plain wrong."

"What choice do we have, Gift?" Miss Heller replied.

"See, that's where we *always* go wrong. All the time. History, I mean. And now us—making the same mistakes that got us where we are now. Why must we always do something unspeakably horrible and justify it by saying we had no choice? How many wars were started that way? How many people have been killed throughout our history because someone believed they had no choice?"

"Gift, I understand. But Miss Heller is correct. We—"

Uncharacteristically, Gift cut General Xiang's words. "No. We *always* have a choice. I mean... Look." Turning to Miss Heller, Gift pontificated, "When we thought the Pioneers were a threat, that's when you said, 'We have no choice but to fight.' I remember those words clearly. *Ciao*, do I remember." How Gift wished she could forget. "Since then, we've made choices. Like those weapons. Our choice was to make defensive weapons that were nonlethal. And with those very weapons, we saved this colony *three times* now... and, and we've killed no one. *Not one*."

It felt good to finally get that off her chest.

"Then we, well, me, I guess... decided to hide for almost three months. Went a little crazy for it, I mean, a bit out of mind." Gift shook her head to come back to the moment. "Then I was being hunted in the N.R.C. but not by the Chinese. It was U.R.M. To remove myself as a target and a potential danger to N.E. and my friends, I threw myself off a *mal'd* building."

"*Seriously?* You tried to kill yourself?" Claudia's voice expressed disbelief for all in the room. "But you didn't. Obviously."

"Not *kill myself*—I hate how that sounds. I was going to... to sacrifice myself. I was the reason they were torturing Mike, Matteo, and Tina." The name of her fallen friend choked her on its way out. "Me and Matteo got trapped... on the roof of a building. I stood on the ledge and leaned forward to neutralize the threat, like we say, to stop them hurting my friends. But then... Matteo... he pulled me back."

"Gift, I... I didn't know." With newly wetted eyes, Oksana barely managed the words.

"It's fine. I mean, it is what it is. What I'm trying to say is... we gotta stop saying we have no choice. We *always* have a choice. And now we need to rise above our history, ourselves, and settle this in a better way than our ancestors did. Without just saying we have no choice but to blow people up."

"A stirring speech, Gift." General Xiang's words came with a hint of sarcasm. "So, what is this choice you say? What are our alternatives?"

"Well... I... I don't know. But that doesn't mean they're not there. We've gotta find them, at least one."

Miss Heller shook her head somberly. "We must take out any ships in orbit if we are to end this. We'll never be safe with them hovering over us, worrying us for the next attack."

"One ship. It's *one* ship, as Aimée said. I trust her intel. And it's got no weapons and barely any personnel. That ship is hardly a threat."

"Even if you are correct about the one ship," The General was about to drop militaristic logic—Gift could sense its approach. "As we all agreed, the larger threat is from ground forces. We successfully stopped a handful here. But we have also shown our hand. That one troop that escaped in the air transport knows all our defenses."

The first syllable of Gift's protest fell flat as Xiang lectured further.

"We must assume the U.R.M. has complete control of the N.R.C. We know many of my people sided with them, perhaps in greater numbers than the Russians. They will advance their mission, they will strike. We possess the means to end this and establish our freedom in victory."

With eyebrows raised in shock, Gift said, "Wait. What... are you saying what I think you're saying?"

"I am sure you do not read minds, as I do not. What I am saying is, if I were leading the joint forces of the United Republic of Mars and the New Republic of China, I would plan an all-out assault on United Africa." The general's palm stopped Gift, lifted on her toes for a rebuttal. "They will take the colonies one by one, increasing their strength each time. They know we are no longer in U.A. and, while they are capable fighters, they are the easiest colony to take. Then, with the assets of the Ubuntu people, they will increase their supplies and resources."

As much as Gift wanted to counter, no words came.

"The Russian Federation will be the next target. They are significantly stronger than us, but they are also more supportive of the U.R.M. occupation, and there are most definitely many loyalists still there." All nodded. "Once they control U.A. and the R.F., they will attack us. With their increased numbers and resources, and knowing our defenses, it will be this colony's end."

Xiang's word choice fascinated Gift. How she used *us*, putting herself in New Europa, and spoke of her own colony as the enemy. While an obvious advantage having General Xiang on their side, as she had proven to be, Gift found her positioning herself as one of them oddly disturbing.

"I don't know about all that." Failing to find anything better to say, Gift felt her reply weak.

Red said, "No, she's right. I mean, of course I hadn't thought it through like her, but it makes sense. They're not done with us. They didn't come all this way just to tuck their tails between their legs and go home."

While Gift had no clue where the tails comment came from, the visual amused her. Heller, Xiang, and Claudia all shot her baffled looks when she chuckled for no reason. Like rubbing the sleep from her eyes to see the morning's time on her display, the logic of the general's words became clearer when Red's sank in. There was no way this was over. Gift had to find the choice that persistently eluded her.

"The choice is rational. We need to take out that ship and the N.R.C." That those words fell from Miss Heller's lips was nightmarish, spoken by a fracture of the woman Gift thought she knew—a ghost slipping through shadows, wearing the skin of a dignified, logical, and compassionate woman. Xiang's words hit much harder, their unbelievability rooted in a vastly different soil.

"I agree with Miss Heller."

From a voice of utter incredulity Gift barked, "*What?*"

"It is unfortunate. Believe me, this is not what I wish. Those are my people, and not all of them have sided with the U.R.M. But enough have. That colony is no longer the New Republic of China but has become the center of their United Republic of Earth. If we wish to stop that from becoming a permanent reality, from taking over this planet, we must destroy their colony."

"I won't do that. I'm sorry... No, I'm not. Why do people say that when they disagree? I'm not going to apologize. I'm right, and I'm *not sorry* about that. First we were going to blow up a ship with Aimée and others on it.

Now we're talking about killing over a hundred fifty thousand souls like we're deciding between noodles or tacos."

Miss Heller's eyes burned through Gift. "I assure you, no one is taking this decision lightly. But I'm sending the order to Frank. He and Sergey will ensure they set the targets and launch those missiles as soon as Raffaella gets access. She must be close by now. We will soon have the means to end this, and we will."

Oksana and Gift looked emptily into each other's eyes with no words needed. Gift could see it on her kid sister's face, assured of her humanity. A humanity Miss Heller tossed aside for the same excuse used for horrific actions throughout history. *For the greater good*. In that moment, Gift realized she needed to get to the bunker.

***

Something about that pitiful patch of grass hidden away in Citadome Three calmed Gift. A soothing balm massaged into an aching muscle. Sitting there with Tom brought a moment of deep reflection like a room full of mirrors showing angles and sides of herself otherwise not evident. She thought it a rare matter to see herself in that way, as eyes were designed to see other people, to judge and evaluate those on the outside. To look inward frightened her and filled her with speculative wonder at what she might discover in there.

Life had changed her. The daily routine of a happy-go-lucky cog in the wheel of progress to humanity's bright and wondrous future was forever gone. A premature death of her character came in the wake of insurrection. Yet it brought with it a resurrection, offering the unexpected grandeur of the Earth outside. It awakened Gift's life to something beyond her wildest imagination. The one who opened that airlock was not the innocent cog blindly following a *For the good of the colony* ideology. A spy, counterterrorist agent, a righteous warrior, opened the door to the world. Then she became someone else.

A prisoner, a liberator, a captive interrogated as her dear friends were tortured. Then a fugitive in exile on the edge of sanity who became a failed martyr. The righteous warrior returned to flee the N.R.C. and save her beloved New Europa, to rescue Oksana from Yuri once again. The corner of her mind's eye saw another Gift but couldn't distinguish the details. It was gone.

"Gift?" Tom said it in a way she should have understood its deeper meaning beyond a designation to identify her. Not that she knew who she was any longer.

"*Huh?*"

"You wandered off again. Been drifting a lot."

"Sorry. Really, I am. It's just..."

As his arm pulled her into his side, Tom said, "I know."

Her head rested upon his shoulder. The silence of a moment, the warmth of the embrace, and the rightness of being with Tom, settled over Gift like warm foam before the full blast of hot water in Oksana's shower. The feeling of total relaxation, of safety, of peace, could have enveloped her for all eternity. While she ached to see Aimée, wished to be with Raff and Mike, groaned at the pangs of grief for Tina and Charlie, she wanted this moment to never end. She yearned for nothing else than to stay exactly where she was, with the man she loved.

"So, you're really gonna go to the bunker?"

"No choice. No... I hate saying that. I mean, yeah, I gotta go. I just, just can't sit by while we exterminate all those people."

"So many must be innocent, not supporting the U.R.M."

"Also too, even for those who are... I mean, how'd *we* become judge and executioner? I gotta go. Raff will figure something out."

After a gentle press of his lips to her forehead, Tom looked longingly into her eyes. "I wish you'd stay. It seems you just get here and keep having to dart off. I don't like saying goodbye."

"Me neither. But I have..."

"I know."

44 | Choice: Day One

Parting is such sweet sorrow. Some young lady called Juliet said that in bidding farewell to her gentlemen caller. Gift vaguely recalled the girl had uttered something about killing the young suitor just before that. Would that have been the sweet part or the sorrow? Whatever the case, the fledgling romance met a tragic outcome as both died in the end. But that wasn't the one where he said, "To be or not to be." Poor Romeo, he was not to be. How Gift wished she could write her own narrative, to end the story of Gift and Tom in a happily ever after.

No sweet lightened this parting's sorrow. It held only nagging uncertainty. What situation would she find when she reached the bunker? Could she even find it as they believed she could? With only a mild degree of certainty, she would have to *best-guess* it as they flew in the general direction. It didn't come close to her ninety-nine percent but she needed to be there when they made the crucial decision to use the weapons.

They've already made the decision.

Gift needed to find her choice.

Oksana's insistence on going with her annoyed Gift at first. While she didn't wish to separate from the young woman, she very much wanted her uninvolved. Her being the only one besides the general who could pilot the flyer got Oksana joined to the dispatch. To free herself of Xiang, Gift used

Oksana's presence and her own limited flying experience as a ploy to reduce their party to two.

With noses and mouths tucked into their elbows, they hurried through the spiraling dust cloud to board the small air transport with its turbines already spinning up toward flight rotation speed. General Xiang sat in the pilot seat waiting for them. *Looks like she gets what she wanted all along,* Gift thought. She tossed an amicable smile at her former interrogator as she and Oksana buckled into their seats.

"So, you get your wish. Going to the missile bunker."

"When I asked you for the location, it was to prevent my colony from being taken over or destroyed. Now, perhaps, you see why this was so important. I am going to do exactly what I wished to prevent. This is no longer protecting my people. I am going to raze my colony to the ground."

"I'm so sorry for that, General. Really, I am. But, if any comfort can be found, that's not what *you're* doing at all. You're taking me there to keep me safe, to guard the location. Raff will get control and then Boss and Sergey will fire the missiles. *They* will be the ones killing nearly two hundred thousand people simply by pushing a button. Also too, I'm desperately looking for a way to prevent that from happening."

Xiang didn't respond. Turning in her chair to face forward, she began her takeoff procedure. The lift pushed the two passengers into their seats as the ground tried its best to hold on to them. Broken free from gravity's pull, they hovered for a second and Gift took in the aerial view of New Europa. A sudden wave of dread swept over her in a single thought. *Will this be my last time seeing home?*

The pilot's silence gave Gift and Oksana needed time for some vital catch-up chat. Patience had been exhausted, and Gift needed to hear of the girl's harrowing ordeal back under her brother's control. Gratitude filled her when Gift learned the extent of Oksana's mistreatment was being tied, gagged, and not fed. Of course, there wasn't a hint of concern for

Stockholm Syndrome this time. When Oksana finished, she pushed Gift to detail her daring run through the N.R.C. as bait and how that culminated in her attempted leap from the roof. That seemed to be all the young lady wished to discuss.

"I am certain we have flown by this set of trees at least once before."

Gift felt the tension rising in General Xiang's words. Her patience had been totally drained as Gift's lack of certainty showed. They would find the bunker eventually... if Gift did, in fact, remember how to do that.

"I told you so many times I didn't *know*. I wasn't lying. Exaggerating, sure, I can *find* it. Pretty sure anyway."

"I am beginning to think it was not necessary to hide you and protect you as we did." A slight smirk twitched Xiang's lip.

"The first time, we were in a ground transport and I never even saw the place. Then I came in a flyer. By then we knew, of course, we needed to keep the location secret. When we flew, we didn't go in a straight line. Didn't go directly there. Someone's brilliant idea not to be followed or tracked. Also too, it would be hard to explain to anyone how to get here as I need visual clues to find it."

Wearing a smug glare under a raised eyebrow, Oksana asked, "And *whose* brilliant idea was that?"

A smile was Gift's only answer, and Xiang didn't need to see it. "I keep saying you are clever. Very smart. And when you offered for me to put you on an air transport to find the complex... you told the truth."

"I did. I actually hoped I'd get to N.E., *not* lead you to the bunker."

"Very clever."

After several turns and course-corrections interspersed with zigzags to augment her fuzzy navigational directions, Gift spotted it. The dirt brown circle of a slightly arched dome covered the bunker they sought. It didn't appear to be much, and notably didn't have any visible missiles or launch platforms.

Pushing her head between Xiang and Gift to see out the windscreen, Oksana said, "This doesn't look like much of anything. Is this the one where those refugees were?"

"Yes. It may not seem like it, but this is the right place."

"Wait. My jerk brother's men were here, right? Then... don't they know how to find it? Why haven't they already taken it?"

"I am clearly missing some details, Gift." Xiang spoke calmly but forcefully, evidently not happy to be going into a situation with limited knowledge. Perhaps that was why they hovered for a while before landing.

"Yuri's men came here to attack N.E. Their navigator died. They never found out what the place was, and by the time Yuri knew, he had no idea *where* it was. Kinda wish we hadn't found it."

"Okay. But then, didn't a whole platoon come with Sergey?" Oksana seemed convinced the secret location wasn't so secret.

"Yeah. They saw a small bunker. Sergey and Tom found the control room, and they kept it to themselves. There are many bunkers and only Sergey had the coordinates, so no one had a clue where it was."

Another smooth landing under the skilled hands of General Xiang reunited them with solid ground. Only then did Gift's stomach settle, not having grown accustomed to flying—convinced she never would be comfortable in an air transport. Gift found it odd when Raff didn't come running out to meet her. It had been so long since they had seen each other. The fluttering in Gift's stomach to reunite with Raff remained after the turbines stopped and she stood again on hard, packed earth.

"Stay alert. It is too quiet. Something is wrong." The general waved a rifle.

"There's only a few people supposed to be here. Raff, Hans Fuchs and Boss. And Sergey came with a couple guys from the R.F."

"Gift, I don't see the Zil." Oksana's observation added to the trepidation. It had been days since Sergey arrived in the Russian ground transport, and it was nowhere in sight.

"The N.E. transport isn't here either," Gift noted.

"We proceed with maximum caution. Draw your weapons."

Slowly they crept along toward the bunker with Xiang taking the lead and Oksana in the middle. Trusting the general, Gift didn't ask why they weren't walking toward the door of the round building. They positioned themselves a few meters from it along the curved wall. Structural supports ribbed the exterior, rising from below the ground and going into the edge of the dome's lip some three meters from the weeds and dirt. The rivet-riddled metal frame reminded Gift of the metallic structure she climbed in Paris but nowhere near as chunky. Every part of the bunker's exterior was brown, like dirt, but slightly redder.

The inexperienced women copied Xiang's posturing when she reached the wall and pressed her shoulders back into it. Not a sound reached Gift's ears besides the breathing of her team. Hugging the curvature of the wall, they stepped toward the entrance hatch. Step by careful step they advance slowly, as if expecting a trap or some hidden danger. Gift had to assume Xiang did. When they reached the hatch, they found it closed but unlocked.

Anticipation beat hard in Gift's chest. A quick hand gesture moved Oksana to the oval hatch's circular latch release. When Xiang gestured two fingers to her eyes and pointed them at the hatch, Gift inferred, *look carefully in there*. An assumption at best, but it seemed to fit the circumstance. Another gesture commanded Oksana to pull the door open.

Gift's squinting couldn't overcome the dark to make anything out. The overcast sky allowed more than enough of the sun's generous illumination through to make the other side of that hatch as invisible as her Box set to blackout mode. Could the General's eyes have adjusted more quickly? Gift wondered if military training could prepare the pupils for rapid dilation.

When Xiang stepped inside, Gift followed, assuming her vision would eventually join them.

Tracking the shadow of the figure moving in the dark, Gift's eyes followed the determined general as she moved deeper in. The space dissolved into seeable images. It reminded Gift of the ridiculously small airlock-style lobby entrance to the N.E. Admin building. Only, this space was three times as large and the wall to her back looked to be twice as long as the wall before her, which had another hatch placed precisely in its center. Oksana stepped up behind her.

They entered the second door following the procedure of the first. Only then did Gift realize how assigning Oksana door pulling duty put her in the safest position, blocked by the solid metal door while the general was first in range of enemy fire, Gift next but shielded by Xiang's body. In retrospect, it was obvious, and Gift felt gratitude for the thoughtfulness shown toward the youngest group member. Creeping through a large open kitchen, rows of storage shelves had been scavenged and left bare but for the film of dust and outlines of their former stock. Scantly dispersed sconces cast an eerie yellow glow.

Tables, chairs, and sofas surrounded them in what appeared to be the primary living space, used for eating, socializing, and entertainment—whatever kept that small group of Pioneers alive and sane for two centuries in such confined quarters. Beyond that, they found the curtain-separated living areas Tom had initially described to Gift, long since vacated. General Xiang took deliberate steps, silent as the night, as if floating ghostly through the space rather than a physical creature moving on two feet. Gift tried her best to keep the same quiet. It was Oksana who kicked something in the darkness, bringing a clatter that reverberated the air around them.

Beyond the living spaces, several doors were opened by Xiang when Gift preferred them closed. A storage room took only a few seconds of the general's attention to clear and move on to the next. The three entered the next door into a large open shower room, square with light blue tiled walls and flooring. A flashback plagued Gift as she lay naked on the floor, pelted by blasts in Chan's icy *shower*. Five shower stalls filled the back wall, all separated by modesty panels but lacking doors. Gift couldn't imagine showering in such a place, her reticence wouldn't allow it without privacy. A memory of showering beside Corinthia countered that notion, and Gift worried for the woman who had let her escape.

"This one is wet... used recently," the General observed as she looked over each one and stopped at the last stall.

"Yeah. Our people have been here for days. I'm sure they're showering. Hope so, anyway." Gift chortled alone at her attempt at humor.

"But where are they?" Oksana's tone reached a slight panic. The same feeling already tingled Gift's skin, raising the tiny hairs on the back of her neck to full attention.

Continuing, they checked a toilet room with proper booths and closing doors and another storage room. The sharp youthful eyes of Oksana spotted a hatch that opened to a set of descending stairs. In the same line—Xiang, Oksana, then Gift—they stepped down like inchworms, tips of their rifles raised. One step, another, and another.

Xiang turned right into whatever space waited below the ground level and Gift followed Oksana off the last step. Faint green lighting concealed the room's detail and heightened anxious suspense. Gift felt her skin moisten, sticking her coverall to her body.

"Hi."

The word was a jump-scare from somewhere hidden in the darkness and Gift jumped out of her skin.

Shot fired.

45

A *theew* immediately returned the startling greeting. Increased lighting unhid Raff standing over Hans Fuchs, his body convulsing on the floor with Gift's stun projectile clung to his chest.

"Sorry," Gift whimpered, shoulders withdrawn.

An energetic rush across the room ended as Raff threw her arms around Gift. The warmth and security of that hug melted her and chased the nervousness of the last several minutes away. Oksana got her hug next, and the General received nothing but a look of surprise bleeding with a touch of anger. Raff knew how Xiang had been helping them, but having her there at the bunker didn't appear at all well-received.

"Miss Raffaella, I am General Xiang."

"I know who you are from our vid message exchanges back when we were somehow enemies. Now you've got your wish after all. Here you are."

"This is not the circumstance I wished for this visit."

"Whoa." Hans Fuchs' moan reminded Gift of his existence—and that she had shot him with the stunner. He pulled himself to his feet. Still dazed, his head wobbled to find clarity.

"Sorry," she said to the man she had sent into violent shuddering as he shook it off and smiled at her.

"It's lovely to see you too, Gift." For the first time since their Union ceremony, Gift found herself pulled into the tight embrace of Hans Fuchs.

Even after shooting him, the friendliness he exuded felt sincere. *Raff is a lucky woman. And so are you... a lucky man, I mean. Stupid brain.*

Freed from his arms, Gift asked, "Didn't you see us coming, or hear the flyer? Miss Heller told you we were coming, right?"

"No cameras were on. They are now, in case anyone else shows up. And yes, Margaret told us you were coming today. Hans and I were about to go upstairs to prepare for your arrival. We sleep, eat, and shower up there."

"We noticed that. So where is everybody? Boss, Sergey?"

"The control room here is solely for the bunker. Took Sergey a good while, when he came here that first time with Tom, to discover this was also a missile complex. Even after Tom reported it and we came, it was hard to find."

Xiang said, "I see nothing of a weapon facility here."

Raff answered, "The storage cache and launch platform are a suitable distance from here, at the base of the mountain about a kilometer north. The launch control room is deeper underground. There's a hidden entrance down here and a hatch leading up to the surface from that room. Frank, Sergey and his two officers are there."

"Everyone who can locate this bunker is here. This is the reason we brought Miss Gift. The location is secure."

"Thank you, General. *Ma*, Gift, is *that* why you're here?"

"I guess it makes sense. Really, *I'm* here because Miss Heller said we have no choice. We keep thinking that, and making bad decisions because it's the only option we suppose we have. But we're wrong."

"Cara, I hope you're right. We're under orders from our Board, confirmed by Nadezhda and Bright. Even Dmytro Melnyk of the Pioneers. All colonies agree this is what must be done, what *we* must do."

"Wait, the Ubuntu? Has Kofi given his opinion?"

"He's not in agreement. *Ma*, he's a minority vote."

"And everyone else agrees, not only for the ship but for the N.R.C. too? *Everyone* really agrees we should wipe out a colony of over a hundred fifty thousand?"

"It must be," Xiang said. "That is my colony, my people, but there is no other way."

Confidently, Gift replied, "We'll see about that."

"Miss Raffaella, I wish to inspect the launch control room, to meet your Russian associates, and to view the platform." The general got right to business. She lived there, always in her official persona as a military leader. Traces of her personality had emerged in the time Gift had been in Xiang's company, but they needed her default in the moment. Gift tried to balance her impression of the formidable woman with those hints of humanity allowed to show through the cracks.

Five entered the bunker control room, a small metal-walled enclosure that made the word bunker even more fitting. Slanted off the side wall, the control panel twinkled with blinking lights interspersed with tablet-sized display screens. It looked modest for an Ops control room and showed nothing related to a missile complex to Gift's eye. When she asked how Sergey ever figured out there was a launch platform anywhere connected to the system, Raff pushed a series of buttons in a pattern.

Turning to a clank from the wall of grey panels opposite the control panel, Gift observed increased disturbance in the floor's accumulated dust. At Raff's "voilà" and final button click, the panel depressed a couple centimeters then slid away to reveal a secret passage. Initial flickering showed Gift glimpses of a revealed tunnel as a child's peekaboo until the illumination steadied in the narrow passageway.

Last in line and with excited trepidation fluttering her heartbeats, Gift trailed Hans Fuchs down the dim earth-bored corridor. The occasional root scratched at Gift's arms, having squiggled through the tight-packed dirt and rock in search of life-sustaining water. *Life struggling to find a way to carry on*. Gift considered it a decent metaphor for her present situation. Some larger rhizomes bore the scars where they had been cut, leaving fragments of dried corpses withered on the ground. Gift fought off any allegories for that.

Eyes popped at the sight that brought Gift's mind to an old vid she watched as a child. It detailed the history of space travel from the first *apestronaut*—her tutor's less-than-clever word—launched in suborbital rockets to the transports taking humans to Mars. Enormous computer rooms with huge screens monitored and controlled the missions. Space-X, MMR, and others entered the so-called *space-race* for Mars until CCTM became the unified global administration to oversee the great migration. Gift used to think it stood for Christopher Columbus To Mars. Her tutor found it cute when an eight-year-old Gift came up with it based on the names of the transport ships: Niña, Pinta, and Santa Maria. Gift wondered momentarily if they were about to blow up one of those historic vessels. How different would her history lessons have been if the native American people had the means to sink Columbus' ships?

Sergey's hug was unexpected in that it happened, and equally in how assuring and comforting it made her feel. Gift's arms welcomed it by squeezing the bulky Russian guard in return. Like a father reunited with a long-lost daughter, Sergey enveloped Oksana and she melted into his embrace. The other two Russian guards were unknown to Gift, so they exchanged introductions. Not good for remembering new people, Gift forgot their names as they said them. Too much on the mind for such trifles.

"Did you get in yet?"

"We're very close," Hans Fuchs replied. "Raff's running a program now that has a few hours to go until completing its data extraction and compilation. It was a breakthrough she found late yesterday."

"I don't get it. Raff, you've been here like... a week. No?"

"No, Cara. It took us almost a week just to get here in our little ground transport. And we had to repair that bridge for the smaller tires. Then it took a day just to get that secret door open. We've been attempting every trick in the book to gain control of this system for three days now. And I think we've got it. We'll know for certain when my subroutines finish running."

"I see. Oh, where's Boss?"

Sergey answered, "Frank is at launch platform. Come, I give you tour while we wait for computers."

The suggestion glowed on Xiang's face like a lamp's reflection as she, Gift, and Oksana followed the tall, broad Russian through another door into what Gift could only describe as a capsule. The solid two-by-one-meter oblong enclosure in polished soft white had gray flooring and a thin shiny pole running horizontally below the ceiling. All copied Sergey in clutching the pole one-handed when he said, "Hold on."

In a jerky fashion that took Gift back to Tina driving the new ground transport for the first time, the capsule moved. A moment of melancholy swept through Gift, contemplating her lost friend who had died to save her life. How much Gift wished to have had it play out the other way—a choice she didn't get the chance to make. Desperately, she needed to find the choice here, to figure out another option besides mass-murder in the name of liberty and freedom.

The one-kilometer ride took just under two minutes. Top rising, bottom half slipping down, the door separated, and the tourists exited with Sergey into a tubular ribbed corridor. To Gift's vivid imagination, she stepped through an open mouth and looked down the throat of an ancient monster's skeleton. When Sergey opened the hatch at the end of the hallway, they entered a massive open space with two control desks under centuries of dust. They appeared to be switched off. Boss extended a hand to Gift, which she shook. She still didn't like the greeting, finding it an empty and awkward gesture.

"Welcome Gift. You are finally here."

"Yeah. I mean, I've been here, in the bunker... but never down here. So, this is the platform then?"

"Yes. Auxiliary controls too. Raff is in the primary systems control center where we'll target and launch."

"Mister Frank, I am General Xiang of the New Republic of China."

"Yes, I know."

"I would very much like to inspect the silos and missiles. Have you verified which type of weapons payload they carry?"

Sergey took that question. "Five long-range missiles carrying Russian thermobaric warheads. There is one decommissioned FOAB. Its nanotechnology explosive is been removed. Is useless to us."

Hearing another puzzling expression, Gift said, "Sorry, an FOAB?"

"Father of all bombs."

"Goodness. Like giving it a clever name makes it less lethal or something. So, these ones with thermo-whatever warheads... they can reach the ship in orbit and hit the N.R.C. from here?"

"Da. If a low orbit, they can reach both targets."

The large open cavern carved from the surrounding rock housed twelve gray cement silos reaching twenty meters from the darkness at the bottom to the roof of steel and rock above. Each had caged ladders running their height vertically.

"Four is enough, if Miss Gift is correct about Aimée's intelligence. One to take out the orbital ship and two for the N.R.C. should be sufficient." An utter lack of emotion in General Xiang's words and a face expressing no sadness confounded Gift as they were talking about slaughtering her people. True, there were some descendants of the Chinese in New Europa, likely some in the U.R.M. as well, but this was as close to genocide as they could get. Gift shivered at the notion. *We've gotta find another way.*

"And that leaves one more, right? We fire three, we have one left." When Oksana spoke, Gift remembered for the first time in a while she was there, part of this new nightmare. What did she think of the whole situation?

Sergey replied, "Da, dorogaya devushka. One left is good in case another ship comes. But we will keep that number secret. Da, a secret for any not now in this place."

"If we use them at all. Gift is still hoping for another option. Maybe we can find a peaceful resolution. We gotta hope so."

"Brava Oksana. *Ma*, he called you 'doro-gaya, devu-shka'?"

"Basically, it means dear girl. He's called me that since I was a baby."

"That's so sweet."

"He's always been fond of me and my mom but never cared for my idiot brother. So, he's a pretty good judge of character." Her words ended in a wide smile, bringing a welcome one to Gift's face.

"How have the Martians not found this place on their own, without me? I mean, it's huge. From a low orbit even, or in flyers. I'd think these would be easy to spot, no?"

"Did you see anything from the air?" Boss pointed up. "And once you did, you made out the top of the small bunker, right...? Could you have identified anything that looked like a missile silo or launch platform? Did you even see any structure besides that little dome?"

Before Gift could answer, Xiang said, "Nothing is visible from the air. Only when we were almost on top of it did we even see the bunker." Turning to Gift she continued, "Weapons platforms like this were designed to be hidden, everything under ground. Hatches above each silo are likely covered in dirt to not be visible until opened. No, if the U.R.M. does not know where we are, they will never find it."

Boss ended the tour. "Come, we've got some time remaining before Raff gets into the system—if that code she's running works. For now, let's get you all settled into living spaces. We may be here a few days still."

46

Delayed expectations weighed upon the last nerve that had escaped being eaten away by Gift's anxiety. The program Raff had written took longer than expected, extending the day well into evening. The women took the first shift in the shower room full of stalls without doors. Like the cleaning crew workroom shower at the N.R.C., these had manually activated water flow levers and bars of soap. With no blast of hot air to dry their skin and hair, they needed to use towels. The cold bite of the water ensured everyone got clean and out in short order.

Dinner was basic rations not unlike what they ate on their expedition to find the Pioneers in the Zil, Gift's first trip away from her colony. A substantial change of life in recent months had her rarely home and missing her little colony terribly. In hiding once again, but not isolated. She, Raff, and Oksana spent the better part of the evening in catch-up conversation and other *girl talk*, as Mike liked to call it. While Gift didn't care for the description, dialogue when no guys were present veered in directions not taken when they were.

Big-Sister-Raff mode engaged and bombarded Gift with questions about her and Tom. When Raff smiled at the relationship's progression, something about that approval became suddenly vital and warmly received. The two nameless Russian guards kept to themselves, only responding if directly asked a question. Hans Fuchs joined Boss and Sergey in a card game, generously sharing Raff with her newly reunited friends. Thoughts then drifted to Charlie and Tina, friends who'd never join a catch-up chat. Stories retold of lost loved ones brought smiles more than tears, and Gift was proud of herself for that.

Seated on the common area sofas, the women were serenaded by songs made by an orchestra of snoring men and one Chinese general. Indiscernible whispers came from the far corner where the nameless men were not yet asleep. Like a frightened child pulling a sheet over her head, Gift sank into the comforting security of having trained guards among their number.

Chirp.

"Has it finished?" Gift anxiously asked. This was what they'd been waiting for, but she needed more time. If they were ready to target and launch before they found their choice, it would be too late. People would die. Determined not to allow it, Gift had no idea how to stop it.

"Looks like it. Let's go check."

The three hopped onto their feet, abandoning the less-than-comfortable sofas, which merited no gratitude from weary bums and stiff spines. They shouldn't have expected luxurious comfort from them. A brief sadness for the Pioneers who had lived there passed quickly as the suspense of descending the stairs to see if Raff had successfully accessed the missile systems took full control of Gift's emotional state.

One of those jutting roots tickled Gift's neck. It was thin and soft, with strings of little hairs corkscrewing off it. The desperate and unstoppable search for life, to keep living, pushed it through rock and packed dirt and into a waterless void of empty air. Yet it wasn't about to give up. Gift knew she had to keep going, find a way to keep those people from being obliterated, stretch her roots farther and deeper and find the way to preserve life. The elusive choice.

"We're in."

"Awesome," Oksana said. "But…"

"I know." Turning to Gift, Raff said, "We didn't find our choice."

"Yeah, *ma*, I mean… everyone's asleep, *right?*" The other two nodded. "No one need know about this until tomorrow."

"Brava, Cara. And we should be asleep now too. So, we won't need to report this to N.E. until morning."

"And like you say, we're in the future. A few hours, right? Gives us extra time before they wake in N.E."

Donning a wide smile, Gift replied, "Brilliant, Oksana."

The teenager replied from a maturity beyond her years, "So, let's keep thinking. We must be missing something. Like you say, there's always a choice. We just need to find it. What else can we do besides launch those missiles?"

Raff said, "We can take the night, but then we must report this. As soon as they wake, the others will learn we got in. It will take some time to get the targeting system online. Even then, we'll need time to find the targets and lock onto them. Without the satellites they were designed to use, we'll have to go with the slower long-range sensors and configure the missiles' adaptive targeting AI. It will take time to track and lock onto the ship and the colony at N.R.C. Plus, the ship is a moving target. Sorting out its orbital course and calculating the trajectory of the missile will take time."

"How much time?" Gift hurriedly asked.

"Not enough, I am afraid." *A male voice. Who? From where?*

The nameless Russian guards stepping into the control room waved handguns at the women. Not stun rifles, they had Russian weapons with bullets. Each held tasers in their other hand. Oksana barely got the first grunt of complaint off her tongue when her body trembled. Quickly moving behind her, Gift softened her fall to the ground, where she twitched uncontrollably. Perhaps rising too swiftly for their liking, portending an attack, Gift received the next pulse and knelt on the ground facing the guard connected to her by coiled wires.

After the violent quivering subsided, everything was fuzzy. Gift's vision was blurred by the aftereffects of the most powerful stun to ever spasm her muscles. Cognition slowly filled her as if guardedly trying not to overwhelm her mind with new thoughts and understanding. She lay on her side, arms restrained behind her back, ankles tied together, not remembering how she'd gotten like that. Raff sat back to the wall, legs stretched out and tied at the ankles and gagged. Only then did Gift note the pull on her own cheeks and the openness of her mouth, the cloth between her lips.

When Gift moaned a grunt that almost made the muffled noise of 'where's Oksana?' Raff motioned her chin over Gift's shoulder. Her eyes found the young woman relatively unharmed, tied and gagged in the same fashion. Yet again, Gift was someone's prisoner. Had they overtaken the men in their sleep, subdued or killed them? Where was General Xiang? Whatever the case, the three women, bound and gagged, lay helpless to the armed men standing over them. *No. We're gagged.*

A clarity came with the thought. The men must have followed the ladies down the steps and into the corridor outside the control room to see if the subroutines had broken into the systems. Once confirmed, they sprang into action, leaving no time to handle the sleeping others. Would they venture upstairs to care for that unresolved loose end now that their first victims were secured? What could Gift do to stop them?

The only thing her brain conceived to do, she did. Moaning through the gag cloth, she summoned the eyes of the guards. One stepped toward her, his boots at her navel. As he lowered himself, his knee came above Gift's cheek but only suggested its potential force. A power-play, no doubt to show his dominance, worked as intended. His head cocked and he looked her in the eye as if to say, *go on*, but without removing the gag for her to speak.

Her noises tried to say, 'What do you want? Let's work together.' The confusion that replaced the harshness on his face told Gift her mumbling wasn't understandable. *Keep them here* played on a loop in Gift's mind. Give the sleepers upstairs time to rouse and come to their rescue. She mumbled some more. Lowering his head closer to hers, his eyes drilled into her, and he addressed her in Russian. The man standing behind him spoke, then the kneeling man engaged him in a verbal volley without breaking eye contact. The words ping-ponging back and forth between them took the tone of an argument. One word reached Gift's ears with understanding as clear as Colony lake on a summer day. *Yuri*.

"Mmmm-mmmm... Mmmm." Her shoulders juddered and her head bobbed to emphasize her plea.

The guard drew his handgun and pressed the tip into Gift's temple and raised a finger over his lips. "If you scream, they hear you. If they hear you, I have no reason to not shoot you. No reason to hide noise. Do you understand?" When she nodded her compliance, he slid the gag off.

"Thank you." She spoke softly to assure her cooperation. "I don't speak Russian, but I heard you say 'Yuri.' You're with Yuri Anoykina, his men? And he's working with the U.R.M. Did you know that's who you're working for?"

"For this, we remove gag?"

"Yeah. I mean, no, not for this. Please, may I sit up?"

The guard helped Gift onto her bum, and she slid back against the wall beside Raff. The eyes of Oksana were upon her, intently observing. It wasn't a plan, more an improvisation being written as it was being enacted. Gift always hated it when some lame *'actors'* thought themselves funny enough to pull that off on open-mic night.

"Thank you. What I mean is it's obvious the U.R.M. are just using him. Whatever they promised Yuri, it's a lie. Has to be. They came to conquer us. All of us. If you give them what they want, what use will they have for you? Think about it."

"You are clever girl. We are not stupid as you think. We know deal Yuri has with Martians. Is good deal. Once they have this place, they rule the world. Is no problem for us. Is good. Each colony needs governor, as they do when they arrive. Yuri is governor for Russia. This is good deal for us. For you, is not so good, I think, da?"

"Zamolchi," the other guard barked.

The guard hovering over Gift replied sternly, "Ty zatknis'."

Gift continued with her attempts at undermining their misguided loyalty. "Yuri might be your friend, but you know he's no leader. And you must realize the Martians see that. And they already have a governor in the R.F. and it's *not* Yuri. Do you really want to bet they will honor their agreement and put that loser of a fool in charge of the second most powerful colony on Earth? *Do* you?"

The face looking back at her went pensive and the guard wearing it holstered his weapon. She was getting through. Even if only to pause him long enough, she had him. The other one, not so much. Gift wondered if he even understood English until he spoke.

"Enough, Pavel. *Ostanovka.* Yes, you are clever girl. And we see this ploy. You try to fool us, trick with words. You will say anything to save skin. We have sent location to Yuri. Waited only for you to get into systems. Now they are *our* systems. *Our* missiles. We are valuable allies. When Yuri arrive with U.R.M. you will see. You will see."

"I'll see you both dead with U.R.M. bullets in your heads. Yeah, they shoot their own guards for not saying some stupid codeword right. *Their own people.* You're nothing to them—used and discarded. And now that you gave them this location, they'll dispose of you like the garbage you are. That's exactly what we'll see. Stupid idiots, both of you. Dead. Stupid. Idiots."

Those words didn't settle well on the standing guard's ears. He lunged forward as if to lean into a strike. Gift saw it as his defeat. When people realized they'd lost an argument or had been outsmarted, they resorted to violence. To let the fists say what the mouth was incapable of communicating meant he was seeing her point but wasn't willing to concede. When the guard kneeling before her shockingly put himself between Gift and her would-be attacker, she was certain she had reached him, planted enough of a seed of doubt, and drizzled a sprinkle of water over it. What that seed would germinate into was unknowable. That it was there was everything.

Little by little, Gift had been raising the volume of her voice, and the angry guard followed suit, outperforming her loudness. Their claims of not being stupid had been clearly overstated. Being pulled completely into heated conversation clouded them, becoming all the moment was, with no regard for anything else. It may not have been enough to traverse the corridor, pass the small bunker control room, and ascend the stairs, but it was worth a shot.

47 | Day Two

Watching the two men arguing, it became clear Gift had sown discord among them. At least they hadn't gone up to kill everyone. Not yet. Unsure of the time, Gift couldn't guess if any of the sleepers had risen or soon would. General Xiang was an early riser, as was Sergey. Perhaps a military thing, though Gift typically got up early herself. Admittedly, her usual 07:00 would be considered late to someone like Xiang.

The men spent impatient minutes on the console through a less-hostile exchange. Not being data operators, engineers, or techs, they couldn't make sense of anything they were seeing. They were guards. And Yuri's guards were barely even that. Oksana's words on the day they met came back to Gift. Sure, they were said in rightful hatred, but they contained truth. She said Yuri and his friends were all idiots and used their guard positions for their own selfish gains. They had indeed proven to be less than clever and not well trained.

Sounds of footfalls waned as the men scurried off, leaving Gift ungagged. Her reactive thought to scream ended when Raff groaned a desperate plea for attention and led Gift's eyes to the control console with her own sparkling greens. As Gift lifted herself to her feet and hopped over to the console, the moan that came around Raff's gag almost formed the word 'alert.' There was a button with a hand-written label, so Gift said,

"Alert button?" and pushed it with her chin when Raff nodded. Nothing happened.

With only her mouth free, Gift hopped to Raff and leaned her face in, pulling the gag down with her teeth. Not dignified or elegant, but it worked. Repeated on Oksana, they were all ungagged and on their feet. They had no plan, not even an idea of what to do.

"Raff, can you lock out the controls?" Gift asked.

"Yes. *Ma*, there's no voice control. I need my hands."

Those words dropped Oksana to her knees behind Raff, teeth her only tool.

"Well done, Cara. You got them squabbling with each other. That one guard was starting to have doubts."

"Yeah, but they went up to kill everyone."

Stopping her chewing, Oksana said, "We don't know that. They said handle them—they were going to handle them. That doesn't have to mean kill."

"Sweetie, in the Russian Federation, *really?* Dai, they meant kill. Like 'at your disposal.'"

"*Gift*. Russians aren't all like that. *I'm* Russian, don't forget. You of all people... I didn't expect such a stereotype from you."

"Sorry... I'm sorry. It's something stupid Nailya Usanova put in my head. Maybe she was teasing, I don't know. I know Russians aren't like that. I can't think straight. No, I'm... it's no excuse. I'm sorry."

Satisfied with the stuttered apology—Gift hoped so, it was sincere—the young lady returned her teeth to working on the zip-tie.

"Wait, Oksana." Raff called her away from her wrists and onto her feet. "You obviously understood all they said." She nodded, said nothing. "So... what did they say?"

"Oh right, you guys still don't understand any Russian. You really should learn, at least a little. So yeah, you got in that one guy's head. Messed him up so much he told the other guy they should stop supporting Yuri and the Martians. Seemed terrified they would kill them once they were no longer useful. Had a U.R.M. guard buddy that went missing."

Gift asked, "And the other guy? He seemed real angry."

"He argued against everything you said. It got heated. Called the other one stupid for letting you mess with his head. Three times he ordered him to go upstairs."

"Did they call Yuri?" Raff asked hurriedly. "Are the U.R.M. on their way here?"

"Yes, they sent a signal, a locator beacon. They'll be here in a few hours."

"Oh mamma. Raff, what do we do?"

Looking to Oksana, Raff asked, "Are you anywhere close to getting through my restraints?"

"Almost there, yeah." She returned her teeth to the task.

"I'll lock out the system, add a security passcode only we will know. That way, if they take the bunker, they won't be able to access the targeting and launch controls. It'll take months to break it."

"Good Raff, that's real good. No one but us. I mean not even Boss and Sergey... If they're not dead. They'll try to launch if they have the code."

"*Ma*, if we're under orders from the Board and haven't come up with another choice? We must give them the passcode."

"Well, sure, okay. *Ma*, buy us a little time. We gotta find another way."

Not pausing her work, Oksana mumbled, "It'd be better if these stupid things never existed."

"Oh mamma, here we go again, giving me knowledge they're gonna want. That's just great." Sarcasm came easier to Gift, though it still left a bitter aftertaste.

"Got it," the youngster declared with teenage excitement.

Hands freed, Raff took to task on the controls to initiate her lockout and passcode. As Raff typed away, Gift speculated the possible horrors happening upstairs, but nothing filtered down to them.

"Okay. We'll need a passcode we'll all remember but won't be guessed. As we cannot write it, it must be easy for us, hard for them."

"Something only we know?" Oksana asked for clarification.

"Esatto."

"Sonia makes good tacos. It was the code you sent to me in the subtitles to tell me it was you."

The look on Oksana's face came from not having the context, though she also liked Sonia's tacos as much as or even more than Gift.

"Va bene. *Ma*, let's make it harder to crack. Sonia, with an uppercase S, dash makes underscore, then in all caps, GOOD slash, then back to lowercase, tacos."

"Can we all remember that? It's a little complicated."

"Easy sweetie," Gift said. "Sonia makes good tacos. *Ma*, just remember dash underscore slash, in that order. Since *good* is the adjective, it gets underscored and capitalized. Sonia dash, makes underscore, uppercase G O O D slash tacos. Easy."

"I think I got it. Thanks."

"Done. No one can access it without that passcode."

Thuds rumbled in, taking Gift aback. "What was that? We should go check."

"No. We have no weapons. If they're losing, we can't help. If they're winning, we'd only get in the way and make things worse."

Raff was correct, but Gift had a choice—at least in this. "That door lock?"

In the control room for a missile launch facility, the door most definitely locked. If nothing else, they could protect the target and launch systems, and themselves, behind a steel door. Not impenetrable, it would be a decent delay at best. The three could access the silo chamber, maybe disarm the warheads before the U.R.M. got in and killed them. They could do something. A choice—if not *the* choice Gift still groped in the dark to find.

Time moved maddeningly slowly. Unable to forget the anxious worry she had suffered for Tom, Gift understood Raff's unease. Well masked, but there. She was a nervous wreck for Hans Fuchs and all his potential outcomes. A knock on the door startled them. Raff offered a hush sound with a finger over her lips.

A crackling voice rained down from above. "Amore, it's me. You alright in there?"

After noticing the small speaker overlaid in tattered gold mesh film above her head, Gift saw the relief dripping from Raff's countenance. When the door opened, she and Hans Fuchs embraced, and tears of joy and offloading dread drained from Gift's eyes watching them. Sergey and Boss rushed in. They were all alive, all safe. *But...*

"Where's General Xiang?" Gift impatiently demanded.

"Injured, but okay," Boss replied.

"A remarkable woman. Remarkable."

Sergey opened with how foolish those two untrained guards were to go up against him, let alone him and a highly skilled Chinese general. Gift interrupted to ask how they figured out the men were traitors and coming up for them. The alert button had triggered a subroutine to signal their handhelds. Hans Fuchs had awoken Sergey, and they had devised a plan in seconds. Sergey would be the bait, making noises of deep slumber, while Boss and Hans Fuchs waited behind the curtains.

That plan changed when Sergey noticed an awake and fully alert Xiang near the hatch to the stairs. He learned later she woke for the second watch, military training not allowing her to have an unguarded night in an unfamiliar location. When she noted the three missing women, Xiang had crept downstairs to check on them and heard Gift's clever commotion.

She positioned herself at the top of the stairs. As Sergey gesticulated an emphatic X with his forearms, the footfalls of heavy boots ascended the stairs.

"The General disappeared. One second there, the next nothing. She was disappeared into darkness. Then rolling thumpings. When I reach steps, she was at the bottom, on top of men, and they were disarmed. I ran down to help; she was fighting both at once and I helped subdue them. The fall had broken her arm, yet she fought. A remarkable woman, as I said. Remarkable."

"Wow," both Oksana and Gift said. It transported them back to N.E. when General Xiang took out the three guards and subdued Yuri in a single blink.

"Oh mamma," Gift exclaimed. "They signaled Yuri. The U.R.M. are on their way here. What do we do?"

"Have you gotten in?" The glint in Boss' eye disturbed Gift, its hunger for vengeance.

Raff's head faced the floor in defeat. "Yes."

"Then we target, and we launch."

Sergey said, "I agree. Is reason we are all here. Begin targeting sequence for ship and then the N.R.C. The ship is the command center. We take it out first."

"Wait," Gift protested. "First, we gotta contact the N.E. Board in the morning, their morning. No harm waiting, we got a few hours before the Martians get here."

"Do we have an *exact* arrival time?"

"No."

Boss stiffened. "This is the directive of the Board. We target and launch *now*."

Already eye-level with Boss, Gift raised herself on her toes. "Actually, no. We're not acting on the orders of the Board. I understand you came here on your own. It was your idea to get Raff out of jail and bring her here. Then Miss Heller... she told us to shoot the ship down and destroy the N.R.C. There was never a discussion by the Board. None of you, none of us has the authority to do this."

"I'm with Gift," a confident Oksana said.

Raff added, "Me too. She's right. Just give us a little time to figure this out."

"We have our orders."

"Miss Anoykina agrees. And General Xiang," Sergey said with a deliberate nod.

Boss added, "And U.A. and the Pioneers."

More assertive than usual, Gift replied, "Again, no. Bright and Mister Melnyk may have said that, but we have no governmental entity authorizing this. And... and... it's just plain wrong."

"Everyone? *Everyone.*" Hans Fuchs spoke in a loud, commanding voice.

A collective "*What?*" was offered by the group.

"I think they're here."

48

Gift had experienced Chan's malevolent hospitality and been a 'guest' of the New Republic of China and then the United Republic of Mars. Now, once again, someone was coming where they didn't belong and were not welcome.

"I think they're here," Hans Fuchs said.

"*What?* I thought we had a few hours," Raff barked at Oksana.

"That's what they said."

"Sweetie, those guards must know who you are." *Perhaps*, Gift thought, *they aren't as stupid as they appeared.*

"Most everybody knows me, yeah. And they were friends of—"

"A misdirect," Raff deduced. "They weren't in China, must have been close, knowing the complex was in this general area."

"Amore, sorry, but what matters now is they're on approach." He was so polite and gentlemanly. Perhaps it was Hans Fuchs' only demeanor.

"What do we do?" The anxiety once again elevated Gift's emotional state, an unrelenting bass drum thumping in her chest.

"We launch," Boss declared as a given.

"But... they're coming. What do we do about *them?*"

"Relax, Gift. We planned for this." No one noticed the general until she spoke, having stealthed her way in the room to everyone's back, her arm in a sling.

"*Huh?* How? You only just got here."

"Sergey, Frank, and I discussed this last night. Sergey had an evacuation plan in place. We wondered why there were no ground transports when we arrived…"

Oksana crinkled her brow. "Yeah, that was odd. Where's the Zil?"

Sergey took to outlining the plan. "The transports are by the emergency egress point above the missile control room. Da, we made escape plan, but we must defend this bunker until we can target, lock, and launch the missiles. I understand this takes Miss Raffaella some time."

"Any idea how many of them are coming?" Boss asked.

Hans Fuchs replied, "One heavy flyer, that's all."

"A Chinese heavy can carry three dozen soldiers," General Xiang said.

"Oh mamma."

While having the highest ranking general of the N.R.C. and the commander of the R.F. Rosgvardiya on the same mission could have been a power struggle, each pushing for dominance and absolute control, the two worked well together. Knowing they were completely outnumbered and outgunned, as Sergey put it, the plan was a simple standoff. The bunker would be hard to breach with the single hatch sealed from inside.

"When we arrived, we entered an unlocked hatch. Those traitorous guards made an exterior patrol before bed." On the General's implication, Sergey took off running. Their standoff plan would fail if the U.R.M. forces just walked right in. "Good." Xiang almost smiled. "Now, we must consider our options. Our time is limited, as they must be carrying something to breach this bunker, having assumed we would not leave the door open—as we nearly did."

"Please don't say we have no choice but to fight."

"No, I would not say this. We cannot defeat them. We would delay them at best and likely take casualties. This is not an excellent strategy. We will use all the time it takes them to blast through the hatch. We will hope to have a launch sequence started by then and we will use Sergey's evacuation plan to flee in the ground transports."

"Um, we've got a flyer," Oksana reminded everyone.

Raising an eyebrow, Xiang said, "It is near the entrance and the first thing the soldiers will take. We will not be able to use it to make our escape."

"We can't outrun them in the Zil."

"Correct, young lady. We expect they will not see us flee the hatch over the control room. They should remain here to gain control of the complex and stop the missiles we will have launched."

"Can they? Stop the missiles?" Boss asked.

Raff said, "We locked the system down. Of course, no security is absolute. They will eventually gain control, but nowhere near in time to stop the missiles once launched."

"Then we launch them all. Better not to hold one back at the risk they do gain control. New Europa would be their likely target."

"Why do you say that, Boss?" The panic rose above all other feelings until it was overtaken by the dread of seeing a mental image of N.E. razed to the ground—a smoldering pile of ruins covering fifty thousand corpses of her people. Gift gasped aloud.

"We're a thorn in their flesh. True, we're working with the R.F. and General Xiang is with us here. But they already control China and seem to still have people in the R.F. as well. U.A. overthrew them, but they're small. And they know our leadership was behind their greatest resistance. They will threaten at first, but will most likely use that last missile on us."

Everyone stood in the missile control room. Cameras, mics, and speakers provided the communication needed for the standoff—a delay tactic all it was. Raff was knee-deep into an argument with Boss, whose volume steadily increased, failing to maintain what composure he had. His bravado was ineffective on Raff, always calm and cool, not at all intimidated by the man. She insisted they get confirmation from the Board at New Europa before unlocking the system with her new passcode. Cleverly, she withheld that Gift and Oksana also knew it.

True to their prediction, a legion of three dozen spilled out of the air transport in disciplined military form. They were heavily armed. As the general anticipated, several guards went straight for the flyer. It seemed pointless to Gift when the rest took aim at the bunker. Even those large guns with real bullets wouldn't do more than spray the two-meter-thick concrete walls with pockmarks. Although, it was an intimidating sight, which was its likely purpose.

They gave Hans Fuchs the job of handling the talking, the stalling part. "People of the United Republic of Mars, you have no business here. We are a peaceful settlement of Pioneers. We advise you to withdraw."

Operating the camera controls, Oksana zoomed in on Yuri stepping from the line of black battle armor, clumsily wearing his own. A smile crossed her lips when he was pulled back and another took the lead position to speak. To Gift's surprise, it was that gorgeous woman who had interrogated her, humiliated her by hanging her from the ceiling in her office and ignoring her. The governor of the N.R.C. under Martian occupation.

"Allow me to correct you, sir, on a few points. We are the United Republic of *Earth,* and we have full jurisdiction over all colonies, settlements, bunkers, caves, tents, and outhouses. And you are no settlement of Pioneers. Your carefully guarded secret is out. We've discovered the location of your missile complex. We'll take control of this bunker and everything and *everyone* inside. If you cooperate and recognize the New World Order under which we operate, you will not be harmed. Open the door so this doesn't get ugly."

"Too late," Gift blurted, relieved to see the mic muted.

While their leader spewed her ultimatum, five soldiers had advanced and gathered around the hatch. Just as General Xiang had predicted, the U.R.M. brought explosives to breach the entrance. Fortunately, several hatches stood between them and the false safety of the control room. Another heavy hatch came after breaking through the exterior one. After that, the remaining doors would be easy enough until they reached the last one, behind which Gift and her team were sheltering.

No matter how Oksana fiddled the camera controls, they had only a side view in front of the entrance, unable to see the hatch itself. When the five soldiers withdrew several steps, a burst of light squinted the observers' eyes. As it flickered and varied in intensity, the bunker squad watched its reflection slowly rise in the lead soldier's visor. Sergey said it was a line of corrosive element making its way around the oval hatch. It took no more than a minute or two for it to fall open. He was spot on.

Only the five advanced into the inner chamber, or lobby. Cameras at their backs found them rolling out a cord of the same element to repeat the process on door two. One soldier cocked his head to stare into the camera in the ceiling's corner and turned back to the hatch. Either they didn't care about being seen or wanted Gift and her team to see the nearness of their oncoming dread. Anxiety climbed inside Gift and all remained silent in the control room, looking on like watching a mystery vid as the villain was about to be revealed.

"Five minutes. That is all it took us to breach the first hatch. We will be through the second and in the bunker in a moment. How many more doors do you think you can hide behind?" Gift's mind answered her former captor, *two standard doors and one more hatch. We've got about ten minutes.* If there had been any gall left in her, Gift lost it on that thought. "My offer still stands to accept your surrender. *Gift?* I'm sure you're in there. I give my word on this. If you come out now, no one gets hurt, and we move forward together."

Pops, like distant tin bubbles bursting, crackled over the mono speaker. The display showed a cloud of smoke where the U.R.M. people were working to take down the interior hatch. The exterior camera counted five soldiers fleeing the bunker's lobby before the crash rumbled and the exterior hatch coughed out clouds of thicker smoke.

"What was that?" Gift asked in hurried panic, imagining a blast blew open the hatch.

"Is part of plan." Sergey wore a proud smile. "Ceiling above ingression chamber collapsed after smoke drove the soldiers out. Smoke was Hans' idea not to kill their men. Now will be much harder for them to enter."

"Can't they just climb over it?" Oksana asked.

"No," Boss said. "They built the room with this security measure. A tactic used since ancient peoples built castles of stone. The wall of the chamber extends up to the roof. A false ceiling just dropped a ton of stone and debris in front of that hatch."

The stern female voice hardened and shouted through the chaos, reaching ears in the control room with greater intensity. "That was most unwise. You cannot keep us out forever. If we do this the hard way, it will not go well for you, I assure you."

Despite Hans Fuchs' protesting arms trying to stop her, Gift slammed her palm on the talk button. "Listen lady, you're not getting in here under any circumstance. You know I tried to jump, don't you? I was going to end my life to keep you from finding this place. We'll do whatever it takes to make sure you don't get in here."

"There you are, Gift. I'm so glad you are addressing me. I must admit, I've missed our chats. And... I have a surprise, just for you. Use your cameras. Look above us."

Frantic teenage hands started panning, tilting, focusing the camera to search the silvery sky for something, anything—what, no one could guess. Oksana found it. An immense gray box, a falling rectangle pushing through the air, jets fighting the gravitational pull wanting to crush it into molten waste. It slowed, hovered for a half-second, then touched down several meters behind the line of soldiers.

"Raff. We need to target, now," Boss commanded.

Gift objected but couldn't lift her eyes from the scene unfolding on the display. "No. We wait for the Board."

Waving his handheld above his head, Boss replied, "We got it. Executive orders by the present members of our Board and full agreement from the other colonies. Target their ship first, launch, then find the N.R.C. and do the same. *Now* Raff."

Raff consented to enter the passcode and unlock the system. Boss and Sergey began the targeting sequence. As Gift braced to launch into a fiery rage-filled denunciation, the fallen rectangle grabbed her full attention. A narrow section outlined in the center pulled away, a hatch or door tilting downward to form an exit ramp to the ground. One man in a blue and gray uniform, no battle armor, stepped out, followed by someone Gift ached to see, but wished it not in this setting.

"It's... That's Aimée," Oksana exclaimed.

"Aimée," Gift shouted. "It's her. She's here."

The tight grip of General Xiang's arm stopped Gift's dash to the secured hatch. Thoughtlessly, she would have headed upstairs to Aimée with no regard for the danger or the ton of rubble blocking the only door to the outside.

"Let us see how this plays out. They brought her here for a reason."

While the general's words were logical, Gift was not in the mood for logic. Her long-lost friend was just outside. Not dead, no longer in orbit, just outside. Before Gift's thought of their escape plan's hidden exit could grow into an idea, that idea into a plan to get her friend, Oksana said, "Look," and pointed at the display screen. Aimée stepped beside the beautiful woman in command—less attractive beside Aimée—and waved her hand at the bunker.

"Gift, I'm here, Love. They brought me down from orbit to talk to you. It's been so long, and I miss you terribly. I know you've been through so much, but it is almost over. Oh Dio, Gift, you need to cooperate. They outnumber us and they have the weapons to destroy us or force us into submission. They don't wish this. They only want to secure this facility to prevent hostilities that will end in needless loss of life. They want peace. Oh Dio, Love, I know you don't want anyone to die."

The general's face went flat, then scowled at Gift. "You said she was not on their side, not a traitor. Now she is telling us they *do* have weapon and you to give up this facility to the U.R.M."

"No, she's not, actually." The thought made Gift smile. "She used our secret code, telling us it's a lie. They're full of crap. They've got no weapons to destroy us and don't outnumber us. And... we definitely should *not* cooperate under any circumstance."

"Impressive. She was able to tell you this in code in that brief message."

"Da, impressive, Gift. But they eventually get in. Then they *will* have weapons. If we are going to defeat them, we need to launch now. Are we ready?" Sergey spoke plainly and looked to Boss for a reply.

"We almost got a lock on the ship. The intel from Amy was correct, as Gift related it. There is only one orbital up there, the rest of the sky is clear. One missile is all we'll need. We have it in sight, but the computer is working on the missile's trajectory based on the ship's current orbit. We should be able to hit it on the next pass, maybe two."

"And the N.R.C. targeting?" Xiang asked.

"We have it. We could use your input on the best strike locations for the two missiles."

"Three," Sergey said to correct Boss.

"Right, three. We fire that last one we planned to hold for another Martian ship."

"Da. The U.R.M. *will* take this facility. Is only a matter for time. We cannot leave one missile here."

"Agreed."

Xiang added, "As do I. They are unloading the explosives to blow through the wall. We must fire all missiles before they do."

"Wait," Gift shouted. "I think we have another choice."

49

Choice in a choiceless situation was what Gift had been desperate to find, unwilling to accept having only one choice, which was having no choice. *Enough of the fighting and violence. No more killing. Basta.* They were supposed to be writing a new chapter for humanity, not rereading the same old story. 'We're a new human species, elevated, and need to have a spirit of cooperation,' Gift once proudly said. Those words fell on the deaf ears of the insane Commander Chan but were no less true. Now the actions of that new human species spoke sternly against such a grandiose notion.

Irritated to no end when Mike brought her own words back against her, holding her to something she said simply by parroting her speech, Gift did it to herself. And in her own words, she found her choice. The choice that had eluded her all this time. She had told that beautiful woman, 'I was going to end my life to keep you from finding this place and we'll do whatever it takes to make sure you don't get in here.'

True, Gift hadn't ended her life when she leaned forward off that building back in the N.R.C. But that was Matteo's fault. Brimming with conviction and resolve and having nerve enough to do it, Gift did it. She leaned forward and would have sacrificed herself to prevent the U.R.M. from getting control of the missile complex. Now they had found it, soon to penetrate the bunker and take the facility. But launching all the missiles wasn't the only way to prevent that. Not the only choice.

"This place has a self-destruct, *right?*"

Boss grimaced. "Gift, that won't solve this. Not giving them the missiles is vital, but doesn't remove that ship, doesn't remove their seat of power in the N.R.C."

"Right. But we know their ship is almost empty, barely a crew on board. And neither it nor the N.R.C. has weapons that can overtake the other colonies."

"She's right," Raff said in clear agreement. "Once word spreads they have no power, no weapons, no other ships, they'll lose what support they have."

Boss stiffened his shoulders and propped on his toes as if to assert a physical dominance beyond his body's ability. "We're under orders. To stop this, we must neutralize the threat. We're locked onto the ship and will fire in under two minutes. Then China."

Heated debate ensued with Raff and Oksana absolutely supporting Gift in favor of the self-destruct option. Less favorable, Sergey sided with Boss and stated the military strategy for what needed to be done for victory. His citation of historical victories included how superior weapons had ended World War Two, the 2037 religious conflict of West Africa, and the second United States Civil War. It brought nods from Boss and General Xiang. Hans Fuchs appeared to want to stay neutral.

Turning from the cameras for the first time, Oksana stared her Russian compatriot dead in the face, creasing her neck to do so. "You know *our* history. That war with Ukraine was a mess, an embarrassment to our people. A so-called superpower, humiliated. It took a while for the changes in leadership and our governmental structure to happen, but *that's* what got us into the colony project. We wouldn't be here to have this discussion if we had kept our *Might-Makes-Right* position."

Pride swelled in Gift for her kid sister, so mature and well-spoken. Equally for how she stood against a violent solution—killing of innocents, of anybody—in the name of freedom and liberty. Given their current divide, Gift could see she and her two supporters wouldn't win this battle of wills. With no other option reaching her mental display, Gift's fingers flew over the keyboard swiftly—not nearly as efficiently as a data operator—to enter the lockout code. The code known only to the three on the side of nonviolence.

"What did you do?" Boss asked in a scolding tone.

"Now we talk." Gift poked at the overhead speaker as if she could activate it with her finger. "Talk to them... outside. See if we can't resolve this peacefully."

"And when they learn the missile has launched?"

"*Huh?*"

Raff said, "He's correct. Once the computer identifies the right orbital pass and works out the trajectory, it will fire at the ship."

"Oh mamma. We gotta stop it."

Moving himself to physically separate Gift from the console, Boss used his body as a wall. "We will do as ordered. Once that ship is destroyed, you will unlock this console and we will target the N.R.C."

"*No.* We need to stop that missile. Raff, can we do that? How do we stop it?"

Without an answer, Raff's face went pale and blank of expression for a second. She turned and ran out the exit toward the capsule to the silo platform. Hans Fuchs said, "I'll get her," and gave chase in pursuit of his partner. He had to wait for the pill-shaped tube transport Raff had taken to return.

"Gift, you *will* unlock this console and let me target that colony. This is treason. We mustn't allow them to control this facility. We must launch before they get in."

On cue from his words, vibrations rippled through the room and up Gift's legs to her gut, swirling the anguish already there like a whirlpool.

The camera showed the blast through the wall. Like sand in an hourglass, within seconds the soldiers funneled through the hole. They were inside the complex. Two simple locked doors and one hatch to blow would have them enter the control room. Hopefully, the confusion of finding the empty Ops room and the puzzle to open the secret passage to the second control room would buy some time.

"No, Boss. I won't do that. We only win this... I mean coming off victorious *as a species* worthy of this amazing and wondrous planet—saving our humanity—if we *don't* launch those missiles. Killing people is *not* the answer. And it's not the *only* choice."

"We preserve our humanity... and the Martians rule the world. Likely they kill all of us and anyone who fought them at New Europa... Like Tom."

That low blow hurt as much as intended.

"No, she is correct," General Xiang unexpectedly said. "I can convince enough of my people. They see defeat as weakness. Not having met their objective to hold the only weapons on the planet will be seen as a disgrace in my people's eyes. They will understand the life these people are promising is not the peace and freedom they claimed. Gift is correct. This will be as powerful a blow as destroying the U.R.M., perhaps even more so."

Shocked looks covered everyone's faces. Gift studied them all. In Sergey's eyes, Gift found contemplation. Boss stubbornly held his ground, unwilling to even consider alternatives. Gift expounded her plan, then noticed Aimée speaking. Her first words had fallen through the speaker's gold mesh screen unheard.

"...in a few minutes. Your time to surrender is running out. Please Gift, do the *right thing* here, Love."

Do the right thing. I'm trying, sweetie. I'm trying. The blip of an orange light on the console contended for their attention, which the group readily gave it. The text beside it was in Russian.

"Launch aborted," Sergey read.

"She did it," Oksana cheered.

Pointing an accusatory finger uncomfortably close in Gift's face, Boss barked, "You'll be kicked off the Board for this! Tried for treason. Or more likely, we'll all be dead soon, thanks to you and your *choice*."

Without the need of thought, Gift hit the mic button. "Aimée. Aimée. Okay, we *will* surrender. We ask only for our release, and the U.R.M. can have the complex. Stop your men coming in and we'll come out." Nothing but a long pause followed the unexpected announcement, only silence piping through the speaker. A hot pink flushed over Boss' face and fury wrinkled his forehead.

"We do *not* accept your surrender," came from the U.R.M. governor's voice. "Very shortly we will take this complex and will have you and your friends in custody. It is too late for negotiations. You see, my dear Gift, now you have nothing to offer us."

"*Me*. I offer me. I told you I tried to kill myself to stop you getting here. Your drone camera saw that. If you bust in here, you'll find us all dead and the systems locked with a passcode you'll never break. You'll get nothing. And you won't get me. You *don't get me*." Raw desperation cracked Gift's voice.

After an agonizing pause, the woman replied, "I accept your terms under two conditions. First, we must find the control systems unlocked. Second, Gift, you were willing to sacrifice your life. Commendable. We ask only for your cooperation. You will come with us to help us solve our medical issues without resistance. Only this way will we let your friends go free."

"Me for Aimée. I'll accept if she goes free too. And everyone else in here. If you give me your word, then I agree to these terms. Me for Aimée or no deal."

"Very well. You have my word."

"Gift, no. You can't." Tears welled up in Oksana's eyes.

Xiang said, "Gift? You know we cannot trust them. Do you have a plan?"

"Yeah. We're gonna set the self-destruct as planned and end this whole thing for good. *Ma*... give us some time to get out and all. I mean, I'll die to protect everyone if needed. Also too, I'd rather not die if I don't have to. We do this right, and we all get out of here before this place blows. Me and Aimée, too."

Breathlessly, Gift raced through her modified plan to escape and save Aimée in the process. She cautiously gaged the look in Boss' eye, finding the dull pointlessness of rage under a glower of stubbornness. *He may be a problem.*

"I say we do what Gift says. Da, is good plan." Sergey looked directly at Boss. He must have noticed the man's countenance as well.

A surprise to everyone, perhaps even to himself, Boss drew a weapon—likely lifted from a subdued guard. The handgun pulled from his waist had no *less* in its lethal. His arm wrapped around Oksana's neck from behind and, with the gun barrel aimed at her head, he cocked the hammer. Unsure of the inner workings of the weapon, Gift assumed he readied it, and it could fire, even by accident.

"*Whoa.* Boss, think this through. Please."

"Gift, you *will* unlock that console now, and then we'll target the ship and that colony and get out by our planned escape route. These are our orders."

"Please, you don't want to hurt that girl."

"So don't make me do that. We need to end this. We do that by using these missiles. Your little negotiation may have given us the time to do what we must and get out. We set the launch as ordered then we do your self-destruct, setting it for just *after* we've fired the missiles. This place goes up with their entire platoon in here. That's how we end this. People like this respond to nothing less than a decisive defeat from which they cannot recover."

While her focus stayed on Oksana, Gift saw—sensed if not physically saw—Sergey and Xiang twitching, desperate for a plan of action to save the young lady and subdue Boss. Gift feared any sudden movement would surely curl his trigger finger, ending a precious young life instantly. She raised her hands in surrender and agreed to unlock the console. Gift keyed in Sonia-makes_ until the commotion froze her fingers.

Oksana's knees buckled and, as her torso lowered, her elbow rose forcefully behind her to meet Boss' groin. A deafening pop. Chips of concrete fell, and gray dust rained over them, flickering like fireflies under the yellow lighting. A one-armed Xiang and Sergey had him in their hands and the gun removed from his person in a split-second. Gift took a deep breath, completed the code entry, and conferred with Sergey on the escape plan as Raff and Hans Fuchs ran in on the commotion.

"What are we doing?" asked a near-panicked Raff.

"You stopped the launch sequence, *right?* We're not gonna fire on the ship?"

"Me and Hans stopped it. *Ma,* what's happened here?"

"Niente. So, now we need to set the self-destruct. Can you do that?"

"*Certo.*"

"*Ma,* give us some time. You know, so we don't all die in here." Turning to Sergey, Gift asked, "Is five minutes enough?"

"Da."

Pressing the mic button, Gift said, "Okay, sorry. There was some resistance to our agreement, but we settled it. We're ready. We do this outside. Your men move back in their line and away from the building. Keep Aimée clearly visible. I'll come to the door... I mean, the hole you blew in the wall. We walk toward each other. Aimée gets safe inside by time I reach you."

"Gift, I know you by now. No tricks. We'll have thirty guns aimed—ten at you and *twenty* at your dear friend Aimée. I assure you, if you try anything, we'll let you watch her die before we take you."

"I see."

"Are we agreed?"

"Yes. Get into position... I'm coming out."

Mic off, Gift said, "Raff, do it, set it for five minutes. Then all of you get out of here, get to the Zil. Sergey, do you have what I need?"

"We must get one thing upstairs first and is ready."

"Okay. Then you gotta hurry to the Zil. Oh mamma, here we go. Wish me luck."

With a handheld patched into the external camera feeds, Gift verified the woman had done as agreed. The soldiers were in line away from the entrance. Two steps before them, the governor stood beside Aimée, clutching her arm. A quick headcount confirmed every U.R.M. person accounted for. In his clumsy guard jumpsuit, Yuri stood out, the only non-soldier there, not even given a weapon. It reinforced to Gift how true her bluff had been when she told his guys the Martians would have no use for him when this was over. Everything seemed to be in place. Hopefully, Gift's nerve would be too. She took a step out and looked her fears in the face.

"Wow, you're so pretty. I'm sure I heard your name, but for the life of me, I can't remember. *Governor*...?"

"Seriously, Gift? We'll be spending lots of time together real soon. We'll get to know each other. Don't you worry."

"Not worried. I just... I can trust people more if I know their name. Please."

"I am Juliette Foster, Chancellor of the United Republic of Mars and now the Supreme Chancellor of the United Republic of Earth."

That surprised Gift. Not only was she a knockout, but she was also so young. As an appointed governor of the N.R.C. it was a stretch. Chancellor of the U.R.M. It blew Gift's mind. Perhaps they elected their leaders based on looks. In that case, the election was likely a landslide. *Back on point, Gift.*

"*Chancellor?* We didn't realize..."

"I'm sure. Our people thought it prudent to keep that a secret. Now, step forward or we'll come for you and end our little arrangement on very different terms. I told you I am a person of my word, but you're trying my patience."

"Just one more thing, if I may. Just to be sure you'll keep your word. No offense... though I don't really care if I offend you, honestly." When Gift unzipped her coverall, eyes squinted over the weapons pointed at her, making them appear more lethal. A black vest with exposed wires running over it revealed itself.

"I'm a bomb. I mean, I'm wearing one. And I have this *Deadman's Switch* in my hand. Or dead woman's, I guess. So, if I don't reach you and Aimée doesn't get inside, you get nothing."

"Most impressive. I shall not underestimate you again. And I assure you I will keep my word. Now, please..."

Right foot first, Gift stepped. Foot over foot, slowly she advanced, being sure Aimée matched her steps, getting closer to safety. Her mind flashed to her hostage exchange for Oksana. Only Xiang wasn't sneaking around their backs to take out three dozen soldiers on her own. No, that plan had played out once, it wouldn't work here. Gift wondered if Yuri had told his Martian friends how he had lost Oksana. *No, he tried to save face. And he's too dim to realize the value of that intel at this moment.*

Tears welled in Aimée's eyes, their first time seeing each other in months. So much had happened to both courageous women. *What must she be thinking? Will this be the only glimpse we have of each other for the rest of our days?* Closer now, one meter apart. Steps came slowly. Each wore long- ing looks. The yearning to embrace burned Gift's heart. Her childhood companion who had become her best friend had almost left her peripheral vision. Gift shouted, "Now."

The tips of the rifles seemed to draw closer in steadied hands. Gift turned and tackled Aimée to the ground, being sure she landed on top as a human shield over her friend's body. Quickly, Gift raised her hand, showing the Deadman's Switch, evoking the vital momentary pause of the soldiers. Before the ants' brains had time to catch up with the ocular input and process the scene, the Zil came flying up at full speed. A blur in the corner of Gift's eye became a flash of light as the sun bounced its rays off the windscreen.

The hefty vehicle rocked forward, then settled quickly as it slid to a full stop to position itself between Gift and Aimée and the line of soldiers. A cloud of dust swirled around the Zil. Familiar metallic pops like steel raindrops pelting it saturated the air, drowning out all other sounds. Opening like a giant mouth, the side door split horizontally as Gift hauled Aimée to her feet. The great metal and glass beast swallowed them as it jumped forward, increasing speed so quickly the two were tossed into the rear storage compartment.

Sergey sped them off for the cover of the forest in case the flyer pursued them. The reunited friends embraced so hard it ached in their bones wonderfully. Oksana jumped in the back to join the unbridled hug with rival enthusiasm. Although they weren't yet out of danger, all the fear had fled, left behind at the bunker.

"They ran inside," Hans Fuchs declared.

"Were they warned?" Gift anxiously asked.

Raff answered, "Yes. I activated the message as the Zil stopped to get you. It's broadcasting the countdown over the comms we used to speak to them. They know it's set to self-destruct."

"But they went in," Hans Fuchs repeated. "That woman, Yuri, and a couple of soldiers."

"The rest?" Gift asked as she pulled off the vest with duct-taped bars of soap and decorative taser coils.

"Scattered like ants and ran to the flyer. I think they'll get away." Hans Fuchs then asked, "How far must we be from it to be safe?"

"One warhead is from three to five hundred meters. I do not think this is increased greatly by being four of them. Plus, they are in the mountain," Sergey explained calmly. Xiang confirmed.

"Yes, but those self-destruct explosives are in the bunker, that's closer." Seated beside Sergey, Boss reminded Gift of his existence and subsequently of his heinous stunt pulling the gun on Oksana.

When the sky turned floodlight white, the shockwave pushed as a gentle shake of the Zil racing off toward New Europa. Finally, Gift was going home.

50 | Colony's End

Home wasn't so much a place, but a feeling. While it had a physical location—her beloved colony of New Europa and her tiny Box—the familiarity was more about the people in her life being there. For months Gift hadn't been 'home.' Partly for being in other colonies, then weeks spent in isolation, and being on the run. The limited social engagement had been the hardest part, the people in her life removed, temporarily or some permanently.

When Charlie died over a year ago, home had changed. A gaping cavity carved into what had been solid, whole. Losing Tina weighed heavily, straining the pericardium and the surrounding ligaments trying their best to support her heart and keep it from sinking into her gut. Her mind drifted from its somber musing to focus on the fear that came as Sergey cautiously guided the vehicle over the scary bridge Gift wished to never have seen again. She hoped no planks would break this time.

With New Europa finally in sight, Gift climbed from the rear of the Zil, over Raff and Hans Fuchs. With her face between Sergey and Boss, she took in the full view. Nothing had changed. In the wake of attacks and occupations that led to revolt and fighting to take back the colony, New Europa looked the same as it had for centuries. Or at least the past year when they first gazed upon its exterior. A warm, gentle smile drew itself on

Gift's glossy-eyed face as she considered the sacrifices of her fallen friends and how Charlie and Tina had helped to preserve their home.

Gift was home.

Tom ran to the Zil as it approached its stop. His form became the most beautiful silhouette Gift had ever seen, coming toward her under the backdrop of the setting sun, its rays glinting off the tear rolling down her cheek. The force of his contact nearly dropped her to the ground if not for his powerful, assuring arms embracing her and removing her feet from the ground beneath them. She floated in the unequivocal comfort of the moment. It felt like home. New, yet totally familiar.

Aimée's parents were steps behind Tom's run to reclaim their precious daughter, back from being gone for months. To Gift's delight, Nadezhda Anoykina was also part of the sprint to the transport, watery-eyed and eager to see her beloved daughter, who had once again been freed from being a hostage. The reunions overwhelmed emotions, taking them to unprecedented levels.

Every moment took forever. Everyone gladly offered the demanded time. It was a return home, to whatever their lives would now become. Firmly grounded in the normal and mundane, Gift hoped. Perhaps that's what home really meant. Belonging, feeling welcome, surrounded by loved ones, brought the most normal everyday comfort of home. This would always be something to be cherished.

Gift was home.

***

Bright and early on her first morning home—with next to no sleep—Gift and Raff entered the Board room for its first official meeting in months. Before being offered to the colonies and peoples of Earth, Gift's proposal needed to pass here. Of course, she had to have her beloved espresso before offering her summary of events that led to this moment. Kavith pulled the steaming shots from freshly ground beans. He ran the best coffee bar in N.E., and Miss Heller's thoughtfulness in having him and his magic espresso machine there was appreciated. That morning, the silky-smooth black with its creamy foam cap tasted especially delicious, the best cup of coffee Gift had ever sipped.

Understanding the effects of what some called 'the heat of the moment' and remembering how it temporarily turned Mike into a warmonger ready to destroy an entire colony, Gift was gentle in the retelling of Boss' interaction in the missile control room. She concurred with his decision to step down from the Board. After giving his full support to Gift's decision not to launch the missiles, he immediately excused himself from the deliberations. It was time for Gift's proposal. Her vision of humanity's future.

"...so General Xiang is on her way to the N.R.C. to offer them what we are about to propose. We already have Miss Anoykina's agreement and the Board of the R.F."

Fred interrupted. His eyes failed to hold Gift hostage as they had in every previous encounter. "As far as we know, the N.R.C. is still under U.R.M. control and many Chinese support them. Losing their governor, or chancellor as it turned out, in her failed attempt to stop the self-destruct and take the complex doesn't mean the Martians are gone or the colony will surrender."

Calmly, Gift replied, "True, Fred. Thank you for pointing that out. Miss Foster was the Chancellor of the U.R.M. and also the ruler of the N.R.C. under Martian occupation. The man below her, James Morris, was much less... *severe* in his approach. We assume he's in charge, the appointed governor working under their, well, their former ruler. She was like some evil emperor or something. And the Chinese supported the U.R.M. because of their promises—all of which have proved untrue—and their dissatisfaction with their own totalitarian rulership."

Softer eyes said Fred started coming around.

"General Xiang is confident they'll accept *her* as leader. Respecting her role in the battle against the Martians, her victories in our fight for freedom. That, along with our proposal, should be enough to sway any lingering support for the U.R.M. to our side."

"I agree with Xiang's assessment and Gift's proposal." Gift appreciated Miss Heller's support and her way to level the discussion and help move it along. "We will know soon how the Chinese and any remaining U.R.M. at the N.R.C. respond."

"Thank you, Margaret." Gift didn't realize how she used the woman's given name for the first time. "That's the key, of course. If General Xiang is successful, we'll be in a better position to offer our proposal to U.A. and the peoples of the settlements—Pioneers and Ubuntu. We cannot move forward on this without a hundred percent agreement. We must be united for this to work."

As Gift articulated her vision, no one interrupted with a counterargument or to disagree. The occasional questions for clarification were welcomed, and Raff helped detail some steps of the plan. Moments before lunch arrived, they had reached a unanimous decision. It appeared they could reach their goal of becoming a new human species, elevated, with a genuine spirit of cooperation. Gift overflowed with gratitude reaching an ecstatic state of hopefulness.

Every known civilization on Earth eagerly supported Gift's restructuring proposal. General Xiang and James Morris quickly reached agreement and the less than four dozen remaining members of the U.R.M. and their many Chinese supporters followed suit. Bright at United Africa, Kofi of the Ubuntu, and Dmytro of the Pioneers gave their wholehearted support and were eager to begin. It would be the dawn of a new era, a glorious new world.

All known governing parties of Earth drafted and signed the new charter. Together they formed a new structure of society and its oversight, and the colonies project officially ended—though in reality, it had ended when the airlock opened, even if no one understood it at the time. Now in practice, they were no longer independent colonies and groups of settlers. They became one people. There would be no grandiose titles for persons or offices, and no individual would have absolute power or control.

Gift had entitled her proposal, "Colony's End."

The charter referred to humanity's Earth, but this was not an official name for their new society. It stipulated they were all humans, sharing the Earth and its resources, working together for its future and theirs. All independent ruling structures were dissolved and one new governing body, a board of twelve chosen two from each colony and people, became the new organizational arrangement for administration and procedures. Members of the new Board would meet each week, and each would be appointed to serve on various of its committees. The plan created an organizational structure more than a government to facilitate the smooth running of everything from climate acclamation to daily food and water supply, work assignments, housing, and educational programs.

Gift suggested participants on the Board should live in their respective locations, being accessible to the people. They would arrange frequent visits and more extensive member exchanges, allowing themselves to absorb the cultures of other groups. As one of few people to have been in all colonies and settlements, Gift considered it a key element of the proposal to help foster an idea of one race, humanity, united in the same goals and ideals.

To cement the concept of unity, Gift led the discussion to change the names of the colonies and settlements to simply identify their geographic locations, making that the only differentiation as such was logistically necessary. While many members of New Europa's former Board were assigned to committees of the new governing body, they unanimously chose Raff and Gift as representatives from New Europa—now simply called Northwest—to be on the new Board of Directors.

Joining them were Nadezhda Anoykina and Sergey Lazarev from Northeast, Dmytro Melnyk and Samantha Hines from North-central, Bright Omoruyi and Joy Alabi from South-central, Kofi Kwarteng and Lilly Blankson from Southwest, Xiang Jei and James Morris from Southeast. The general thought it best to include him, even though his people were such a small number, to allay any residual resentment of the failed occupation, revolts, and subsequent changes in administration. Plus, if the future brought repatriated Martians home, they would be more at ease, not feeling unrepresented.

It delighted Gift to learn Corinthia had shifted her mindset, and she arranged a catch-up vidChat with her in coming days. If her attitude toward cooperation persisted, she would be a valuable member of one of the upcoming subcommittees Gift planned to propose.

They held the first meeting of the governing body of Earth over video conference. Weekly meetings would be held mostly in this way. All came to an agreement not to have a seat of oversight in one physical location to quell any notions of a capital or elevate one location or people over any other. The first order of business was getting the committees established, clearly defining their roles, and appointing Board members as chairpersons. Gift finagled getting herself on at least one committee each with Aimée, Mike, Matteo, Oksana, Sakura—a given for medical research—and Marco. Her friends, who were more than that. Each had proven accomplished at their professions and had shown fidelity to the same ideals that would shape humanity's future. Their loyalty to and loving support of Gift were also unquestioned.

Next came an agenda point Gift feared could have been controversial. It was one of many reasons it elated her not to be the chairperson of this new Board of Directors. By unanimous decision, that duty fell upon Raffaella. As with many of her anxieties—futile but unstoppable—Gift soon discovered she had spent time needlessly worrying about what would not come to be.

"*Allora*. Then we have unanimous agreement to invite the colonists of the U.R.M. to return to Earth if they wish?"

A show of hands confirmed, and group secretary Dmytro noted the decision. Word had been sent to Mars, informing them of the results of their first venture to Earth, the misguided efforts of their former Chancellor, Juliette Foster, and the succession of James Morris to her office. A small crew of those formerly known as Martians headed by Commander Ryan would return to the currently unmanned but still orbiting Santa Maria for a return trip to Mars.

That Aimée was joining to speak for Earth was the sour aftertaste of the otherwise delicious outcome. They could expect the first of the repatriated colonists—and Aimée's return—in about a year, so preparations began immediately to expand the living quarters in each location. This allowed the returnees to blend into human society, making their new homes among all settlements. Excitement surrounded everyone when plans were approved for external habitats for current and soon-to-be-arriving residents of Earth.

There was so much to be done, but it came with an electrifying excitement, a power greater than caffeine that energized Gift in the weeks that followed. Seeing those seeds of this new, elevated, human race germinate into a truly new world on their restored and magnificent Earth overwhelmed Gift whenever her mind mused over it. She gave in entirely to the joyful abandon of allowing that to happen often.

Gift was truly home.

| Epilogue |

When he claimed he had finally mastered Matteo's recipe for pancakes, it happened. The call of his name stopped Tom and turned him quickly, spinning his heels in his thick house socks. Gift had been playing with little Charlie on the floor of the dining area when she stood him up and let go. It was too early for first steps, but the excited couple considered what he did to be just that. Both grandmothers rushed over to see it. They had been so helpful in those first months when Gift suffered from loss of sleep and the overwhelming anxiety of being a new mom.

One job only Gift could do was feeding him. Another of her so-called miracles made her the first mother in over two centuries able to breastfeed her baby. Conceptually strange and awkward at first, it became the most natural thing in the world once she got the hang of getting him to latch on. The way their eyes met when he nursed at her breast joined them in a beautiful and deep connection she cherished.

Later that evening, she and Tom would celebrate their two-year anniversary. Gift insisted on a simple gathering of their closest friends and family, and Tom desperately wished to try out his new pizza oven in the garden beside their home. The modest 3D-printed house—dozens had been built and occupied—sat beside Colony Lake with a twelve-step path to the shoreline, ten for Tom.

Raff and Hans came just after breakfast to prepare the pizza dough, Raff insisting it needed the hours to rise to make perfect wood-fired Neapolitan pizzas. Rolling the flour from a mush into a semi-firm ball took extra effort for Raff, leaning over her massive belly. Hers would be the seventh pregnancy to follow Gift's "natural way" with Sakura's treatments. Gift basked in the confidence that Raff's daughter and Charlie would be as close as brother and sister.

Oksana arrived next. She had been spending a lot of time over the last two years with Gift, especially that first year while Aimée had been away on her trip to Mars. It still blew Gift's mind to think of those words, *Aimée's trip to Mars*. An evening with friends was an evening with family. Gift made sure Charlie would be raised in such an environment with Zia Raff and Uncle Hans, Aunt Aimée, Uncle Mike, Uncle Matteo, Aunt Oksana who called herself Tetya to Charlie, even Uncle Marco. When he claimed the teenage crush from Matteo, Big Sis Gift found it cute.

Margaret wouldn't be able to attend the evening's festivities as she, along with Sergey and Xiang—in Union almost as long as Gift and Tom—were en route to Brazil to make the first contact visit with the newly discovered colony. Aimée would normally be on such a trip but wouldn't miss Gift's anniversary party for the world, consistently stating her regret for missing the first one for Mars. Her role as spokesperson proved just as vital as ever, or perhaps more so. Not only for resident communications and news, which helped keep everyone united, she also established contact with new colonies.

Expanded communications and long-range flyer expeditions had located other colonies outside of their project, and Aimée had visited each of them to establish first contact. All had joined them as residents of Earth, adding members to their Board of Directors for each. Now Margaret hoped for a similar outcome in Brazil. Recent communication had gone unanswered, but Gift had made tremendous progress at leaving problems that were out of her control to the involved parties. Perhaps being a mom taught her that balance.

The guests joined just before the eye-watering sunset. Everyone loved the pizzas as Tom pulled them out of the inferno that was his new stone pizza oven. Gift's mom smiled wide the entire time, amicably taking turns holding sleeping Charlie. Gift lovingly gazed over Tom's parents, Oksana, Sakura, Matteo, Mike, and Marco. Seeing Sakura with Hiro took some getting used to. Observing how happy Charlie's widow looked felt right, what her dear old friend would want for his beloved partner.

Sara came as well as Melody and Anton, those two now promised in Union. Bright and his wife traveled to join the party, bringing Blessing's children who had been calling Gift *Auntie Gift* since before their mom had died. Kofi and Paulina came on the same transport and brought cards of congratulations from their children and a lovely stuffed giraffe for Charlie. Uncle Mike checked it for choke hazards.

When Charlie fussed in Oksana's arms, Gift waved her over and took the baby with his crinkled little nose and puckered lips. He was ready for his next meal as the adults washed their pizzas down with sips of beer or water. Watching her friends and family in her garden, the warming sensation of the familiar, of normalcy, of home, wrapped around her as if everyone she loved joined their arms to envelop her in an endless hug. In the distance, Gift saw Tina and Charlie smiling in a memory that brought nothing but joy, and she whispered a silent 'thank you.'

Wonderment dominated Gift fully as she imagined this world, this life, seen through the saucer eyes of her innocent little Charlie. What did they absorb looking over this perfect moment? A scene filled with incredible people, friends and family both—the heart and soul of their lives—with Earth's splendor as its glorious backdrop under a star-filled sky. Lost in contemplation of his future, the one she and his dad along with their dearest friends had bravely forged for him, optimism and hope flooded into her, and Gift gave herself fully to the soothing sensation. This was her life, as wondrous as it was amazing.

Locking eyes with her son, Gift said, "Charlie, my love, welcome to this incredible life."

THANK YOU

I'm truly blown away by your support as a reader. I would be delighted to learn if you enjoyed the exciting conclusion of Colony's End. I loved ending this one on a note of optimism and hope you found it uplifting for the human condition and what we can become.

As an indie author, it means a great deal to me that you enjoyed my work enough to read this trilogy. If you enjoyed the New Europa series, please tell a friend.

Stories by indie writers like me don't always find the audience that will enjoy them. It means so much to us, to me, to have reviews. Please consider taking just a couple of minutes to review this book.

Follow my writing and engage with me at: www.glassauthor.com/dawn

As a 'thank you' for subscribing, you will receive a free copy of *All Lies*, a New Europa novella exploring the beginning of Boss' misfit group of conspiracy theorists.

ABOUT THE AUTHOR

Reading is a passion; writing is an obsession.

And *IT consulting is a job*. While N Joseph Glass enjoys the challenges of managing a virtual infrastructure, backups, email systems, and cloud environments, crafting stories is his cherished second job.

Born and raised in Brooklyn, NY, Glass lives and writes in Milan, Italy. A fan of science fiction and other genres, he loves to expound stories that are driven by relatable characters on meaningful journeys.

Drawing from personal experiences enriches the writing process and leaves readers feeling like they know the characters they spend time with in a story. That human connection between his characters, readers, and himself, fuels his drive as an author.

Optimistic views of the future through art always interest him, as Glass believes ours will be bright.

www.glassauthor.com

www.ingramcontent.com/pod-product-compliance
Lightning Source LLC
Chambersburg PA
CBHW071217300726

48975CB00002B/257